Burning for Her Kiss

Serpent's Kiss, Book 1

By

Sherri Hayes

Burning for Her Kiss
Serpent's Kiss, Book 1
Sherri Hayes

Copyright 2015 by Sherri Hayes
ISBN: 978-0-9909596-2-5

This is a work of fiction. Names, places, characters and incidents are the product of the author's imagination and are fictitious. Any resemblance to actual persons, living or dead, events or establishments is solely coincidental.

Other Books by Sherri Hayes

Finding Anna series

Slave

Need

Truth

Trust

Daniels Brothers series

Behind Closed Doors

Red Zone

Crossing the Line

Serpent's Kiss series

Welcome to Serpent's Kiss

Burning for Her Kiss

Single Titles

Hidden Threat

A Christmas Proposal: A Hidden Threat Novella

Acknowledgments

Writing a book is always a journey and I'm lucky to have had some wonderful people along for the ride on this one.

First and foremost, thank you to my beta, Riane Holt. She's the first to see the story and gets to experience all the road bumps I encounter along the way.

This is my second self-published book and I was very lucky to have two of the editors I've worked with for the last few years back on board. Thank you to Wyndy and Andrea for helping make my books the best they can be.

A big thank you to Sara Eirew, my photographer and cover designer. Her beautiful pictures never cease to amaze me. Picking the one picture that would be the cover for Burning For Her Kiss was difficult because there were so many great ones to choose from.

Publishing a book is only the first step. In the weeks leading up to a book's release, and after it's out, there is a lot of marketing to be done. People won't read your book if they don't know it exists. I'm lucky to have some very dedicated members on my street team who spend hours every week helping to spread the word about me and my books. Thank you to Andrea, April, Shannon, Elke, Rosie, and Lee for all your work. And an extra special thank you to Rae. She stepped up to be my PA and has done a wonderful job organizing my street team and just about anything else I've asked her to do.

I'm rather picky when it comes to accuracy in my books. Although I'm writing fiction, I like for the stories to be somewhat believable and as true to life as possible. I want to thank Mack for reading through all the BDSM scenes in the book to make sure I got them right. He puts up with the romance even though it's not his usual choice of reading material.

When I began writing Burning For Her Kiss, I set out in search of some information regarding the St. Louis Fire Department. Little did I know that I would end up talking to Captain Garon Mosby, in charge of PR for the SLFD. A huge thank you goes out to him for his help in making my hero's job as realistic as possible. He spent hours on the phone with me answering all sorts of questions from scheduling to uniforms to the number of trucks that would be called to a fire.

Last but not least, I want to thank one of my local firefighters, Justin. I ran into him at a farmers' market and ended up with an invitation to stop by the station for a look around. It was a great experience and it included my getting to see them respond to a call. Thank you for taking time out of your day to show me around and answer my questions no matter how strange.

Dedication

Thank you to all the readers out there who have supported me through my journey as a writer. You have no idea how valuable you are.

Chapter 1

Drew Parker had finally drummed up the courage to come to Serpent's Kiss by himself four weeks ago. He'd been anxious about walking into a kink club. The idea of going alone terrified him. In the end, after a lot of internal arguments, he'd done it. He'd made the leap into the unknown.

In the months leading up to his first trip to the club, Drew attended a few local munches. That had been daunting in and of itself. He hadn't known what to expect, but the people were more welcoming than he'd thought they'd be—especially John and his mistress, Allison. They seemed to sense his need for guidance and had taken him under their wing, so to speak.

It was through John and Allison that Drew found out about the club. Serpent's Kiss was a private club in the heart of downtown St. Louis. On the outside, it appeared to be an old warehouse. No one would know it was a BDSM club unless they paid close attention to the people who came and went on Friday and Saturday nights.

With the help of his new friends, he was introduced to the club and its owner, Mistress Katrina. Drew was a little surprised a woman owned and ran a kink club. He wasn't sure why, but he'd just assumed a man would be in charge. The joke was on him, however. If he'd ever been in doubt as to his submissive tendencies, they'd disappeared after his interview with Mistress Katrina. The moment she began questioning him from behind that big wooden desk, her tone of voice changed and he felt his heart pick up its pace. She seemed to get a kick out of his reaction, and after a few more questions, she'd shown him around the club.

While Mistress Katrina's dominant nature got his blood pumping, that was where his reaction to her ended. There was no physical attraction. He was confident part of that was because the dungeon mistress was a busty blonde. He preferred leggy brunettes with a little extra cushion in the back end.

Thinking of his first meeting with the club's mistress made him squirm in his seat. She was certainly nothing like he'd expected her to be. Then again, most of the Dommes he'd met weren't what he'd expected. Allison was a perfect example. The Dommes he'd seen in online videos barked orders at their submissives, and seemed to take pleasure in humiliating them at every turn. Allison was nice. Drew had no doubt that, if pushed, she could be hard as nails, but she'd been nothing but pleasant to him. She'd even offered to do a scene with Drew if he wanted. Although it was tempting, he wasn't sure if he was ready for that step yet. For the time being, he was content to watch. Everything was still so new to him.

To be honest, Drew was relieved to discover not all Dommes were like the ones he'd seen online. While he wanted his lover to be in control in the bedroom, public humiliation wasn't on his list of desires. He wanted to serve his partner—to worship her body and mind. Meeting Allison and John gave him hope.

As Drew glanced around the main room, he spotted some familiar faces. It was a typical night. The main room was scattered with people talking and sipping on drinks. Submissives were in various stages of undress. Some were on leashes kneeling on the floor next to their masters or mistresses. Others were sitting beside or on top of their master's or mistress' laps. Mistress Katrina was near the bar talking to a male Dom and his female sub. Drew recognized both of them, but he didn't know their names.

There were also a handful of people Drew had met at the munches he'd attended. While he'd met a few others since coming to the club, the atmosphere was different. Munches were for socializing. Serpent's Kiss was for playing.

The club was divided into sections, which was one of the things Drew liked the most. There were plenty of seating areas scattered around the main floor, as well as a bar along one wall, a small dance floor, and a raised platform. He'd been told the platform was used for demonstrations, but he'd yet to witness one of those since he'd been a member. As for kinky play, very little beyond the occasional spanking or some other light impact play occurred in the main room. Everything else took place upstairs.

A couple of weeks ago, he'd drummed up the courage to climb the stairs and take a look around. The upstairs rooms looked completely different with people in them than they had when Mistress Katrina had shown him around during the club's off hours. The sounds alone charged the atmosphere.

Although Drew didn't consider himself a voyeur, he couldn't help himself. He was drawn into watching some of the scenes. Most of the items in the rooms were things he'd seen online in his initial research into the lifestyle. Some of them appealed to him. Some of them didn't.

Drew had the desire to submit to a mistress, but he wasn't looking for just the physical aspects of submission. Maybe that sounded cheesy, but he'd done the whole sex-only thing in the vanilla world. There was physical gratification, yes, but he'd never truly felt connected to a woman before. Drew knew part of that was his desire to give up control to his partner. He was twenty-eight, and he wanted someone he could share his life with.

As a firefighter, he saw death and tragedy on a regular basis. He didn't want to wake up ten years into the future and still be searching for someone who could give him what he needed. That was why he'd decided to plunge headfirst into this new lifestyle instead of dragging his feet in the regular dating pool. Even still, Drew knew it was going to be an uphill battle. There were more male subs than there were female dominants. Even at the club, there were five male Doms to every one Domme. But as his new friend John had reminded him on multiple occasions, if Drew didn't put himself out there, he'd never find the woman he was searching for.

Drew watched as John sat at his mistress' feet with his head in her lap. It wasn't demeaning in any way. It was affectionate, and Drew wanted that for himself.

Allison moved, getting John's attention. "Get me a drink, my boy."

John was swiftly on his feet. "What would you like, Mistress?"

That was the last of their exchange Drew heard because his attention had shifted to the door. He vaguely registered John leaving the cozy sitting area, but Drew was too focused on the woman who'd walked through the club's main entrance.

The new arrival surveyed the room. From the way she was carrying herself, Drew was almost positive she was a Domme. If he was being honest with himself, he was hoping she was a Domme. Whether she was or not remained to be seen.

She looked to be about five foot six or seven, but the black heels she had on added a good three to four inches to her stature. Her long hair was pulled up into a high ponytail and looked almost black in the dim club lighting. The black corset and jeans she wore accented her curves to the point where Drew was afraid he might be drooling.

Only a few seconds passed before the woman strolled with confidence over to the bar and ordered a drink. Drew continued to stare. She chatted with the bartender for several minutes, even after he'd handed the woman her drink. Drew didn't recognize the woman as anyone who'd been to the club since he'd joined, but the bartender seemed to know her. Of course, that didn't mean anything. For all Drew knew, the mystery woman and the bartender lived next door to each other. Then again, this was a private club. In order to be here, she had to be a member. Especially since she'd come alone.

Drew's eyes followed the woman as she headed to a booth across the room. She sat down with another group of people similar to the one he was with. He recognized most of them. They were all regulars.

Abruptly, John sat down next to him on the couch having returned with his mistress' drink. "I wouldn't get your hopes up."

Drew reluctantly pulled his gaze away from the woman. "What?"

"Don't *what* me. You're staring at Lady Beth."

Then what John said registered. "What do you mean I shouldn't get my hopes up? She is a Domme, right?"

"Oh yes, definitely a Domme."

"She doesn't like male subs?"

"She does." John drew out the two words, and Drew knew there was a 'but' coming.

He sighed, frustrated. "Then what's the issue?"

John lowered his voice to a whisper so no one around them

could hear the information he was about to disclose. Drew doubted his friend would tell him anything ninety percent of the club didn't already know, but he decided to play along. One of the first things Drew learned was that word traveled fast in the small community—especially if it was something bad. "She used to come here all the time with her sub, Ben. They'd been together for years, from what I heard, before Mistress and I began getting involved in local events. Then, three months ago, they both suddenly stopped coming. To the club. To munches. Everything."

Drew couldn't help himself. He was intrigued. "What happened?"

"Ben traveled a lot for his business. Sometimes he was out of town for weeks at a time going to all sorts of places. Apparently, his trips weren't business related. At least, not completely. Lady Beth found out he had a wife and daughter in Florida."

"That's insane. It's like something you hear on TV." Drew shook his head, trying to digest the information he'd received.

"I know. He'd lied to her the entire time."

Drew's gaze drifted back to Lady Beth. He couldn't imagine what it would be like to have trust broken in such a way.

John's voice pulled Drew out of his musings. "I don't know if she's ready to dive back into a relationship, man, and I know that's what you want."

It was true. Drew did want a relationship, but he was willing to work for it. One step at a time, right? So the first thing he had to do was find a way to introduce himself.

***

Beth Davenport tried to ignore all the stares she received when she entered the club. It had been three months since she'd stepped foot inside Serpent's Kiss. She knew showing up would mean she'd be the hot topic of gossip for the evening. Her best friend and fellow Domme, Nicole, had warned her about the rumors floating around. They were surprisingly accurate as far as rumors went except no one knew how Beth had come to find out about Ben's lies. Only Nicole knew the whole truth, and Beth wanted to keep it that way.

Domme or not, finding out a large portion of the life you'd been living for the last three years was a lie left Beth broken in a lot of ways. She wasn't even sure why she'd come to the club. Oh, that's right. It was Nicole's hounding over the last two weeks. Nicole had insisted three months was enough moping.

Every Friday afternoon for the last month, Nicole had called Beth asking if she was going to put in an appearance at Serpent's Kiss. Each time, Beth had weaseled out of it. Her friend had even enlisted Katrina's help more than once.

The club mistress was a formidable woman in her late forties. She'd been married to a man who wanted no part in her kinky ways. Beth didn't know her back then, but the way the story went was that at forty-four, her husband was diagnosed with a rare form of cancer. He'd died within two months. The sudden change in Katrina's life prompted her to take stock. Six months later, she opened Serpent's Kiss.

While Beth admired Katrina and her take-the-bull-by-the-horns attitude, Beth wasn't sure she was ready to be back at the club. Unfortunately, when Katrina had put her on the spot, Beth hadn't been able to say no. Both Katrina and Nicole had been incredibly supportive after what had happened with Ben. While Beth had no desire to put herself back out into the dating world—it was the last thing she wanted at the moment—Nicole and Katrina had convinced her that she needed to get out and mingle. She had friends here, and it wasn't right for her to turn her back on them because Ben had been a class-A jerk.

So here she was, sitting with Nicole and a group of their friends. Beth was the only Dominant in their group without a sub. It was a little awkward, but she tried to ignore it and have a good time. Nicole was right about one thing, Beth had missed her friends. She wasn't going to let what Ben did tarnish that.

"I think you have an admirer," Nicole whispered in Beth's ear, jarring her from her thoughts.

"What?"

Nicole scooted closer to her. "There's a guy across the room that hasn't been able to take his eyes off you for the last fifteen minutes. I'd say he's interested."

Beth didn't even bother to look. "I'm not."

"Oh, come on. He's hot, and I happen to know he's a sub."

"That doesn't change anything. I'm not ready to get back into the dating pool again."

Her friend rolled her eyes. "Well, you don't have to date him, you know."

She shook her head. "I'm not into playing with random subs and you know it. Even if I was, I don't think I could even do that after everything."

Nicole frowned. "You have to get back on the horse sometime."

Beth sighed in defeat. "I know. Maybe in a month or so—"

Her friend placed a hand on her arm, stopping Beth mid-sentence. "I don't think he's going to wait a month or so. He's coming over."

"What do you mean he's coming over? Here?"

Nicole nodded and turned back to their group, effectively leaving Beth to fend for herself. Taking a deep breath, Beth prepared herself for whatever line this guy was going to try to sell her.

Her heart pounded as she felt him drawing closer, but Beth refused to show any outward signs that she was aware of the man. It would only encourage him.

To her surprise, instead of coming over and trying to sweet-talk her, the guy sat down in the chair to her right and said nothing. It was odd to be sure, but since she wasn't interested in the slightest anyway, Beth decided to ignore him and refocus on her friends' conversation. Maybe he'd eventually get the idea and go away. Or maybe she was only being paranoid and he didn't walk across the room for her at all.

Ignoring him turned out to be more difficult than Beth originally thought. Although he didn't attempt to engage her in conversation, she felt his presence beside her. Even with her eyes purposely averted, Beth knew he wasn't a small man. She'd seen enough in her peripheral vision to know he was tall and nicely proportioned.

No matter how aware she was of his presence, Beth outwardly ignored him. That was until she finished off her drink. She scooted forward in her seat, preparing to head to the bar for a refill, but he moved, too, inevitably drawing her attention. "May I, ma'am?"

Beth tilted her head to look at him for the first time, and all the moisture seemed to disappear from her throat. Cute did not begin to describe the man sitting next to her. He was tall and lean, but she wouldn't call him lanky with his broad shoulders and muscled arms. His hair was a light brown and he was clean-shaven, but it was his eyes that drew her in. They were the most amazing baby blue.

When she didn't respond, he repeated his question. "May I get you a refill on your drink, ma'am?"

"Y-yes." Then, catching herself, she spoke again with more confidence. "Um. No. Thank you. I don't know you from Adam."

He extended his hand. "Drew Parker."

She raised an eyebrow.

"Allison and John will vouch for me. No funny business. I promise." He tilted his head toward another Femdom, Allison, and her longtime boyfriend and sub, John. Beth knew them both, although not well.

Beth waited until Allison looked in her direction, and gave her a questioning look. Allison smiled and nodded.

Reluctantly, Beth handed her glass to the man sitting beside her.

"What would you like?" he asked.

"The bartender knows. Just tell him it's for Beth." Her answer came out more clipped than usual. She wanted him to take his leave as quickly as possible before she went and did something stupid. Beth kept her gaze on him as he walked away. Her stomach was doing flip-flops and she didn't like it one bit.

He returned a few minutes later and handed her a small glass filled with half Coke and half Sprite. Beth rarely drank alcohol, and never at the club. Whenever she came to Serpent's Kiss, she was either playing with Ben or she was alone where she'd have to drive home. Either way, she didn't drink.

After taking the glass from Drew, she turned back to her friends, effectively ignoring her unwanted admirer once more. Nicole had a knowing smirk on her face that Beth desperately wished she could wipe off. Maybe she could borrow one of the club's floggers. It had been a while since she'd thrown one, and she had to admit the thought of having the leather in her hands again was appealing.

For the next hour, Drew continued to sit beside her in silence as she chatted with her friends. Everyone in their small group brought Beth up to date on what was going on in their lives. Meanwhile, her new admirer said nothing. And although he did little more than sit there, he was making her uneasy. Every one of her nerve endings seemed to be aware of him.

Finally, Beth couldn't take it any longer and turned to face him. "I don't know what you're looking for, but let me spell out exactly what I'm *not* looking for. I'm not looking for a submissive and I don't play with random partners."

"I understand." His voice was smooth, and it sent tingles down her spine. This was not good.

She quirked an eyebrow at him. "You understand?"

"Yes, ma'am."

Beth waited for him to leave, but he remained where he was. "So if you know I'm not looking for a relationship or a play partner then why are you sitting here?"

"I'd like to get to know you, if you're agreeable." He sounded sincere.

"You want to be friends?" she asked.

"Yes, ma'am."

"Why?"

He shrugged. "You seem interesting."

Beth gave him a hard look trying to decide if he was telling the truth or not. She never used to question her judgment, but after Ben, everything was different. "Do you have a mistress?"

"No, ma'am. I'm pretty new to the lifestyle."

"How new?"

"A few months." His gaze never left hers.

"Have you ever played with a Femdom before?" Why she was asking was beyond her. It wasn't as if she ever planned on playing with him.

"No, ma'am."

Again, she had no idea why she was pressing for information, but the questions kept coming to the forefront of her mind and she kept asking them. "No vanilla girl out there for you?"

"I've tried vanilla relationships and they don't work for me. I want a woman to take control."

The image of him tied to a bench completely at her mercy flashed in her mind before she squashed it. No. She would not go down that path.

If he wanted to be friends, she could try, she supposed. But there would have to be ground rules—no seeing him outside the club being the number one. She had no idea if he frequented the local munches or not. If so, she would have to be careful. Munches were more laid back. That could open up a whole new set of problems— especially since she was already having a physical reaction to him.

Theirs would have to be a lifestyle friendship only. If Drew had questions about BDSM or needed help finding a Domme, she could maybe give him advice. That was it, though. Beth wasn't ready to get tangled up in another web of emotional attachment.

Taking a deep breath, she offered her hand, and introduced herself. "I'm Beth. Beth Davenport."

He wrapped his fingers around hers almost reverently. "It's nice to meet you, Beth Davenport."

Chapter 2

Drew's alarm woke him bright and early at six. He didn't get in until almost two, and he was feeling it. Originally he'd planned on leaving the club at eleven—he had to work Saturday, after all—but after laying eyes on Beth, getting a full night's sleep became less of a priority. She'd stayed until one thirty, so he had as well. The thought of leaving before her didn't cross his mind.

Padding into his bathroom, Drew stepped into the shower, and turned on the spray. He adjusted the temperature so it was a little cooler than normal hoping it would help wake him up.

As the fog lifted from his brain, he recalled the end of his night. When he'd offered to walk Beth to her car, she'd looked at him with shock, and then panic. He wanted to comfort her, but he was at a loss. She wasn't his mistress. They'd agreed to be friends, and he'd gotten the impression she wasn't entirely comfortable with that much. He had to be cautious. As much as he wanted to touch her, he knew it wouldn't be a good idea.

Drew smiled as he rinsed the shampoo out of his hair. Turning off the water, he grabbed a towel, and swiftly dried himself off. Beth hadn't sent him away. Friendship wasn't exactly what he wanted, but he could work with it. She'd been hurt. He could understand that, too. Drew's last girlfriend, Mya, hadn't understood his need to relinquish control. Although at the time he didn't completely understand it himself, he'd tried to explain it to her. She'd lashed out at him, and they broke up.

Their fight was the driving force behind Drew's exploration into BDSM. He needed someone who understood what he needed, what he craved. Trying to fake it wasn't working for him anymore.

Drew pulled up to the fire station with five minutes to spare. He parked his car and grabbed his duffel bag from the backseat. He worked in one of the larger stations in St. Louis, and they were in the middle of a shift change. People were coming and going from all directions. Everyone he passed acknowledged him in some way. Being a firefighter was like being part of a large family. Sometimes it even reminded him of a college frat house.

"Parker!"

He whirled around and looked up. Chief Franks was leaning over the second-floor railing. "Morning, Chief."

"I need you to grab your crew and head down to Crawford Street ASAP. Madison's crew is still there holding a scene until an inspector gets there."

"Is the fire out?"

"Yep. All I need you and your guys to do is sit on your pretty asses until the inspector gets there and takes over the scene."

"Arson?"

Chief Franks nodded. "Looks like."

"Let me put my things in my locker, and I'll grab the guys."

Without another word, Chief Franks headed back into his office.

Drew worked his way to the locker room. Baily and Irwin, two of the guys on his crew, were already there. "Hey. We need to grab our gear and head over to Crawford. Shawn and his crew are holding a scene until one of the inspectors show up, and we need to go relieve them."

"The fire's already out?" Baily asked.

" 'Fraid so."

Both Baily and Irwin sighed and shut their locker doors.

Drew focused on putting his own things away. "Do you know if Romeo's made it in yet?"

"Looking for me, Cap?" Eddie Romero—otherwise known as Romeo—strolled into the locker room right on cue.

"Put your things away, and then grab your gear. We've got to go relieve Shawn's crew."

"Fire?"

"It's already been put out, man," Baily said.

Since Drew had an SUV, they all piled in and drove over to the scene. The mood was a lot more somber than it would have been had there still been a fire to fight. As it was, all they would be doing was standing around twiddling their thumbs.

The warehouse was less than five miles from the station. A lot had changed in the area over the last ten years. Most of the old warehouses had been converted into apartments and storefronts. Drew supposed they were lucky the building the arsonist chose was still abandoned.

He parked along the curb behind the truck. His buddy and fellow captain, Shawn, and his crew were lounging against the side, waiting. When he saw Drew pull up, he pushed off the truck and sauntered over to meet them. "I was hoping you'd be the inspector."

"Any idea what's taking so long?" Drew asked as he rounded the vehicle to unload their gear from the back.

"Not a clue. Dispatch said they were on their way, but so far nothing."

With their gear unloaded, Drew handed his car keys over to Shawn. "I guess we wait, then."

Thirty minutes later, they were still waiting. Drew was about to radio dispatch again to see what was going on when a dark blue sedan pulled up in front of the fire truck. A woman exited the vehicle, her head tilted down looking at something. He began striding over to her, not sure who she was or what she was doing at the scene.

She looked up, and Drew nearly tripped over himself. It was Nicole from the club. Beth's friend. And someone he knew for a fact was a Domme. From the way her eyes widened, Drew guessed Nicole was as shocked to see him there as he was to see her.

Nicole recovered quickly and walked toward him. "Good morning, gentlemen."

His crew mumbled hello while Drew got his bearings. He wasn't sure what to say or how he should handle the situation, so he decided to play dumb, remembering what Mistress Katrina had told him about the privacy of the club's members. "Can I help you, ma'am?"

Drew didn't miss her smirk. "Nicole Owens. I just transferred to the Fire Marshal's office. I understand we have a suspected arson."

"You're the fire inspector?"

Amusement lit Nicole's eyes at his question. "Yes."

"Okay." Drew was still shaken, but he knew he needed to buck up and do his job. "Baily, Irwin, stay with the truck. Romeo, you're with me and the inspector."

They spent the next few hours combing through every inch of the building. The pictures, or what he could see of them through the digital camera Nicole was using, downplayed the damage, in Drew's opinion. It looked as if the building had been in the process of being remodeled. All the new internal structure was ruined. The building was only safe to be walking around in because of its brick exterior and the quick reaction time of the responding stations.

Nicole followed them down, out of the building, and back onto the sidewalk. "Thank you for going over everything with me. I think it's safe to say this was arson. I'll get this turned over to bomb and arson so they can take it from here."

Romeo smiled, and Drew realized his friend was smitten with the new fire investigator. Too bad he was married and Nicole was currently spoken for. "It was our pleasure, ma'am."

During their walk through the building, Drew and Nicole had done their best to keep things professional. They spoke when needed, but that was where it ended. It was for that reason the next words out of her mouth stunned him. "I'm starving. What would you guys say to some lunch? I know a little place around the corner."

Before Drew even had a chance to respond, Baily was answering for all of them. "Sounds great. Lead the way."

***

Beth had been running around like a mad woman all morning. She hadn't gotten nearly enough sleep, and Tommy showed up late. Of course, the lack of sleep was entirely her own fault. Beth should have left the club well before midnight. She didn't want to dwell too much on why she'd stayed until almost two.

It was a little before noon and the Saturday lunch rush was already in full swing. Half the tables in her café were occupied and they had several patrons at the counter waiting on their orders. What she wouldn't do for a break, or even better a nap, right about now.

Too bad that wasn't likely to happen in the next two hours. Lucky for her it wasn't a weekday. They were so busy sometimes during the week that she didn't make it home until almost dinnertime.

She piled the roast beef on a slice of still warm rye bread. Most of Beth and Tommy's customers were locals. They were lucky. Even on Saturdays they were usually busy. With the revitalization going on in the area, they were hoping to stay that way for many years to come.

The bell above the door jingled announcing another customer, and Beth tried to hurry. Getting behind would only make it worse.

"Hey, B. You have a visitor," Tommy yelled.

Beth sighed. She hated when he called her that, but telling him did no good whatsoever. Tommy was twenty-three and felt the need to give everyone a nickname. She had to admit B was better than the first nickname he'd come up with for her—Bumble Bee.

Cutting the sandwich in half, Beth placed it along with chips and a homemade pickle on a plate and brought it out with her to give to Mr. Keller. "Here you go."

He smiled back at her and took the sandwich. "Thank you, dear."

Beth wiped her hands on her apron and started toward the counter where Tommy was chatting with someone. When she saw who it was, she grinned.

Then Beth noticed the man standing behind Nicole. Drew Parker.

No. No, no, no, no. This was not supposed to happen. He wasn't supposed to be here. He wasn't supposed to know anything about her life outside the club . . . the lifestyle.

The only thing that made her feel a little better was the look on Drew's face. Clearly, he hadn't been expecting to see Beth any more than she'd been expecting to see him.

"Nicole. What are you doing here?" Beth asked through gritted teeth.

Her friend acted as if nothing were amiss. "We were working in the area and got hungry. I told Captain Parker and his crew that I knew of a great place for lunch, so here we are."

Beth was going to strangle her.

Putting on her best hostess smile, she tried to keep the irritation out of her voice. "What can I get you?"

Nicole ordered her usual, turkey on wheat, and then stepped aside so Drew could order. Beth tried really hard not to react to him, but it was impossible. Her heart was hammering in her chest. She hadn't missed that he was wearing a polo shirt with the St. Louis Fire Department logo on it. They hadn't talked about jobs the night before. Beth wasn't sure how she felt about him being a firefighter.

That thought brought her up short. What the heck was she doing? What did it matter if he was a firefighter or not? It was his life. It had nothing to do with her.

"Hi," Drew said.

"Hello." She adjusted the straws displayed on the counter, and then stopped herself. Why was she fidgeting?

He smiled and cleared his throat. "I've never been here before. What's good?"

"Everything's good. We bake all our breads and pastries fresh daily."

"Hmm." Drew glanced up at the menu behind the counter. "I think I'll try the pulled pork."

"Make that two," the man standing behind him said. The sad part was, Beth had completely forgotten about the rest of them.

"Sure. Two pulled pork sandwiches coming right up." Beth swallowed and looked to the other two men. "And what can I get you two?"

The one on the far left spoke up first. "I'll take a roast beef sandwich."

"Turkey, please, ma'am," the blonde said. In response, his buddy rolled his eyes.

Beth nodded absentmindedly. All she wanted to do was get out of there as soon as possible. "I'll be out in a few minutes with those."

Disappearing into the back, Beth helped Tommy with the sandwiches, and then made him take them out front. She hid in the kitchen until Tommy yelled for her again. "I'm busy."

"Oh no, you're not." Beth looked up to find Nicole standing right inside the kitchen with her hands on her hips.

Reaching for the nearest towel, Beth began tidying up. "Yes, I am. Tommy was late this morning, and we're behind. I'd like to get out of here at a decent time today."

Nicole propped her hip against the metal counter less than a foot away from where Beth was pretending to clean. "That may be true, but it's never stopped you from coming out to visit me for a few minutes."

"You have people with you today. You don't need me interrupting."

Her friend shook her head and clicked her tongue in disapproval. "You can't fool me, Beth Davenport. The only reason you're hiding in here like a chicken is because of that man out there."

"I don't know what you're talking about."

Nicole went on as if Beth hadn't said anything. "Which tells me that, as much as you claim to have no interest in him, you do. A lot of interest, if I'm not mistaken. So stop being a coward and go out and say hi to the man."

Beth dropped the towel and hunched her shoulders. "It's not that easy."

"Oh sweetie, yes it is. He's not Ben."

"You don't know that. You don't know any more about him than I do."

Nicole edged closer. "I know he's been a firefighter for seven years and was recently promoted to captain. I know he's got an eye for detail. When we walked through a building today, he spotted a few things that both me and his buddy missed. And I know from the looks he was giving you last night and how he kept glancing over his shoulder to see if he could catch a glimpse of you throughout lunch that he's interested."

"I can't. I'm sorry. I know you mean well, but I just can't. It's too soon."

Her friend sighed. "Okay. I don't agree with you, but . . ."

"Thank you."

"Well, I'd better get back out there. Don't want them to think I ditched them or something." Nicole winked and turned to go.

"Nicole?"

"Yes?"

"You don't think he'd say anything, do you? I mean, he's new. He knows not to . . . I mean . . ."

Nicole grinned. "I don't think he'll say anything. We were both shocked when we met this morning. I figured if he was going to let the cat out of the bag, he would have done it then. He didn't say anything. Didn't even act like we knew each other. I'd say you're safe."

"Okay."

"Anything else?"

"Yeah. If you ever pull anything like this again, I'm going to ask to use Katrina's cat-o'-nines."

Nicole laughed and ducked out of the kitchen. "You'd have to catch me first."

Beth threw the towel in her friend's direction. She missed, and it landed on the tile floor a few feet shy of the doorway. Sighing, Beth ambled across the room to retrieve the towel. Throwing it in the hamper, she went to the closet to get a clean one.

The door closed behind her and she was alone in the small supply closet. Instead of going to the back of the room, she lowered herself onto the step stool they kept right inside the door. Moisture welled up in her eyes, and before Beth knew it, she was crying uncontrollably. It made no sense, and yet it did. The tears weren't for Ben or her lost relationship. Beth was scared. Terrified. Nicole was right. Drew was interested, and Beth couldn't deny she was attracted to him as well. And he was a sub. It should be perfect. It would be perfect if not for the nightmare she'd experienced with Ben.

She wiped at the tears, but for every one she banished two more came in its place. Interested or not, Beth couldn't risk it. If Drew hurt her, she didn't know if she'd be able to survive it. Ben, and his wife and daughter, nearly killed her. Beth took her role as a mistress seriously. It wasn't a game to her. She not only wanted the physical connection it provided, but the emotional one as well. Beth had loved and trusted Ben, and he'd taken both and trampled it.

There was a knock on the door, and Beth jumped up. "B? You in there?"

She rushed to the back of the room to get the towel she'd originally come to retrieve. "Yeah. I'm just getting a clean towel. I'll be there in a minute. You need some help with something?"

When she emerged from the storage room, Tommy was washing dishes. He paused mid wipe, and frowned. "Are you all right?"

Beth knew she must look a mess. She quickly turned her back to him. "I'm fine. Did you need me to watch the counter for a while?"

"Beth?"

"Hmm?"

"It's two thirty. There's only a few tables left, and they're finishing up."

She glanced at the clock on the far wall. Sure enough, it was two thirty. Beth had been in that supply closet for almost two hours.

"Are you sure you're okay?" Tommy asked.

Beth nodded. "Yeah. I'm fine. Really. I'll just go check on the tables we have left and then I'll be back to help you."

Tommy was right. Guests at one table were getting up, and the other two were almost finished with their lunches. Beth walked over and asked if she could get them anything else. It was the least she could do after abandoning Tommy and her business for two hours.

Chapter 3

Beth felt horrible. Tommy had been swamped with customers throughout the lunch rush. So much so that he didn't have time to search for her. Luckily, since it was a Saturday, most of the lunch-goers were regulars. She had no idea what would have happened if she'd flaked during a weekday.

As soon as the last customer was out the door, Beth sent Tommy home. He'd protested, of course, but she put her foot down and made him leave. Besides, she needed a little time to herself.

It took her twice as long to wipe everything down and prep for Tuesday. Most of it was mindless work—cleaning surfaces, filling containers. Things she could do in her sleep. It gave her way too much time to think.

Drew had been in her café. He knew where she worked. And thanks to Nicole, he'd breached the careful boundary Beth had placed upon their relationship without even trying.

Nicole. Beth was still cursing her best friend. Then again, maybe she should be rethinking their entire friendship after Nicole threw Beth under the proverbial bus. She didn't understand why Nicole was pushing so hard for her to get back in the dating scene. It wasn't as if she had a vested interest in anything. It was Beth's life, after all.

By the time she headed home, Beth was on edge. She'd

promised Nicole she'd put in an appearance at Serpent's Kiss later, but she was rethinking that plan. All she wanted to do was go home and curl up on the couch with a bowl of ice cream.

Beth was still debating the issue three hours later when there was a knock on her front door. It was Nicole. "What are you doing here?"

Nicole brushed past Beth into the two-story house. She'd bought it the year before as a present to herself for her café making it past the five-year mark. At the time, Beth had envisioned kids running through the house laughing—kids she'd planned to one day have with Ben. Realizing having children might never happen for her was depressing. She was thirty years old with no real prospects on the horizon.

The memory of Drew sitting beside her the night before flashed in front of her eyes. Her pulse began to race thinking about him. It was crazy. Nuts. She had to be out of her mind reacting like this to a man she didn't even know.

"Penny for your thoughts?" Nicole asked.

Beth shut the front door and forced the memory of Drew out of her head. She leveled a not-so-pleasant look at her friend. "I'm thinking of all the ways I can torture you for the stunt you pulled today. What the hell were you thinking bringing him to my café?"

Nicole shrugged as if it were no big deal. "We were in the area and it was lunchtime. Where else would I take them?"

"Why not let them fend for themselves? They seem capable enough. I'm sure they could handle it all on their own."

Her friend chuckled. "I'm sure they could. But where would be the fun in that?"

Beth threw her hands up. "Why are you doing this?"

"I don't know what you're talking about. Doing what?"

"Trying to throw this guy at me."

Nicole turned on her heel and headed in the direction of Beth's bedroom. "Did you already have something picked out to wear tonight?"

Beth followed. "I haven't decided if I'm going or not. And stop avoiding the question."

"I'm not avoiding anything. What I'm doing is making sure you get out of this house and back into the land of the living."

Nicole's comment hit its mark. Beth had been living like a

hermit these last three months. When she wasn't at the café, she could usually be found at home, sitting in front of the television. Beth couldn't say how many movies she'd watched in that time. More than she'd probably watched the first thirty years of her life.

"I'm not ready." It sounded feeble even to Beth's ears.

Her friend threw several items onto the bed, and lowered herself to the floor to go through Beth's shoe selection. "No one says you have to do anything more than socialize. Not even with Drew, although I could tell by the way you reacted to him last night and today he must do something for you. Be that as it may, Drew's working tonight so he won't be there. You're safe."

For some reason that made Beth feel better. She wasn't ready to see him again.

"Besides, I need some company. Jeff had to go help his sister move into a new apartment, so I'm on my own tonight."

Beth sighed and picked up the dress Nicole had selected. It was sexy, but certainly not the most provocative thing Beth owned. "Girls' night?"

Nicole smiled. "Girls' night. Now come on. Katrina is giving a demonstration tonight, and I don't want to miss it."

***

An hour and a half later, Beth was sitting in the club's main room with a drink in her right hand. The furniture had been rearranged for the evening's activities. While they were waiting, a few people wandered over to say hi. Everyone was friendly, saying they were glad to see her back.

It wasn't until Nicole got up to get another drink that Daniel, a Dom in his early fifties, came to say hello.

Beth smiled when he lowered himself into the chair beside her. "How have you been?"

"Can't complain. What about you? It's good to see you back."

Daniel was one of the nicest men Beth had ever met. He'd been in the lifestyle for over twenty years, and he was full of helpful advice. It was too bad she wasn't a submissive. Daniel was one of the few men Beth trusted.

"I'm good."

He raised one eyebrow. Beth had seen him give that look to subs many times.

"I am. The café is doing well. I'm keeping busy." Beth took a sip of her drink.

Daniel didn't beat around the bush. "Have you heard from him?"

Beth didn't need Daniel to clarify who 'he' was. She knew he was referring to Ben. "No. Not since I kicked him out."

He nodded. "Maybe I shouldn't say anything, but if it were me, I'd want to know. He came by the club about two months ago."

Beth spat out her drink.

"Don't worry. Katrina asked him to leave and made it very clear he was no longer welcome. In fact, I think she promised him the end of her whip should he make another appearance." Daniel grinned.

Although Beth knew she shouldn't ask, she couldn't help herself. "What did he want?"

Daniel shrugged. "No idea. Katrina didn't let him get more than a few feet inside the door. The only reason I know as much as I do is because she asked Sam and I to back her up."

Beth rolled the glass between her hands, looking down into the dark brown liquid. "Thanks for telling me."

Nicole sat down on the other side of Beth. "Hey, Daniel."

"Nicole. How's the new job?"

"One word: paperwork."

They all laughed.

Before any more could be said, the lights dimmed and Katrina made her way to the front of the room. "Thank you all for coming to our demonstration tonight. We've had a number of individuals ask about wax play, so tonight we're going to go over all the dos and don'ts. I'll stop periodically to see if there are any questions, but I ask that everyone please wait until those specific times so as not to break my, or my submissive's, concentration during the scene."

Katrina motioned toward a man who had been standing off to the side. He looked to be about Beth's age, maybe a little younger. Beth had never seen him before, which surprised her. Katrina didn't have a single submissive she regularly played with but in the past she'd usually used Ryan for stuff like this. Then again, Beth had been out of the loop for a while. Maybe things had changed.

The man walked over and knelt down in front of Katrina. She walked around the man, taking her time. Once behind him, Katrina ran a hand down the length of his back, and then back up into his short-cropped hair. "As with many other forms of play, touch is extremely important. It can tell you things you might miss otherwise. Is your sub tense? Are they scared? Excited? Learning to read your partner is one of the greatest gifts you can give yourself and them."

She moved to retake a position in front of him. "Go lie facing up on the table, Wes."

The man stood and strolled over to the table. Doing as he was told, he lay down with his back on the padded surface.

As Beth continued to watch the scene, she couldn't help but think about Drew. What would he look like laid out like that? Did he have as many muscles under his shirt as he seemed? What would he feel like under her hands?

Wes sucked in a deep breath as the wax hit his chest. Other than that, however, he didn't react. Knowing Katrina as Beth did, she smirked as the club mistress redirected the candle lower. Wes cried out as hot wax dripped down his stomach to his cock. It was fully erect. He was obviously enjoying Katrina's torture. From the look on her face, Katrina was having fun as well.

"I might have to try that," Nicole whispered.

Beth snorted, but otherwise let it go. Her mind was still on Drew. Nicole said he was working. He could be out fighting a fire as they sat there watching Katrina hold a burning candle over her willing victim.

Without thinking, Beth sent up a silent prayer Drew would be kept safe. She wasn't sure she wanted a relationship with him, but she was quite certain she didn't want to see him harmed either.

***

Drew didn't have much time to think about Beth during his shift. They'd not been back fifteen minutes on Saturday afternoon before they were called out to a car accident. Once they got that cleaned up, the guys headed back to the station. They were less than a minute away when the call came in for a small grease fire.

By the time they got back and cleaned their gear, they were all ready for some downtime. Unfortunately, there was still work to be done. His lack of sleep the night before was beginning to wear on him. As soon as the clock struck nine thirty, Drew made a beeline for his cot, and crashed. Lucky for him, the next call didn't come until four hours later. He rolled out of his bunk and hit the ground running.

Shawn cornered him the next morning. "I heard it was a busy shift."

"All minor stuff." Drew shrugged. It had kept him occupied. That was probably a good thing.

"So. What's with you and the lady at the café?" The two of them were alone, but they wouldn't be for long.

"Nothing."

"Sure. I heard you were craning your neck all throughout lunch trying to get another glimpse of her. You gonna ask her out?"

"Gonna ask who out?" Johnson, one of the stations EMTs, asked.

Two other guys followed Johnson in and Drew became the center of attention.

Drew sighed. The last thing he wanted was to draw the guys into this. For one thing, he couldn't explain how he knew Beth. Or how he knew she wouldn't be thrilled if he asked her out.

Before he could figure out how to answer, Shawn did it for him. "Parker here had to babysit a scene yesterday until the inspector got there, and apparently the new inspector took them all to lunch at this little café. Rumor has it he was taken with the woman behind the counter."

"Was she hot?" Martinez asked.

Romeo chose that moment to join the conversation. "An eight or a nine, I'd say."

The guys whistled.

Drew shook his head. It was useless. "I'm outta here. See you guys tomorrow."

On his way home, Drew took a detour and drove by the café. All the lights were out and the doors locked. According to the sign, they were closed on Sundays and Mondays.

He wasn't sure if he was disappointed or relieved. Drew wanted to see Beth again, but what exactly would he say? He supposed he could apologize for the day before, but even that sounded lame. Nicole had blindsided them both.

Drew didn't know what to make of Nicole. Never in his wildest imagination had he dreamed of running into her, or anyone else from the club for that matter, on the job. Maybe that was naïve of him, but it had thrown him for a loop.

He had done his best to remain professional throughout their examination of the building. She hadn't brought up their connection, even when Romeo was out of earshot. Katrina had explained to him the importance of privacy for many of the club's members when he'd joined. He was completely on board with that. Drew couldn't imagine the ribbing he'd get from the guys if they ever found out he wanted a woman to dominate him. He'd never live it down.

The week seemed to drag. It had nothing to do with work. They had plenty of calls to keep them busy. Most of them were medical, but something was better than nothing.

Drew did a lot of thinking over the course of the week, and most of it revolved around Beth. It had been a while since he'd pursued a woman. Being a firefighter had its perks. When he was younger, it was great. Find a pretty woman in a bar, tell her how you rushed into a building and saved someone's life, and more often than not, she was enamored.

It was great for the first five years or so. He'd been more concerned with getting laid than finding a long-term relationship. Drew wasn't sure if it was because he was getting older or not, but he was ready for something more meaningful. He didn't want to wake up ten years into the future and not have someone waiting for him at home. He wanted a wife—a family. Was Beth the right woman? He didn't know, but he wanted to find out.

Friday night Drew put on his best black jeans and a dark blue T-shirt his ex-girlfriend always said made his eyes pop. He was hoping Beth would be at the club. Drew still wasn't quite sure how to cross that line Beth had drawn in the sand regarding their relationship, but he knew he had to figure out something.

The first thing he did when he walked in the door of Serpent's Kiss was look for Beth. It took a minute, but he found her in the corner laughing with Katrina. Drew smiled. She looked happy. Relaxed.

As if Beth could feel his eyes on her, she turned her head in his direction. Her smile faltered, and his heart sank. She wasn't pleased to see him.

A second later, Nicole was in front of him. "Don't get discouraged."

He blinked. "What?"

"Beth. Don't let her attitude discourage you."

"Oh. Okay."

Nicole smirked. "Come. Let's get a drink."

Without a better option, Drew allowed Nicole to lead him across the room to the bar. She ordered herself a drink, and he did the same.

They found two bar stools and sat down. "You handled last Saturday well. If I didn't know any better, I would have thought we'd never met."

"Well, we hadn't. Not officially."

She smiled. "True."

The bartender placed their drinks in front of them, and Nicole twirled the little umbrella between her fingers. "What are your intentions, Drew Parker?"

He nearly choked on his drink. "Excuse me?"

"You heard me. I'm sure you've heard Beth's story. Or at least part of it. I don't want to see her hurt. So I'll ask again. What are your intentions?"

Drew thought for a moment. He could refuse to answer, but he wasn't sure that was the best idea. So far, Nicole had been his best ally. "I want to ask her out."

"And?"

"And I don't know. As I'm sure you know, I'm new to this. I don't really know what comes next. Or if I'm overstepping some unwritten rule. All I know is that I'm attracted to her. I'd like to see if there's more."

"Are you looking for a relationship, or someone to scratch your itch?" Nicole asked.

Drew had to hand it to her. She wasn't pulling any punches. "I'm looking for a relationship. Is Beth that woman? I don't know yet."

Nicole took a sip of her drink and grinned. "Fair enough. And honest. Okay, I'll help you. But if you break her heart, I'll break your balls. Got it?"

The look she gave Drew had him swallowing nervously. He had no doubt she meant it. "Got it."

"Good. Now, go mingle with your friends. In about an hour, find her and say hi. Keep it light."

"Anything else?" he asked.

She slid off the stool and patted him on the back. "Turn on that firefighter charm all you boys are famous for. It might make a small dent in that wall of hers."

Drew snorted, and watched as Nicole strolled across the room to join Beth and Katrina. They spoke for a few minutes before the club owner excused herself. Beth leaned in and whispered something to Nicole. He figured Beth wasn't happy he and Nicole had been chatting.

Following Nicole's advice, Drew went to find John and Allison. They were upstairs watching a scene in one of the semiprivate rooms. The Dom had his submissive in a spread-eagle on a Saint Andrew's cross. It was obvious he'd been working on her for a while. Her back and ass were red, and he was in the process of inserting a butt plug.

"You made it." John smiled, and nodded toward the large viewing window. "Mistress wanted to see the scene. You just missed the flogging. Very intense."

"Looks like it."

"Daniel is one of the best at flogging, especially Florentine," Allison supplied.

They stood there watching the rest of the scene, which concluded with the sub hanging limp in her bindings after several screaming orgasms. By the time it was over, Drew was hard as a rock. He knew he couldn't seek out Beth with his cock straining against his jeans.

He excused himself and headed back downstairs. Instead of going into the main room, he turned the corner, and found a spot along the wall. He leaned back against the vertical surface and took several deep breaths. He had to calm down—a difficult feat in a club shrouded in sex.

It took a while, but he got himself under control. He strolled out into the main room of the club and scanned for Beth. She was sitting next to Nicole near the center of the room.

Taking his time, he made his way over to her. "Hello again."

Beth glanced up.

He wasn't sure what to make of the look on her face. "May I sit down?"

"Um. Sure."

"Thanks." Drew sat beside Beth on one of the love seats. "How have you been?"

Instead of answering, she said, "You didn't tell me you were a firefighter."

"No. I suppose I didn't. You didn't tell me you worked in a café either."

"I don't work there. I own it." Her voice held an edge he didn't understand.

"Impressive. The food was great, by the way." He had no idea what had caused her sour mood.

Beth relaxed her shoulders a little. "Thank you."

"So are you going to answer my question?" he asked.

"And which question is that?"

He smiled. "How have you been?"

She glanced down at his crotch. Drew didn't need to follow her gaze—he already knew what she would see. He was hard again. Not as bad as he'd been after watching the scene, but enough that it would be noticeable.

Beth smirked. "Probably a little better than you at the moment."

Chapter 4

Beth was having difficulty containing her amusement. As she continued to stare at Drew's lap, the bulge in his jeans became more pronounced. She knew she should probably look away, but she was enjoying the show too much.

"Sorry. I was watching a scene upstairs. Guess I'm still a little worked up."

She forced herself to meet his gaze. He seemed embarrassed, although she couldn't fathom why. Most of the males walked around the club in various stages of arousal. It was par for the course given the club's vibe.

Beth knew she should let it go, but she couldn't help herself. "And what about the scene had you worked up?"

He shrugged. "I don't know. The whole thing, I suppose."

"Do you know who it was?"

"I don't know the Dom's name, but I've seen him around the club. I didn't recognize the submissive. John said I missed a pretty impressive flogging."

Although Beth was curious to know more of the specifics, and to dig deeper into what had aroused him about the scene, she let the subject drop. She was already having too many thoughts of her own about what she'd like to do to Drew. The last thing she needed was to add to it.

Silence stretched between them for several minutes. That didn't mean she wasn't extremely aware of him. She'd been too aware of him from the moment he'd sat down beside her.

Beth was scrambling, trying to figure out how to break the lull in conversation when he cleared his throat. "So what do you like to do for fun? When you're not here at the club, I mean."

As topics went, Beth figured this was a relatively safe one. "I like history."

"History?" His eyes widened in shock.

"Not what you were expecting?"

"No, it's just . . ." He shook his head. "Okay, yeah, I wasn't expecting that."

"I'm sure there are a lot of things about me that would surprise you." As soon as the words left her mouth, Beth wished she could take them back. She didn't need to be flirting. It would only encourage him, and that's not what she wanted.

He smiled, and her stomach did a little flip. "I'm sure there are."

Beth needed to regain control of the conversation, and fast. "What about you? What do you like to do when you're not here or out fighting fires?"

"Anything outdoors—hiking, camping, that sort of thing. Have you ever been camping?" he asked.

"Not since I was ten. That's when I started realizing the importance of dry clothes and a warm bed." Beth cringed again. Why did she keep putting her foot in her mouth?

Drew grinned. "The last part is only an issue if you're sleeping alone."

"Well, seeing as how that would be the case, I don't see where it matters." Her words came out sharper than they should have.

"I'm sorry. Did I say something wrong?" He was frowning, and Beth hated to admit how much she wanted to see him smiling again.

She sighed. "Drew, we can't be anything more than friends."

"I know."

"Do you?" she countered.

"Yes."

Beth raised her eyebrows, broadcasting her doubt.

He met her gaze. "I'm not going to lie."

"That's good, because I detest liars."

Drew nodded. "Would I like to take you out on a date? Yes. But if friendship is all you're offering, then I'll take it."

She wasn't sure what to make of his statement. Was he telling the truth, or was it only a ploy to get her to let her guard down? "Why?"

"Why what?"

Was he intentionally being dense? "Why would you be okay with friendship? And why are you wasting your time sitting here with me when you could be off finding yourself a Domme?"

He shrugged. "I enjoy talking to you."

Beth was expecting him to elaborate, but he didn't. "Are you not interested in finding a mistress? If you sit here all night talking to me, that isn't likely to happen."

Drew smirked. "I'll take my chances."

She looked him over, head to toe. "Are you sure you're a sub?"

"Pretty sure, yeah. Why?"

Beth was trying to figure out a nice way to say it, but decided to throw caution to the wind. There was no reason to hold back. She was who she was, and if he didn't like it, he could take himself somewhere else. "Because you're awfully cocky for a submissive."

He laughed. "That's probably the firefighter in me. We tend to be a rather cocky bunch."

If what he said were true, whomever his mistress ended up being would have her hands full. Too bad it wouldn't be her. "How did you decide to become a firefighter?"

His smile grew wider. "I used to go camping with my dad when I was younger. By the time I was eight, I was begging him to let me build the fire. I'd take my time, making sure it was just right, and then once I had it perfect I'd sit there and watch it burn until my dad would tell me it was time to turn in. Dad said I was so fascinated with fire I'd either grow up to be a firefighter or an arsonist."

"I'm betting he's happy you chose firefighter."

"Yeah." Drew chuckled. "So what about you? What made you want to own a café?"

She began to relax. This was the kind of stuff friends talked about. This was safe. "That's a long story."

He shifted his weight, which brought their legs closer together. "I've got time."

Beth hated to admit it, but she was more aware of him than she'd like—even when having such a mundane conversation. "Um.

Well, the short version?"

"Sure."

"I used to work in a bakery, but after the owner died it closed up. I was trying to figure out what to do with myself. One day I was having lunch with a friend at a little restaurant across town. When they brought out our sandwiches, they were less than stellar."

"And you thought you could do better?" Drew asked.

"Not exactly. My friend thought I could. And by the end of our lunch, she had me thinking seriously about opening up my own place."

He grinned. "And you did."

Beth couldn't help but grin back. "I did. It was the best decision I ever made. Lots of hard work, but definitely worth it."

Drew cleared his throat. "I should apologize for last week—for just showing up in your café like that. I had no idea you'd be there."

Beth sighed. "I know you didn't. It's fine."

"So you're all right with me maybe stopping in to get a bite to eat once in a while?"

Was she? To tell him no would be rude, but look at what happened the last time. She'd ended up hiding out in the supply closet for two hours.

"That was the wrong thing to ask, wasn't it?"

"No. I mean, of course it's fine. Why wouldn't it be?" Oh, maybe because his appearance had thrown her off for the rest of the day? She couldn't tell him that, though.

"Okay. Good. I'm glad." He gave her a smile that had her heart racing.

"Nicole told me you've been a member of the club for a little over a month." She needed to get their conversation back on track.

"Yes. It's been a good experience so far."

"You said you're new to BDSM."

"That's right."

Before either of them could say any more, Nicole sat down across from them. "My feet are killing me. I never should have worn these new boots."

"That's why you never play in new shoes," Beth said.

Nicole slipped off one of her boots and began massaging her arch. Her submissive, Jeff, appeared a moment later with a drink for her. She took a sip and sighed. "Thank you, love. That's just what I needed."

Without words, she lifted her foot slightly and rotated it. Jeff got the message and lowered himself to the floor. He adjusted Nicole's foot so that it was resting in his lap, and he began gently kneading her flesh.

The rest of the evening was spent with the four of them talking about an upcoming spanking event scheduled the following week. Nicole and Jeff dominated the bulk of the conversation. Spanking was one of their main kinks, and both of them were looking forward to the event.

While Beth enjoyed spanking, she didn't get as into it as some of the other Femdoms. There were other things one could do to a sub that were a lot more fun, in her opinion.

As the conversation continued, she found herself watching Drew's reactions. He seemed interested. Beth wondered if he'd ever had an erotic spanking before. It was a foolish train of thought, but one she was beginning to realize was inevitable. She was attracted to him. No matter how much she tried to deny it, facts were facts. That didn't mean she had to act on it.

By midnight, Beth was ready to call it a night. Like last weekend, Drew offered to walk her to her car. She opened the driver side door and turned around to face him. "Thank you for the escort."

Drew smiled. "You're welcome."

There was a moment of tension before Beth broke it by sliding behind the wheel. "Good night, Drew."

"Good night, Beth."

***

Drew continued to replay the conversation he had with Beth in his head the next day as he did some laundry and tidied up his apartment. Was he being too aggressive in his pursuit of her? Did that make him less of a submissive? He didn't know the answer to that.

But what was the alternative? Beth had made it clear she wasn't interested in anything more than friendship. He, of course, was, and Beth knew that. Still, he'd been honest. If friendship was all she was comfortable giving him, then he'd take it and hope she grew to trust him enough to make herself vulnerable again.

As the day wore on, he grew more and more restless and all he could think about was going to the club again that night. Would she be there? And if so, would she be happy to see him? He didn't know the answer to either of those questions and it was slowly driving him insane. Maybe he was more of a masochist than he thought.

All his worrying had been for nothing. When he arrived at the club a little after eight, he realized Beth wasn't there. By nine thirty, he knew she wasn't coming. Whether or not that had anything to do with him, he didn't know. He hoped not.

By the time Monday rolled around and he returned to the station for his next shift, he was running scenarios in his head of what he'd do the next time he saw her—what he'd say. His mind was so full of Beth it had taken him twice as long to finish the paperwork on his desk. Most of the guys hated this part of the job, but Drew didn't mind it. Not usually. The thing with Beth was playing havoc with his brain, though. He couldn't concentrate.

As he was settling into his cot for the night, he remembered how she'd smiled when he told her about camping with his dad. Beth was beautiful—and even more so when she let her guard down.

Although there'd been some tension on Friday night, it was less than the week before. He wondered if that would have held true had Nicole not interrupted them. It seemed as if Beth was more comfortable keeping the conversation casual. Anytime it began getting too personal she would tense up, which was the last thing he wanted. Then again, he also wanted to know everything about her.

Taking a deep breath, Drew tried to push his inquiries out of his mind. He needed to rest. It was already after midnight.

Unfortunately, his sleep was interrupted two hours later by the alarm. Jumping out of bed, he joined the rest of his crew down on the main floor as they donned their gear. Although they'd all been awakened from sleep, it didn't take long for the adrenaline to take over as word came over the radio from dispatch about the blaze. They were sending eight trucks, which meant it had to be of significant size. It would probably keep them busy for the rest of the night.

Sure enough, Drew and the other firefighters on the scene spent the next four hours putting out the flames and making sure all the hot spots were extinguished. He hadn't been able to spend much time analyzing the burn patterns, but given the location and what little he'd seen, Drew wouldn't be surprised if it turned out to be another target of the arsonist.

By six, the scene was secure, a fire inspector was on scene, and they were ready to head back. Drew grabbed hold of the rigging to pull himself up onto the truck when his gaze landed on two people watching from about three blocks away. Even though she was wearing a pink apron with what looked to be flowers, he recognized her instantly.

Hopping down from the truck, he hollered to the guys that he'd be right back, and then jogged over to where Beth stood. "Hi."

"Hi." Her eyes were wide, although her voice was steady.

He looked down at himself and took in all the soot. Only then did it occur to him how he must look after spending the last four hours inside a burning building. He shouldn't have crossed the street to her. "I'm quite a sight, aren't I?"

It was the young man beside her who answered. "We couldn't believe it when we came into work this morning. I wasn't sure I would even be able to get to the café with the roads blocked off."

Drew didn't want to take his eyes off Beth, but he didn't want to be rude either. "Yeah, it was a hot one, that's for sure. It was safer to keep everyone back until we got it under control."

"Was it the arsonist?" Beth asked.

"Too early to tell." Of course she would know about the arsonist. She was friends with Nicole. Besides, it wasn't as if they could keep something like this out of the news. Several camera crews were on scene during the fire, but luckily, the officers who responded had kept them away from the action.

She nodded.

"I should probably get back. Need to get the truck ready to go before the next shift comes on at eight."

"Cool." There was a little more enthusiasm in the young man's voice than was warranted. Drew could see a bit of hero worship in the man's eyes as well.

Drew turned to go. He'd taken two steps when Beth stopped him. "Drew?"

He met her gaze, and realized there was still something about the way she was looking at him. "Yeah?"

"I have some muffins about to go in the oven. They should be ready in a half hour or so. If you're free."

A slow smile spread across his face. "Good to know. Thanks."

"Yo, Parker. Come on man. You can flirt on your own time," Baily yelled from inside the fire engine. His voice echoed off the surrounding buildings even from so far away.

Drew took another long look at Beth, and then hustled to rejoin his crew. The whole way back to the station he couldn't wipe the cheesy grin off his face. Beth had invited him to return to her café for muffins after his shift. He tried to remind himself not to get his hopes up—it was only breakfast. It didn't mean anything. Maybe if one of the other guys had trotted down the street she would have extended the same invitation.

Even as the thought crossed his mind, he knew it wasn't true. He could maybe see her handing out something already made as a thank you, or even offering to have all the guys stop in later, but that's not what she'd done. She'd given him a personal invitation.

With that in mind, he worked quickly to clean and stow his gear so he could head back over to Beth's café as soon as possible. His crew noticed his rush and had to give him a hard time about it. He laughed it off and concentrated on what he was doing.

It was after eight thirty before Drew made it back to the café. He'd had to take a shower, which slowed him down, but he didn't want to show up smelling, and looking, like a burnt piece of charcoal.

He opened the door and walked into the brightly lit space. There were a handful of customers seated at the small tables, and one at the counter talking to the young man who'd been standing beside Beth earlier. As Drew strolled toward him, he noticed the man was wearing a nametag that said Tommy.

"Hey, you made it," Tommy said, catching sight of Drew.

"I couldn't turn down the offer of fresh baked muffins, could I?"

"Beth makes the best muffins," said the woman standing beside him, waiting for her order.

"Is that so?" Drew had to admit he was curious as to what this woman had to say. Clearly, she wasn't a first-time customer. The way she said Beth's name was too casual.

"Oh, gosh, yes. There's nothing like one of her blueberry muffins hot out of the oven and a cup of coffee. The best way to start your day, I tell ya."

Drew's stomach took that moment to protest. He hadn't had

anything to eat since dinner the previous night.

The woman giggled as Tommy handed her a brown paper bag. She patted Drew's arm as she went to leave. "Get one of the cinnamon rolls. I promise you won't regret it."

With the woman gone, Drew turned his attention back to Tommy. "You have some loyal customers."

"Beth does. She has a talent for baking. I just help her out and follow her recipes."

Although he knew he shouldn't, Drew had to ask. "Have you two been working together for a long time?"

"I used to work with her at the old bakery when I was in high school. She was starting this place up, and found out I was looking for work, so she asked if I wanted to come help her. I've been here ever since."

Drew was about to ask another question when Beth came through a set of swinging doors. She stopped when she spotted him. "You made it."

"An offer of fresh muffins is hard to pass up." He smiled, hoping it was having the effect on her he wanted.

"I suppose it is." Beth slid a tray of chocolate chip cookies into a glass case and wiped her hands on her apron. "Did you want some coffee? Or we have milk or juice."

"Coffee sounds great."

She nodded. "Why don't you go sit down and I'll bring it out to you."

Before he could say anything else, she disappeared through the swinging doors again. He shook his head and went to find a place to sit as far in the back as he could. When Beth brought his breakfast out, he was hoping she might stay and visit with him for a few minutes. A guy could dream, right?

Chapter 5

What had she been thinking? After completely freaking out the last time Drew came into her café, she went and invited him to come have muffins? Was she crazy?

Apparently.

As she placed two muffins on a plate—one blueberry, one banana nut—she tried to regulate her breathing. She could do this. She would do this. It was only breakfast.

After seeing him earlier that morning in his firefighter gear and covered in dirt and grime, Beth had experienced a jolt of fear. Whether it was fear for him or fear of what could have happened had they not been able to contain the fire, she didn't know.

The fire he'd help to put out was a little over two blocks from her café. She was no expert, but Beth knew in places with buildings so close together it wouldn't have taken much for the fire to spread. What would have happened if it had made it to her café?

Carrying the muffins and a carafe of coffee out to the dining room, Beth tried to push her thoughts about the fire aside. She and Tommy were safe, as was her café—thanks to Drew and the other firefighters.

He grinned as she walked toward him. Beth felt a fluttering in the pit of her stomach seeing him sitting there in his white T-shirt and jeans. The thought of what he would look like naked flashed through her mind. She ignored it, and set the plate down in front of him.

"Thank you," he said.

"You're welcome. I hope you like them." Crazy as it sounded, Beth really wanted him to like her muffins. It was completely irrational, but there it was just the same.

She cleared her throat. "Well, I'll let you eat. Just let Tommy know if you need anything else."

As she turned to go, his voice stopped her. "Will you join me?"

"I don't . . ."

"Please? I won't bite. I promise."

Beth chuckled. "I thought you preferred being the bite-*e*."

Almost instantly, she started to blush. Why in the world had she said that?

Drew glanced down, and then back up to meet her gaze. "Touché."

Their eyes locked for several moments before Beth lowered herself into the chair beside Drew. "Sorry about that. I shouldn't have—"

"It's all right. Besides, it's the truth. At least, I think it is."

Drew picked up the blueberry muffin and took a large bite. While he chewed, Beth was drawn to how his throat moved as he swallowed. His skin was smooth. He'd shaved before he came.

She lowered her gaze to the T-shirt he was wearing where it was pulled tight against his muscles. For some reason, Beth was having trouble looking away.

"Wow. This is amazing." His exclamation roused her from her thoughts.

Beth felt the blood rushing to her cheeks again. "Thank you."

He took another bite, chewed, and then took a drink of his coffee. "Do you mind if I ask you something?"

She had no idea what he wanted to know, but given the gratitude she was feeling, Beth figured she'd take a chance. "All right."

"Is it me, personally, that you don't want to date, or is it men in general? Because of what happened, I mean."

Looking down at where she had her hands clasped on the table, Beth thought about how she should answer. If she told him it was only him, she was fairly positive he would go on his way and not bother her anymore. But could she do that? As much as she didn't want to date anyone at the moment, Drew had revived something in her she thought was dead.

Taking a deep breath, Beth glanced up. "It's not just you."

He nodded and took another bite.

As Drew was tearing into his second muffin, the timer she had attached to her apron went off. "I need to go check on something in the kitchen."

"I'll let Tommy know if I need anything. Thank you again for breakfast."

"You're welcome." As she stood to go, Beth felt reluctant to leave. It made no sense, and it certainly wasn't what she wanted. Too bad her mind and body weren't on the same page.

Forcing her legs to move, she hurried into the kitchen, and leaned back against the wall. She needed to get a hold of herself. He was only a man, and other than him being a firefighter and a sub, she knew very little about him. Getting too involved could land her in a world of hurt. Again. She couldn't let that happen.

Her secondary timer went off on the oven, and Beth rushed over to remove the bread before it burned. She didn't know what she was going to do about Drew. She really didn't.

A little after noon the next day, things became even more complicated when a man showed up with a bouquet of spring flowers for her. The flowers were beautiful. Simple, yet lovely.

"Who are they from?" Tommy asked as he followed her into the back.

"I don't know." It was true. She didn't know. She hadn't dared look at the card yet. That didn't mean she wasn't ninety-nine percent sure.

Tommy huffed. "Well, open the card already. The suspense is killing me."

She laughed. "It's killing you?"

"Yes."

Beth shook her head and plucked the card from where it was nestled in some baby's breath. "Well, I don't want you falling dead on my kitchen floor, so . . ."

He rolled his eyes. "Come on, B. You never get flowers. I bet it's that hunky firefighter. I saw the way he was looking at you."

"And just how was he looking at me?"

"Like he was imagining what you looked like with your clothes off."

"Tommy!"

He chuckled. "Well, it's the truth. Now, are you going to open the card or not?"

Beth toyed with the idea of not opening it for about two seconds, before running her finger along the envelope's seam. Whether she liked it or not, she was curious.

Slipping the card out of the envelope, she flipped it open.

> *Beth,*
> *Thank you for breakfast.*
> *Drew*

"Well?" Tommy demanded.

She fought a smile, and lost the battle. "They're from Drew."

"The firefighter?"

"Yes."

Tommy did a fist pump. "I knew it."

It was Beth's turn to roll her eyes.

"So?"

"So what?" she asked.

He sighed. "Sooo. Are you going to go out with him?"

"Just because he sent me flowers doesn't mean we're going out on a date."

"Pfft. A guy doesn't send a woman flowers he doesn't have the hots for."

Beth moved about the kitchen to get some water for her flowers. "Don't you have customers to wait on?"

Tommy gave her a hard stare. "Yes. Probably. But, B, give this guy a chance. I like him."

"Why? Because he's a firefighter?"

"No. Because I've met him three times now and not once has he talked down to me."

She knew what Tommy was saying. Ben would often come into the café for free meals when he was in town. Whenever Tommy was at the counter, which was almost always, Ben would make Tommy feel as if he were little more than a child—at least that was Tommy's view. Whenever Beth would ask Ben about it, he would deny doing any such thing. And, of course, Beth never witnessed the interactions personally. Ben was always on his best behavior when she was out front.

"I'll think about it, okay?"

Tommy smiled.

"Now, get out there and take care of our customers," Beth ordered.

He stuck out his tongue, and jogged away.

Alone with her flowers, Beth read over Drew's card again. It wasn't anything fancy—very direct and to the point. But if she was honest, she liked that he wasn't all about the frills. If Beth did this again, she wanted real. She wanted honest.

Placing her flowers on the table beside where she was working, Beth went back to preparing the mixes they'd need for the next day. As she worked, her eyes kept going back to the flowers. Could she take a chance on Drew? Could she trust him not to break her heart?

The problem was she didn't know the answer. There were too many what-ifs—too many unknowns.

By the time she and Tommy closed everything down for the day, Beth was finally coming to a decision. Although she'd told Drew they could be friends, she'd kept him—and their friendship— at arm's length to protect herself. Maybe that wasn't the best idea.

She and Ben hadn't been friends first. They'd jumped into a relationship right from the start. She'd trusted everything he'd told her on blind faith. That obviously hadn't worked well, so maybe it was time to change things up.

As she drove the short distance to her house, Beth knew she and Drew would need to sit down and talk, really talk, if he was truly interested in her. She would offer friendship. A *real* friendship. They could see where things went from there.

Pulling into her garage, Beth turned off the engine, and retrieved her flowers from the passenger seat. She hoped Tommy was right— that Drew was different. Only time would tell.

***

Drew had arranged for the bouquet of flowers to be delivered to Beth around noon on Wednesday. He'd watched the clock all morning. Then he spent the entire afternoon wondering what she'd thought of them.

When he'd asked her the day before if it was him or guys in general, her answer gave him hope. She'd been burned, and he understood her caution. That didn't mean he was willing to give up. There was something about her that sucked him in. He couldn't explain it. Yes, she was gorgeous, but it was more than that. The way she gave him that look—the one that made him excited and edgy all at the same time. It was damn close to how he felt when they were responding to a fire. He could only imagine what it would be like to play with her.

He'd watched a few scenes with Dommes and their male submissives. One he witnessed stood out above the others. It wasn't so much what was being done, but more the connection between the players. He'd later found out that the two had been together for almost twenty years. Drew wanted that.

Shawn found him on Thursday morning as Drew was filling up his coffee mug. "Saw your girl yesterday."

"What?" Drew wasn't sure he'd heard Shawn correctly.

Shawn took a mug out of the cabinet above the sink and reached for the coffee pot. "You heard me. I stopped in at that café you had lunch at last week. The one on Crawford Street."

As curious as Drew was, he tried to play it cool.

When he didn't respond, Shawn continued. "Yeah. And your girl was there. Looks like you may have yourself some competition."

"Really? How's that?" Drew said, leaning back against the counter.

Shawn raised his eyebrows up and down several times. "Someone sent her flowers."

"And?"

"And? Come on, man. Don't try to tell me you're not interested. If half of what Romeo and Baily are saying is true, you were practically drooling over her. Heed my advice, if you want in on that, you're going to have to make your move, but quick." Shawn had ten years on Drew, but the two had developed a friendship over the last few years. It was Shawn who'd encouraged Drew to apply for the captain's position when it opened up.

"I'll keep that in mind." Drew tried not to let it show how pleased he was that not only had Beth received his flowers, but that it was done in such a way that her customers had noticed. He needed to change the subject, though, or he was going to give himself away.

"So what brings you in early? Didn't you want that extra hour's sleep?"

His buddy smiled. "Chief called. You and me have a meeting in his office first thing. Hope you didn't have any plans this morning."

"Just a date with my bed," Drew said as he pushed himself away from the counter and headed toward the chief's office.

"Be better if you had someone there to keep it warm for ya."

Drew gave Shawn a playful shove. "Sure. Keep rubbing it in that you have a woman at home."

Shawn laughed. "Could be you, too, buddy. Just saying."

"Yeah, yeah. Come on. Let's see what the chief wants."

Turns out, the chief wasn't the only one waiting for them. Nicole was also in Chief Franks' office along with the other captains assigned to the station, and another man Drew didn't recognize.

The meeting was brief. The man he didn't know was from bomb and arson. It had been confirmed that both the fire from two weeks ago and the one over the weekend had been arson, and they looked to have been set by the same person. The mayor was all over this. So far, they'd been lucky—the arsonist seemed to be targeting abandoned buildings. Sooner or later, someone was going to be in the wrong place at the wrong time. The mayor wanted the guy caught before that happened.

By eight thirty, Drew was headed out to his car with his duffel bag. He tossed it in the backseat and was about to get behind the wheel when someone called his name.

He pivoted to see Nicole striding toward him. "I'm glad I caught you."

"Something wrong?"

She smiled. "Nope. Not a thing."

Drew was confused. She'd sought him out to tell him everything was good?

"Don't give me that look. I just wanted to let you know that I think the flowers you sent to Beth were perfect."

"Thanks."

"I wanted to find out what your next move is." she said.

"I don't know. I haven't really thought that far ahead. The flowers were a gamble."

Nicole looked serious. "You got any plans for today?"

He shook his head. "Just sleep."

"Good. Why don't you stop into the café for a late lunch—say, around one thirty?" There was a gleam in her eye Drew wasn't sure he liked.

"Why one thirty?"

The evil look in her eye spread to the rest of her features. She had a wicked grin on her face. "Because the café closes at two. It will give you enough time to eat and linger. Maybe you can offer to help her close up. Show off some of those service skills."

He snorted. "You're pushing awfully hard for this relationship. Why?"

Nicole's face fell. "You didn't see her . . . after. Although she's been cautious with you, there's finally some life in her again."

Drew guessed that made sense. "I'll see what I can do."

Before Nicole could add anything more, Drew lowered himself into the driver's seat.

"Take care of my girl," she said.

He nodded and drove away.

When he arrived at his apartment, Drew was struck at just how bare it was. Some of it could be explained by him being a bachelor with no woman in his life. Even that, however, was a stretch. His one-bedroom apartment didn't contain more than the basics. He had a bed, a dresser, a small table with two chairs, a television, and a recliner. That was about it when it came to furniture. He'd always intended to make more of an effort, but had never gotten up the energy to do it. After all, who was going to see it?

If he was thinking about pursuing a relationship with Beth, maybe he should finally do something about the place—spruce it up a little. He couldn't imagine she'd be all that impressed.

Strolling into the kitchen, he downed a glass of water before going into his bedroom. Although it was almost nine in the morning, he quickly went through his bedtime routine. Lowering himself to the bed, he reached over and set his alarm for twelve thirty. It would only give him a few hours' sleep, but given the option of catching a few extra hours of sleep and seeing Beth again, he'd pick the latter.

Slipping between the sheets, Drew leaned back onto his pillow. His bed was the one thing he'd splurged on when buying furniture for his apartment. Although the cots at the station weren't horrible, they certainly didn't scream luxury. The mattress and box springs had cost him a pretty penny, but it had been worth it. Settling in, he enjoyed how the material conformed to his body.

Drew closed his eyes and sighed, letting sleep take him.

His alarm went off waking him from an amazing dream. He was lying on his bed, hands tied to the headboard with Beth sitting astride him. She had this look on her face that sent his heart racing and had his cock stiff.

Reaching down beneath the sheets, he wrapped his hand around the part of him that was aching. It had been months since he'd been with a woman—something he couldn't have imagined a couple of years ago. This was different, though. It wasn't a faceless woman he was imagining. It was Beth.

Closing his eyes, he let his mind wander as his hand worked up and down his shaft. The pressure in his balls built quickly, and before he knew it, he was on the verge of exploding.

Throwing the sheet off him with his free hand, he ran his thumb over the head of his cock as he pulled up once . . . twice . . .

A surge of energy sprang up as he released, covering his hand and stomach. Tilting his head back, he took several deep breaths to calm himself down before reaching over to grab the towel he'd taken to keeping beside his bed.

With the majority of the mess cleaned up, Drew made his way into the bathroom. After throwing the soiled towel into the hamper, he turned on the water, and stepped into the shower. As the spray pounded his back, Drew couldn't shake the memory of Beth on top of him. His dreams of being with her got more detailed as time went on.

He had to hope the reality would be better than the fantasy. Drew had never wanted to get his hands on a woman more, and knowing that, even if they did end up in a relationship, she could deny him was driving him even madder. But it was also thrilling.

Drew knew he had to be patient. His dad always told him that the right woman was worth the effort, and Drew had a feeling Beth was that woman. At least, for him.

Chapter 6

Drew had to admit he was a little nervous as he stepped inside the café. He homed in on Tommy behind the counter. When the man saw him, he smiled. That eased some of Drew's anxiety. At least Tommy was glad to see him.

"You come for lunch, or to see Beth?" Tommy asked.

"Both, actually."

Tommy beamed. "Tell me what you want to eat, and then I'll run back and get Beth for you."

After placing his order, Tommy gave Drew his change, and handed him a glass.

"Go ahead and have a seat. I'll let Beth know you're here and have her bring your food out to you."

"If she's busy, I can wait." The last thing Drew wanted was to take her away from her job.

"No worries. We're slowing down. She's probably starting to clean up already."

Before Drew could say another word, Tommy had disappeared into the back. What was it with people lately?

Shrugging it off, Drew went to get his drink and find a table. He chose a spot in the back again. Although there weren't many people in the café at this time of day, Drew still wanted them to have some privacy. That, of course, was all based on the assumption that Beth was going to come out and talk to him.

As the minutes ticked by, Drew watched most of Beth's few remaining customers file out of the café. By the time Beth appeared with his sandwich, only one other table near the front was occupied. As far as Drew was concerned, it was perfect.

Without saying a word, Beth set the plate down in front of him and took a seat.

"Thank you," he said.

Beth nodded. "Thank you for the flowers. They were lovely. And rather unexpected."

He smiled. "You're welcome. I'm glad you liked them."

Silence filled the space between them as he dug into his lunch. He wasn't sure how much he should push and how much he should let her lead.

Luckily, before he came to a decision, she spoke. "I don't know how much you know about what happened. With me and my ex, I mean."

"Not much, but I know enough."

"Do you?"

There was an edge to her voice, and Drew was hoping he hadn't overstepped again. "I know you were hurt, that he betrayed your trust."

"I see. And did Nicole tell you that?"

"No. John did that first night I met you at the club."

She sighed. "I guess I'm not surprised. Bad news travels fast."

"John said he didn't know the details, but he wanted to give me a heads-up since . . ."

Beth smirked slightly, and then frowned. "Since he realized you were interested in me."

Drew met her gaze. "Yes."

She was quiet for several minutes, and he took the opportunity to finish his meal.

When she spoke again Drew had the urge to hug her, but he resisted. "I can't offer you anything more than friendship right now. I'm sorry. I just can't."

"I understand."

"You keep saying that."

"And I mean it. Like I told you before, I'm willing to take what you're offering. No strings," he said.

Beth snorted. "You sent me flowers."

"So?"

"So that isn't exactly something a friend would do."

He pretended to be offended. "Says who?"

She chuckled and shook her head. "Says me, that's who."

"You've never had a friend send you flowers?" he asked.

"Not the point." She rolled her eyes at him.

Drew had to admit he was having fun, and since she seemed to be right there with him, he continued. "Sure it is. You mean to tell me Nicole has never sent you flowers?"

"Yes. She has. For my birthday. But Nicole is not you." There was a light in Beth's eyes—a sparkle—and he loved seeing it.

"Ah. So I'm not special enough to send you flowers. I see how it is."

Beth rested her face in her hands and laughed. "You're impossible."

He grinned. "Am I?"

She looked up at him, amusement the most dominant emotion on her face. "Yes. You know exactly what I mean, and you're intentionally missing the point I'm trying to make. You're a guy. Guys don't send flowers to women they're friends with."

His expression sobered. "Would you rather I not have sent them?"

Beth paused and seemed to consider his question. "No. I liked the flowers. I just don't want you to get your hopes up."

"I'm not." He'd said it before, and if she needed him to, he'd repeat it every day until she believed him.

***

Beth wasn't sure if she should believe what Drew was saying or not. It was obvious he wanted more than friendship from her. Looking like he did, she couldn't imagine why he'd be willing to settle for friendship when he could probably go down to the local bar and find several women willing to give him whatever he wanted.

It irked her how much that thought turned her stomach. Although she wasn't ready for a relationship with Drew or anyone else, the thought of him with another woman made her ready to pounce. Even she knew that wasn't fair. Beth had no claim on him.

He was free to date, and even sleep with, whomever he wanted.

She stood quickly, sending the chair scraping along the floor. "I should get back to work if I want to get home at a decent hour."

Drew arose and picked up his plate. "Want some help?"

"That's all right. Tommy and I—"

"Please? I took you away from what you were doing . . . put you behind. Let me help."

Beth tilted her head to the side and considered his offer. If Nicole had offered to help her close down for the day, Beth would have jumped at the chance and would have immediately put her to work. If she was going to allow Drew into her circle of friends, shouldn't she treat him the same?

"All right. Follow me."

Without looking back, Beth made a beeline for the kitchen. Tommy was already at the sink doing dishes. When he saw Drew behind her, he winked.

She rolled her eyes and grabbed the tray they used to close down the dining room. Filling up the small bucket with warm soapy water, Beth handed it over to Drew. "Think you can handle wiping off all the tables and filling up the salt and pepper shakers?"

"Yeah. I think I can handle that."

"Good. I'll be out to check on you in about twenty minutes. And don't forget to check underneath the tables."

Beth thought she heard Drew chuckle before he headed back out to the dining room.

"Going a little hard on him, aren't you?" Tommy asked.

"No."

"Come on, B. Don't play that game with me. I've known you for too long. You like the guy. Admit it."

Picking up a clean towel, she wet it and began scrubbing the kitchen counters. "Yes, I like him. I know I shouldn't, but I do. Satisfied?"

"Maybe."

Beth groaned. "You're as bad as Nicole, do you know that?"

Tommy laughed so hard he had trouble catching his breath. "I'll take that as a compliment. I like Nicole."

As much as she wanted to comment, Beth kept her mouth shut. Tommy knew a lot about her life, but he had no idea that both she and Nicole were into BDSM. Tommy was young. Okay, he was twenty-three. Still, he was young enough for her to feel the need to keep that part of her life away from him. She'd known him since he was sixteen, and in many ways, she still viewed him that way.

Trying her best to ignore the satisfied grin on Tommy's face, Beth concentrated on getting her work done. Once she had everything cleaned and put away, she went out to the dining room to see how Drew was doing.

She found him near the front of the café. Even though she hadn't told him to, he'd flipped all the chairs upside down and placed them on the tables. To her knowledge, he'd never been to her café after hours. Maybe he'd worked in a restaurant when he was younger. That or he paid attention to details. When she'd worked at the bakery, putting the chairs on the tables was something all the new employees had to be told. More than once someone would just try to vacuum around the chair legs and call it done.

"You put the chairs up. That's good."

He glanced up. "Figured it was easier to do it as I went. I didn't see a sweeper anywhere, though."

Beth took a long look at the table she was standing next to. The salt and pepper shakers had been filled and arranged neatly at the center of the table beside the sugar. She walked to the window and flipped the sign to closed before turning her attention back to Drew. "It's in the supply closet. I'll show you."

She turned on her heel knowing he'd follow her. When she heard his footsteps behind her, Beth grinned.

Opening the door, she stepped into the small room, and turned on the light. Everything for the restaurant that wasn't food-related was stored in this room. She spotted the vacuum on the far wall and was about to retrieve it when Drew brushed past her. The area he'd touched—albeit briefly—left behind an almost electric charge.

He must have felt it, too, because he stopped and turned to face her.

They stared at each other for several moments before Drew cleared his throat. "Do I need anything else while I'm in here?"

She swallowed and shook her head. "No. The vacuum should be it."

Not waiting for a response, Beth left the room, and went to find Tommy. He was up front stocking supplies behind the counter. "Having fun with the firefighter?"

"Shut it. Now, what else needs to be done up here?"

Tommy chuckled and pointed to the large display case.

"Left that for me, did you? Thanks so much." Beth took a wet rag and began cleaning the large glass case they used to display the baked goods. It was perhaps her least favorite part of running the café. Everything had to be taken out of the case, wiped down, and put back. Sounded simple enough, but when jelly or icing dripped and then dried on the metal racks, it sometimes meant scraping it off.

As she was prying some icing from the center rack, she heard the vacuum turn on. Beth didn't need to look up to see Tommy was smiling—the amusement was vibrating off him. He was enjoying this thing with her and Drew way too much.

Before long, everything was as it should be, and Beth found herself standing outside the back door with Drew and Tommy. Beth knew she and Drew needed to talk, and figured this was as good a time as any. "Thanks, Tommy. I'll see you in the morning."

He glanced back and forth from her to Drew, and then nodded. "Call me if you need anything."

She didn't miss the thumbs-up Tommy sent her way as he was getting into his car. Beth sighed as she faced Drew and tried to prepare herself for what she was about to do. "Would you like to take a walk with me?"

"Sure."

Drew seemed a little surprised, but he followed her down the alley and out onto the sidewalk that ran along the front of the café. She turned left, setting a leisurely pace. As they continued to walk, Beth realized he was intentionally keeping himself a step behind her. "You can walk beside me. I'm not your mistress, and we aren't playing. There's no protocol."

Beth actually thought she saw him blush.

"Sorry. I don't . . ." He shook his head. "Sorry."

He lengthened his step a little and fell in beside her. "Thank you."

"It's my fault. I feel like I keep screwing this up," he said.

"You're not. If it were anyone else, I'm sure it wouldn't be this complicated."

Drew shot her one of his killer smiles. "Maybe I like complicated."

She laughed.

They passed several more storefronts before either of them spoke.

Beth took a deep breath. "I want to apologize to you."

"For what?"

"I told you we could be friends, but so far I've done a really crappy job at holding up my end of things."

"That's not true."

"It is." There was no room for argument in her tone. "Although I said it, I didn't mean it. Truthfully, I was hoping you'd lose interest and go away."

"Is that what you want?" Beth didn't miss the hint of disappointment.

She groaned. "This isn't coming out the way I wanted it to. I wanted to apologize, and then offer for us to start again. Somehow I've even managed to screw up the apology."

He stopped, so she did, too.

Drew's brow was furrowed. It looked as if he was deep in thought about something. "So what does that mean, exactly?"

Beth released a harsh breath. "It means that before when I said we could be friends I didn't really mean it."

"And now?" he asked.

"And now? I'd like for us to try to be friends. Real friends. I still can't offer you more than that right now, but . . ."

He didn't answer right away. "How would this *real friends* thing work? As opposed to the fake friends thing."

When she realized he wasn't upset, she relaxed a little. "I suppose it means we would talk, hang out, that sort of thing. Isn't that what friends do?"

"It is. I guess I'm just wanting to make sure I know the ground rules."

Beth nodded and started walking again.

Drew fell into step beside her.

"Okay. Rule number one. While we can hang out, it can't be anything remotely like a date."

"So no showing up at your door with flowers. Got it."

She grinned. "Exactly."

"All right. What else?"

"Let's see. No inappropriate touching. Or kissing, of course."

"Of course."

One side of his mouth pulled up, and she knew he was fighting a smile. He was taking this much better than she thought he would. Maybe this could work after all.

"Is there anything besides no kissing or date-like behavior that's off the table?" he asked.

Beth shook her head. "Not that I can think of. If something comes up, I'll let you know."

"Fair enough."

They'd covered almost six blocks when Beth turned left to head toward the local farmers' market. She rarely bought anything, but she liked to stroll through the stalls to see what the vendors were selling—especially the ones hawking baked goods.

She knew the moment Drew realized where they were going. "Do you come to the market a lot?"

Beth shrugged. "I try to get here once a week. It's good to check out your competition once in a while."

"Ah. Good idea."

As they strolled through the stalls, Beth wondered what was going through Drew's mind. She'd laid out their friendship, and on the surface, he appeared to be content with the arrangement. But was he? She knew he wanted more. How long would he be happy with what she was willing to give before he became fed up with her and moved on?

"May I ask you a question?"

They were passing by a vendor who was selling a variety of apples. "Sure. And you don't have to ask permission. We're friends. You can ask me whatever you want. If I don't want to answer, I'll tell you."

He nodded. "How long have you been a . . . a . . ."

Beth smiled. "About six years."

"So you were in your early twenties?"

She chuckled. "Are you fishing for my age?"

"Maybe." Drew's eyes sparkled with mirth.

"I'm not like some women. I have no issues telling my age. I'm thirty." Beth glanced over at him. "And you?"

"I'm twenty-eight. My birthday is next month, though."

"So you're a young thing," she said, teasing.

"Not that young."

Beth nodded.

"Does me being younger bother you?"

"Not at all. Why would it?" Beth asked.

"I don't know. Just thought I'd ask."

"Are you asking as a friend, or are you asking if it would bother me if we were more than friends?" She was fairly sure she knew, but she wanted him to spell it out for her.

"I'm curious if it would make any difference if this thing between us did develop into more. Eventually," he hurried to add.

She made him wait for her answer, and as they rounded the corner to the last row of stalls, she could feel his tension growing. "No."

"No?"

"No. It wouldn't matter to me."

Beth heard him release a large burst of air from his lungs. "Okay. Good."

The two of them finished at the farmers' market and headed back toward the café. When they arrived at her car, Beth leaned against the metal to face Drew. "Thank you for walking with me."

"No thanks needed. I had fun. It was a good way to spend an afternoon."

"When do you have to work again?" she asked. If they were going to be friends, she should probably get an idea of what his schedule was.

"Tomorrow. I work twenty-four-hour shifts. One day on. One day off. After three days on, we get four days off. It's a nine-day rotation." When he saw her confused look, he shrugged. "I know it's a little confusing at first."

"That's okay. I think I get it."

They stood in silence for several moments.

"Any plans for tonight?" Beth had no idea why she was asking.

Drew shrugged. "Not really. I'll probably watch a little TV and turn in early."

It sounded a lot like the evening Beth had planned for herself. "Well, I'll let you get on with it, then."

She moved to get into her car, but he stopped her. "Beth?"

"Yes?"

"Does this new friends thing include us exchanging phone numbers?"

Beth thought about it for a moment. Although giving him her

phone number gave her pause, she wasn't as nervous about it as one might think. Katrina was really good at screening applicants for the club. She'd even found Ben's marriage certificate when they'd applied for membership. The problem was Ben was good at lies and procuring fake documents. When the subject came up, he was able to produce a very legal-looking certificate of annulment dated about a month after the marriage. Unfortunately, neither Beth nor Katrina had thought to question it. They'd both learned a very hard lesson.

No, nerves had nothing to do with Beth contemplating Drew's request. Even without the background check Katrina would have done on him, she knew he was a firefighter. She knew where he worked, and even if he hadn't told her, with Nicole's help she would be able to find out. What was holding her back was the thought that it would be one more thing linking them together—one more step into opening herself up to trusting a man again.

"You don't have to if you're not comfortable," Drew said.

"It's not that. Okay, it is that. A little. But you're right. Friends do typically exchange phone numbers."

Before she could second-guess herself, Beth took out one of her business cards and a pen. Flipping it over, she scribbled both her home and cell numbers onto the card and handed it to him.

He looked it over, and then tucked it into his wallet. "Do you have another one of those? I don't have anything with me to write on."

Beth gave him another one of her cards, and he quickly jotted down his numbers. "The cell number is usually better. As long as I'm not out on a call, I'll answer."

She took the card and slipped it into her pocket. "Thanks."

"I should let you go. Thank you again for this afternoon. I had fun."

He waved, and she waved back before getting into her car. Every time she saw Drew, she got in deeper. How long would this 'just friends' thing hold?

She didn't know the answer to that. But for the first time since Ben exited her life, she was beginning not to care. Drew wasn't anything like her ex, which was good. The last thing she needed was another fake submissive who played with her and her emotions. She wanted real, and for all of Drew's cockiness and his inexperience with being a sub, he was real.

Driving home, Beth tried not to let the possibilities weigh too heavily on her mind. She would let this thing with Drew play out. Hopefully, if he turned out to be another Ben, she'd find out before it cost her another broken heart.

Chapter 7

After she got home from the café Beth second-guessed giving Drew her phone number. Although the rational side of her brain kept trying to talk her down, the irrational part wouldn't shut off. Thoughts of her phone ringing every five minutes soared through her head the entire drive.

By the time Saturday night rolled around, Beth began to calm down. Drew hadn't called. Not once. It had only been two days, but for some reason she'd expected him to utilize her phone number or show up when she least expected it. He did neither and she was adamantly ignoring the tinge of disappointment it caused.

As Beth dressed to go to the club, she eyed her phone where it lay on her dresser. She knew that in all likelihood Drew would be there, and she was trying to convince herself that she wasn't anxious to see him.

Readjusting her necklace, Beth took a final look at herself. She'd chosen one of her more provocative outfits—not for Drew's benefit, of course. Her top wrapped around her torso, coming to a deep V that ended a few inches above her navel. It showed off her breasts nicely as well as her waist. The leather skirt she'd chosen clung to her hips, and ended roughly four inches above her knees. It covered everything it needed to, but also showed off her long legs. To enhance the effect, she'd chosen black stockings and her favorite boots. The boots were also leather and had a three-and-a-half-inch heel.

She picked up her jacket and slipped it over her blood-red top, which also happened to match her lipstick. The outfit made a statement, and on some level Beth knew she was playing with fire. But for the first time in more than three months, she didn't much care. She was going to enjoy herself. She was going to prove to herself, and to everyone else, that Ben no longer had any sway over her life. Tonight had nothing to do with Drew. It was about her taking control of her life again.

Now, if she could just believe that, she'd be all right.

Twenty minutes later, Beth pulled into the parking lot outside Serpent's Kiss. The space was nearly full. From the look of it, there would be a decent crowd inside the club. Then again, it was Saturday night, so that was to be expected. Katrina had created a safe, fun environment for kinksters to both socialize and play.

Beth crossed the short distance to the club's entrance, and stepped inside the small foyer. She removed the red and black plastic card from her purse, and slid it through the card reader beside the door. Two seconds later, the light on the reader turned green and the interior door unlocked, allowing her to enter.

She stepped into the second room—this one larger than the first—and was greeted by Ali, a woman not that much older than Beth herself. Ali had been a member at the club for a little over a year. She didn't have a Dom, but every now and then she would volunteer for a demonstration. Beth knew Ali was on the lookout for a more permanent play partner, but as far as Beth knew, she hadn't set her sights on anyone specific. "Good evening, Lady Beth."

Beth removed her jacket and handed it to Ali, who was manning the coat check for the evening. "Thank you, Ali. Looks like the club is rather busy tonight."

"It is. There's been a steady stream of people for the last hour or so." Ali paused and glanced down for a moment. "I believe I even saw that new sub, Drew, come in a short while ago."

"Is that so?" Hearing he was inside made Beth's heart rate kick up a notch.

"Yes, ma'am."

Nodding, Beth headed for the door that would lead her to the club itself. Squaring her shoulders, she opened the door, and entered the main room. She immediately began searching through the crowd. Beth told herself she was only looking for her friends, but that wasn't entirely true. Sure, she was looking for Nicole and the other members of the group she typically hung out with, but she was mainly scanning for Drew. Ali said he was there, which also told Beth that everyone in the club knew he'd set his sights on her. For some reason, knowing that didn't bother her as much as it probably should.

Ignoring her nerves, Beth continued her search. She wanted to find him first. She wanted to be the one to set the tone this time around.

Right when she was about to give up and head to where she'd seen Nicole and Jeff sitting across the room, she spotted Drew. He was sitting with his friends, Allison and John.

Beth hesitated, but then Drew looked up. She knew the exact moment when he found her in the crowd. His eyes went wide, and his lips fell open. Before she could lose her nerve, Beth took a deep breath and walked toward him.

***

Drew about lost it when he caught sight of Beth. His cock jumped to attention and began straining against the confines of his jeans. The closer she got to him, the worse his condition became. Beth was wearing a curve-hugging leather skirt and black boots that ended right below her knees. He couldn't see the rear view, but his imagination had already taken over and then some.

If the skirt and boots weren't enough, the top she had on was downright sinful. It was deep red and dipped low, showing off her cleavage. Drew knew he was going to need some serious alone time later. He only hoped he could make it home first.

When she was about ten feet away, he stood. He had to ball his hands into fists to keep from reaching for her. The fact he couldn't touch her at all was driving him crazy—especially when she showed up looking like this.

She came to a stop in front of him and smiled. "I was wondering if you'd be here tonight."

He shrugged, trying to appear calm even though he was anything but. "I try to come on my nights off. Gets me out of the house and keeps me out of trouble."

Drew had meant it as a joke, but when Beth's eyes sparkled with amusement he knew something was coming. "You come to a kink club to stay out of trouble?"

Heat rushed to his face, and Drew couldn't believe she was actually making him blush. "I guess you have a point. Maybe that was the wrong choice of words."

Beth chuckled. "Maybe."

He felt something nudge his foot, and glanced down. Although John wasn't looking at him, Drew knew his friend must want an introduction. It wasn't as if Drew had talked about anything besides Beth the last few weeks. Considering John was the only friend Drew had he could talk to about her, he'd taken full advantage.

Clearing his throat, Drew angled his body so Beth could get a clear view of John and Allison. "I don't know if you know my friends. This is Allison and John."

Allison nodded in Beth's direction. "We've met. It's good to see you back at the club."

"Thanks. It's good to be back," Beth said.

Allison grinned and tilted her head toward John. "I'm not sure if you've met my boy before."

"No. I don't believe so."

"Did you want to join us?" Drew asked.

Beth turned her attention back to him. "I was thinking about getting something to drink and then heading upstairs."

Although Drew knew he shouldn't, he couldn't pass up the opportunity to spend time with her. "Care for some company?"

"Sure."

They said a quick goodbye to Allison and John before making their way across the room to the bar. Drew hadn't missed the encouraging look John had given him as they strolled away. His friend was one hundred percent behind his pursuit of Beth.

Drew followed Beth's lead as they stepped up to the bar. Katrina was very picky about who ran her bar. She had a strict policy of no more than two of what she considered 'soft' alcoholic beverages and one of what she considered the hard stuff per person per night.

Although he wasn't much of a drinker, he'd found out on his first night at the club just how serious Katrina was about the policy.

He'd been nervous and needing a little liquid courage, so he'd ordered a shot of whisky. When he joined, he'd been told about the rules, but at the time, he hadn't really thought much about it. That was until he was told all they could give him for the rest of the night were drinks that contained absolutely no alcohol. It had made for a very long first night.

Beth rested her forearms on the bar, stretching her top even more, and Drew had to bite back a groan. She was killing him. Absolutely killing him.

The bartender, Brandon, strolled over to them. "Hey, Beth. What can I get you?"

"Just the usual for me."

She turned to Drew, waiting. "I'll take a water, please."

"Coke and Sprite, and a water. Comin' right up."

As they waited, Drew searched his mind to come up with something relatively safe to say. What he wanted to do was ask if he could kiss her, but he knew that probably wouldn't go over well.

He was still pondering when Brandon returned with their drinks. Beth reached for her membership card.

"Let me get it?" Drew asked.

She stopped, met his gaze for a long moment, and then nodded.

He handed over his membership card. Within a few seconds, Brandon had swiped the card, and handed it back to him.

They took their drinks and headed upstairs. He wasn't sure if Beth wanted to watch a specific scene, or if this was a purely voyeuristic venture. Either way, he was happily along for the ride as long as it meant he was by her side.

The first room they came to had two people inside he didn't recognize. It was a male Dom and a female submissive, but unlike the scene he'd witnessed the week before, this one seemed a little awkward. The Dom's movements were less fluid, and the submissive didn't appear to be completely relaxed.

"First public scene."

Drew jumped a little at the sound of Katrina's voice. He hadn't noticed her come up behind them. "Oh."

"Have they been playing together long?" Beth asked.

Katrina shook her head, but didn't take her eyes off the couple in the room. "No. They're both fairly new to the lifestyle."

The Dom selected a blindfold from the table and secured it over the sub's eyes. She tensed, and he placed his hand on the top of her head in a comforting gesture.

"Decent instincts," Beth said.

"Yes. I didn't get any bad vibes from either of them. They're just very new. It will take time for them to establish a rhythm," Katrina agreed.

As he stood there, Drew tried to take it all in. Although the couple was still feeling their way around, he could also see the hidden connection there in the way the sub reacted to her Dom's touch. She might be unsure of what he was going to do, but it wasn't that she lacked trust in him. It was most likely trust in herself she was struggling with.

Drew could relate to that. Since he'd never participated in a scene before, he had no idea how he'd react. Even though he wanted to give up control to his partner, actually doing it was something altogether different. In all honesty, as much as he and Beth being friends frustrated him, he was grateful for the opportunity to get to know her before they ventured into anything like what he was watching unfold before them. He needed to be able to trust her completely, and no matter how much a person said they trusted another, true trust didn't happen overnight. It was built and tested over time.

Several more minutes passed as the Dom inside the room circled his submissive with a crop. Every now and then, he'd swat her leg, arm, or breast. It was completely random, and the sub was having a hard time keeping still. She was anxious. But what shocked Drew was that he was, too. His skin was tingling with every hit the crop made to the submissive's flesh.

Someone came up behind them, pulling Drew out of the moment. He took a deep breath and tried to find his balance again.

The man addressed Katrina. "Sorry to interrupt, but your presence is being requested in room five."

She nodded and then turned to Beth and Drew. "If you'll excuse me?"

A moment later, Katrina was gone, and he and Beth were alone again.

When Drew turned back around to look into the room, the Dom was kneeling in front of the sub. From this angle, he couldn't tell what the Dom was doing, but then he saw the sub's intake of breath and knew clamps were most likely being attached to her nipples. Drew had heard the reaction often enough in the club.

"What are you thinking?" Beth asked.

Drew met her gaze. "Wondering what it will be like. My first scene, I mean."

She stared up at him, and Drew once again felt that spark that always seemed to be lurking when Beth was near. He wondered if she felt it, too. When he noticed the vein in her neck pounding, he knew she did. It gave him courage. He took a step forward—the scene they'd been watching totally forgotten. "Beth . . ."

Before he could do anything else, a door slammed shut at the end of the hall, jarring them both. Beth blinked and stepped back. She edged past him and hurried down the hall.

Not knowing what else to do, he followed after her. She kept moving until she reached the last door on the right. Stopping for only a moment to glance inside, Beth hurried through the doorway and out of his sight.

Drew had to admit he was worried. Everything had been going well until a moment ago.

When he arrived at the open door, he looked inside. She was standing in the center of the room with her back to him. He wasn't sure what to do, so he stood a foot or so inside the door and waited.

Beth didn't react outwardly to his presence although he knew she had to realize he was in the room. Just when he was ready to break the silence, she spoke. "Shut the door, please."

Startled, he did as she asked without thinking. The door clicked as it latched into place, the sound echoing off the walls. Drew felt as if he were missing something.

Several minutes passed before Beth set her drink down, strolled over to the wall, and removed a crop. It looked identical to the one used in the scene they'd been observing.

She held the crop in her right hand, and ran her left down the length of it. "Do you know this is the first time I've picked up one of these in four months?"

Drew wasn't sure what to say, so he remained silent.

"We were in the middle of a scene."

He was confused. "I'm sorry?"

Beth turned around to face him. "Ben and I. We were in the middle of a scene when his wife showed up."

Drew felt bile rise in his throat. "You don't have to tell me this."

"I want to. You need to know what you're signing up for."

He still wasn't sure he wanted to hear it, but he nodded anyway.

She returned the crop, and reached for some items he wasn't familiar with—a few of which looked as if they could be painful. "We were in my bedroom. I had him secured to the bed, and I was flogging him."

Although he knew about her previous sub, it was weird hearing her talking about playing with another man.

"Someone rang my doorbell. At first, I ignored it since we were in the middle of playing, but the person persisted. I figured it must be pretty important, so I released one of his cuffs, and threw on a robe to go see who it was."

She sighed and dropped her hands down to her sides. "When I opened the door, I came face-to-face with a very angry woman I didn't know. She pushed me out of the way and began searching my house. I was furious, of course. I followed her, demanding to know who she was and why she was in my house."

During the few weeks Drew had known Beth he'd never seen her look as vulnerable as she did at that moment. He couldn't imagine what she'd been thinking when the woman burst into her home.

"Eventually she found Ben in my bedroom. He was still in my bed—both feet still secured to the bedposts." Beth looked up to meet his gaze. "After that the details get a little fuzzy. There was a lot of shouting as she released the remaining cuffs. But it ended with her slapping me, calling me a pervert, and telling me to leave her husband alone. She dragged him out of my house in his underwear."

"I take it that he never mentioned he was married."

Beth snorted. "No. He didn't."

Drew felt helpless. He wanted to comfort her, but wasn't sure how.

"Ben showed up at the café the next day. He tried to apologize. Explain himself. That's when I found out that he didn't only have a wife, but a daughter as well."

When Drew heard the catch in her voice, he threw caution to the wind. Leaving his water on a long table right inside the door, he crossed the room to her in three long strides. He stopped a foot in front of her, and opened his arms in offering—giving her the choice to take his comfort or not.

She hesitated for only a moment before stepping into his embrace. It was the first time he'd been so close to her. While he hated seeing her in distress, he couldn't help but take in the feel of her body against his. If only he could take the hurt and betrayal he knew she must have felt away from her, the moment would have been close to perfect.

"Thank you," she whispered.

"Any time."

She pulled away, and he couldn't help but feel the loss. "I haven't told that to anyone besides Nicole. Katrina knows some of it, but . . ."

"Thank you for telling me." He felt honored that she'd shared something so personal with him.

"I figured you should know, in case . . ." She took a deep breath and released it. "In case it changed your mind about me."

He was confused. "Why would it change my mind? He lied to you. He betrayed your trust."

Beth looked down at her hands, and then back up at him. "He broke me, Drew. I know you want a mistress. And I know you're hoping I can be that for you one day. I just don't know if that's possible. I don't know if I can . . ."

Drew extended his hand, and she took it. He gave her fingers a squeeze. "I'll take what you are willing to give."

She opened her mouth to speak, but he cut her off.

"Whatever you're willing to give, all right?"

Beth studied him for several moments before nodding. It was a small step, but he'd take it.

Chapter 8

They retrieved their drinks and made their way downstairs. Drew was acting as if what she'd told him didn't matter. Maybe it didn't, but it still didn't change the facts. She wasn't ready to be anyone's mistress again.

As they neared the bottom of the staircase, she took in the number of available Femdoms in the club that would be willing to take on a new male sub. There were at least three that she could think of off the top of her head. If Drew was a masochist, she could add a couple more to the list.

Beth knew she should encourage him to shift his attention to one of these Dommes, but the thought of actually speaking the words made her feel as if she'd eaten something that didn't agree with her. Ready or not, she wanted him for herself. Even though she had no idea how long it would take her to feel up to a relationship again, she couldn't bring herself to suggest another mistress.

"Is something wrong?" Drew asked.

It was only then that Beth realized she'd come to a dead stop at the bottom of the stairs. "No. I'm fine. I should find Nicole, though. She's probably wondering where I am since I told her I'd be here tonight."

He nodded and glanced down at her glass. "Did you want me to get another drink for you?"

"I think I'm good for now." She paused and considered her next words carefully. Although she wanted to spend time with him, she didn't want him to feel obligated to stay by her the entire night. "It's all right if you want to go hang out with your friends. I don't mind."

If she hadn't been watching him as closely as she was, she would have missed the disappointment that flashed in his eyes. "Is that what you want?"

She swallowed, and looked him square in the eye as she spoke. "No."

He grinned, and the butterflies were back to fluttering in Beth's stomach. Why did she have such a strong reaction to him? It would be so much easier if she didn't.

Before Beth could lose her nerve, she stepped forward, and leaned in close to whisper in his ear. "Thank you."

The muscles in Drew's neck moved as he swallowed. "For what?"

She tipped her head enough to meet his gaze. "For having patience with me."

Drew closed his eyes. "Beth."

"Yes?" She knew she was teasing him, but she couldn't help it.

He opened his eyes, and the look in them nearly burned a hole in her soul. "I so want to touch you right now."

Her only response was to lick her lips.

Beth heard him groan, which caused her to chuckle. She'd missed this. She'd missed this a lot.

Backing away, she shot him a heated look, and then turned on her heel.

She had a huge grin on her face as she strutted across the room toward Nicole. Her friend must have seen at least part of the exchange, because she smirked at her as Beth sat down.

"Having fun?" Nicole asked.

"As a matter of fact, I am."

Nicole snapped her fingers, and Jeff crawled to her side. She brought his head into her lap and began running her fingers through his hair before turning her attention back to Beth. "About time."

Beth felt Drew lower himself into the space next to her. He didn't say anything, but she could feel the energy flowing off him. She knew she was on dangerous ground, but it didn't matter.

They passed the rest of the evening talking about some new toys

Nicole had acquired. Although her friend could sometimes be slightly more sadistic than Beth, she and Nicole had a lot in common when it came to play. When Beth had been with Ben, she and Nicole had often shared ideas. Since the demise of Beth's relationship, Nicole had toned it down. Yet another thing Ben had taken from Beth that she wanted back.

During most of their conversation, Drew had sat beside her and listened. He didn't need to be the center of attention. That was good. Beth wasn't into bratty, attention-seeking submissives.

By the time Drew walked Beth out to her car at the end of the night, she was feeling pretty good. They'd had a nice time. She hadn't felt pressured to be anything other than herself.

Beth was still riding her high on Tuesday morning when she strolled into the café. Tommy picked up on the change in her mood. "Tell me you have a date with that fireman?"

She laughed and shook her head.

He groaned. "What in the world are you waiting for?"

Beth shrugged and slipped her apron over her head.

Tommy rested his hands on his hips and sighed. "Do I have to have a talk with him? Is he not stepping up?"

She stopped what she was doing and leveled a hard stare at him. "Don't you dare. This is none of your business. Do you hear me? You stay out of it."

He rolled his eyes, and stuck out his tongue at her before reaching for a bowl. "I just don't get it. He's single, right?"

"As far as I know."

"Then what's the problem?" Tommy asked.

"I don't know if I'm ready." Her reply was barely above a whisper, but she knew he heard her.

"If I ever see Ben again, I'm going to punch him. I should have done it the day he came in here begging you to hear him out." Tommy rarely got angry. He was one of the most easygoing people she knew. But she had no doubt if Ben were to walk through the door at that moment, Tommy would follow through on his threat.

Beth dropped the dough she'd just removed from the refrigerator on the counter, and pulled Tommy in for a hug. "Thank you for caring, but I'll be okay. I promise. I just need some time."

Tommy snorted. "I still want to punch him."

She smiled. "I know you do, and that means a lot."

Sighing, he went back to work on the mix he'd been making when she'd come in. "I just don't want to see you miss out on something because of him."

There wasn't really anything Beth could say in response to that, so instead she nudged him with her hip to lighten the mood. It worked. He grinned back at her, and hip checked her in return.

The two of them worked quickly to prep for the morning rush—neither one bringing up Beth's relationship issues. Once the doors opened, the steady stream of customers seemed to keep coming nonstop. By ten thirty, they were nearly wiped out of all their pastries. She hated to tell people they were out of something, so it was a good thing it was almost lunchtime. Even though they occasionally sold a muffin or two during the afternoon, most customers made their selections based on what was left in the case.

She disappeared into the kitchen to remove the last two loaves of bread from the oven when Tommy peeked his head in the back. "You have a delivery."

"What?" She looked toward the back door, but it was secured, as it should be.

He chuckled. "Nope. Out front."

Before she could respond, he was gone.

Sighing, Beth placed the bread on the cooling rack, and then went to see what he was talking about.

There on the front counter sat another bouquet of flowers. These were purple and white with some greenery mixed in. Unlike with the previous delivery, Beth didn't hesitate to reach for the card. She knew they were from Drew.

> *Beth,*
> *Thank you for trusting me.*
> *Drew*

The grin that spread across Beth's face made her cheeks hurt.

"Tommy, can you watch the front for a few minutes?" She took her flowers, and the card, into the back without waiting for a response. Digging through her purse, she found Drew's number, and dialed before she could have any second thoughts.

"Hello?"

"Drew, it's Beth. I didn't catch you at a bad time, did I?"

There was a hesitation, and then the sound of a door closing. "Not at all. I was just hanging out with some of the guys from the station. We were getting ready to start up the grill."

"Oh. Okay. Well, I won't keep you, then. I only wanted to let you know that I got your flowers, and I wanted to say thank you. They're beautiful."

"Don't apologize. I love that you called me. And that you like the flowers. Lunch will wait. You can call me anytime you want. As long as I'm not in a burning building, I'll answer."

"Still, you're with your friends. I won't keep you."

"Beth?"

"Yes?"

There was a long pause. "Thank you for calling. I'm glad you like the flowers."

***

Drew was flying high when he stepped out onto the deck in Romeo's backyard. That was until three sets of eyes turned in his direction and seemed to be waiting for something. "What?"

"Got something to tell us, Parker?" Baily asked.

"Not at all."

All three of them scoffed.

"You ran out of here with that phone to your ear awfully fast, Captain. You got a hot date you aren't telling us about?" Romeo teased.

Drew strolled over to the cooler and grabbed a bottle of water. He downed it before answering. "Why would I tell you knuckleheads if I did, hmm?"

Luckily, Sophia, Romeo's wife, chose that moment to bring a large platter of meat outside. Conversation pretty much became nonexistent as everyone focused on the food.

His reprieve didn't last long, though. About five minutes into the meal, the eating slowed, and the conversation resumed. Of course, his phone call was still at the top of the subject list.

"At least tell us if it was a woman? It was a woman, right?" This time it was Baily who chimed in.

Drew sighed. Not answering would only work the guys up more, but he didn't want to say too much either. His relationship with Beth, whatever it was, was private. "Yes, it was a woman. Your sister, actually. She wanted to know if I was free tonight."

Irwin and Romeo laughed. Baily scowled. "Not funny, man."

"Yeah, it really was," Romeo said.

With a few well-placed comments, Drew was able to deflect the conversation away from his phone call. He doubted it would last indefinitely, though.

Sure enough, the next day the guys started in with little comments. First it was Baily asking if he needed to sit down and have a heart-to-heart with Drew about the birds and the bees. Then it was Romeo with an offer of dating advice. The only one who kept his opinions to himself was Irwin.

"Come on, guys. It was just a call."

"Yeah, 'cause I go running for privacy when my friends call," Romeo hollered from the top of the truck.

"Maybe I just didn't want to make them listen to all your whining," Drew shouted back.

There was a collective laugh.

Before the guys could get started again with the questioning, the alarm went off and they all abandoned cleaning the rig to respond to a small kitchen fire a couple of blocks from the station. The entire call took a little over an hour. It was enough to get the guys' minds off Drew's personal life, but he knew not to get his hopes up. That's why as soon as they were back at the station, he cleaned his gear as quickly as he could, and then barricaded himself in his office.

Throughout the afternoon, there were knocks on his door from not only his crew, but nearly every one of the guys at the station. It was almost as if they'd developed a rotation and brainstormed excuses to bother him. He wasn't sure if they were waiting for him to extend an invitation for one of them to come in and talk, or if they were hoping to catch him on the phone again. Either way, they were disappointed. He would answer their question and then send them on their way. After a while, he began thinking of assignments to keep them busy. Once they realized bothering him was getting them more work, the interruptions became less frequent.

When dinnertime rolled around, Drew grabbed his food, and headed back to his office. He wasn't in the mood to socialize even though he knew doing so would only invite more questions. What he really wanted to do was talk to Beth, but he didn't think calling her so soon would be a good idea. He didn't want her to think he was a stalker or anything.

Sleep was a long time coming that night. He'd waited until most of the guys had gone to bed before heading for his assigned cot. Even then, he'd heard a couple of coughs and mumbled words as he made his way to his bed.

Although he wished the guys would let it go, Drew knew that wasn't going to happen. It wasn't the way things were done. He was acting strange, and they all knew it. Drew was going to have to figure out something to tell them. It would be different if he and Beth were already in a relationship. This friendship of theirs was a little more complicated to explain.

If he and Beth did end up in a relationship, he was sure she'd meet the guys eventually. It was sort of inevitable. He wasn't worried. Beth could hold her own. Drew had no doubt about that. It was the fear that if his buddies found out what Beth was—what he was—Drew had no idea if it would change how they viewed him.

It ended up being a slow night. They'd been called out a little after one to a possible heart attack. The EMTs had taken the man to the hospital, and then they'd all returned to the station. Nights like that were rare, so Drew counted his blessings.

Five days later, he walked into his apartment around nine with an arm full of groceries. Before leaving for his shift the day before, Drew noticed his refrigerator was disturbingly empty. Granted, he didn't cook much outside the station—it was only him, after all—but that didn't mean he wanted to eat peanut butter on stale bread for every meal. Plus, he was off for the next four days, and the last thing he wanted to do was eat frozen dinners the entire time.

Setting the bags down on the counter, he went to work putting everything away. Drew placed a couple of tomatoes on the counter beside a bag of onions and some garlic. One of these days he hoped Beth would let him cook for her. Of course, there were a lot of things Drew was hoping she'd let him do for her.

His thoughts began drifting into X-rated territory when he heard his phone beep. Digging it out of his pocket, he checked the message he'd just received. His heart skipped a beat when he saw it was Beth. He hadn't heard from her since they'd spoken on the phone the week before, and he hadn't been able to make it to the club on Saturday. When he hadn't heard from her again, he'd debated calling her, but had hesitated. He was trying to let her set the pace.

**I hope I didn't cause you any problems with
your friends. - Beth**

Drew quickly typed out a response.

You didn't. I was happy you called.

Okay. - Beth

Her reply didn't give him much to work with, but he wasn't
willing to end their conversation yet—even if it was only via text.

The café is closed today, isn't it?

Yes. - Beth

He took a deep breath, and plowed ahead. She'd made first
contact. He was going to take a leap of faith.

Do you have plans?

Not really. - Beth

Did you want to catch a movie?

She didn't answer back immediately.

Together? - Beth

Yes.

There was another extremely long break in the exchange, and
Drew was thinking he'd put his foot in his mouth again.

Friends? - Beth

He released a loud sigh of relief.

Of course.

All right. What time? - Beth

Drew was shaking with excitement. He could barely type his response back to her.

I just got home. Let me check movie times, and I'll text you back. Anything you want to see?

I hate to admit this, but I don't really know what's out right now. Been a while since I've gone to the movies. -Beth

Okay. I'll put together a few options.

As quickly as he could, Drew finished putting away his groceries, and then went to the bedroom to retrieve his laptop. It took him a few minutes to pull up movie times for nearby theaters. He wanted to give Beth as many options as possible, so he chose a location that boasted twenty-four screens. They had five different movies all starting within a half hour of each other. He figured he and Beth could find something suitable to watch from the choices.

He texted her back with the movie names and times.

Did you want me to pick you up?

She answered almost immediately.

No. I'll meet you there. What time? - Beth

Now? LOL

Didn't you work last night? Don't you need to sleep? - Beth

I can sleep anytime.

You need your rest. 2? - Beth

Okay. I'll see you at 2.

Sleep well, Drew. - Beth

I will. Now.

By the time Drew plugged his phone into the charger on his nightstand and slipped into bed, he felt as if his face would fall off from grinning so much. He had a date with Beth. Okay. Not a date. It was two friends going to see a movie together. Still, he was going to be spending time with Beth outside her work or the club. He couldn't see a downside.

Unfortunately, his enthusiasm for his afternoon with Beth made for a restless sleep. Thank goodness it had been slow at work the night before or else he might have found himself dozing during the movie. That was unacceptable. Drew would have begged on his hands and knees for this time with Beth. He wasn't going to waste it.

The entire time he was getting ready, he kept telling himself that he needed to calm down. They were going out as friends. It wasn't a date.

That was true enough. He also knew that if the outing didn't go well this afternoon, then the chances of him ever getting her to agree to go out on an actual date with him were slim to none. Talk about pressure.

Drew threw on a nice pair of faded jeans and a T-shirt. He had thought about stepping it up a little, maybe nice khakis instead of jeans, but decided that might not be the best idea. He couldn't do anything that would suggest they were on a date.

After swiping his keys, he made the short drive to the movie theater. Getting out of his car, he saw her already waiting on a bench not far from the main entrance. She was beautiful, but she always was. Her hair was down, and for the first time he saw how it looked as it framed her face. He wanted to run his fingers through it and see if it felt as soft as it appeared.

He made it halfway to where she was before she saw him. Drew picked up his pace and crossed the parking lot. "Sorry I wasn't here sooner. Did you have to wait long?"

She smiled, but it seemed off somehow. "No. I got here a few minutes ago."

They stood in awkward silence for a moment.

"Should we go inside?" he asked.

"Yes. I mean, no. I mean . . ." She shook her head and huffed. "I hate feeling so out of sorts."

Disappointment began to take hold. "Did you change your mind?"

"No. I agreed to see a movie with you, and that's what I'm going to do. But we've agreed this isn't a date, correct?"

"Correct. It's just two friends going to see a movie together."

Beth nodded. "That means I pay for my ticket, and you pay for yours. I don't need there to be any blurred lines."

Although the notion of him not paying for Beth's ticket rubbed him the wrong way, he agreed, and motioned toward the ticket counter. "Shall we?"

She looked up at him with a much more relaxed expression. "You know, I was thinking maybe that action flick. You like action movies, don't you?"

"Come on. I'm a guy. Of course I like action movies. What's not to like? Fighting? Guns? Explosions?"

Beth laughed, and Drew felt a warmth spreading through his chest. So far so good. He had one goal for the day—to make sure Beth had a good time—and he was going to do everything he could to make that happen.

Chapter 9

Beth didn't know what to expect when she'd accepted Drew's invitation. All she knew was that when he'd asked, she really wanted to go. So throwing caution to the wind, she'd texted him back agreeing to meet him at the theater.

It turned out to be a very good decision. After getting their tickets, Drew had guided her over to the concession stand saying that they had to have popcorn. He'd gotten a large bucket—insisting he hadn't eaten anything since breakfast—and a large soda. She'd ordered herself a drink, and tried to get him to let her pay half for the popcorn as well, but he was adamant that it wouldn't be fair since he'd most likely eat the majority of it himself. Short of arguing with him in the middle of the cinema, Beth let it go. Sometimes Drew didn't act very submissive.

While they were waiting for their movie to start, they munched on popcorn and commented on the theater ads that were showing. It was laid-back and natural. After a while, Beth started to relax.

The movie turned out to be pretty good. As advertised, there was a lot of action. What she hadn't expected, however, was the tearjerker ending. The credits began rolling on the screen, and Beth was sniffing and wiping tears off her cheeks. How utterly unattractive.

"You okay?"

Beth nodded and reached into her purse for a tissue. "Yeah, I'm fine. I don't know why they always make these movies with endings that make me cry."

Drew shrugged. "They probably figure they've gotten the men with all the violence, so they need to appeal to the women as well with something emotional."

She chuckled. "That's rather sexist, you know."

"Or honest."

Beth had to give him that. And he was probably right in any case. Ninety percent of the movie was all about killing and blowing things up. While she had nothing against an action-packed movie, Beth preferred if there was a little more to it—a little heart. Which, of course, explained the tears she was currently wiping off her face.

They waited until everyone else had exited the theater before leaving. It gave her time to pull herself together and get rid of any evidence of her emotional outburst.

As they left the cinema, the bright sunlight nearly blinded Beth. Her eyes were extra sensitive after spending such an extended time in the dark. She had to blink several times before her vision returned to normal.

Drew stayed close by her side, but made sure he kept a friendly distance. While there was a part of her that wanted to close that gap, she was pleased that he was respecting her wishes. Maybe he wouldn't make such a bad sub after all.

"Um." He cleared his throat. "I'm still kinda hungry. That popcorn didn't really fill me up. Did you want to grab a bite to eat?"

Here they were on shaky ground once more. "What did you have in mind?"

He released the tension in his shoulders, and she realized he must have been anxious about asking her. "There's a burger joint around the corner?"

"It's a little early, but I could probably eat."

And there was that smile of his again—the one that had her stomach all tied up in knots the other night. It was having a similar effect now.

"Lead the way."

Drew didn't waste any time guiding her the short distance to a restaurant that looked as if it had been transported through time from the 1950s. There were even little jukeboxes on the tables. A sign right inside the door indicated that customers were to seat themselves. He paused for a moment, taking in their options. "Booth or table?"

"Booth." Beth was impressed he'd asked.

They settled into a booth along the back wall, and a server came over to get their drink orders and give them menus. After the woman returned with their sodas, Beth and Drew put in their orders. Listening to him rattling off what he wanted to the server made her realize he hadn't been exaggerating about being hungry. Even if she were starving, she wouldn't be able to eat everything he'd ordered. Not by a long shot.

"Are you really going to eat all that?" she asked.

He grinned. "Probably."

They both grew quiet for a few moments. There was an awkwardness hanging between them, and Beth knew it was mostly her fault. She'd placed parameters on their relationship, and now they were both trying to figure out how to navigate without overstepping.

Beth took a sip of her water. "Do your parents live in St. Louis?"

Drew shook his head. "They live on a farm about an hour away, but I have a brother that lives here."

This was the first time Beth had thought to ask about his family, and to say she was interested was an understatement. "Is he a firefighter, too?"

He laughed. "No. Seth is ten years older than I am, and he enjoys his comfy job at his law firm."

"So he's a lawyer?"

"Yeah. Corporate law, mostly. He's tried to explain it to me, but to be honest, I usually end up tuning him out. While I don't mind the paperwork that comes with my job, I couldn't imagine weeding through pages of contracts looking for loopholes and technicalities. Seth loves it, though."

They both leaned back as their food arrived. Beth had kept it simple ordering a turkey club and fries. In contrast, three plates were set in front of Drew—each completely full. She guessed she had to hand it to him that at least one of those plates contained a salad, even if it looked as if lettuce was a minimal ingredient.

For the next several minutes, they both concentrated on their food. When the conversation resumed, it was Drew who broke the silence. "What about you? Do you have any family in the area?"

"No. I grew up in Ohio, and my parents still live there, along with my brother and sister."

Drew took another bite of his burger and swallowed. "Are you the oldest?"

Beth nodded.

"What brought you to St. Louis?"

She swallowed before answering. "School. I had no idea what I wanted to do, so I applied to a dozen or so schools all across the country. I got into most of them, but the University of Missouri offered me a partial scholarship."

"So you came here." His smirk was back.

"So I came here." She twirled her straw between her thumb and index finger with a glint in her eye. "What about you? Did you go to college?"

"Community college. I knew I couldn't join the fire department until I was twenty-one, and my parents refused to let me sit around and do nothing for four years."

Beth chuckled. "Smart parents."

"They are. And they completely supported my decision to become a firefighter. You should have seen my mom when I was promoted to captain. You would have thought I'd won an Oscar or something."

It was obvious by the look on Drew's face that he loved his parents. "She was proud of you. As she should be."

"Thank you."

Drew finished off his food, wiped his mouth, and laid his napkin on the table. "Can I ask you something?"

The tone of his voice had her a little worried. "Sure."

"Does my job bother you?"

She had to admit his question had caught her off guard. "No. Not really, anyway."

When he gave her a questioning look, she knew she was going to have to elaborate, even though she really didn't want to. "Yes, I've worried a little on occasion, but in the general sense, no. I figure you must know what you're doing."

He released a heavy breath. "I do. We're always training and making sure safety procedures are followed."

Beth smiled, hoping it came across as encouraging.

"I mean, I didn't think you had a big issue with it, but I figured it was best to ask. I've had women in the past who, while they initially loved the idea of dating a firefighter, the reality of it was too much for them."

"But we're not dating." The statement was said with less conviction than she knew it should.

"I know, but I'm hoping . . ."

Drew let that linger in the air as they stared at each other.

Despite all her reservations, Beth felt that pull toward him she always did. It was getting harder and harder to keep him at bay when there was a voice in her head—that was getting stronger by the minute—telling her to take a leap of faith and go for it.

As much as she wanted to do just that, the fear of another broken heart still made her question whether or not it was smart to get involved. "I like you, Drew. A lot. I really do."

"Is it because I'm new to this . . . the lifestyle, I mean?"

"No. If anything it helps." She gave him a weak smile. "I enjoyed today. Maybe we can do it again sometime."

He gave her a grin that made her heart skip a beat. "How about tomorrow? I'm off for the next three days."

Beth shook her head and laughed. "You're incorrigible, do you know that?"

"Is that a yes?"

"I have to work tomorrow." She was dragging her feet to see what he'd do.

"I can wait."

Grabbing her purse and the bill the server had left on the table for her food, she slid from the booth, and stood. "It's good practice for you."

He picked up his ticket and followed her toward the front of the restaurant. She could tell he was dying to press her, but kept his mouth shut.

Beth made him wait until they were standing in front of her car. "I'll meet you here at three thirty. Don't be late."

Before he could respond, she got behind the wheel and shut the door. Beth spared him a glance in her rearview mirror as she drove away. He looked pretty pleased with himself, and Beth wondered if she really knew what she was getting herself into. And for the first time she considered what would happen if she couldn't get past her fear. Drew had made his interest in her clear—his desire for a relationship. What would happen if she couldn't deliver? She'd been so afraid that he'd break her heart, but what if she broke his instead?

***

Drew was humming as he walked joyfully to his car. He had another movie date with Beth the next day. Okay, not a date, but that was a technicality. She was opening up to him, and his mind was racing with the possibilities.

"Hey, Parker."

Turning, he came face to face with one of the guys from his crew. His good mood quickly dwindled. Although he normally wouldn't care, Drew wasn't ready to share Beth with the guys. They'd want to know everything about her, and well, he was still trying to figure her out himself. "Hi, Baily."

Baily looked around as if searching for something. "You meeting someone?"

Before Drew could answer, the little girl standing next to Baily spoke up to get her father's attention. "Daddy, are we going to go see the princesses now?"

Taking advantage of the opportunity, Drew opened his car door. "I don't want to make you miss your movie. I'll catch you later."

"You coming by Romeo's house tomorrow to help with the pool?"

Crap. He'd completely forgotten about that. "Got something in the afternoon, but I'll be there for a few hours. You?"

Baily, of course, didn't let it go. "Got a hot date?"

Drew decided to make a joke of it. He winked at Baily, and slid in behind the wheel of his car. "Something like that."

The next morning, Drew contemplated the wisdom of showing up to Romeo's at all. Sure, he said last week that he'd help, but that was before Beth had agreed to spend any kind of time with him outside the club. He had no doubt that by the time he got there his 'hot date' would be the main topic of conversation. Drew had to figure out what he was going to tell his crew about the woman he wasn't actually dating.

Pulling up in front of the two-story house, he could see that

Baily and Irwin were already there. Taking a deep breath, he turned off the engine, and made his way into the backyard where he knew they'd be waiting.

The teasing began as soon as they saw him.

"Hey, hey. He made it," Baily said.

"Up late last night?" Romeo asked wiggling his eyebrows up and down suggestively.

Drew ignored their comments, and reached for one of the blueberry muffins laid out on a table set up along the back of the house. "You said eight thirty, didn't you?"

The guys chuckled, but settled down some when Sophia stepped into the backyard carrying a pitcher. "Thought you boys might like some juice to go with your breakfast. I've got some coffee brewing as well. I'll bring it out when it's ready."

Romeo took the pitcher from her and kissed her cheek. "Thanks, baby."

She smiled and disappeared back inside the house.

After stuffing their faces with muffins, coffee, and the apple juice Sophia had provided, the four of them got to work. By the time lunch rolled around, they had the ground cleared and leveled with sand, and the pool lying in parts on the lawn. Overall, it was a very productive morning.

At noon, Romeo fired up the grill and cooked some burgers and brats. They lazed on the back patio eating and shooting the bull. It was then that the subject of his upcoming afternoon activities resurfaced.

"You going to tell us what's so important that you're abandoning us this afternoon?" Irwin asked.

Kyle Irwin was the quietest guy on his crew. He usually kept his head down and went along with whatever was going on. For him to be speaking up, Drew knew what the main topic of conversation had been before he arrived that morning.

He shrugged. "I just have plans, that's all."

"Girl plans?" Baily asked.

"Not exactly."

There were a lot of suggestive noises followed by Romeo lifting his beer in salute. "Well, don't let us get in the way of you getting some pussy."

While Drew knew he shouldn't let the guys get to him—

especially since it was nothing he hadn't dished out before himself on occasion—it irritated him all the same. Beth wasn't some random hookup. "It's not like that. We're friends."

"You're blowing us off to go hang out with a girl you're not banging? Something wrong there, man," Baily said.

Drew let it go and finished off his burger. He tossed his trash in the garbage bag Sophia brought out earlier that morning, and headed into the house to use the bathroom. On his way back out, he ran into Sophia. She had her arms full with two more pitchers. The sun was beating down on them, and they'd been downing water almost as fast as she could bring it out to them. "Here, let me help you."

She smiled, and handed him one of the pitchers. "Thanks."

He opened the sliding door for her, and waited until she was outside before following. The rest of his crew, already several feet away, was huddled around the various parts that would eventually make up the pool.

Sophia took the pitcher from him and laid it on the table. "Eddie tells me you've got a hot date this afternoon."

"Not you, too."

She chuckled. "You know they'll find out eventually. The more you keep it from them, the more they're going to tease you."

"I know."

Going up on her tiptoes, she kissed his cheek. "You're a good guy, Drew Parker. I hope whoever she is that she's good to you."

Drew nodded. "I should probably cut out. I need to stop at home and grab a shower. Thank you again for keeping us in food and drinks."

"Anytime. You know that."

After saying a quick farewell to Baily, Romeo, and Irwin, Drew jumped in his car and drove to his apartment. Once inside, he peeled himself out of his dirty clothes, threw them on top of the washer, and padded naked toward his bathroom. He took his time taking a shower, making sure to wash off all the dirt and grime.

Satisfied he was once again clean, he dried himself off, and then wrapped the towel around his waist so he could shave. Date or not, he wanted to look his best for Beth.

By two thirty, he was ready. Unfortunately, that meant he still had an hour before he needed to meet Beth at the movie theater. He thought about driving to the café and seeing if maybe she wanted to ride to the cinema together, but he wasn't sure how she'd react to that. The last thing he wanted to do was mess things up.

He lowered himself onto a tan couch, the newest addition to his living room, and tried not to let his nerves get the better of him. Needing a distraction, he pulled out his phone and dialed his parents' number. His dad was most likely out in the barn, but he was hoping his mom would be home.

"How are you, sweetheart?"

Drew smiled when he heard his mom's voice come through the phone. "I'm good. How about you?"

"Same old, same old. Not much changes around here."

He knew that all too well. It was one of the many reasons why he'd left the farm for the city. Although Drew enjoyed the space, he had no desire to shoe horses or milk cows for the rest of his life. "Is Dad staying out of the heat?"

"Oh, you know your father. Ain't nothing going to keep him away from his animals."

"Yeah, I know."

"Don't worry too much about your dad. He can take care of himself. And when he can't, he's got me." She was full of confidence. His mother had always been a take-charge type of woman.

"I still worry about you guys."

"And you don't think we worry about you and your brother?" she asked.

"I know you do."

"Speaking of worrying, are you coming home for the barbecue this year?"

Drew knew she was talking about the annual Memorial Day barbecue his parents held at their house. It was a big deal. All his cousins would be there, as well as many of the surrounding farmers. "I'm not sure yet. I'm going to try to make it, but if I come, I'll have to leave before dark. I have to work Tuesday."

"Don't worry about that. We just want to see our son."

"I'll see what I can do."

He talked with his mom for a few more minutes before he realized it was already after three and he needed to go. "I'm sorry, Mom, I'm meeting someone at three thirty, so I need to go."

"A woman?"

Drew bit back a groan.

"Andrew Raymond Parker, are you holding out on me? Have you met someone?" He could hear her hope.

"She's just a friend."

Of course, his mother heard what he didn't say. "But you're hoping it will eventually be more than that, right?"

He didn't answer.

"Invite her to come to the barbecue. I'd love to meet her."

"Mom, I can't—"

"Yes, you can. You said she's a friend, right? Well, we'll have a bunch of friends here. She'll fit right in."

Drew wasn't so sure about that.

"Well?"

"I'll think about it."

"You do that. Now, go meet this girl of yours. If she's the right one for you, she'll know what a catch you are."

He laughed. "You're biased, you know?"

"Of course I am. Doesn't mean I'm wrong, though."

Drew shook his head.

"What are you still hanging on the phone for? Go. Scadoodle. I want grandbabies one of these days before I'm too old to enjoy 'em."

"Goodbye, Mom."

It was her turn to laugh. "Goodbye, Drew. Take care of yourself. We love you."

"Love you, too. I'll call back soon."

He hung up the phone and lowered his head. So much for keeping Beth a secret for a while, until they figured everything out.

Chapter 10

Most days flew by for Beth while she was at the café. There was plenty of work to keep her busy, and for the months since the fallout with Ben her business had been the only real bright spot in her day-to-day life. Her customers were always able to lift her spirits.

Today had been different. From the moment she awoke, Beth's mind was on her upcoming meeting with Drew. She'd enjoyed her time with him the day before, and despite her reservations, she was looking forward to seeing him again.

She worked doubly hard to stay on top of her work throughout the day so that she could leave a little early. Even Tommy noticed and commented that she must have a date with her firefighter. Beth tried to ignore him, but inside she felt a little giddy. Every time she caught herself getting too worked up, she'd remind herself that she still didn't know all that much about Drew. But even she knew that excuse wasn't going to hold true much longer. He'd told her about his job, his family, and some of his hobbies. How much more did she need to know?

The sad reality was that no matter how cautious she was, there was always the chance that he'd hurt her—especially now that he was worming his way into her heart. It was crazy really. The man would be a handful for whatever mistress chose to take him on. So why was she beginning to consider it?

Even with the extras she'd done throughout the day, it was after two thirty by the time she was able to leave the café. Having rushed home, Beth jumped into the shower and got herself ready as quickly as she could for her non-date with Drew. She chuckled to herself as she pulled one of her favorite pairs of shorts up over her legs and took a glance in the mirror to see how they made her backside look. Each meeting with him felt more and more like a date no matter how much she insisted otherwise. She cared about her appearance. She cared what he *thought* of her appearance.

After a final check in the mirror, Beth grabbed her purse off the table and headed for her car.

She spotted him standing near the entrance of the movie theater as soon as she pulled into the parking lot. After finding a place to park, she went to meet him. "Hey."

"Hey." He smiled, but it wasn't the full of life smile he normally flashed her. This one didn't set off butterflies in her stomach.

"What's wrong?" she asked.

Drew shook his head. "Nothing. Are you ready to go in? There are a couple of movies starting soon."

"I'm not concerned about the movies at the moment. I want to know what's wrong."

"I told you. It's nothing."

She gave him a look that made it clear she wasn't buying what he was selling.

He ran his hand through his hair. "Look, can we not talk about this here?"

Beth glanced around. While there weren't a lot of people in their general vicinity, there were enough within hearing distance.

"Where would you feel comfortable talking?" She tried not to think too much about the leap of faith she was taking. Or what it would mean in regards to their relationship.

"We don't—"

"Where?"

Drew sighed. "There's a park a few miles from here. Would you be up for a hike?"

"I'll follow you there." Without further comment, she turned back toward her car, and waited until he maneuvered his own vehicle out into traffic.

The drive wasn't far. As Drew said, the park was only a few

miles away. There were three other cars in the small lot, but no sign of people. She guessed they were already on the trails.

Beth turned off the engine, exited her vehicle, and joined him a few feet away. "Lead the way."

He released another loud sigh, and began walking across the parking area to a marked trail.

They trekked down a small hill and around a bend before Drew started talking. "I want you to know that I've been completely honest with you in regards to our friendship. I'm completely okay with us being friends."

A tinge of unease began creeping up her spine. "Why am I sensing a *but*?"

"I called my mom before I came, and I sort of let it slip that I was meeting you this afternoon."

He looked incredibly guilty. While Beth wasn't sure how she felt about his mom knowing about her, she didn't understand what was causing him to react the way he was.

"I tried to explain that we're just friends, but you know how mothers are." He stopped to meet her gaze. "Anyway, I'm supposed to invite you to my family's Memorial Day barbecue. It's a huge affair with all my cousins and many of the surrounding farmers."

Not what she'd been expecting.

"I don't expect you to go . . . not that I don't want you to . . . I do . . . but . . ." He shook his head and began walking again. "Mom will want to know if I asked you the next time I talk to her, and I don't like lying to my mom."

"So you knew you needed to ask."

"Yes."

They strolled side by side in silence for several minutes. Beth didn't know what to think of the invitation. Of course, she knew that his mother thought they were an item even if Drew had told her otherwise. And Beth thought it was incredibly sweet that he was nervous about saying something to her, yet he did it anyway because he didn't want to have to lie to his mother. It said a lot about him.

"I'll think about it and let you know."

He stopped again. When he faced her, his eyes were wide with disbelief. "What?"

Beth tried to stifle her laugh. "I said I'd think about it. I'm assuming it's on Memorial Day, correct?"

"Well, yes. It's—"

"So I have about three weeks before I have to make a decision."

When he realized she was really considering going to meet his family, he perked up considerably. "You mean you might actually want to go?"

This time she restarted their forward progress. "This *thing* between us. I've been thinking a lot about it. I'm not sure I'm completely ready yet, but I'll admit, I'm getting there. At this point, I think we should play it by ear and see what happens."

Drew groaned.

"What?" Beth couldn't imagine what she could have said that would make him react like that. She thought he'd be thrilled. Wasn't that what he wanted?

"I have an insane urge to kiss you right now."

This time she didn't hold back her laughter.

It took a few seconds, but eventually he joined her. "Sorry, but it's the truth."

When she got a hold of herself again, she was feeling lighter than she could remember being in a long time. "I know it is, and believe me I appreciate it. I'm getting there. Just please be patient."

He reached out and touched her arm, causing her to halt her movement. The look in his eyes caused her breath to hitch, and all thought of patience and waiting flew out the window. She took two steps forward, closing the gap between them. Beth could feel his warm breath brush against her face.

She lifted her right hand and ran her index finger along the seam of his lips. They were soft, and they parted as she continued to rub back and forth. It was as if something was drawing her in . . . something unseen yet irresistible.

Drew closed his eyes, and her gaze fell to his mouth. Despite her earlier assertion, she wanted to kiss him. It was almost a craving it was so potent. She'd never felt anything like it before.

Beth was moments away from succumbing to what she wanted when the sound of someone coming jarred her back to reality. With it came the knowledge of what had almost happened . . . what she'd almost allowed to happen.

Allowed. That was comical. She'd pursued it. She'd let her growing feelings for him and the situation to completely unarm her. What was happening to her?

Frustrated with herself, Beth took off at a faster than natural pace. It didn't take long for her to hear Drew racing to catch up.

"Beth. Wait. Please."

As much as she wanted to run away and forget it ever happened, that wasn't her style. She slowed down and waited until he was beside her again.

"I'm sorry."

She looked over at him, but didn't stop walking. "Why are you sorry? You didn't do anything."

"I stopped you. None of that would have happened if I hadn't—"

"Drew, you have nothing to apologize for. That was all me. I set up these rules for our relationship and, apparently, I can't seem to follow them. That's my fault, not yours."

"Still."

They were coming to the end of the trail. She wasn't sure if she was glad about that or not. "Maybe there are a few things we need to talk about."

"Okay." He sounded as if he were waiting for her to chastise him or something.

"What you did—stopping me—was perfectly normal. I'm the one who stepped over the line and didn't stick to the limits we'd both agreed to. Just because you're a sub doesn't mean you have to be the one always to apologize. It's me who should be apologizing to you, not the other way around." She was hoping he understood the weight of what she was saying. Although they were technically alone, she didn't want to get into a full-scale discussion about the lifestyle out here in the middle of the woods.

"I understand what you're saying but, Beth, I just told you that I wanted to kiss you. I'm pretty sure that would qualify as a green light on my side of things. And it was your limit, not mine. I have no issues with you kissing me anytime you feel the urge."

When she glanced up at him, the sparkle in his eyes was back. "Fair enough. But still, if I mess up, now . . . or later . . . don't hesitate to call me out on it."

"I can agree to that."

"Good."

The trail opened up and Beth realized that they weren't back at the parking area as she'd originally thought. It was a large open space. The grass had been mowed, and there were a couple of tents along the opposite tree line. Apparently, their hike wasn't over.

***

Drew had walked the path they'd taken many times over the years. It led to one of his favorite local camping spots. Granted, he had a few, some a lot more remote, but this was where he liked to come if he was limited on time but needed to get away for a day or two. It had seemed logical to bring Beth here.

She glanced up at him and then back at the campsite. "Do you come here a lot?"

"At least once a month when it's nice. It's not too far from home, but it's away from the noise of the city."

Without further comment, she started toward the small pond on the far side. It was a good distance away from the tents, and it would give them privacy to continue their conversation.

She found a large rock and sat down. Instead of joining her—because if he did he was afraid they'd end up right back where they'd been a few minutes before—he strolled over to the bank and knelt down. "I've spent many hours fishing here."

"Did you use to fish with your dad when you were younger?" Beth asked.

He picked up a stick that had washed up along the bank, tossed it out into the water, and stood. "Almost every Saturday morning when there wasn't snow on the ground."

"I've noticed that you never mention your brother when you talk about these trips with your dad. Why is that?"

Drew waited to answer her until he was back at her side. She scooted over to make room for him. He sat down, and he instantly felt that electric pull toward her. Taking a deep breath, he looked out across the pond, and tried to concentrate on the conversation. "He used to go when I was younger, but as Seth got older, he lost interest. By the time he was sixteen, he was off doing his own thing, leaving me and Dad on our own."

"You would have been six then, right?" Beth smiled, and he felt the muscles in his stomach clench.

"Right." He swallowed and pressed his hands into his thighs to keep from reaching for her like he wanted to. "The age difference meant we didn't have much in common. I think that was part of the reason he didn't want to go camping and fishing with us. I mean, what fun is it when you have your six-year-old little brother tagging along?"

"I bet you were cute when you were younger."

He drew back and pretended to be offended. "Are you implying I'm not cute now?"

Beth pressed her lips together and studied him in a way that had his entire body vibrating.

The air around them felt as if it could ignite at any moment. Drew didn't know what it was about Beth, but being with her was both comfortable and excruciatingly frustrating at the same time.

She closed the gap between them once more. This time her lips came within an inch of his. Drew held his breath waiting to see what she'd do.

Her eyes met his. "I'm not sure I'd use the word *cute* to describe you."

His palms were itching, but he tried to remain still. All those years of learning to work under pressure were coming in handy. Who knew he'd be relying on his crisis management training to navigate a relationship? "What word would you use?"

"Hmm. I have a few words I could use, but I think I'll keep them to myself for now."

The look in her eyes had him desperate to close the distance between her lips and his.

Right when he thought he couldn't take it anymore, Beth's mouth made contact with his own. Before he knew what was happening, she was framing his face between both of her hands and straddling his lap.

Instinctively, he brought his arms up to embrace her.

"Hands on the rock. Keep them there," she ordered.

It was absolutely insane, but her words caused his cock to swell. He groaned in frustration, but did what he was told.

She plunged her tongue inside his mouth and took what she wanted. It was the hottest thing Drew could ever remember experiencing in his life.

The kiss didn't last more than a minute or two, but it was long enough for him to know he wanted more.

Beth rested her forehead against his. She was breathing just as hard as he was. Her chest was heaving up and down, brushing against his chest. Not to mention that she was still straddling his lap.

"Please tell me you want to do that again."

She laughed. It was so nice to see her happy and carefree.

"Is that a yes?"

"Don't get cocky on me now." She ran a single finger down the side of his face and over his lower lip.

He closed his eyes, trying not to push.

"Open your eyes," she whispered.

When he met her gaze, he noticed the amusement was gone. He was instantly on alert. "What's wrong?"

Beth shook her head. "Nothing's wrong. I'm just . . . considering my options."

"Options about what?"

"You."

"Oh." He wasn't sure he liked the fact that thinking over her options had banished the fun they'd be having.

Before he could formulate another question, she explained. "Things between us are moving faster than I thought they would."

"Is that bad?" He needed to know. In his opinion, things between them weren't moving fast enough.

She sighed. But Drew also noted that she hadn't removed herself from his lap. That was good, wasn't it?

"I don't know. Maybe. Maybe not."

Since they were no longer in the heat of the moment, he took a chance and brought his hands up to rest on her hips. She didn't protest, so he settled in and enjoyed finally being able to touch her. "We're friends, right? So talk to me."

Beth released a single, rather sarcastic-sounding laugh. "Last time I checked, friends didn't do what we just did."

He decided to try to lighten the mood. "Well, some friends do. At least, that's what I've heard."

She gave him a small smile. "I don't do friends with benefits."

"Good," he said in all seriousness. "Neither do I."

They were both quiet for several minutes. As much as he wanted to say something, he knew she had to process this thing between them in her own time. He was hoping after the kiss they shared that she'd be ready to move to the next level with him. As much as he enjoyed their friendship, he wanted more with her. And after that kiss, he knew the potential was there.

Beth sat back, resting her ass on his thighs. The serious look was still there, and he wanted to wipe it away. He wanted to go back to when he'd seen the passion and teasing in her eyes.

"What's your schedule this week? I know you said you had the next couple of days off."

He had no idea why she was asking, but he'd gladly tell her anything she wanted to know. "I work Friday, Sunday, and Tuesday. Then I'm off for four days."

"So you don't have to work this Saturday?" she asked.

"No. I get off around eight in the morning and don't have to be back in until about seven Sunday morning."

She nodded, and he waited to see what she'd say next. "Did you still want to go out on that date?"

Was she serious? "Yes. Of course I do."

Beth nodded. "Okay."

He tried to contain his excitement. "Does this mean you want to go out on a date with me Saturday? A real date? Not just meeting up at the club?"

"Yes, if you want to."

Without thinking, Drew pulled her against him and gave her a solid kiss.

Luckily, she didn't seem upset.

"Thank you. For trusting me, I mean."

She wrapped her arms around his neck and gave him another kiss. It wasn't as heated as the first one, but this time he was able to hold her in his arms. Drew couldn't imagine it got much better than this.

Chapter 11

They sat for a little longer, enjoying their peaceful surroundings before making their way back to the trail. Drew couldn't wipe the smile off his face. Never in a million years could he have imagined that a short hike to talk about an invitation to his family barbecue would result in Beth agreeing to go out on a date with him. And that kiss. Heaven help him, but he wanted more of those. Well, he wanted more, period, but he had confidence that it would come in time. He only had to be patient.

Beth walked quietly beside him as they wound their way back down the path that led to their cars. She seemed . . . pensive.

"Something wrong?"

She glanced over at him and then back up at the trees. "No. Just thinking."

"About?"

There was a twinkle in her eye when she met his gaze this time. "I'm trying to decide how fast I want to take things with you versus how far . . . and fast . . . you'd want to go."

Although she said it with a hint of levity, Drew knew she was being serious. They would need to talk about things if their relationship was changing. Given the BDSM aspect they both wanted, it would mean a more detailed conversation. "I'll be honest. Other than the basics and what I've seen at the club, I don't know much. And the more I do learn, the more I'm realizing most of what's online is wrong."

Beth nodded. "If you don't know the specific sites to look for, you mostly end up with porn. It's a bad example of what the lifestyle really is."

He snorted. "That's for sure. I was so nervous the first time I got up the courage to go to a munch."

"It was nerve-racking for me as well, even though I didn't go by myself."

"Was it with . . . Ben?" he asked, almost afraid saying his name would somehow shatter the progress they'd made.

"Yes."

They both grew quiet as they reached the top of the hill and stepped out onto the grass surrounding the parking area. He could see their vehicles parked side by side about thirty feet away. Soon they would be going their separate ways, and it was the last thing he wanted. Drew wasn't ready to say goodbye to her yet. "Did you still want to catch a movie?"

Beth didn't answer until they were in front of their cars. She shook her head. "I'm not really in a movie kind of mood anymore."

"Hungry?" He didn't want to sound desperate, but let's face it—he kind of was.

She chuckled. "I could probably eat."

"So could I. Would you care to join me? I know a place not far from here. We could ride together and I could bring you back to your vehicle when we're done." He paused. "Or you could follow me."

After a moment's consideration—Drew thought it was more to toy with him than anything else—she sashayed over to the passenger side of his vehicle. He grinned and went to unlock her door. Beth smiled a thank you, and then slid inside.

While he could cook for himself, he was no stranger to eating out. Being a bachelor meant he knew a lot about the local places to eat. For their date on Saturday, he planned to take her some place nice, but he figured he should keep it casual for tonight. This wasn't a date. Or officially it wasn't.

They pulled up in front of a small family-run restaurant, and he turned off the engine. "Ever been here before?"

She looked up at the sign. "I think so. But it's been a while."

After exiting the vehicle, they met around front before heading toward the entrance. As soon as they were through the door, an older lady greeted them. "Welcome. Two of you this evening?"

"Yes, ma'am," Drew answered.

The hostess escorted them to a table along the wall and handed them menus.

Beth scanned the dining room and grinned. "I have been here before. I remember that green counter along the wall."

He glanced over to see what Beth was referring to, and had to chuckle. Most of the décor in the place had been done in the seventies, including the mint green counter that separated the kitchen from the dining room. "I guess it doesn't hurt business."

She took in the other diners. "I guess not. You'd think it would, though. I mean mint green?"

Drew couldn't argue with her. The décor was tacky at best.

Their server came a few moments later, and they put in their orders. Once they were alone again, Beth clasped her hands together on the table in front of her. "Are you sure you want to go forward with this?"

When he tilted his head to the side in confusion, she clarified. "The non-vanilla part, I mean. Did you want to keep things . . . normal for a while first, or—"

"I've done *normal*. Normal doesn't work for me."

Beth nodded. "Okay. Katrina has a limits list on the club's website that you can download. Fill it out and bring it with you Saturday. We can go over it and see where we want to go from there. Sound good?"

"I can do that." Nervous excitement was coursing through his body. This was really happening.

She smiled as the server brought their salads. When the woman walked away, Beth cleared her throat. "Were you surprised that I kissed you?"

He nearly choked on his food. After taking a sip of water, he met her gaze. "A little. But I'd be lying if I said I wasn't hoping for a repeat performance when I drop you off at your car."

Beth smirked and dug into her salad again. "I might be able to arrange that."

Drew turned his attention to his food, but inside he was counting down the minutes until he would be able to get his hands on her again.

"Why don't you tell me more about your family? I should probably know what I'm getting myself into if I decide to spend Memorial Day with them."

"Not much to tell. I mean, we're a fairly normal bunch. Dad farms and takes care of his animals. Mom runs the house." Drew shrugged, not sure what else to say. Overall, his family was pretty boring.

Beth shook her head. "There has to be more to it than that. I mean, you grew up on a farm. What was that like? Were your parents strict or did they let you get away with everything? Inquiring minds want to know."

He finished his salad and pushed his plate to the side. "It was a lot like you'd expect. It was just my parents, Seth, and I, until Seth went away to college. Our nearest neighbors were almost a mile away, so until I was old enough to go to school I didn't play with other kids my age much. We went to school, did our homework, and our chores."

"Did that bother you?" she asked. "Being so far away from other kids, I mean. Given there was such a big age gap between you and your bother, I imagine it could be pretty lonely."

"Not really." He paused as their server returned with their meals. When they were alone again, he continued. "There was always plenty to do. If I wasn't helping Mom or Dad, I was running around the farm pretending to protect our home from approaching enemies and wild animals."

She laughed.

"Then, once I started school, I made a few friends and they'd come over on the weekends and they'd help me defend the farm."

"It sounds like a very normal childhood."

"It was. I was very lucky. My parents have been together since they were in their early twenties and are as much in love today as they were then. I couldn't ask for better."

They grew quiet for several minutes as they ate. After talking about his own family, Drew couldn't help but wonder about hers. "What about you? Was your childhood normal?"

Beth shrugged. "I suppose you could call it *normal*. My parents didn't get married until they were in their early thirties. They had me seven months later."

"Were you the reason—"

"That they got married? Yeah." Beth hesitated. "I mean, they loved each other—still do—but I sort of rushed things along."

"And your siblings?" he asked.

"I think they were more planned than I was." She took a bite and swallowed. "We were all loved and cared for. Even when my dad lost his job and we had to move in with my grandparents for a few months, they made sure we had what we needed."

It was nice to hear more about Beth and her life. Although he'd gotten to know her some over the last month, he loved that she was opening up to him.

They lingered over coffee and shared a piece of apple pie. Being with Beth was easy.

Although he didn't want to, Drew let her pay for her dinner. When they went out on their date on Saturday, he was paying and she'd just have to deal with it.

The drive back to her car was too short. They'd spent the last five hours together, yet it wasn't enough. He felt as if he'd only scratched the surface and he wanted to know more. He wanted to know everything.

When she got out of the car, he followed her. They were alone in the parking lot. All the other vehicles were gone.

Drew was trying to decide whether to ask if he could kiss her or just do it when she reached up to cup the back of his head. She pulled his mouth toward hers, and he didn't resist. Seconds after their lips connected, he had her pressed back against her car, and her leg was wrapped around his waist. This time he didn't hold back. His hands were on her back, her legs, her ass. She felt amazing, but there were too many clothes between them.

Beth was the first one to break the kiss. When her mouth left his, she trailed her lips down his jaw to his neck. She grazed her teeth right where his pulse was pounding beneath the skin. Part of him wanted her to bite down so he could know what it felt like. Instead, she teased him, holding him on the edge, not giving him what he wanted.

He dug his fingers into her hips and ground his pelvis into the heat he could feel coming from between her legs. Ever since he noticed her across the room that first night, he'd wanted to get his hands on her. Now that he was able to touch her, he didn't want to stop.

Finally, she clamped down on his neck with her teeth, and his cock pulsed almost painfully. He was hoping she wouldn't make him wait too long before he was able to feel her pussy surrounding his cock. But thinking about her pussy did nothing to help calm him down. Neither did her snaking her hand between them to cup his erection and give it a squeeze.

"Mmm," she hummed against his neck.

He swallowed. "I want you."

"Patience." Her breath ghosted along his neck, sending a chill down his spine.

He moaned.

She ran her fingernail down the side of his neck, and released her hold on his cock. He didn't know if that was better or worse.

Drew took a deep breath and nodded. It would be getting dark soon, and he knew she should be on her way. The park closed at dusk. "I should let you get home."

Beth rose up on her tiptoes and brushed her lips against his. "I'll see you Saturday. And . . . you can call me." She was teasing him, and he loved it.

"I'll call. Let you know what time I'm picking you up for our date." He hadn't let go of her, and she didn't seem anxious to pull away.

She nodded and brought their mouths together once again.

This kiss was all soft lips and gentle suction. It did nothing to dampen the fire inside him.

She pulled away before he was ready, so he followed her with his mouth, seeking more.

Beth laughed. "I promise the wait will be worth it."

"My cock feels like it's about to explode."

As if to test his assertion, she wrapped one hand around his cock and the other cupped his balls. She squeezed each three times, and he nearly fell over. He dug his fingers into the sides of her hips and closed his eyes. "Beth . . . please."

"Please what?" she asked against his lips.

Before he could form a coherent thought, her hands were gone and she was moving away from him. He opened his eyes to find her slipping behind the wheel of her car. She grinned up at him and waved. "Call me."

Drew stood without moving as she drove away, his cock

painfully hard. Making it to Saturday was going to be torture. Pure torture.

***

Beth was pulling into her driveway when Nicole called. "Hey."

"Hey, yourself. How'd your movie date with Drew go?" Nicole asked.

Tucking her purse under her arm, Beth hurried inside, and kicked off her shoes. "It didn't."

"What do you mean it didn't?" Nicole demanded.

Beth sighed, and flopped down on her couch with the phone to her ear. "I mean we ended up going for a walk instead. Apparently, he let it slip to his mom that he was meeting me this afternoon, and was told to extend an invitation to me to the family's Memorial Day barbecue."

"Meeting the family, huh? That's a big step. You gonna go?"

"I haven't decided. I told him I'd think about it." Beth rolled over and propped herself up on her elbow. "Oh. And we're going out Saturday."

Nicole got real quiet for several moments. "Going out as in meeting up again to hang out or going out as in going on a date?"

Beth didn't answer right away. She wanted to let Nicole stew a while. "The second."

"Finally!"

"It's only been a month."

"A very long month," Nicole insisted.

"If you say so."

They both chuckled.

"So tell me, how did a walk turn into plans for a date?"

Beth eagerly filled her best friend in on the details of her time with Drew, including what turned out to be the first of several kisses. Nicole was riveted, and pumped her for details. Her friend burst out laughing when Beth relayed the heated good-night kiss she'd shared with Drew. "I would have paid to see that."

"I don't think we're ready for an audience."

"Beside the point." Nicole released a contented sigh. "I'm happy for you."

"Let's not get ahead of ourselves. It's just a date."

"And several kisses. Rather passionate kisses. We can't forget those," Nicole said.

Beth rolled her eyes. "Whatever you say."

"So does that mean you'll be coming to the club together Saturday night?"

The thought had crossed Beth's mind. "I don't know. We have a lot to talk about. That is, if the date goes well."

"Don't jinx yourself. Why wouldn't it go well?" Nicole asked.

"I don't know. Just nerves, I guess. Look, I should go. I have a few things to do before I turn in."

"All right. Sleep tight. And dream of that hunky fireman of yours."

Beth shook her head. "Good night."

"Good night."

Disconnecting the call, Beth headed for her bedroom, placed her phone on the charger, and booted up her computer. She located her limit list and opened the file. It had been a while since she'd read over the list, let alone updated it. She and Ben had been together for three years. At the beginning, it had been a useful tool in helping them navigate the kinky side to their relationship, but after a while they'd foregone their lists entirely and relied solely on verbal communication. If something came up that interested one of them, they brought it up and discussed it. It showed a level of comfort . . . of trust.

Beth snorted. *Trust.*

She took a deep breath and pushed Ben out of her thoughts. This wasn't about Ben. It was about Drew. Her and Drew. And in situations like theirs, lists were good. They had to start somewhere, and knowing what kinks interested each of them was better than guessing. She needed to know what Drew wanted to explore. Who knows? They might find out that their kinks weren't compatible. It wasn't as if they'd talked about them in any detail.

As it turned out, most of the changes she made were minor. They consisted of changing things from 'want to try' to 'like' or 'dislike'. The vast majority of it, however, stayed the same. What happened with Ben made her more cautious, but it didn't change what she enjoyed.

She saved her new list and logged off the computer. Knowing she needed a little me time before turning in for the night, Beth headed for her bathroom and began filling her tub with water.

Once she made sure the temperature was right, she opened the bottom drawer of her vanity. Tucked into the back underneath several hand towels were two of her treasured bathroom accessories. One was a dildo. The other a vibrator. Both were waterproof and perfect for some underwater fun. There was nothing like a nice long soak in her bathtub, and two of her favorite toys, to relax her.

With her bath ready, Beth removed her clothes, twisted her hair up into a bun, and lowered herself into the tub. The warm water surrounded her. Baths were something she cherished. Before she'd bought her house, she'd lived in a one-room apartment that only had a small shower. The only time she was able to take a bath was when she went home to Ohio, and that wasn't often. One of these days she was going to have one of those soaker tubs installed so she could stretch out and still have the water come up to her chin.

Beth leaned back and closed her eyes, letting her mind drift. It didn't take long for Drew's image to flood her vision. She could still feel his hands on her back, her hips, her butt. His cock pressing against her, wanting desperately to be let out.

She ran her hands down her torso, lingering on each one of her breasts, tugging at her nipples. What would it feel like to have him sucking and licking every inch of her? Beth planned to find out.

By the time she grazed a finger over her clit, she was ready. Beth reached for her toys and positioned them exactly where she wanted them. The soft hum of the vibrator could be heard even through the water as it massaged her pussy. It felt good, but she needed to be filled. Since she didn't have a real cock at hand, a fake one would have to do.

The silicone dildo stretched her inch by inch as she pushed it inside. While she enjoyed toys, there was nothing like the real thing. Beth let her imagination take over and pretended it was Drew pushing his way inside her. Drew making her breath hitch. Drew pumping in and out of her faster and faster.

She approached her peak and increased the pressure against her clit. It was enough to send her barreling over the edge.

As her high faded, she was struck with a fit of giggles. Over the last few months, she'd pleasured herself plenty. None of them had been as intense as what she'd just experienced. She had no idea if it was because of the afternoon she'd spent with Drew, or if it was because she'd imagined it was him, instead of some faceless man who happened to have a very talented appendage. Either way, she was feeling extremely sleepy.

Beth opened the drain and forced herself out of the tub. As she dried herself off and got ready for bed, she began humming. It was crazy how happy she was. Nothing had even happened with Drew yet. Okay, that wasn't true. They'd kissed. And, boy, what a kiss it was. There was definitely chemistry there. She'd felt it down to the tips of her toes.

She strolled naked into her bedroom and plucked one of her favorite nightshirts out of her dresser, humming the entire time. After running a brush through her hair, she slipped under the covers. There was a lot she'd need to do before her date on Saturday, but she'd worry about that tomorrow. Letting her eyelids close, she fell into a peaceful sleep.

The next morning started normal enough. Her alarm went off at five, and by six thirty she was elbow-deep in bread dough. She was in the process of taking a fresh loaf of bread out of the oven right before noon when Tommy popped his head back in the kitchen. "Delivery."

Beth made sure nothing was in immediate danger of burning before going out front. She had a feeling she might be getting more flowers, and she was right.

"Are you going to read the card?" Tommy was in his element.

"Well, of course I am."

She had her hand poised inches above the card when it dawned on her that every customer had their eyes trained on her. Every one of them stared at her full of curious anticipation. Mrs. Carlisle—an older woman who came into the café almost every morning—was sitting at a table not far from the counter with her husband of nearly forty years. She held her hands clutched to her chest, a huge grin on her face. They were all waiting.

Heat flooded Beth's cheeks. She grabbed her flowers and made a mad dash toward the kitchen.

Unfortunately, she didn't get far before she heard a familiar voice. "Who sent the flowers?"

She looked up and all signs of her blush vanished. There, standing near the door, was Ben.

"You need to leave." Beth resumed her path toward the kitchen and didn't look back.

She heard some rustling and raised voices, but remained hidden. Maybe it was cowardly, but Ben was the last person she wanted to deal with. Not now. Not when she was finally getting her life in order.

Beth had no idea how much time had passed, but she didn't think it was more than a few minutes when Tommy came back to check on her. "Are you all right?"

She nodded. "I'm fine. Is he gone?"

"Yeah."

"Thank you."

Tommy reached for some gloves, and she realized he was planning to work on the sandwiches she was supposed to be making.

"I can get those," she said. "Why don't you go back out front and make sure no one needs a refill on their coffee. I'll make sure everything is taken care of back here."

He looked unsure. "I can help."

Beth shook her head. "I've got it. Promise."

The smile she gave him was weak, but it was the best she could do. Ben showing up had thrown her. The last time she'd been somewhat prepared. This time . . .

She placed the fresh loaf of bread in the slicer and began assembling the sandwiches for her customers. Why was he here? Why now?

As quickly as she could, Beth rushed the sandwiches out to the customers who ordered them. She didn't miss the sympathetic looks she received from her regulars. Many of them had been around when she and Ben had been a couple. They all knew things had ended between them. Some even knew it ended badly. She hated their looks of pity.

Plastering a smile on her face, she finished her task, and then returned to the kitchen. Her gaze fell on the flowers Drew sent. Ben had taken that moment of joy away from her and she hated him for it.

She ran her fingers over the delicate blooms—tulips this time— and extracted the card.

> *Beth,*
> *I hope you enjoyed our hike as much as I did.*

Drew

Simple and to the point. So why did her chest clench? Drew seemed to know exactly what to say and do to break through her defenses. She felt moisture trail down her cheeks, and swiftly wiped it away.

Before she could second-guess herself, she dug her phone out of her pocket, and shot Drew a text.

Got the flowers. They're beautiful. Thank you. - Beth

Only seconds passed before he responded.

You're welcome. Call you tonight?

She didn't hesitate to reply.

Yes. - Beth

Smiling, she laid her phone down on the counter, and got back to work. Ben was her past, and as far as she was concerned, he was going to remain there. She had the potential of a new relationship with Drew. A relationship that wasn't built on lies. She was going to concentrate on that and forget Ben ever existed.

Chapter 12

"You holding out on me?"

Drew shoved his phone back in his pocket and picked up the nail gun he'd been using before answering Beth's text. "Why do you say that?

Shawn had called Drew late the night before and asked if he could help put on a roof. He used to work with Shawn a lot on his days off back when they were on the same crew. Now, more often than not, they had conflicting schedules.

His former captain and friend dropped another bundle of shingles onto the roof and leveled a stare at Drew. Shawn raised his eyebrows. It was a look Drew had seen often. It was the you're-full-of-shit look.

While he was reluctant to tell anyone about Beth, he knew he could trust Shawn. "Her name's Beth."

"Is it serious, or just fun?"

It was a valid question. Shawn knew all about Drew's wilder days. He also knew Drew had settled down over the last two years. "Hopefully serious. We'll see what happens Saturday."

Shawn began laying down another row of shingles. "Big date, huh?"

Drew grinned and continued to work. He'd been thinking a lot about his upcoming date. It couldn't be overly complicated since he had to work the next day, but he wanted to make sure it was memorable at the same time. "I've been trying to figure out where to take her."

They worked side by side for several minutes before Shawn responded. "What does she like?"

"She likes history." Drew shrugged. "We haven't talked about it all that much. And I know she likes movies. I guess I could take her to a museum, but she doesn't get off work until three. That doesn't leave us much time."

"This is a first date, right?" Shawn asked.

"Yeah."

Shawn nodded. "And you want to make a good impression?"

"Of course."

"Take her to a concert in the park. You can pack a picnic dinner for you both. Women love that sort of thing. Plus, unlike the rest of us, you can actually cook."

They both chuckled. Drew had taken some ribbing from the guys at the station when they found out he wasn't a total slouch in the kitchen. That was until they were the ones benefiting from his knowledge.

The more Drew thought about Shawn's suggestion, the better it sounded. It would be nice to spend the evening under the stars with Beth, listening to music.

The sun was dipping low in the sky by the time they'd finished the roof and cleaned things up. Drew said goodbye to Shawn and drove home. As soon as he walked in the door, he stripped out of his clothes and headed for the shower. Once he didn't feel as if he were sporting a second skin of dirt and sweat, he fully intended to call Beth. He'd been dying to talk to her all day. Seeing her the previous two days had spoiled him.

He rushed through his shower and threw on some shorts before settling in on the couch with his laptop and his phone. After he'd pulled up information on concerts in the park, he scrolled through the contacts on his phone until he found Beth's name. He smiled as he pushed the call button.

"Hello." Beth's voice was husky. His mind began racing with the possibilities. The only time he'd come close to hearing her like that was after their kiss when they'd both been breathing hard.

"Did I call at a bad time?" He really hoped she would say no.

She sighed. "Not at all."

"Okay. It's just . . . you sound . . ." Funny? Weird? Incredibly sexy?

Beth giggled. "And how do I sound exactly?"

"Um . . ."

"Yes?" She was clearly enjoying tormenting him.

"You sound . . . you sound like you're really turned on." There. He'd said it.

This time she laughed. "You're close. I just finished spending some quality time with my favorite vibrator."

Drew's head fell back against the couch and he groaned. All thoughts of his Internet search went out the window. Without conscious thought, he moved his hand closer to his groin where his cock was tenting his shorts.

"Does that turn you on? Knowing that I was pleasuring myself?" she asked.

He swallowed. "You have no idea. Just imagining you touching yourself like that makes me hard."

"Mmm. I remember what you felt like all hard and ready."

"You'd think I hadn't jacked off in weeks," he admitted.

She hummed. "I'll take that as a compliment."

Drew shifted in his seat. Her voice still had that husky tone and it wasn't helping his current condition. "You most definitely should."

There was a long pause, and then her voice dropped even lower. "What do you think about when you're getting yourself off? Anything you want to share?"

"You." Was he imagining it, or did he really sound out of breath?

"What about me? Am I doing anything special?" Her voice was barely above a whisper.

He cupped his hand over his erection and pressed down. "This morning, I imagined that I was tied to the bed, and you were sitting on my face."

"Hmm. I like the sound of that. Is that something you'd like me to do to you?"

"Yes." It was one of his many recurring fantasies. Most involved him being tied up. Everything else varied. Sometimes she was riding him. Other times she had her pussy covering his face . . .

grinding against his tongue until he couldn't smell or taste anything but her. That's what had filled his vision earlier that morning.

"Are you alone?" she asked.

"Yeah. I'm home. In my living room."

"Good. If you're wearing any clothes, take them off." She was completely serious.

"Now?"

Beth sounded amused by his question. "Something wrong with now?"

"No. I just . . . give me a sec." He picked up his laptop and placed it safely on the coffee table, then stood and removed his shorts before resuming his place on the couch. "Okay."

"Put me on speaker and get comfortable. I want your hands free, but I still want to be able to hear you."

It took Drew a minute or so to get everything situated. In a way, the whole situation was a little strange. He'd had phone sex before, which he was pretty sure was what was going to happen, but always in the past he'd been the one giving the instructions. This was different. Different, but not in a bad way. "Okay, I'm good."

"I want you to spread your legs as wide as you can. With one hand, I want you to hold your cock against your stomach. With the other hand, I want you to touch your balls."

She paused a moment, giving him time to do as she'd instructed.

His balls were heavy in his hand. It was crazy how worked up he was considering he came both the night before, and then again that morning. He shouldn't be this hard.

Whether he should be or not was irrelevant. He was.

"Now, I want you to roll your balls around in your hand. And every now and then I want you to give them a little tug."

He did what she said. It was something he'd done before. He was sure most guys had. When your junk was right there in front of you every day, you got curious. But for some reason, Beth telling him to do it made it feel ten times better.

"How does that feel?"

"Good." More than good, if he was being honest. The only thing that would make it better was if he was pumping his cock at the same time.

She must have read his mind. "I want you to take the hand holding your cock and begin moving it up and down. Slowly. We don't want you to come too fast now, do we?"

A groan escaped his throat before he could stifle it.

Beth chuckled. "If you're going to be my submissive, you're going to have to learn patience."

He closed his eyes and tried to concentrate on not coming.

"Tell me what you're thinking about right now."

That was easy to answer. "I'm imagining it's you touching my cock and balls."

"What am I doing? Am I between your legs? Straddling you?"

"You're between my legs."

"Mmm. I think I like that." She sounded as if she was smiling. "I'm going to lick your cock now. Run your thumb over the head of your cock and imagine it's my tongue."

"Gah! I don't know how much longer I can hold on. Beth, please."

"Please what? Tell me what you want." She was taunting him. Teasing him. And he found that he loved it. He was hard and pulsing in his hand. His balls were full and tight, ready to explode.

"I want to come. Please. I don't want to disappoint you, but I don't think . . . I don't . . ."

"Let it go. Let me hear you come for me," she whispered.

Drew picked up speed, pulling and pumping like a mad man. It didn't take long. He saw red and white and . . . well, he couldn't quite remember. Light flashed before his eyes as he spilled out his cum over his hand and stomach.

"You still with me?" she asked.

He breathed deep. "Yeah."

Beth laughed. "Go clean yourself up, and then we can talk."

"Be right back." He jumped up off the couch and raced into the bathroom. It took a few minutes to get everything back to normal again. He had to admit it was the best phone sex he'd ever had.

As he returned to the living room and slipped back into his shorts, it dawned on him that Beth hadn't come. At least, he didn't think she had. Granted, he'd been a little distracted at the time.

He took the phone off speaker and held it to his ear, his joyous euphoria fading. What kind of a jerk didn't make sure a woman he cared about got hers first? "I should probably apologize."

***

Beth was feeling pretty happy after listening to Drew. Sure, she could have joined him—her toys were still out and easily accessible—but that hadn't been the point. She'd wanted to see how he'd react to being dominated, even if it was only over the phone. From her end, he'd seemed to enjoy it, which was why she was confused by his comment. "For?"

"I should have made sure you came first. I didn't even think—"

Out of all the possibilities that had been swirling in her head, that hadn't been one of them. "It's fine."

"No. It isn't." He blew out a loud breath. "It's been a long time since I've left a woman hanging like that."

"I'll let you make it up to me. How about that?" She hoped he could tell she was teasing.

"I guess I can deal with that."

She laughed. "I'll look forward to it."

Neither said anything for several moments.

Beth stretched out on her bed, and then raised herself so she was sitting up against her headboard. "So tell me, Drew Parker, have you ever had phone sex before tonight?"

"Maybe a time or two." He chuckled. "Okay, maybe more than that, but it's been years. Since being out on my own, in-person encounters are much more desirable."

"Agreed."

"That's not to say that I didn't enjoy what we just did. Or what I just did, I guess. Because I did. Enjoy it, I mean."

It was cute to see him nervous. "I'm glad you liked it. In your past experiences with phone sex, had you ever had your partner tell you what to do?"

He snorted. "No. Not at all. Usually it was me telling her what to do."

"What did you think of the role reversal? Other than our kiss, this was your first real taste of domination, wasn't it?" From what he'd told her in the past, she was almost positive this was the case.

"Unless you count the one time I tried to talk my last girlfriend into tying me up and having her wicked way with me."

"This would be the same girlfriend who broke up with you because you wanted to be dominated?"

"One in the same," he said.

"Then no, that doesn't count."

There was a pause, and when he began speaking again Beth could tell he was smiling. "I'm glad my first experience with this will be with you."

Was he being honest or trying to butter her up for something? She hated that her mind automatically went there. Another by-product of Ben. Drew had never given her any reason to question his sincerity.

He must have noticed her silence. "Was that the wrong thing to say?"

"No. I was just thinking. Maybe . . ." She glanced up at the ceiling. "Maybe this isn't such a good idea."

"Don't say that."

She closed her eyes and took a deep breath. "Do you know what my first thought was when you said that you were glad your first experiences would be with me? I wondered if you were telling the truth or trying to pull the wool over my eyes about something."

"That's understandable, I guess. I have to earn your trust. But Beth, I promise you that I'm not like him. I mean, I invited you to come meet my family. If I had something sinister to hide, why would I do that?"

Beth took a moment, and he waited for her to gather her thoughts. Damn Ben. He was still screwing up her life. His showing up at her café hadn't helped either. She had no idea what he wanted, and quite frankly, she didn't care. She just wanted him to go away and let her get on with her life.

"Don't back out of our date. I promise we'll have a good time. If we don't, I'll go away. If that's what you want."

It didn't take a genius to know how hard those words were for him to get out. She'd seen the look on his face when she told him that she'd go on a date with him—something she knew he'd been wanting since they met.

Pushing down her fear, she tried her best to get things back on track. It wasn't fair to keep making Drew pay for Ben's mistakes. "Have you decided where we're going Saturday?"

"I have something in mind, but I'm still hashing out the details." She didn't miss his sigh of relief.

"Anything you'd like to share?"

"I'd rather surprise you."

"I guess that would be acceptable." She was trying to bring back the teasing atmosphere from before her anxiety had put a damper on their conversation. "Should I dress up?"

"Not if everything goes as planned. I'll text you once I confirm everything."

"I'll need to know what time you're picking me up, as well. Don't forget I have to work Saturday." Although he knew that already, she felt the need to remind him. A part of her wondered if maybe it was her way of keeping things on a level she could handle. Everything with Drew was moving so fast.

"I remembered." He grew quiet. "I've been working on my list."

Beth knew there had to be a question in there, so she gave him some time.

"What if we compare lists and we're not . . . compatible? What happens then?"

There wasn't any question of their chemistry. After the kiss they shared, that question had been answered loud and clear. Kinks, however, were a different thing entirely. His question was valid. What happened if he wanted something she couldn't give, or vice versa? "I guess we'll have to cross that bridge when we come to it."

He snorted. "I don't think I've ever felt so unsure of myself in a relationship before. You'd think I was a teenager again fumbling my way around the backseat of a car with my first girlfriend."

That made her laugh. "I wouldn't go that far."

"It's true."

"Drew, just be yourself. Do what comes naturally—what feels right. Everything else will figure itself out."

"So what you're saying is that I need to relax."

She chuckled. "Something like that."

"I should let you get ready for bed. It's getting late, and I know you have to be up early."

Beth glanced at the clock and realized that it was already after ten. They'd been on the phone for almost two hours. Her gaze landed on the bouquet he'd had delivered to her earlier that day. She'd put the flowers in a vase with some fresh water and placed them on the stand beside her bed. "Thank you again for the flowers."

"You're welcome."

There was a long pause, and she wondered what he was doing. "You have to work Friday, don't you?"

"Yep. I have to be there at seven."

As things with Drew heated up, that little voice in the back of her head that worried about his safety got stronger. "Be safe, okay."

"Always."

She reached over and ran the tips of her fingers along one of the petals. "Good night."

After Beth hung up the phone, she scooted off the mattress, and began getting ready for bed. That included cleaning the toys she'd used earlier. As she washed the silicone dildo, her thoughts returned to Drew masturbating to her instructions. Hearing him had been such a turn on. She couldn't wait to get her hands on him.

Unfortunately, that thought was quickly followed up by another memory of Ben. Why wouldn't he leave her alone and why had he shown up wanting to talk to her? It had been bad enough when she'd found out he came to the club months ago, but if he'd been looking for her, why hadn't he sought her out at her house or the café then? Why had he waited until now? Did he hear she'd found someone else? And if so, how? As far as she knew, he was living in Florida with his wife and daughter. Was someone feeding him information? Was he trying to destroy her new relationship before it even got started?

Beth felt the beginning of a headache coming on.

Gritting her teeth, she finished what she was doing, and left her toys out on the counter to dry. It was one of the advantages of living alone.

She finished going through her nightly routine, and snuggled beneath her sheets. Beth forced her mind to more pleasant thoughts, such as Drew and the fantasy he'd shared with her. Rope bondage wasn't something she excelled at, but she knew the basics. She also had several sets of leather cuffs. If he liked to be bound, she could work with it. And if rope was something he wanted to explore more, she could certainly find someone at the club to help her expand her skills. She had no idea what else would be on his list, but so far he hadn't revealed anything she viewed as a hard limit.

Releasing a deep breath, she closed her eyes and let thoughts of Drew tied to her bed fill her mind. She was dying to know what he looked like underneath all that clothing. To have him at her mercy caused her body temperature to rise and moisture to pool between her thighs.

Before she could change her mind, she snaked her hand beneath the sheet. Saturday night couldn't come soon enough for Beth. She had no idea if they would attempt to play that night, but if things went well, she had every intention of taking Drew up on his offer and letting him return the favor.

Chapter 13

By the time Saturday afternoon rolled around, Beth was becoming nauseous from all the ups and downs she'd experienced in the last day and a half. One minute she was looking forward to her date with Drew. The next minute, she was debating whether or not to call it off.

Nicole had been her saving grace. Every time Beth started to get cold feet, she'd call her best friend and get reassured that she wasn't being stupid by giving Drew a shot. Honestly, she was making herself sick with all the dependency, but she needed a shoulder to lean on and Nicole got the luck of the draw.

"You ready for this?" Nicole asked.

It was four fifteen and Beth was standing in front of her bathroom mirror fixing her hair and makeup. She had her friend on speakerphone so she could get ready and talk at the same time. Drew had sent her a text on Friday letting her know that he'd pick her up at five on Saturday evening. Giving him her address had taken more resolve than giving him her phone number, but she'd done it. His reply back to her, including a smiley face and a 'see you tomorrow', had her grinning and all feelings of unease disappeared.

With less than an hour until he was due to show up on her doorstep, she'd needed Nicole's support yet again. "I think so. I just hope I'm making the right decision. The friends thing was working well. What if this ruins it?"

"What if it makes it better?" Nicole countered.

"I know. I'm just worried about all the what-ifs. I can't help it."

"Considering what that jackass Ben did to you, it's not surprising. Speaking of which, he hasn't shown up again, has he?"

Beth had told Nicole about Ben showing up at the café earlier that week. Her friend had wanted to track him down and have a nice long chat with him. It was a sweet notion, and Beth appreciated it, but she also knew it wouldn't help anything in the long run. If Ben showed up again, she would most likely have to look into getting a restraining order. That wasn't a pleasant thought, but she couldn't have him continuing to show up at her shop and disrupt her and her business.

"No." She finished running the brush through her hair, and debated whether or not to put it up or leave it down. "I just wish I knew what he wanted. First the club, and now the café? And why so much time in between? It doesn't make sense."

"No, it doesn't. But you know what they say. Curiosity killed the cat."

She laughed. "Thanks. I'll try and remember that."

Deciding to leave her hair loose, Beth cleaned up the counter, and went to her bedroom to start getting dressed. Drew said they would be keeping things casual, so she was opting for shorts and a fitted T-shirt.

"Just remember to relax and have fun. It's just a date. And Drew seems like a nice guy."

Beth waited until she'd pulled her shirt over her head before answering. "So did Ben, at first."

"You have to learn to trust again sometime."

"Maybe I need to have that tattooed across my forehead or something."

"Nah. If it was on your forehead, you'd only see it when you looked in the mirror."

As usual, talking to Nicole had lightened her mood considerably. "Okay, I think I'm ready. And . . ." Beth glanced at the clock beside her bed. "I have over twenty minutes to kill. Just enough time for me to psych myself out again."

Nicole snorted, and Beth could almost see her rolling her eyes. "Do you have any idea where he's taking you?"

Beth strolled into her living room and took a seat on her couch. "I asked, but he said he wanted to surprise me."

They spent the next several minutes throwing out ideas on where Drew might be taking her on their date. It had started with things such as dinner and a movie, but by the time a knock sounded on her front door, they were both giggling and making jokes about outrageous costumes and scavenger hunts.

"I think he's here."

"Relax, and have fun. Oh, and call me tomorrow. I want details." With that, Nicole hung up, not giving Beth time to respond. Sighing, she tucked her phone into her purse before going to answer the door.

Drew stood on her front porch with a small bunch of red flowers. They looked a little like lilies, but she'd never seen lilies that color before.

"Hi."

"I hope I'm not too early. I couldn't wait any longer." He gave her that smile she loved so much.

"Eager, huh?" Was it wrong that she had the urge to grab him by his shirt and yank him inside?

"Just a little." He handed her the flowers. "These are for you."

She took his offering and brought them close enough to inhale their scent. "They're beautiful. Thank you."

Drew surprised her when he reached up and ran his hand along the side of her face. His fingers left tingles in their wake where they touched her skin. Her body heated, and her desire to kiss him overruled everything else. Throwing caution to the wind, she grabbed hold of his shirt with her free hand and pulled him to her.

He offered no resistance as her mouth sought his.

The kiss was brief but intense. When she took a step back, they were both breathing hard. Her body and her mind were at war. They'd been dancing around their attraction for over a month. Her body knew what it wanted. But she had to be strong. Things needed to be discussed before they went any further—what they both wanted, what each expected.

She released him and backed away. "Let me put these in water, and then we can go."

Beth took a few extra minutes in the kitchen to calm herself down. Her libido was in overdrive.

When she walked back into the living room, Drew was mumbling to himself.

"Everything all right?"

He snapped his head up to meet her gaze. "Yeah. Fine. Are you ready to go?"

"Sure."

Beth locked up and followed him out to his vehicle. He opened the car door for her, and waited until she was settled in the passenger seat before closing it and rounding the car to get behind the wheel. Drew was being a gentleman, and she had to say that so far, she was impressed. Not that he hadn't been a gentleman before. He'd always been polite and attentive when they were together, but this was more than letting her walk through a door first. She felt valued. Beth really hoped it wasn't all an act.

"So do I get to know where we're going?" she asked.

He shot her a quick smile before refocusing on the road. "We're having a picnic. There's a concert at the park tonight celebrating the beginning of summer."

Definitely not what she'd been expecting. But the more she thought about it, the more appealing it sounded.

It didn't take them long to arrive at their destination. The park was divided up into various areas. Given it was a beautiful Saturday evening, there were a lot of people milling about. Most of them, however, were congregated around the soccer fields.

"Did you want to walk around a little first, or we could scope out a spot near the stage?"

Although Beth would have loved to have taken a look around—it had been a while since she'd been to this park—she'd been on her feet all day. "I think I'd like to find a place and sit. It's been a long day."

Drew headed to the back of the car to gather the blanket and food he'd brought. "Did something happen?"

She shook her head as they made their way around most of the people to a grassy area not far from a small stage. "No. Just busy. The warmer weather means more people are out and about. I really shouldn't complain. It's great for business. But I think I'm going to have to hire some help soon. It's getting to be too much for Tommy and me by ourselves."

He laid out the blanket a good distance away from where the

band would be playing. While they were here to see the concert, he also wanted them to have a little privacy. It was a date, after all. "That's probably a good idea. I mean you've had a good number of people in there every time I've stopped by. Have you even had a vacation since you opened?"

Once he had everything on the blanket, he motioned for her to have a seat.

"No. The only days I have off are the days we're closed. Tommy's taken a few days here and there, but not many. We've both been working hard to make the café a success."

"It sounds like it worked." His grin was back, and Beth felt that fluttering in her stomach.

She swiftly looked away, trying to keep a hold on her emotions. Besides, they were in public. "So what about you? How was work yesterday?"

Drew began removing items from the cooler he'd brought. "Slow. We had a few med calls, but that was about it."

"Is it like that a lot?"

He quirked an eyebrow at her.

"Slow, I mean." He held out a container filled with tiny sandwiches, offering her one. "Thanks."

After removing a sandwich for himself, he replaced the container inside the cooler. "Water? I would have brought some wine, but they don't allow glass here, and I've never felt it quite right to drink wine out of a plastic cup. It reeks of high school kids sneaking into their parents' liquor cabinets."

He wrinkled his nose, and she chuckled. "Water's fine."

Drew twisted the top off the bottle and handed it to her. The whole situation was quaint and different, but she found she liked it. This was something she could see them doing over and over again.

***

Shawn had thought a concert in the park was a great date idea, and Drew was beginning to think his friend was right. The longer he sat next to Beth on their blanket, the more he realized that he owed Shawn. Drew had picked a spot in the back near a cluster of trees to give him and Beth a little privacy. He knew, as the time for the concert got closer, every inch of grass in front of the stage would be packed with people.

"Wow."

Beth's exclamation brought his attention back to her. She'd bitten into one of his sandwiches and was staring at it with wide eyes.

She met his gaze. "This is amazing. Where did you get this?"

"I made it." A feeling of pride spread through him.

"Remarkable. Do you cook, too?" she asked.

He shrugged. "A little. When I have the chance. I wouldn't call throwing together a picnic cooking, though. It was mostly just slicing, chopping, and mixing."

Before he knew it, she was on her knees. "What other goodies do you have in there?"

He motioned toward the cooler and sat back as Beth opened it to look inside.

A few moments later, Beth had pulled out and opened several containers. She took a bite of each of their contents. "This is really good."

"Thank you."

"No, Drew, I mean seriously good. Are you sure you're a firefighter?"

He laughed. "Pretty sure."

She shook her head as if she'd heard some private joke, and then lowered herself back down next to him. "Where did you learn to make stuff like this?"

"Desperation, mostly." He picked up a strawberry and popped it in his mouth.

"Most of the guys I've met either order takeout or warm up TV dinners when they get desperate for food." He wasn't sure if the look she was giving him was one of pride or skepticism.

As they continued to eat, he explained. "I guess my mom spoiled me. She used to cook these amazing meals when I lived at home. Then I came to the city and . . . well, like you said, it was mostly takeout and TV dinners. After a while, I couldn't take it, so I asked my mom if she had any simple recipes I could make. Things kind of grew from there. I found it wasn't as hard as I thought it was."

"I'm impressed. I mean you could open your own café and give me a run for my money with these sandwiches."

He grinned. "That's nice of you to say, but I think I'll stick to my day job. Cooking is just a hobby."

She surprised him with a hard kiss that lingered.

When she pulled away, he took a deep breath, inhaling her scent. "Not that I'm complaining, but what was that for?"

It was her turn to shrug.

Deciding to test the waters, he leaned in and kissed her this time. She didn't resist in the slightest, and their lips mingled together for several minutes before they broke apart.

"Thank you for agreeing to tonight," he said as he picked up his sandwich again.

Beth didn't comment, but there was a twinkle in her eye. He had no idea what the night would hold for them, but he wasn't going to worry too much about it. They were together—on a date—something he hadn't thought would happen for a good long while. He was going to enjoy every minute of it.

By six thirty, they were still nibbling on the food he'd brought as the area in front of the small stage began to fill in with people. Some brought blankets like Drew and Beth had, while others had lawn chairs. As the number of people grew, so did the noise. Even the hint of privacy had disappeared.

"There're more people than I thought there'd be."

She glanced in his direction as she took a sip of her water. "How did you find out about it?"

"Shawn. He's a good friend, and he was my captain for seven years." Drew couldn't help smiling as he remembered some of the crazy stuff that had happened to them during the time they'd worked together. Shawn was like a brother to him. He was the same age as Drew's brother, but unlike Seth, Shawn hadn't pushed Drew aside. Shawn had taken Drew under his wing when he'd joined the fire department. Drew didn't know if he would have made it through that first year if it hadn't been for Shawn.

There was a knowing look on Beth's face. "You're close."

"We are. I used to work with him a lot on our days off. It doesn't happen much anymore, though."

"That's too bad. You should always have time for friends," she said.

He nodded. "What about you? I know you and Nicole are pretty tight."

Beth snorted. "Yeah. You could say that. I mean we were close before, but after . . . well, let's just say if not for her, I'd still be sitting in front of my television in my PJ's with a quart of rocky road ice cream."

Drew wasn't sure what to say to that. He knew she had to be referring to her ex, but the last thing he wanted to do on their first date was talk about what he knew was a sore subject for her. "Did you meet at the club?"

"We did. It didn't take long for us to start hanging out outside Serpent's Kiss, though. A girl always needs a shopping partner."

He was glad to see that sparkle back in her eyes. The sun still glowed bright in the sky, and created a sort of halo around her face as she stared back at him.

"You're so beautiful." His voice was soft . . . reverent. "The way the sun is shining down on you, you look like an angel."

She looked over her shoulder, and then leaned in close to whisper in his ear. "Is that what you want? For me to be an angel? I thought you were looking for something a little . . . naughtier?"

Her breath washed over him, and he shivered. Or maybe it was her words that caused his reaction.

Before he could figure it out, the band took the stage, and welcomed everyone to the show. Drew was listening, sort of, but he couldn't take his eyes off Beth. She was smirking back at him. "Beth . . ."

She placed a single finger over his lips. "Later."

There was a part of him that wanted to drag her back to the car and make out like a couple of teenagers. He wasn't sure how well that would go over with Beth. It was the only thing that stopped him.

Taking a calming breath, he nodded.

Beth grinned and removed her finger.

The band began to play, and she turned her attention toward the stage. Drew, however, continued to watch her. Everything about Beth was appealing to him. He loved her eyes. When she looked at him, he felt as if he had an acrobat inside his stomach doing somersaults.

Of course, that didn't lessen the effect her body had on him. Everything from the silkiness of her hair and how it flowed down around her shoulders, to the way the clothes she wore seemed to accentuate her curves. Whenever he was near her—and even when he wasn't—he wanted to bury himself in her softness.

As if she knew he was thinking about her, Beth reached for his hand and brought it to rest on her lap. It looked completely innocent. And at first, it was. Then she shifted a little, spreading her legs. Heat he had only dreamed about radiated from between her legs. He closed his eyes and tried to keep from embarrassing himself.

"You okay?" she asked.

"Yes." He didn't open his eyes. He couldn't. But he also wasn't willing to remove his hand either.

"You sure?" He didn't miss the amusement in her voice.

He glanced over at her. "You're enjoying this."

"Just a little." There was no hiding her smile.

Drew sighed and tried to concentrate on the band. He couldn't say he was very successful since it was impossible to ignore the woman sitting beside him.

It was getting close to eight thirty, and he could tell the concert was winding down. A few people who had chosen to sit closer to the back had already begun packing up their things.

"Did you want to stay 'til the end?" he asked, hoping she was as ready to go as he was.

Without a word, she began gathering their things. He took the cue and finished packing everything into the cooler he'd brought.

Once they had everything, Beth and Drew made their way back to the car. The parking lot was less crowded than it had been before. The soccer fields were empty, and with the exception of two young kids with their mother, so were the playgrounds. He went to the back of the vehicle and opened the trunk.

No sooner had he tossed everything into the trunk, he felt her press against him from behind.

He sucked in a breath, unsure of what to do. They weren't exactly alone.

All thought left him as Beth cupped his erection—the one he'd been trying to tamp down for the last two hours. "We need to talk about our lists. Are you up for that?"

She squeezed him a little, and he nodded.

"I can't hear you." She squeezed again. Harder.

"Yes. Please."

Beth chuckled and released him.

He groaned when the cool air hit him as she moved to her side of the car. Never had he wanted a woman quite like he wanted Beth. Then again, he'd never wanted a woman like Beth before.

Giving himself a moment, he made sure he wasn't going to be giving anyone a show before closing the trunk. The sooner they went over their lists, the sooner he could get some relief. At least, he hoped.

Chapter 14

Beth tried to stay calm as Drew parked his car in front of her house and they strolled up the walkway to the front door. She'd been stupid pushing the physical like she had when they needed to talk about things. But they'd been dancing around their attraction for a month. When given the chance, she hadn't been able to keep her hands to herself.

Which was what had led to her current dilemma. They needed to talk, but doing so with their adrenaline pumping wasn't smart.

"Something wrong?" he asked.

She shook her head and opened the door.

When they stepped inside, she started to walk toward the kitchen, but he stopped her. "What's wrong? And please, don't tell me it's nothing. I can see it in your face. Something's bothering you. Are you having second thoughts?"

Taking a slow, deep breath, she stepped toward him. Without saying a word, she reached up and pulled his head down to hers.

Drew responded by wrapping his arms around her waist and pulling her closer.

As she slid her tongue inside his mouth, she felt his body respond. Blood surged through her veins, and she knew there would be no way to have a rational discussion until they released some of the sexual tension that had been building since the night they met.

She took a step back, urging him to follow her. He met her step for step, not releasing his hold on her. It was almost as if he were afraid she'd disappear if he eased up. That was perfectly fine with her. She didn't want him going anywhere either.

When her knees hit the back of the couch, she pulled away, and lowered herself down. He followed her, not allowing her to get too far away.

Drew hovered over her, his face inches from hers. She turned his head slightly and nipped at his earlobe.

"I seem to recall you promising to make it up to me."

"What did you have in mind?"

Beth wiggled her shirt up over her head and tossed it to the side. His gaze went directly to her breasts. She wondered if he could tell how hard her nipples were behind the black bra she wore.

Running her hand along his face, she directed his attention away from her chest and back to her face. "I want you to know that I'm clean. I've been tested twice since . . . well, since everything happened. I—"

"So am I, Beth."

She cut off his words by smothering them with another kiss. He began kissing her back in earnest. Her body was pulsing, and all she could think of was what his mouth would feel like in other places.

With that in mind, she leaned against the cushions and arched her back, pushing her breasts against him.

He took the hint and moved his lips down along her neck until he reached her bra-covered breasts. Beth didn't waste time once he arrived at his destination. She reached behind her to unhook her bra, and with a little maneuvering, it was out of the way without too much effort.

Drew took the removal of her bra as all the invitation he needed, and latched onto one of her nipples. She tangled her fingers into his hair and held him tight to her chest while he licked and sucked.

"Harder," she demanded.

He did as instructed and drew her flesh further into his mouth. It felt amazing. She'd dreamt of feeling his tongue lave at her tits for weeks.

Ripping his mouth away from her left breast, she guided his attention over to the one on the right. The cool air hit her wet nipple, causing it to stiffen even more. Both of her breasts were aching for his attention, and she needed it from him—now.

He brought his hand up to cup the breast he'd just abandoned, and began massaging it. Every nerve ending in her body was tingling, and her pussy was begging for attention. She just wasn't sure if she was ready for him to stop playing with her breasts yet. He didn't show any sign of getting bored or frustrated with his current endeavor, so she decided to let him worship them for a while.

With every tug his lips made, Beth felt herself getting wetter. She scraped her nails along his neck and back, encouraging him. "Do you know how many times I've imagined what your mouth would feel like?"

Drew groaned, but otherwise made no move to change his position or what he was doing. That was good. She wasn't ready for him to stop.

Reaching between them, Beth popped the button on her shorts, and lowered the zipper. When Drew realized what she was trying to do, he used his free hand to help her push her shorts down her legs.

Naked, she pressed her pelvis up against his clothed body letting him feel the heat and wetness. His hand gripped her hip and held her against him. "Do you like that?"

He hummed.

She let him dig his fingers into her hip while she ground against him for several minutes. Then, when she couldn't take it any longer, she pushed his head away and repositioned herself on the couch so she was lying down with one leg bent against the back of the couch and the other spread wide with her foot flat on the floor. She was completely open to him. "I want you to make me come with your tongue."

Apparently, she didn't have to ask twice. As soon as the words left her mouth, he was there between her legs. He spread her open further and ran his nose along the inside of her thigh before slowly licking up her slit. Beth knew she was wet, but she hadn't realized just how wet she was until he reached the top of her cleft and met her gaze. Already his lips were glistening with moisture.

He swirled his tongue around her clit, and her body responded in earnest. The pulsing in her belly began building into a pressure she knew would eventually explode into the most wonderful orgasm.

Cupping his head, she let his tongue work its magic. Beth hadn't had many lovers, but she'd had a few. The best one at cunnilingus had been Ben. That, however, was after lots of practice. Drew wasn't as skilled, but he showed great promise. That and he seemed to love having his mouth on her pussy.

As she got closer, she dug her hands into his scalp and began grinding her pussy against Drew's face. He held tight to her hips, securing himself, and kept licking as if his life depended on it.

Beth felt her orgasm coming and embraced it completely. She tossed her head back and let out a strangled cry.

For a few moments, she felt as if she were floating. It was heavenly.

A gentle pressure drew her attention as she came back down to earth. Drew was still between her legs, his tongue massaging her still swollen flesh. She reached down and ran her fingers through his hair. "Thank you."

Only then did he look up and meet her gaze. The entire lower half of his face was covered in her juices. "No, thank you. Just say the word and I'll do it again."

Beth grinned. "Good to know."

Pushing herself up on her elbows, she looked down at the erection he had pressing aggressively against his pants.

He followed her gaze.

"That seems to be a habit when I'm around," she said, smirking.

Drew chuckled. "What can I say? He likes you."

"Mmm. Well, let's do something about that, shall we?" She sat up, and he followed suit.

Without giving him time to process what was going on, Beth straddled his lap, took his face between her hands, and drove her tongue into his mouth. Her scent was everywhere. Not only could she taste herself, but she could also smell her heady odor as her nose brushed against the side of his face. She loved that she'd marked him. Whether she liked it or not, she wanted him. Not just his body. She wanted to mark him as hers and watch him lose himself in his submission to her.

He clutched at her hips, holding tight to her ass.

"Do you like my ass?" she asked, having noticed he went for it every chance he got.

"Yes. I love your ass. Then again, I can't think of any part of you I don't love. You have a fantastic body."

She ran a hand down his chest. "Trying to suck up, are you?"

Drew shook his head. "Not at all. I could touch you for hours and it wouldn't be enough."

"Yes, well, you've done a fair amount of touching tonight. I'd say it's my turn."

Scooting back, she took hold of the hem of his shirt and lifted. He leaned forward to make it easier for her to get it up his torso and over his head. Once removed, she threw it over to join her discarded shirt.

She backed herself up further until she could place her feet on the ground. He looked a bit disappointed that she was no longer within his reach, but that would soon be remedied. Placing her hands on his knees, she knelt down in front of him and went for the button of his pants.

It didn't take long before Drew figured out that the evening's tryst wasn't over yet. He helped her shimmy his pants down his hips and legs, and then watched intently as she laid them nearby.

Beth placed her hands on his knees again, and this time she pushed them wide apart. Looking him straight in the eye, she ran her palms up his legs until they were settled on either side of his erection. "I'm going to suck your cock now. You'll have to let me know if I do better than your hand."

***

He watched as Beth lowered her mouth to his cock. The anticipation of her lips made it feel as if it were happening in slow motion. When she finally made contact, he sucked in a sharp breath.

She ran her tongue along the slit in the top of his cock, and then along the ridge of its head. Even when she did finally take him into her mouth, it was only the very tip. She seemed perfectly content to take her time.

His palms itched with the want to touch her, but he didn't know if he should. They hadn't talked about anything yet. Hell, at the moment he was doing good to think, period.

Beth snaked one hand between them and began playing with his balls. It was just like what she'd had him do when they were talking on the phone. The difference, however, wasn't lost on him. This time it wasn't his hand milking his cock. It was her very warm, and very wet, mouth.

When he couldn't stand it any longer, he placed one hand on top of her head and tangled his fingers in her hair. She didn't object, but she did take him in a little farther and scraped her teeth along his length. He got the message loud and clear. Even though it might seem as if she was in a subservient position, she was still in charge. It was crazy how much knowing that turned him on.

Drew closed his eyes as she worked his cock and balls. He didn't even care as she gradually increased the pressure and the suction. Everything felt right.

She bobbed her head up and down taking him in until he felt the head of his cock hit the back of her throat. He knew he should feel a sense of power knowing all it would take would be a quick thrust of his hips to plunge his erection down her throat, but instead he felt vulnerable. Beth held his cock in her mouth. She could cause him pain or pleasure. It was completely up to her.

He moaned as he felt his orgasm building. "Beth . . ."

She didn't let up. If anything, she increased her efforts.

Within a few moments, he was no longer able to hold back. "I'm coming. Beth, I'm . . ."

She gave a gentle tug to his balls, and he felt a burst of energy shoot straight up his cock. He groaned as he released into her mouth, letting go of all the pent-up sexual frustration he'd been experiencing since seeing her walk into the club over a month ago.

Beth glanced up at him from her spot between his legs and grinned. "Well?"

He huffed out a laugh. "Oh yeah. Definitely better."

Pushing herself up onto her feet, she sashayed across the room to get her clothes. Drew's eyes went right to her behind. He'd had that ass in his hands, and it felt as good as it looked.

She bent over and wiggled her backside. "Enjoying the view?"

"You have no idea. I've been trying to picture what you'd look like naked for weeks now."

Slipping her panties up her long legs, she pulled them over her hips before walking back to where he sat on the couch. She placed one knee on the cushion beside his thigh, and then the other, straddling his lap. Her breasts were inches from his face before she lowered herself down onto his legs. Drew couldn't help himself. His hands went immediately to grab that perfect ass of hers.

She grinned and leaned in to brush her lips against his.

He pulled her to him, enjoying the closeness. It was strange. In some ways he already felt closer to Beth than he had his last girlfriend. He attributed that to the fact that he didn't have to try to hide what he liked, or at least that he preferred the submissive side of things. Being able to let go and know that she would lead was liberating and arousing at the same time.

"We should get dressed," she whispered. "We have things to talk about."

Drew wasn't quite ready to let her go. "Why can't we talk like this?"

Beth chuckled and sat up. "As appealing as that sounds, we do need to talk about our lists and doing so when we're in a sexualized state isn't wise. Being aroused alters your thought processes. We both need to be thinking rationally."

As much as he hated to admit it, what she said made sense. When she'd had her mouth on his cock earlier, he would have agreed to just about anything.

He let his hands drop to the couch, releasing his hold on her. Beth ran a hand down the side of his face and placed one last kiss on his lips before backing off his lap and standing up. She went back to gathering her clothes and getting dressed. He reluctantly did the same.

Once they were fully clothed again, he followed her into her kitchen.

"Have a seat, and I'll get us both some water," she said.

Drew pulled out a chair and took a seat. While she busied herself getting their drinks, he realized that not once had he pondered what the inside of Beth's house would look like. All his dreams about Beth had revolved solely around her and maybe a single piece of furniture such as a bed or a couch . . . or even a table. And even now, as he sat in the middle of it, he was trying to mesh what he was seeing with the woman he'd gotten to know over the last month.

She set a glass of ice water in front of him, and sat down on the opposite side of the table. "You seem to be thinking hard about something."

He took a drink and shook his head. "Just looking around. Your house is very . . ."

"Normal?" she offered.

While that wasn't exactly what he'd been trying to say, he

supposed it was as good a word as any. "I guess you could say that. It doesn't look that much different from my mom's. She has a similar setup. The table is even in the same location."

"Ah. I thought maybe you were thinking I'd have floggers on the wall for decoration or something."

Her tone was lighthearted, joking, and he found himself smiling at how relaxed he was with her. "Not exactly. Although I am curious. I mean, you did say you played in your house, right?"

She took a sip of her water before answering. "I keep a chest in my bedroom with the majority of my toys. Most are portable, though."

There was that glint in her eye again. He was feeling himself becoming worked up again despite the distance between them. "That's . . . good."

Beth stood and strolled over to the refrigerator. She poked her head inside and returned to the table with a container of fruit and cheese. "We might as well have a snack while we talk."

He swallowed and nodded. As much as he didn't want to admit it, he was a little on edge.

"Did you bring your list with you?" she asked.

"Yes. It's out in the car." He should have thought to bring it in with him, but he'd been distracted at the time. The only thing he'd been able to think about the entire way back to her house was how long he'd have to wait before he would get to touch her.

"Why don't you go get it? I'll grab mine, and we can sit here and go over everything."

She smiled down at him, and then walked out of the room, leaving him sitting at the table. He wondered if it was intentional.

Taking a huge gulp of his water, he placed the empty glass back on the table and stood. This was what he wanted. Now all he had to do was hope he didn't chicken out when they both laid all their cards out on the table.

Chapter 15

Beth had printed her list out the night before, so all she had to do was retrieve it from the drawer where she'd stashed it. She heard the front door open and close as she pulled the sheets of paper out of their hiding place. Drew had presumably gone out to get his list.

She took her time as she made her way back downstairs to the kitchen. Setting the papers on the table, Beth picked up both their glasses and refilled them. They might as well be comfortable while they discussed things.

It was hard to believe that she wasn't more nervous. Leading up to their date, she'd nearly driven herself crazy with all the what-ifs. Sure, they were still there, but they weren't nagging at her as much as they had been. Okay, that wasn't true. She was still worried. About the future. About whether they could make things work between them. But what they were about to talk about—their limit lists—that wasn't worrying her so much. Given their fun on the couch, she guessed they'd be able to figure out how to make a sexual relationship work pretty easily. It was the rest that was questionable.

Drew walked back into the room as she was returning their glasses to the table. She could tell he was more anxious than he'd been before, but he also looked resolute.

"Have a seat," she said.

He released a heavy breath and lowered himself into the chair he'd been in earlier.

Beth joined him at the table. "I know you've never done this before, but I have to say this is one of the things about this lifestyle that I like the most. Honestly, I think if more vanilla couples did this, they would be much happier."

Drew smiled and relaxed his shoulders a little. "I'm trying not to stress too much about it, but it's strange putting all your wants and desires out there even though I know you're already aware of some of them."

"The first time is always the hardest. It will get easier." She picked up her list and scanned the first page. "Let's start with something simple. As far as the D/s dynamic is concerned, what are you interested in? Given what I know about you so far, I can't see you wanting something 24/7."

He grinned. "No. Not only would that be difficult with my job, I just can't see myself being submissive all the time. I'm not even sure I could be that way most of the time. My fantasies usually revolve around bedroom activities, so I think I'd like to confine it to that. For now, at least."

Beth nodded. "So bedroom only. That works for me, although I would be interested in expanding that some in the future if that is something you want. A 24/7 relationship doesn't appeal to me either. Frankly, it's too much work. But I do like the idea of you kneeling at my feet while we watch a movie, or maybe even having you do things around the house while I keep you in line with my crop."

"That could be interesting."

"Very." Beth couldn't help but picture Drew on his hands and knees cleaning up some mess she'd intentionally made for the sole purpose of watching him do her bidding. He'd be naked, of course, and she'd have fun playing with him while he was busy trying to get her floor spotless.

Drew cleared his throat. "If I'm working, we can't play. I can't jeopardize my job."

"I would never want to put your career in danger, Drew. Nor would I want you distracted when you're working. Your job is dangerous enough as it is."

He frowned. "My job still worries you."

Beth sighed. "I'm not sure that will ever change. I mean, if I were rushing into a burning building as part of my job, wouldn't you be concerned about me on some level?"

"You're right. I would."

She grinned, trying to lighten the mood a little. "Let's get back to our discussion. We've figured out when we don't want to play, so now we need to figure out when we do. I know your schedule is . . . well, for lack of a better word . . . strange."

He chuckled.

Beth rolled her eyes. "It's the truth. I'm going to need a calendar to keep track."

"You get used to it."

"I suppose I will." She reached for a couple of grapes and popped them into her mouth. "But that still leaves the question as to *when*. Between your schedule and mine, it could get a little hairy."

Drew picked up a cheese square and took a bite. "My single days off can be hectic. Also, I have to be at work by seven in the morning."

"So I'd say those days are out."

He frowned again.

"What?" she asked, not understanding his reaction.

"I want . . ."

"Yes?"

"Beth, I want a relationship with you. I want the other stuff, too, but I want us to date and . . . and be together as a couple."

She knew this. If all he'd wanted to do was play, she was sure he would have been able to find another Domme at the club to experiment with. The man was easy on the eyes and she'd seen more than one Femdom looking him over. She wasn't sure what his wanting a relationship had to do with their playtime, though. "I know."

He grinned. "Good."

"So it's agreed that we only play during the stretches when you have at least four days off, and during the rest of the time we're just a regular couple."

"Agreed." He paused. "That means we can still do normal couple things during the non-play times, correct?"

It took her only a moment to get what he was asking. She burst out laughing. "Are you asking if we can still have sex if we're not playing?"

Drew's cheeks turned a bright shade of pink.

Beth shook her head. "You are such a guy."

He puffed his chest out. "I would hope so."

This only made her laugh harder.

Drew joined her.

It took them several minutes to regain their composure. When they did, it was Beth who spoke first. "I think tonight we proved that we can have perfectly good sex without getting kinky."

His eyes widened. "Good?"

"What? You didn't think what we did tonight was good?" she asked.

He snorted. "Tonight is probably up in my top five sexual experiences ever, and I didn't even get my cock inside you. Plus, it still felt as if you were in control, and I liked that. I don't want that to change."

"Good. Me either." She looked down at her papers and tried to hide how much his words thrilled her. *One of his top five.* She wouldn't deny she was feeling pretty pleased with herself. "So we've talked about the when. We should probably talk about the what."

Drew pushed his list across the table in her direction. "Being that I work mostly with guys, I figured there wouldn't be any sexual term I hadn't heard before. This proved me wrong."

She chuckled and did a quick scan of what he'd marked. It was what she'd expected for the most part. He was interested in bondage, although he had no personal experience with it. Impact play was also on his *want to try* list as well as sensation play. She was happy to see that humiliation and degradation were listed as 'not interested'. The one thing she was surprised to see, however, was that he'd marked 'maybe' beside CBT. She hadn't pegged him for an interest in cock and ball torture.

"CBT?" she asked.

He shrugged. "I've seen it done at the club. It looks extremely painful."

"It can be."

"I made a comment to John once saying how I couldn't understand how a guy could want that done to him. He explained that there was a heightened sense of giving up control associated with it. She quite literally has you by the balls and can do with you what she wants." He leaned forward and picked up another piece of cheese. Instead of eating it, he rolled it between his thumb and index finger. "I don't know if I'll like it, but it's something I'd like to try. Eventually."

Beth could take or leave CBT. It had its place, and it was fine once in a while, but it wasn't something she normally did. "Maybe we can explore that in stages. There are many different types of CBT. We'd have to discuss the specifics and just how far each of us wanted to go with it."

He took a deep breath and ate the cheese he'd been toying with.

She handed her list to him and picked up several more grapes. "I don't see any major conflicts. Many of the things you want to try I've done before."

Drew nodded as he looked over her list.

"Do you have any questions?" she asked.

"How do we know where to start?"

Beth grinned. "I'd like for you to leave your list with me. I'll look over it in more detail tomorrow and come up with a game plan."

"Okay. That makes sense."

"Is there anything specific that you'd like to try first?"

"Bondage." He had the answer out almost before she was able to finish asking the question.

Beth chuckled. "I think that can be arranged. You're off on Monday, correct?"

"Yes. But I have to work Tuesday. Then I'm off Wednesday through Saturday," he said.

"Why don't you come over on Monday? I'll make us dinner and we can talk some more. You can take my list home and look it over in more detail as well."

"I like the sound of that," he said.

"Good. I can have dinner ready by five. That will give us plenty of time after."

***

Drew was reluctant to leave Beth on Saturday, but he hadn't felt comfortable asking if he could stay the night. They weren't there yet. Besides, he had to work the next morning. With her work schedule, Sundays and Mondays were her only days to sleep in. He didn't want to take that away from her just to satisfy his own selfish want.

His apartment was dark when he arrived home. He must have forgotten to turn on the outside light in his haste to get out the door. Turning the key in the lock, he pushed open the door, and flipped on the light.

The sight that greeted him was not what he'd expected. His buddy, Shawn, was curled up on his new couch with a blanket draped over him. "Shawn?"

Shawn rolled his large body to face Drew and then sat up slowly. It was only then that Drew noticed several empty beer cans beside the coffee table. "Hey. You're back."

Drew shut and locked the door behind him. "What happened?"

"My old lady kicked me out. Said I'm afraid of commitment or some shit." Shawn ran his hands through his hair, causing it to stick up in all directions. "Do you think I can crash here for a few days? I start my rotation tomorrow, so I won't be able to look for a new place until Friday."

"Sure. Whatever you need."

"Thanks."

Walking into the kitchen, Drew realized he still had Beth's list in his hand. He quickly folded and tucked it into his front pocket. The last thing he needed was for Shawn to get curious. Trust was one thing, but he didn't want to have to lie to his friend. He also wasn't ready to put his sexual preferences out in the open to be scrutinized.

"Were you out with your girl tonight? The one you were telling me about?" Shawn asked.

Drew took two glasses and filled them with water. He had no idea how much Shawn had had to drink, but if what he could see on the floor was any indication, his friend was going to be feeling it tomorrow.

Handing one of the glasses to Shawn, Drew sat down a few feet away on the recliner. "I was. And before you ask, it went well. She's making me dinner Monday night." He couldn't hide his joy about that, so he didn't even try.

"I'm happy for you. You deserve it."

"Thanks."

They were both quiet for several minutes.

"I hope you don't mind that I used the spare key you gave me,"

Shawn said.

"Of course not. I gave it to you to use if you needed it. You obviously needed it tonight."

Shawn gulped down half the water in his glass. "Yeah."

"You want to talk about it?" Drew asked. Shawn had certainly listened to Drew's women troubles over the years.

"Not much to tell." Shawn shook his head and downed the rest of his water. "I was over at Mickey's helping him set up a swing set for his girls for most of the day. Came home around five and Jill had my bags packed and waiting for me at the door. Everything was fine last week. I don't know what happened."

"Didn't you mention she'd been out of town or something?" Drew asked, trying to help his friend make sense of what appeared to be the end of his relationship. Shawn and Jill had been together since Drew had been a firefighter—longer.

"Yeah. Her sister's been sick, so she was in Denver helping take care of her sister's kids. She got back late last night. I was hoping we'd get to sit down and enjoy a nice evening together before I went back on rotation."

Drew didn't know what to say. "I'm sorry, man. I really am."

Shawn nodded and looked around the apartment. "Are you sure you don't mind me crashing here for a few nights?"

"Of course not. We're both on duty tomorrow, then between sleeping and having dinner at Beth's, I won't be here much Monday either."

"I owe you."

"Pfft. How many times did you save my skin in the last seven years?" Drew asked.

His friend laughed. It was good to hear.

"Exactly. So don't sweat it. Crash here as long as you need."

Considering it was going on eleven, Shawn helped Drew clean up some of the clutter and downed a few ibuprofen before climbing back on the couch. After making sure everything was locked up tight and that the lights were out, Drew made his way into his bedroom. Only then, with the door closed, did he fish Beth's list out of his pocket.

She had very few things marked as 'want to try'. Then again, she'd been in a BDSM relationship before. Although he knew that, seeing it in black and white was quite different. He felt the jealousy peak inside him and tried his best to push it away. It was completely irrational. She was with him now. *Officially.* There wasn't any use getting upset about her being and doing things with another man. Especially a man who ended up being a lying, cheating bastard.

Drew was so caught up in his internal argument that he almost missed something Beth marked on her list as 'love'. He ran his finger down the page to be sure he wasn't reading it incorrectly.

He wasn't.

Beth loved knife play.

Racking his brain, he tried to remember what he'd put for that. Dislike? Hate? He couldn't remember. During his two months as a member of Serpent's Kiss, he couldn't recall ever witnessing knife play.

Before he lost his nerve, he pulled out his cell phone and sent Beth a text.

Knife play?

It took her a few moments to respond.

Yes. -Beth

It sounded crazy to admit it, but he was curious.

Why?

Instead of her sending another text in response, his phone rang. He answered it quickly and held it up to his ear. "Hey."

"Hey, yourself."

"You didn't have to call. I was a little shocked, that's all. I wasn't expecting you to be into that," he said.

Beth hummed. "I noticed you marked it as *dislike* on your list."

He guessed that answered his question. "I've never seen it done, but I'm not sure I'd like something like that."

"I didn't think I would either until I saw a demonstration. Once I tried it myself, I was hooked." She paused. "If you're not comfortable with knife play we can take it off the table for now. There's no pressure, Drew. I get that this is new to you."

While he understood and appreciated that, he felt he needed to be honest. "I'm torn. A part of me is curious since you ranked it so high on your list, but having a blade that close to my skin . . ."

"It isn't about that. Or at least for me it isn't. It's a mind game. I'm not going to cut you, but I could. The possibility is always there."

"Thanks."

She laughed. "Just being honest, remember."

He was quiet for a moment. "I'll think about it."

"Fair enough."

A knock sounded on his bedroom door and it caused him to jump.

"Yes?" he yelled in the direction of the door.

"Do you have an extra toothbrush lying around somewhere?" Shawn asked through the door.

"Yeah. Just give me a minute and I'll get it for you," he responded back to Shawn. To Beth he said, "Can you hang on?"

"Sure. But I can let you go if you—"

"No." He hesitated. The last thing he wanted to do was sound desperate. "I'll be right back."

As swiftly as he could, Drew headed out into the hall to the bathroom, dug through his linen closet until he found an unopened toothbrush, and then grabbed the tube of toothpaste from the medicine cabinet. It was one of the few lessons his brother had imparted to him. Always have a spare toothbrush in your closet for overnight guests. The last thing you want is to French kiss a girl goodbye in the morning when she hadn't yet brushed her teeth.

With Shawn's issue taken care of, Drew rushed back into his bedroom. He made sure his door was shut firmly behind him, and then went to the bed to resume his phone call with Beth. "I'm back."

"Everything okay? I didn't realize you had houseguests."

"It was a surprise to me, too." Drew debated how much to tell her. "Shawn was here when I got home. His girlfriend kicked him out."

"That's horrible."

"Yeah. It is. They've been together for years," he said.

Beth grew quiet. "Does that mean you're going to need to cancel for Monday night?"

"No. Shawn can take care of himself. I'll be there."

"I guess I'll see you then." He could tell she was smiling, and he wished he were there to see it. "Good night, Drew."

"Good night, Beth."

With a spring in his step, Drew plugged his phone into the charger, and then went to get ready for bed. It had been an amazing day, and he couldn't wait for Monday when he could see Beth again.

Chapter 16

When Drew's alarm woke him up at six the next morning, he jumped out of bed with an excess of energy. He loved his job, but it had been a while since he'd had such a spring in his step. The renewed energy he felt was an obvious byproduct of his date with Beth. Or Beth herself. Things had gone better than he'd expected, and they were moving forward with a relationship. He couldn't have asked for more than that.

His mind on other things, Drew opened his door and headed toward the bathroom. It wasn't until he heard movement in his kitchen that he remembered he had a houseguest.

Seconds later, Shawn turned around and caught Drew standing there buck-naked. Shawn smirked and pointed a piece of toast at him. "I like you, Parker, but not that much."

Drew held up his middle finger and continued on his way to the bathroom.

Figuring he'd get his shower out of the way, he turned on the water, and stepped into the spray. As he worked the soap down his body, he smiled remembering Beth between his legs. He had no idea what the future held for them, but he knew he'd do just about anything to feel her mouth on his cock again.

Although it was tempting, Drew decided it probably wasn't a good idea to jack off in the shower with Shawn in the other room.

Besides, his friend would most likely want to shower as well before heading into the station, so he probably shouldn't use all the hot water. Finishing up, he dried off, and wrapped a clean towel around his waist.

Shawn was just finishing his breakfast of toast and orange juice when Drew strolled out of the bathroom. "It's all yours."

His friend nodded, and Drew darted into his room to get dressed.

They drove separately to the station. Shawn wasn't ready for the guys to know that Jill had kicked him out. Drew could relate to that. These guys were family to him, but there were some things you didn't even want family to know.

It was midmorning before they got their first call. There was a gas leak in an assisted living facility. All seventy apartments had to be evacuated. Since the residents were over the age of sixty-five, many had to be helped out or even carried. Once everyone was safe, it was a matter of securing the area until the leak could be fixed.

When they arrived back, everyone fell into their normal routines making sure the trucks and all the equipment were cleaned and ready for the next call. Drew gathered his crew for a quick debriefing, and out of the corner of his eye he could see Shawn talking to his guys as well. Everything had gone well, all things considered, so there wasn't much to discuss. When he dismissed his crew, though, he glanced over to where Shawn had been but he was gone.

Drew found his friend in the kitchen. It was lunchtime, but given they'd all been out on a call for the last two hours nothing was ready. He washed his hands and pitched in to help.

"Thanks," Shawn said.

The two worked together to get lunch on the table as soon as possible. Drew didn't know about everyone else, but he was starving. He'd learned long ago to make sure he ate well at every meal. A call could come in at any time, so you took advantage of the food put in front of you no matter what it was.

They'd barely taken a few bites of the lunch they prepared when another call came in. It looked as if it was going to be one of those days. He shoved a last bite in his mouth while he listened to the dispatcher rattle off the information they would need. Then they were off—their half-eaten lunch left sitting on the long table.

Three hours later, Drew worked alongside his crew as they

finished their daily chores around the station. It was only then that he had time to think on Shawn's situation. Jill had complained that Shawn was afraid of commitment. The two had never gotten married. They weren't engaged. Yet they'd been together for over seven years. Drew had always thought that was a mutual decision, but apparently it wasn't.

Thoughts of Shawn's relationship inevitably led back to Drew's newly established one with Beth. He knew she'd been hurt by her last relationship, and that she had trust issues. Would that translate into a fear of commitment? She hadn't showed any signs of that last night, but things had moved rather quickly. Maybe once she had time to ponder everything she'd change her mind. He really hoped not.

Shawn came up on his left. "You got a minute?"

"Sure." Drew tossed his rag onto the bench and followed his friend outside.

Shawn kept walking until they were several feet away from the open bays. It wasn't likely anyone would hear them out there.

"I got a text from Jill while we were out earlier."

From the look on Shawn's face, she hadn't been messaging to ask him back. "What did she say?"

He leaned back against the building and ran a hand over his face in frustration. "She wants me to come get the rest of my stuff tomorrow. Says she wants a clean break so she can move on with her life before it's too late."

Drew moved to stand beside Shawn. "I'm sorry."

For the first time in the seven years Drew had known him, he thought Shawn might break down.

He didn't. Instead, he took a deep breath and looked across the street where a couple of kids were playing. "I know you have a date tomorrow night with your new girl, but do you think you can go with me to move my stuff? It shouldn't take more than a few hours. Most everything in the house is hers anyway."

"Sure. Did you want to go first thing in the morning, or would you rather get some sleep first?" Drew asked.

"I think I'd rather get it over with, if you don't mind."

"Of course not."

Shawn nodded. "I'd ask some of the other guys but . . ."

"But you'd rather they not know yet. I get it."

Shawn snorted. "I suppose you do. How long do you think you're going to be able to keep your new girlfriend from everyone? Given that cheesy grin I've seen on your face a few times today, and your late night phone call . . . I'm thinking a week, tops." The change in subject had brightened Shawn's mood considerably.

Drew rolled his eyes. "We'll see."

"She must be something if she has you mooning after her already."

He smiled. "She is."

"I'm happy for you." Sadness crept back into Shawn's features.

"Do you think you and Jill can work it out?" Drew asked.

"I don't know. She seems pretty determined it's over." Shawn bent down, picked up a stick from the sidewalk, and began tearing off the bark. He'd quit smoking about six months ago, and Drew figured he was probably trying to distract himself from wanting a cigarette. "Tell me about Beth. What's she look like?"

Drew grinned and lowered himself down beside Shawn. "She's about five six. Long, dark brown hair. It's almost black it's so dark. Her curves are what dreams are made of, and her legs . . ." Drew sighed as he remembered having his hands on her hips as he licked her pussy and watched as she shuddered around him.

Shawn whistled. "You've got it bad. Maybe a week's too long."

Drew shoved his friend, stood, and brushed himself off. "We'd better get back in there before someone comes looking for us."

Nodding, Shawn threw the battered stick down on the sidewalk. Drew thought he'd push himself up off the wall and that would be the end of their conversation. He was wrong. Shawn looked up at him, squinting in the sunlight. "If she's the one, don't let her get away. Don't make the same mistake I did."

Before Drew could respond, Shawn was up and headed back into the station. Drew had no choice but to follow him. Shawn always had liked to get in the last word.

Aside from an EMS call around nine that night, things were quiet. Drew settled into his cot a little before eleven. He closed his eyes and tried to relax. It had been a busy day. He should've fallen asleep in minutes, but at eleven thirty he was still awake. Of late, he would have blamed it on his libido, but that wasn't the problem this time.

He was worried about Shawn. His friend had gone through the

motions during their shift. Normally he was a pretty laid-back kind of guy. He could be serious when the situation warranted it, but otherwise he didn't let much bother him. The apparent end of his long-term relationship was weighing on him. Shawn's parting words rang through Drew's head once more. He knew his friend was right. If Beth was the one, then he had to do everything he could to hold onto her. He had to show her she was appreciated and that he wouldn't take her for granted.

Rolling over, he dug his cell phone out of his pocket, and scrolled through his contacts until he found Beth's name.

I hope you had a relaxing day. I'm looking forward to tomorrow night.

There was no reply. He hadn't expected there to be. Beth was most likely asleep.

Feeling better since he'd reached out to her, Drew tucked his phone back into his pocket, and tried to get some sleep while he could.

***

She found Drew's message the next morning when she checked her phone. Beth smiled at his words. If she wasn't careful, she could see herself falling for him. Who was she kidding? She was already well on her way.

After making herself a quick breakfast, she headed to the grocery store. There were a few items she would need if she was going to make dinner for the two of them this evening. She was going to keep it simple—steak, baked potatoes, and salad. What meat-loving guy didn't like that?

Beth was on her way out of the store when her phone rang. The moment she saw Drew's name on her screen, her stomach did a little flip. "Morning."

Drew chuckled. "Good morning. I didn't wake you, did I?"

"Nope. I've been up for a while. I was just doing a little shopping for our dinner tonight."

"That's actually why I'm calling." His voice took on a serious tone.

She frowned. "You aren't canceling on me, are you?"

"No. Not at all. But I had to do something this morning, and it's taking longer than expected. I haven't even been home yet to change out of my uniform," he said.

It was on the tip of her tongue to ask for details, but she held back. "Is everything all right? Are you okay?"

"Yeah. It's nothing like that. A buddy of mine just needed my help with something." He paused. "I need to go. I'll see you tonight. I promise. I just might be a few minutes late."

"Okay. I'll see you tonight."

He seemed reluctant to hang up. She was about to ask again if everything was all right when she realized he'd disconnected their call.

Trying not to let it bother her, Beth put her shopping bags into her car, and drove home. She had a lot to do before he arrived, including going through her toy box. While they wouldn't be playing tonight, she did want to talk about what their first scene would be. If all went well, and he agreed, their first session would be Wednesday evening. It was the start of his four days off, and it would give him some time to deal with any lingering effects of their play.

The hours passed quickly as she worked around the house and prepped dinner. By the time five o'clock rolled around, everything was as ready as it could be. All she needed now was Drew.

Only twenty more minutes went by before she heard a car pull up out front. She watched as he climbed out of his vehicle and made his way up the driveway. He had a small bouquet of flowers in his right hand.

When he reached the front porch, Beth opened the door to greet him. He looked up at the sound, and smiled as soon as he saw her standing there. Despite his smile, she hadn't missed the worry that had creased his features before he realized she was there. Something was troubling him. While their relationship was still new, she hoped he would open up and share whatever it was with her. If they were going to have the type of relationship they both claimed they wanted, communication was key. Especially if they weren't only going to be play partners.

He stepped through her door and extended his arm, offering her the flowers. "Sorry again. I was hoping I wasn't going to be late, but . . ."

"It's fine. Why don't you come into the kitchen with me while I finish putting everything together?"

Drew grinned and motioned for her to lead the way.

She strolled over to the refrigerator while he took a seat at the table.

"Anything you need me to do?" he asked.

"Nope. I cooked the potatoes and made the salad earlier. All I have to do now is cook the steaks." She glanced back at him and smiled. "Thank you for offering, though."

He sat patiently as Beth removed the potatoes from the oven and then adjusted the setting to broil. She seasoned the steaks and laid them aside before going back to the refrigerator for the salad. It was a simple meal, but one she thought he'd enjoy.

Once everything was cooking, she joined him at the table. She was trying to come up with the best way to broach the subject that had been eating at her all day when he spoke up. "I guess you're probably wondering what all that was about today."

"I am a little curious." A *little* was putting it mildly.

Drew sighed. "Remember when we were talking Saturday night and I told you what happened with Shawn and his girlfriend?"

Of course she remembered. "Yes."

"Well, she sent him a text Sunday while we were working wanting him to come by today and clean out his stuff. He asked if I'd help him."

"That was nice of you." It was nice, but from everything she'd learned about Drew so far, it fit his character.

He shrugged, brushing off the compliment. "He'd do it for me."

Beth figured that since he'd brought up the subject, she'd go ahead and jump in with both feet. "Is that what you were thinking about then, when you were walking up to the door?"

"Yes and no."

He was quiet for a few moments, and Beth took the opportunity to get up and put the steaks in the oven. When she turned around to return to her chair, Drew was standing behind her. Without a word, he reached out, pulled her into his arms, and kissed her.

"I missed you," he said, resting his forehead on hers.

She wasn't sure if she wanted to admit it yet, but she'd missed him, too. Everything seemed to be happening so fast between them. "I'm here now."

Drew took a deep breath and then lowered his mouth to hers once more. She wrapped her arms around his neck and gave as good as she got. If she wasn't ready to say she missed him, she had no problems showing him.

Things quickly got out of control as their tongues mingled and hands explored. Beth ran her fingers through his hair as he lowered his mouth to her neck. All thoughts of food quickly left her mind until she began to smell the meat as it broiled in the oven. She placed her hands on his shoulders and pushed a little to get his attention. He pulled back with a questioning look on his face.

Beth smirked and held up one finger.

Turning her back to him, she leaned over and turned off the oven. As appealing as dinner sounded, Drew was even more so. Sure, she could wait, but she didn't want to. And from the looks of it, Drew didn't either.

When she faced him again, she had a plan. "I know we agreed that we wouldn't play when you have to work the next day, but are you up for a little mild bondage?"

His eyes lit up, and she could have sworn she saw his cock twitch. "Yes."

She nodded and placed her palm flat against his chest.

He got the message and began walking backward. Within a few steps, his knees hit the edge of the chair he'd been sitting on a few moments before.

Beth ran her hand down the length of his chest until she reached the hem of his shirt. She took hold of it and worked it up over his torso. When he realized what she was doing, he raised his arms over his head to help her remove it.

Then she went for the button on his pants. He kept his hands out of the way as she worked. Normally she would take her time if she was undressing a sub as part of foreplay, but she wasn't worried about either of them being ready for the main event. She was already wet and aching to feel his cock inside her, and from the way his erection stood at attention, she would guess he was more than ready as well.

Once he was completely naked, she directed him to sit down. She could tell he was curious, but eager as well.

She walked around behind him and opened a drawer where she kept various items. Beth had learned not long after she and Ben had started playing that it was a good idea to have kinky items, or at least pervertables, in each and every room. Toward the back of the drawer, she found what she was looking for. It was an old scarf. Someone had given it to her years before at a Christmas party. It was orange and rather ugly looking. She'd found it one day and was going to throw it out, but then had gotten inspiration to keep it for times such as this.

Grasping the scarf in her hand, she went back to stand behind Drew. She took hold of his arms and guided them behind the back of the chair. "I'm going to tie your wrists. If something doesn't feel right, just say red and we'll stop. I'll untie you and that will be it."

He nodded. "Got it."

Beth waited a spilt second before she bent down and secured his wrists with the scarf. "How does that feel?"

"Amazingly good."

She chuckled.

Moving around to his front, Beth released the top button of her blouse. The muscles in his jaw flexed a moment before she saw him swallow hard. Oh yeah, this was going to be so much fun.

Chapter 17

Drew couldn't believe this was happening. His heart was pounding in his chest as the reality of what was about to occur sank in. Beth stood before him slowly unbuttoning her top. He could already see a hint of the purple bra she was wearing. She toyed with the next button that would give him a full view of her chest. He wanted her to hurry. He wanted to see, to touch, to taste.

In reaction to his thoughts, he leaned forward. The motion tugged at the scarf that bound his wrist to the chair—reminding him that he wasn't, in fact, free to touch. He groaned and the burning in his groin increased. His reaction didn't make any kind of sense, but it was there just the same.

Beth must have heard him groan. She stepped forward and bent over to whisper in his ear. Her breast was inches from his face. "See something you like?"

"Yes." It was all he could do to get out that one word when she was so close to him.

Without moving away, she popped the button she'd been playing with a few moments before. He took a deep breath as he watched her work through the remaining buttons before discarding the shirt. She hadn't backed away during the process. Her tits were right there. So close, yet far enough away that he couldn't easily reach. Not with his arms bound as they were.

Her chest vibrated, and he glanced up to find her grinning down at him.

This teasing was torture.

He loved it.

She cupped the back of his head and positioned herself so that his face was nestled between her breasts. He wasted no time nuzzling his nose into her cleavage and running his lips along the seam of satin and lace. Beth wasn't overly endowed in that area, but she had more than enough in his opinion. Her bra pushed her tits together, and he ran his tongue along the valley it created.

Beth reached up with her free hand and pushed one satin cup out of the way. He didn't need an engraved invitation. In less than a second, his lips were covering her nipple, sucking it into his mouth. She dug her nails into his scalp as he continued to lick and suck and tease. With only her body, she told him what she wanted and how she wanted it.

Somewhere along the line, she released her hold on him long enough to reach behind her back and unclasp her bra. It fell away, and she guided him to the other side. He'd never been a breast man, but there was something about having Beth's tits in his mouth— feeling her fingers in his hair—that turned him on more than playing with a woman's breasts ever had in the past.

The sound of a zipper caught his attention. He stopped and began to pull away.

"I don't remember telling you to stop." Her voice was firm but breathy at the same time.

He went back to what he was doing, but he had to admit that he was imagining what that sound meant and the fact that he was tied to a chair and not able to get his hands on her luscious ass.

"Something wrong?" she asked.

"No. I was just . . ."

She tilted his head up and brushed her lips against his. "Did you not want me to take off the rest of my clothes?"

There was a gleam in her eye, and Drew realized that he'd screwed up. Even though all they'd agreed on was some light bondage, he'd told her he wanted her to take charge when it came to the bedroom. "Sorry. I guess old habits are hard to break."

Beth hummed and trailed her mouth along his jaw until she captured his earlobe between her teeth. "I shall forgive you." She bit down enough to cause a slight measure of pain. "This time."

He got the message. Tonight was only a little fun and exploration of something he'd wanted to try. In the future, there would be consequences.

Before he could dwell too much on what had just happened, she lowered her mouth over his again, and thrust her tongue inside. There was no sweetness to this kiss. Teeth clashed as she continued her assault, holding his head in the exact position she wanted it.

Gradually she eased her grip, and softened the kiss. There was still no doubt, however, as to who was in control. He met every caress of her tongue with one of his own.

Drew was so lost in the kiss that he almost missed the movement of her hips as she straddled him. It was only then that he realized her skirt and panties were gone. He'd heard the zipper, yes, but how had he missed her shedding the rest of her clothing?

His breath caught in his throat as she rubbed her bare pussy over his cock. Her juices covered him as she rocked her hips and continued to kiss him. He wanted to be inside her. He wanted to feel that heat surrounding him.

"Beth."

He tried to break free from their kiss, so she moved her mouth lower to his neck. Drew didn't know if that was any better as she ran her teeth along his skin, biting and sucking as she went. He was on fire and he felt as if he would go mad if he didn't have her soon.

When he didn't think it could get any worse, it did. Beth reached down between them. He couldn't see from the position he was in, but he could feel it. She lifted enough to fit her hand between them, and plunged her fingers into her pussy. Drew couldn't tell how many, but it didn't matter. She was fucking herself right there on his lap.

"Please. Please, Beth. I want to be inside you. I need to . . ."

The next thing he knew, those same fingers that had been in her pussy were at his lips. He eagerly opened his mouth and took the offering. Tasting her only made him want her more. He was so aroused, he was afraid he might not last long even if she did give him what he wanted.

She removed her fingers from his mouth and brought his lips to meet hers. He moaned deep in his throat and his nostrils flared as he tried to keep himself in check. At the same time, he didn't want to.

All he could think about was her.

Beth pulled back enough to rest her forehead against his. Her eyes were dilated and she was breathing hard. The tips of her nipples brushed against his chest, sending sparks through him with every touch.

"I'm going to fuck you now." It was all she said before she took hold of his cock and lined it up with her entrance.

He gritted his teeth and closed his eyes as she lowered herself down.

"Open your eyes. I want you looking at me."

Drew did as she said, and he was so glad he did. Her eyes glazed over as she took him all in. He wouldn't have wanted to miss that.

Once she had taken every inch of him, she began to move. First it was only a rocking motion. Then she rested her hands on his shoulders and began lifting and lowering herself on his cock. It was only by watching her face, knowing that he wanted her to get there first, that he kept his orgasm at bay.

Seeing her pleasure build was a fascinating sight. As she got closer, her eyelids drooped. Her head fell back, breaking their eye contact, and her mouth opened to form a silent O.

Her speed picked up and he had to close his eyes again to keep himself from coming. It was the only way.

Again, he felt it when she slipped her hand between them to touch herself. This time she used two fingers—one on each side of his erection—to rub. He forced his eyes open so he could see the motion of her hand as it moved.

Watching her hand was nearly his undoing. Knowing she was touching herself combined with the movement of his cock sliding in and out of her pussy made all the moisture leave his mouth. For the first time since she'd bound his wrists, he made a conscious effort to get free. He wanted to touch her. He wanted to hold her hips in his hands and impale her with his cock over and over until she exploded all over him.

Not only did her tie hold, but also his actions weren't needed. Beth took what she wanted from him. She ground herself against him with a fierceness and abandon he'd never seen from a woman before outside porn. He knew porn was fake. Beth wasn't faking. She was as caught up as he was.

Her breath hitched and her fingers picked up their pace. A few moments later, she released a strangled moan as her muscles pulsed around him. Her orgasm seemed to go on forever.

When she finally stilled and opened her eyes again, he was still hard and teetering on the edge. It wouldn't take much to make him come.

Beth smiled and gave him a long, languid kiss. And while she kept their bodies joined, she remained amazingly still. He needed friction.

In that vein, Drew lifted his hips.

She broke the kiss and stood.

He nearly cried.

That is until Beth turned herself around and began to lower herself onto him again—this time giving him a prime view of her ass.

***

Beth had almost forgotten how much fun this was. Okay, that wasn't true. She hadn't forgotten. Not really. But she didn't realize how much she'd missed this feeling of being in complete control of her pleasure as well as her partner's.

Given that she had Drew exactly where she wanted him at the moment, she figured she'd provide him a nice view as she milked his cum from him. They'd talked about him being an ass man, and he'd more than proven it to be true over the short time they'd been together. At every opportunity, his hands went straight for her backside.

As soon as she seated herself on his cock again, his breathing picked up, and he began to buck his hips. She could only imagine how badly he wanted his hands free. It would be interesting to see how he felt about the restriction . . . after.

She braced her hands on his knees, and rocked in time with him. It felt good, and another orgasm began to build low in her belly.

His thrusts became more aggressive and she knew he was getting close. She shifted her weight to one hand and began massaging her clit.

"Please tell me you're close. I don't know if I can hold on much longer," he panted.

Beth was close. Closer than even she realized.

Her second climax hit her without much warning. One moment she was climbing the peak, and then the next she was flying. She cried out as her orgasm claimed her.

A few moments later, as she was coming back down to earth, she realized Drew was chanting her name. Running her hands along his inner thighs, she nudged his balls out of the way, and began rubbing his perineum.

He went off like a rocket—her name left his lips in a gasp.

She gave him some time and then twisted around so that she could see his face. He looked up at her and blew out a shaky breath.

Beth chuckled and reached behind the chair to loosen the scarf. "I'm going to go clean up. I'll be back in a minute."

Drew nodded, and she lifted herself from his lap.

The loss she felt was frightening. She'd always enjoyed sex . . . even more so after she'd discovered kink. This was something altogether different.

Trying not to dwell too much on what she was feeling, she gathered up her discarded clothes, and strolled into the half bathroom right off the kitchen. She took a few minutes to go to the bathroom and clean herself up.

When she walked back into the kitchen with a damp cloth, Drew was standing beside the chair, still naked, with a huge grin on his face. She laid the cloth on the counter and took a quick look at his wrists. There were a few red marks, but nothing that would last more than an hour or two.

After her brief inspection, he glanced down at both his wrists.

"You may want to roll your shoulders a few times. It will help prevent stiffness," she said, reaching for the cloth and handing it to him.

"Thanks."

Once he'd cleaned himself, he did as she suggested and rolled his shoulders several times. She took the opportunity to go back to preparing dinner. It was already after six thirty. Now that she wasn't ready to jump his bones, her body was making its other needs known.

She heard him moving around behind her as she turned the oven back on to warm the steak and potatoes. The potatoes would be fine—she wasn't worried about that. The steak was a completely different story. It had only been cooking for four or five minutes before she'd turned everything off. Hopefully, it wouldn't be too chewy.

Turning around, she came face to face with Drew. Before she could say anything, he wrapped his arms around her, and buried his nose in the crook of her neck.

Beth didn't hesitate to return the hug. It felt good to have a man's arms around her again. Even if she was still scared of getting hurt.

"That was amazing," he murmured against her skin.

"So you enjoyed your first experience with bondage?"

He pulled back enough to see her face, and ran a hand along her cheek. "It was . . . well, it's hard to describe. Not being able to touch you when I wanted to was frustrating. But knowing you could do anything you wanted to me and I couldn't stop you"—he brushed his lips against hers—"I'm not sure I've been so turned on in my life."

She smiled. "So you'd like to do it again?"

Drew kissed her. He took his time, and she felt herself melting into his embrace. "You can tie me up anytime you want."

Beth laughed and circled her arms around his neck. "Good to know." They stood there for several minutes touching and kissing until the timer she'd set went off.

Drew laid out the plates and silverware while she got the food out of the oven and brought it to the table. By the time everything was in place and they were ready to sit down and eat, it was almost seven. He held out her chair for her. When he'd set the table he'd made sure to seat them side by side rather than across from each other as they'd been on Saturday night. Throughout the meal, he continued to touch her. Sometimes it was little more than a brush of her hand or arm. With every caress, she felt her libido revving up again.

She cleared her throat. "We should talk about tonight."

He took a bite of his food. "What about it?"

"Was there anything I did that you didn't like?"

His answer was immediate. "No."

"Nothing?" she asked.

"I'll admit you did a few things that surprised me, but considering I don't remember the last time I came like that . . . no, I can't say there was anything you did that I didn't like."

She was quiet for a few moments. "Speaking of coming, I know we didn't really talk about protection. I get a shot every three months, but we still should have talked about that. I'm sorry. I got caught up—"

"It's fine," he said, laying a hand on her arm to stop her rambling. "We'd already talked about us both being clean and I trust that you'd be careful about pregnancy."

"Still, it was irresponsible of me."

He finished the rest of his dinner before he responded. "I could have said something, too. It wasn't as if you had me gagged or anything. I am an adult, remember. I have a condom in my wallet. My dad taught me always to carry one. Just in case."

She grinned. "Very good advice."

"It was. And it came in handy more than once over the years." He turned to face her. "When I realized that you weren't going to use anything, the only thing I felt was happiness that there wouldn't be anything between us. I'm twenty-eight and I've never had sex without a condom. The main reason for that was that I've never been in a relationship before where I intended it to last for any length of time. It was something I'd considered with my last girlfriend, but then things fell apart and I'm glad I decided not to go there. Maybe, deep down, I knew how she'd react to my desires and that's why I never broached the subject."

Even though he didn't say it, she knew what he was implying. Drew was making a commitment to her. To them. He didn't have plans to go anywhere anytime soon. It left her with mixed feelings. She didn't want him to go anywhere, but at the same time it was a big step given they'd only been on one official date.

Deciding it was best not to dwell on it, she changed the subject. "Wednesday starts your four days off. Did you want to try a scene or would you rather wait?"

"If it means you having your wicked way with me again, then yes. I want to try a scene."

Beth ignored his flippant response. "I was thinking we should keep it simple. Since you enjoy bondage, we could work that in as well as some impact play. Are you up for that?"

He must have realized how nervous she was because he clasped her hand and squeezed. "Beth, I trust you. I wouldn't be here if I didn't. As long as it's not a hard limit, I want you to do what you want. I promise that I'll use my safewords if it gets too much. That's what they're there for, right?"

She nodded. "Right."

Drew was quiet for a moment. "You're not having second thoughts about us, are you?"

"No." She smiled and gave his hand a reassuring squeeze. "Ben and I had been dating a few months before we started playing."

"I get it. It took me four months to get the courage to bring up something as simple as bondage in my last relationship."

"And I tied you to a chair on the second date."

He laughed. "Yeah."

Drew hadn't let go of her hand. Their eyes met, and he moved closer, drawing her in.

"Did you want to spend the night?" she asked as his lips drew closer to her mouth.

"I have to work tomorrow," he whispered. "I have to be in at seven, and I don't have any clothes here."

She placed her palms flat on his chest and began moving them lower. "What I have in mind wouldn't involve clothing. And besides, my alarm goes off at five. Surely that would give you enough time to get home and change."

His response came in actions rather than words. He stood, taking her by the hands. "How fast do you think we can get this cleaned up?"

Cleaning up was the last thing she was worried about given the heated look he was giving her. "It can wait until tomorrow."

The words were barely out of her mouth when he began leading her toward the stairs.

Chapter 18

While the alarm had gone off at five, they hadn't made it out of bed until after five thirty. Saying goodbye to Beth had taken another twenty-five minutes—not that he would have changed anything. It was the first time in the last seven years that he'd wanted to call in sick. He knew his crew was counting on him, however, so he made himself do what he had to do.

He made it home at six twenty-four. Shawn was already gone. Drew took one of the fastest showers of his life, threw on his uniform, downed a bagel and some orange juice, and jogged back out to his car.

The station was buzzing with activity when he arrived at ten after seven. Several of the guys greeted him as he made his way to the locker room. It was in the locker room that he ran into Shawn.

"Good morning." His friend shot him a knowing smile.

"Morning." Drew tried to act normal as he stowed his keys and wallet into his assigned locker, but the writing was already on the wall. Shawn was aware that he hadn't come home last night. He also knew Drew had had a date with Beth. It didn't take a rocket scientist to put the two together.

His friend waited until the other guys exited the locker room before he started in with the questioning. "Last night went well, huh?"

"Yeah."

Well didn't begin to cover it. After they'd gone to her bedroom, they'd had another round of hot and heavy sex. That time he was able to touch her to his heart's content. Afterward, they'd talked more about what they wanted to explore when it came to the BDSM side of their relationship. For some reason, he'd always envisioned negotiations taking place across a table like you see on those cop shows—stark interrogation room, harsh lighting, that sort of thing. This was about as far removed from that as could be. They'd talked for hours tangled in each other's arms.

Shawn whistled, causing Drew to look up. "Must have been some night if you're daydreaming about it already."

Drew felt the heat surging in his cheeks. He turned his head so his friend couldn't see.

Patting him on the back, Shawn walked toward the door. "I'm happy for you. Enjoy it."

After shutting his locker and taking a deep breath, Drew went out to meet with his crew—and maybe get a little more breakfast. They had work to do, and if they weren't too busy with calls, he wanted to get some training in as well. The training was more for his benefit than theirs. Drew needed to keep busy. The faster the next twenty-four hours went, the better.

***

Normally when Beth was late to work, it threw her entire day into a tailspin. She hated being late.

Tommy, who had known her for almost seven years, knew this about her. That was why he immediately became suspicious when she floated around the kitchen humming to herself during morning prep, even though she'd come in nearly twenty minutes late. He stopped what he was doing and stared her down.

"What?" she asked when she noticed him looking.

"I'm trying to figure out why you're so cheery this morning."

She grinned as memories of the night before came back to her.

"Ah." Tommy smiled and nodded. "Things are going well with the firefighter."

Beth had no reason to deny it. "They are."

"Good. I'm glad." He reached around her to grab a large mixing bowl from the shelf. When he returned to his position beside her, he nudged her with his hip. "Make sure he treats you right."

Although she didn't comment, the look on her face must have been answer enough for Tommy.

When the doors opened at seven, people began flooding in. Almost every week they were busier than the one before. She'd been considering hiring another employee, if for no other reason than to give her and Tommy a break every now and then.

It was as they were closing the café down that afternoon that Beth broached the subject with Tommy. "What do you think about me hiring someone to help us around here?"

He looked up from where he was wiping the front counter. "You mean another employee?"

She nodded.

"I think it's a good idea. If things keep picking up, you and I aren't going to be able to handle it on our own."

"I know. And with summer just around the corner, it's probably going to get even busier."

On her way home that evening, Beth swung by the store and picked up a help wanted sign for her front window. Maybe she'd get lucky and have someone see the sign and apply. If not, she'd have to place an ad in the local paper. She had plenty of foot traffic, though. Odds were someone who frequented her café was either in need of a job or knew someone who was.

That night she opened her toy chest and laid everything on her bed. Beth sorted the items based on what Drew had put on his checklist. Everything not on his list she tucked away in the bottom drawer of her dresser. The rest she cleaned and then returned to the chest so they would be easily accessible when she needed them.

With that accomplished, Beth made herself some dinner, and then curled up on the couch to call Nicole.

"Well, how was it? Please tell me you fucked that boy senseless."

Beth laughed. "Well, hello to you, too."

"Pfft. Save the pleasantries for later. Come on. Spill. You two did have sex, didn't you?"

She rolled her eyes. "Yes."

"And?"

"And . . . we'll be doing it again tomorrow." Beth picked up the bowl of ice cream she'd brought into the living room with her.

"It's about time."

"It was only our second date."

"Maybe technically. But tell me you didn't want to see him naked the first time you laid eyes on him."

Beth chuckled as she licked the ice cream from her spoon. "I think half the women in Serpent's Kiss wanted to see him naked."

"You think that's changed? Something tells me the first time you two scene at the club you're going to have an audience."

"I figured. Somehow, I don't think Drew is all that into exhibitionism."

"He'll get over it."

Although Drew didn't strike her as a man who had issues with his body, it was one thing to be comfortable in your own skin. It was another to have a dozen people watching you get your rocks off. "We'll have to talk it over. Honestly, it's not even something I'm thinking about yet. We need to get through our first scene before we add anything else to the mix."

"Something holding you up? I would have thought you two would jump right into it."

"His schedule. He's in the middle of a rotation," Beth said, figuring Nicole would understand since she knew how their scheduling worked.

"Makes sense. It wouldn't be good if he experienced subdrop in the middle of a shift."

The thought had crossed Beth's mind. She worried about his safety enough as it was. It was one of the reasons she'd asked him to spend the night. "We're going to try on Wednesday evening. He's coming over for dinner, and then we'll see how things go from there."

"I'm happy for you."

"Yeah, well, don't count your chickens yet. He might realize after he gets a full taste of submission that he doesn't like it."

Nicole let out a noise that sounded somewhere between a whine and a snort. "You actually believe that?"

"It could happen."

"And pigs could fly."

She was right. It was a long shot. Especially given his reaction to being bound. "I know you're right. I just—"

"Stop worrying. Things are going great, right? Just go with it."

"I'll try."

Nicole sighed. "Don't try. Do."

Beth rolled her eyes. "Okay, Obi-Wan."

"I suppose I should give you credit for at least getting the movie reference."

"Why, thank you so much for your generosity." Beth chuckled and went to put her empty bowl in the dishwasher. She glanced over at the clock and was surprised to see how late it was. "I should probably let you go and get myself ready for bed."

"You do want to be fully rested for your big night tomorrow."

Beth groaned. "Don't put more pressure on me than I already feel."

Nicole laughed. "Good night."

"Good night."

It took Beth several minutes to walk through the lower level of her house and make sure everything was turned off and locked up for the night. As her day wound down and she got ready for bed, she couldn't help remembering the previous night.

She slid beneath the covers and reached for the pillow Drew had used. A faint hint of his smell still lingered on her sheets. And if she closed her eyes, she could almost imagine him there, lying beside her again.

Beth was surprised how right it had felt for him to be in her bed. The first time Ben had spent the night with her, it had been awkward. He'd been restless, which in turn had caused her to be restless as well.

Drew, however, had no issues falling asleep in her bed. He'd rolled over, curled up against her back, and fallen asleep within minutes. His comfort had in turn made it easy for her to relax and drift off to sleep herself. She hadn't been plagued by self-consciousness or uncertainty as she had with Ben. Then again, all her cards were on the table with Drew. He knew she was a Domme and liked to be the one calling the shots in their sexual relationship. She hadn't tried to downplay her desires. Instead, she'd embraced them and so had he.

Tucking the pillow he'd used the night before under her chin, Beth turned onto her side, and closed her eyes. Drew would most likely spend the night tomorrow after their scene. While she realized it wasn't good to be overly attached to him so soon, she already knew she was going to be helpless to stop it. Wise or not, her heart wanted Drew. She'd welcome him into her bed as often as she could have him.

***

"Any plans for your days off?" Baily asked to the room at large. The new shift had arrived so Drew and his crew were about to head home.

Romeo clasped the necklace he always wore around his neck when he wasn't on duty. Once it was secured, he tucked the gold cross beneath his shirt. "I'm sure I have a 'honey-do' list waiting for me when I get home."

All the guys laughed. Whenever Romeo had his four days off, his wife always had a new project . . . or two waiting for him.

Baily nodded toward Irwin. "What about you? Got any plans?"

"Nah. Not really. I might see if my brother-in-law needs some help at the restaurant."

"Trouble in paradise?" Romeo asked.

Irwin shrugged. "I don't know. Maybe."

They strolled out of the locker room and headed toward the parking lot.

"What about you, Cap? Got a hot date with your café lady?" Baily asked.

Drew tossed his duffel bag into the backseat of his car and shut the door. He waited until he was opening the driver door and about to slide into the seat before answering. "As a matter of fact, I do. See you all bright and early Sunday morning."

While they were still gaping wide-eyed back at him, he started the engine, and drove away. He knew there would be hell to pay during his next shift, but for the time being, he couldn't wipe the grin off his face.

He was about to slip into bed an hour later when Shawn ambled through the door. "Hey."

Drew leaned against the doorjamb outside his bedroom. "Hey."

Shawn walked into the kitchen and reached into the refrigerator. He pulled out a beer and took a large swig.

"You all right?" Drew asked.

"Yeah. I'm fine."

He didn't buy that for a second. "Something happen? Is it Jill?"

His friend took another long pull on his beer before turning around to face him. "I figured I'd go by the house this morning. See if maybe Jill and I could talk."

"And?"

"I pulled up to the curb in time to see a guy I didn't recognize stepping out to get the morning paper."

"Oh, man. I'm sorry."

"Yeah. So am I." Shawn stared down at the floor. "How could I have missed this? How could I not have known she was seeing another guy?" He looked at Drew as if hoping he had an answer for him.

"I don't know."

Shawn nodded as if he had expected Drew's response.

Silence filled the air for several minutes before Drew cleared his throat. "I'm supposed to go over to Beth's tonight. I can call her and cancel if—"

"Don't you dare. Go. Spend time with your woman."

"Are you sure?" Drew asked.

Shawn drained the rest of his beer and threw the bottle in the recycle bin. "Sure I am. No reason why we both have to spend the evening wallowing in self-pity."

"That isn't reassuring."

"I'm fine. Really. Or, at least, I will be." Shawn sighed and headed toward the bathroom. "Go get some rest. I'm sure you'll need it for tonight."

Drew stood there and watched his heartbroken friend disappear into the bathroom. He was torn. Tonight would be his and Beth's first real foray into BDSM—and his first ever. It was something he'd dreamt about since laying eyes on her. But Shawn was one of his closest friends.

With a sigh, Drew stepped into his bedroom and closed the door. Aside from the call that woke them all up at five o'clock this morning, he'd gotten a decent amount of sleep during his shift. His anxiety over his upcoming evening with Beth had made it a bit difficult to fall asleep, but after that, he'd been out until the alarm sounded. He figured it was a good idea to try and get at least a couple more hours of sleep, given the evening they had planned.

Shawn was right. If things went well with Beth later, he would need all the rest he could get.

He rolled out of bed a little before two in the afternoon. Although he was still concerned about Shawn, at least he felt rested.

Drew stretched, feeling the pull of his muscles. As he laced his fingers behind him to stretch his arms and back, a knowing grin pulled at the corner of his mouth. He wondered if Beth would tie him up again.

The thought of Beth caused him to look over at his phone. It was showing he had a voice mail message.

Holding the phone up to his ear, he checked his messages.

It was Beth.

"Good morning. I hope you're ready for tonight." There was a level of seduction in her voice, and he felt his pulse quicken in anticipation. *"Be at my house at five. Bring an overnight bag. I don't plan on letting you out of my bed before morning."*

He swallowed and instinctively reached down to cup his groin.

She lowered her voice, but instead of lessening the effect, it did the opposite. *"No touching yourself until I say."*

There was a long pause in her message, and he could feel the blood pumping through his veins. He removed his hand from his growing erection even though it was the last thing he wanted to do. This was what he'd signed up for. This was what he'd wanted.

After several moments of silence, she finished her message in a lighter tone. *"I'm looking forward to tonight. See you at five."*

Beth's message ended, and the automated voice came on asking if he wanted to save or delete the message. He hovered over the delete button, but then changed his mind and saved it instead. There was no real reason to. She hadn't left a list of instructions he was unlikely to remember. If he was being honest with himself, it had more to do with having access to her voice whenever he wanted it. And the best part about the message was that she showed both sides of herself—the Domme and his girlfriend.

He chuckled as he laid the phone back on his dresser and went to get some coffee and a light lunch. Drew was still grinning when he strolled into the kitchen. He stopped short, however, when he saw Shawn sitting dejectedly on the couch.

Shawn opened his eyes and sent Drew a weak smile. "Sleep well?"

"Yeah." Drew walked over to the coffeemaker and flipped it on. "You?"

His friend shrugged.

"You need your sleep. You have a shift tomorrow."

"I'll be fine," Shawn said, waving him off. "We weren't that busy last night, so I got a good four hours at least. That's enough."

While Drew wasn't convinced, he wasn't Shawn's babysitter either, so he let it go. Instead, Drew moved about the kitchen gathering what he'd need to make scrambled eggs and bacon. He somehow figured he'd need the extra protein later.

Shawn folded the blanket he was using and placed it, along with his pillow, at one end of the couch before joining Drew in the kitchen. Falling into the same routine they were used to at work, Shawn gathered what was needed to set the table. Drew carried the food over when it was ready, and they dug in.

"What time are you supposed to meet your girl?" Shawn asked.

Drew was still unsure if he should leave his buddy alone, but if Shawn didn't want him there, he wasn't going to push. "Five."

Shawn shoveled in a few more bites. "Want to head over to the gym before you go? I feel the need to pummel something."

"Sure." Drew lowered his head so Shawn couldn't see the smirk on his face. There was no doubt in Drew's mind whose face his friend would be picturing as he planted his fist in the gym's punching bag.

Chapter 19

Beth had everything ready for Drew's arrival, even the food. She wondered if he'd gotten her voice mail, and how he'd reacted. They'd discussed orgasm control as they lay in her bed on Monday night. Although their arrangement was bedroom only, he'd liked the idea of her deciding when he would be allowed to come. If it came to their sex life, he wanted her to be the one in charge. She'd experimented some regarding that aspect of domination with Ben. He didn't much care for it, so it was put in the strongly dislike column.

A knock sounded on her front door and she shook off the memory of her ex. Tonight was about the future—hers with Drew. The rest was water under the bridge.

Butterflies began swirling in her stomach when she drew closer to the entry. She paused for a moment with her hand on the knob to steady herself before opening the door.

Drew stood on the porch smiling at her—a duffel bag slung over one shoulder and a single daisy in the other. "Hi."

"Hi," she said, moving out of the way so he could come in.

He brushed past her into the foyer. She shut the door and turned around to find him close.

"I brought you a daisy."

Beth could feel his breath on her face and it had her head

whirling. Drew was all man. There was no doubt about that. "It's beautiful. Thank you."

"It means loyalty. Commitment. I thought it was fitting given our plans for tonight."

"You seem to know a lot about flowers. Are you trying to impress me?" Beth didn't know if she wanted him to say yes or no. She didn't need frills, but she had to admit it was nice.

Drew's lips curled up into a sheepish grin. "Maybe a little. My mom loves flowers. She has a wide variety growing around the farm. I used to help her weed the beds when I was younger and she would tell me all their different meanings."

"Does she still have them? The flowers, I mean?" Beth asked.

"Yes. When she's not in the house cooking, you can usually find her in her flower beds."

Hearing this new insight into his family relaxed Beth even more. Drew was sharing things with her about himself and his childhood. Taking the offered flower, she raised it to her noise, and inhaled its fragrance. "Does your mom have any daisies?"

"She does. Daisies are one of her favorites."

Beth went up on her tiptoes and brushed her lips against his before giving him a soft kiss. "I can't wait to see them, then."

He blinked. "Does that mean you're going to the barbecue with me?"

She nodded.

Before Beth knew what was happening, he had dropped his duffel bag to the floor and picked her up. She laughed as he twirled her around.

When he finally set her feet back down on solid ground, he was grinning from ear to ear.

"I'll make sure you're not back too late. I know you have to work the next day," he vowed.

Beth gave him another hard kiss, and then began walking toward the kitchen. "Don't you have to work as well?"

"Well, yes, but I'm not worried about that."

She glanced back at him. "I just don't want you getting hurt because you're dead on your feet."

He chuckled and took the plate she'd picked up off the counter out of her hand. "Not to worry. I once pulled a twenty-four-hour shift with zero sleep."

When she gave him a questioning look, he continued. "Right when things were beginning to settle down for the evening, we got a call for a possible injury accident. Took us about an hour to get that all cleaned up and head back to the station. We were about ready to head up to our bunks when the next call came in. It pretty much kept up like that all night. I think we rolled into the station at around six in the morning. By that time, there was no point in going to bed. We all chipped in to get things prepped for the next shift, and then started on breakfast."

"Wow," she said, taking the food out of the oven and placing it in the center of the table.

"Luckily, that doesn't happen often. It was a rare night."

Beth grabbed the pitcher of ice water and sat down.

Drew followed. "It smells great."

"Thank you." She motioned that Drew should help himself while she filled both their glasses. "Are you ready for tonight?"

"I think so. I'm more anxious than anything."

"Anything in particular you're anxious about?" she asked.

He shrugged. "The usual, I suppose. I don't want to mess up."

"If you *mess up*, then we'll deal with it. You're learning. It's to be expected. Who knows? I could be the one to mess things up."

Drew snorted before taking a bite of his food. "I doubt that."

"It could happen."

He watched her for several moments. At first, he looked as if he was going to comment, but then he must have changed his mind.

Beth decided to jump on her chance to change the subject. The last thing she wanted to do was get into the self-doubt Ben had left in his wake. "Do you have any questions before we get started?"

"When will we start?"

It was a good question. "When we've finished eating, I'll show you to the guest room. You can put your stuff in there and do anything else you need to do. Once you're done and ready to get the evening underway, I want you to meet me in my bedroom."

Drew blew out a heavy breath. "Okay. Anything else?"

She reached over and ran her hand up the inside of his thigh. "When you come to me, I want you naked. You will enter the room with your gaze on the floor. After that, you just need to do what you're told."

The muscles in his throat contracted as he swallowed.

"Drew?"

He looked up to meet her gaze.

"We're going to have fun tonight."

"We haven't started yet, right?" he asked.

"Right."

Without warning, Drew placed his hands on either side of her face and brought his mouth down on hers. She moaned as her body reacted to the feel of his lips, and heat spread throughout her body.

Just as suddenly as he began the kiss, he ended it. They were both panting, and Beth was tempted to say forget about the scene and take him in the kitchen chair as she'd done before. The only thing that stopped her was a curiosity to see just how powerful their connection could be in a full scene. "I'm going to make you pay for that, you know."

He chuckled. "I can't wait."

Beth glanced over at his empty plate. "Finished?"

"With food."

She felt her body temperature rise a few degrees more. "Follow me. I'll show you to the guest room."

Not waiting for a response, Beth stood, and made her way to the stairs. She knew he was behind her even though she didn't look back.

At the top of the stairs, she made a left. When she'd bought the house, there had been four bedrooms. The master, of course, had its own bathroom, but the other three shared a communal bathroom at the end of the hall. That was why one of the first things she did after buying the house was to renovate the upstairs. She lost a bedroom in the deal, but gained two additional bathrooms. It was a fair trade, and given the nature of their relationship, Beth had felt Ben needed to have his own space—including his own bathroom.

Beth strolled into the guest room. She stopped a few feet inside the door and waited for Drew to enter.

He threw his bag on the bed and took in his surroundings. "Nice. But I think I like your room better."

His cocky smile was back. She was going to have some fun with that attitude of his. "If you're good, I promise you'll be seeing the inside of my bedroom a lot."

"Promises, promises."

She shook her head and turned toward the door. "You have ten minutes. Don't be late or I'll have to punish you."

Drew's smile grew bigger. "I'd better hurry, then."

Beth rolled her eyes and walked to her bedroom where the night's activities would take place. She removed her shirt and skirt, leaving her in a purple corset with a matching set of panties. Going to her closet, she retrieved the black boots she'd worn to the club a few weeks ago. They were her favorites. Satisfied with her attire, Beth took a final look around to make sure everything was in place.

She was closing the lid on the small cooler filled with ice that she'd brought upstairs earlier when she heard Drew enter the room. Beth looked in his direction and saw he had followed her instructions. The erection he was already sporting told her how excited he was. Heat flared in the area between her legs. She couldn't wait to get her hands on him.

***

Drew wanted to look up and feast his eyes on Beth. He'd only gotten a peek at what she'd been wearing as he'd entered the room and then dutifully lowered his gaze. Even that small glimpse was enough to have his cock standing at attention.

"Come over here," she ordered.

He obeyed, keeping his head down.

Beth cupped the side of his face with one hand and looked into his eyes. She must have seen whatever it was she was looking for because she nodded, released her hold on him, and took a step back. "On your knees."

Lowering himself to the floor, he waited to see what she'd do next.

Nothing happened for several moments. All he could hear was his own breathing. Her scent was all around him, though, and as she moved closer to him, he could smell it even more. She was aroused and his mouth moistened in anticipation of being able to taste her again.

Placing a hand on the top of his head, she began to move. Beth combed her fingers through his hair and then down his back as she walked to stand behind him. Her touch felt so good. It was exactly what he needed after everything that had been going on with Shawn and work and . . .

He must have tensed or something, because the next thing he knew she was whispering in his ear. "Shh. Whatever's going through your mind, let it go. Tonight you are mine. You're here to serve me. Nothing outside this room matters. It will still be there later to worry about."

"Yes, ma'am."

"Good."

It sounded as if she was pleased with his answer. He wondered if she was smiling.

She went to her dresser and retrieved something before returning to stand behind him. "Raise your chin."

He did as he was told. Seconds later he felt something wrap around his neck. A collar.

"This is a training collar. I thought it might help you get into your submissive mindset. To remind you that your body belongs to me tonight."

She waited.

Drew realized she wanted him to answer. He decided to try out her new title. They'd talked about it. She was going to be his mistress, after all. Still, this would be the first time he'd actually called her that. "Thank you, Mistress."

A moment later, he felt something slide against the back of the collar followed by a click. He realized it was a lock.

Taking several slow deep breaths, he relaxed and let what she'd said sink in. As he did so, he felt the stress of his day begin to fade. This was their time and he was going to savor it.

Beth stood before him and he was able to get his first good look at her. She was stunning. The corset she was wearing hugged her curves and lifted her tits. He wanted to bury his face in her cleavage. Then there were her panties. The tiny scrap of material that covered her front made him salivate for a view of the back. Drew could only imagine how her ass would look.

"Had a good enough look?" she asked.

He met her gaze and saw that she was amused by his perusal. "I could stare at you all day."

"I'll keep that in mind." Looping a finger in the O-ring he hadn't noticed on the front of his collar, she pulled up. "Stand."

There was a part of him that fought against her ordering him around, but there was a larger part that wanted this.

She led him over to the wall. It was then he noticed the large X with cuffs attached to it. "Stand facing the wall with your arms raised and your legs spread."

He got into position and held still as she secured his arms and legs. There was still plenty of room between him and the wall. Beth took advantage of the space by grasping his cock. "Did you touch yourself today?"

"No, Mistress."

She ran her hand from base to tip three times, making his cock swell even more.

He had to bite back a groan when she took her hand away.

"Tonight we are going to do some experimenting," she said.

Drew had no idea what that meant, but he'd told her that he was up for trying anything he'd marked on his list and he'd meant it. There was a lot he'd seen at Serpent's Kiss that he was curious about. This was his opportunity. He had what he wanted—a relationship with a woman willing to dominate him.

A sting to his behind brought him back to the present. It didn't hurt exactly, but it had returned his focus.

The first sting was followed by several others in various places on his ass and thighs. Only when Beth trailed the flat leather tip along his spine before landing another blow to his butt cheek did he realize she was using a crop on him. It felt different than he'd expected. As she continued to hit different places on his body, he felt his skin warming.

Beth pressed herself against him from behind and ran her nails over his ass. It wasn't the first time she'd touched him like this, but it felt different after she'd used the crop. Everything was very sensitive. He could feel every movement—every scratch.

"Did you like that?"

"Yes."

Beth allowed her hands to drift lower. She raked her nails along the inside of his thighs, and he sucked in a breath.

He felt her lips against his back. "Don't worry. We're just getting started."

To his great disappointment, she removed her warmth from him and went to grab something else. This time he knew what she was using with the first strike—a flogger. The falls licked at his flesh, making his already sensitive skin tingle. She mixed soft, almost tickling caresses with hard blows that thudded soundly against his back, ass, and legs. He felt the stress of the day leaving his body completely as he became lost in the sensation.

Drew was so caught up in what he was experiencing that the feel of something much firmer hitting his backside caused him to snap his head up.

Beth laughed. "That got your attention."

She hit him with it again and he felt the bite of the leather. It hurt, but it wasn't altogether unpleasant. His body was singing at that point and whatever she was using only added another note to the symphony.

After ten strokes with whatever she was using, something soft caressed his overly sensitive backside. He closed his eyes and let the feeling take over.

Right when he was getting used to the gentle touch of whatever she was using, the flogger was back. Then, moments later, the softness returned. It was a game trying to anticipate which he would feel as she moved back and forth between the two. He found that he yearned for the feel of both.

Hands splayed across his chest and trailed down over his abs to wrap around his cock. Lips pressed against his back as the hands pumped his erection. It felt wonderful, but it wasn't enough. He needed more. In that vein, Drew flexed his hips into the hands.

Almost instantly, the hands were gone.

"Uh-uh. None of that." Beth's voice grounded him.

"Sorry, Mistress."

"Hmm. It's just as well. I have other plans for you this evening." She bent down and released his ankle cuffs, and then stood to free his wrists as well. "How are you feeling?"

"I think every nerve ending I have has been awakened."

"Does that mean you're ready to continue?" she asked.

"Yes. Please."

Beth smiled. "Remove my panties."

He eagerly dropped to his knees and looped his fingers in the sides of the purple underwear he'd been admiring earlier. Inching them down her legs, he worked them over her boots, and deposited them on the floor.

She lifted her leg, resting it on the blanket chest at the end of the bed. The new position opened her up to him and her pussy was staring him right in the face.

No words were spoken as she laced her fingers through his hair and guided his mouth to where she wanted it to be. He'd been dreaming since their date about the next time he'd get to taste her. Drew would be happy to do this for her every day if she'd let him.

Beth rested her hand at the base of his neck and began grinding her pussy against his tongue. Her wetness coated his face as he licked and sucked her, drawing out her pleasure.

He knew she was close when she shifted her hips, placing his tongue directly over her clit. Drew flicked his tongue rapidly, edging her closer. Her grip on his neck tightened and her hips jerked moments before her breath hitched and he felt a flood of moisture on his chin. There was such a sense of satisfaction in serving her this way. And when he gazed up into her eyes, he knew he was exactly where he wanted to be—on his knees serving her.

Chapter 20

Beth tried to catch her breath as her orgasm faded. Drew's head was still in between her legs, licking and nuzzling her pussy. She had half a mind to let him get her off a second time. But as much as she wanted to come by his mouth again, she wanted him inside her more. Reaching behind her, Beth retrieved the leash she'd placed on the end of the bed, and attached it to his collar.

Drew froze and looked up.

She smiled down at him and gave the leash a firm tug. "Get on the bed and lie down with your hands behind your head."

He hesitated briefly and then did as she'd instructed. This was going to be a test to see how well he obeyed without being bound.

Beth climbed onto the bed and straddled his waist. The end of the leash was wrapped around her hand. She kept enough of a pull on it to remind him it was there.

She brushed her mouth against his before running her tongue along the seam. He groaned and parted his lips. Beth took the offering and dipped her tongue inside his mouth. The taste of her arousal filled her senses. Drew was hers and tonight she was going to claim him.

Their kiss continued. She was in no hurry. They had hours to play, and she planned to enjoy every minute of the time they had.

After a while, though, he became impatient and started to reach for her. Beth broke the kiss and jerked on the leash. "Did I tell you to move your hands?"

Drew blinked up at her as if waking from a daze.

She knew the moment her words sank in. He placed his hands back into position and lowered his gaze. Beth remained where she was, waiting to see what he'd do. It was almost as if she could see the words forming in his mind as he centered himself once again.

Releasing her hold on the leash, she got up off the bed, and went to fetch the items she'd placed on the dresser. Drew's eyes followed her movement. Normally for sensation play, she'd blindfold her partner, but since this was his first time, she decided that she wanted him to see what she was doing to him. Tonight's exercise was about obedience.

Beth set the cooler, flogger, nipple clamps, and cock ring next to the bed. She made sure to lay each item down slowly so he could see them. Other than furrowing his forehead some when she opened the cooler, he didn't react.

The end of the leash laid flat against his stomach. She left it there and chose to grasp the leather about a foot from where it connected to the collar around his neck. Pulling his head up away from his hands an inch or so, Beth gave him a hard kiss before releasing him. She left the leash in place, however, just in case.

"Keep your hands where they are. If you move them again, I will have to punish you."

"Yes, Mistress."

Satisfied, she placed her palm on the inside of his thigh. "Spread your legs."

She stood by the bed while he moved his legs. Once he was where she wanted him, she took his cock and worked the silicone ring down the length of his erection. The constriction caused him to harden further and she dipped her head down to lick the tip of his penis.

He sucked in a breath as she ran the tip of her tongue through his slit. "Like that?"

"Yes, Mistress."

Beth covered the head of his cock with her mouth and circled it with her tongue before releasing him. "If you're a good boy, maybe I'll use my mouth on you more later."

Drew nodded, and she could tell he was trying very hard not to move. He wanted more and he was used to calling the shots in the bedroom. She had to remember that this was all new to him.

With the cock ring in place, Beth reached for the nipple clamps. Although he'd seen them used many times, this would be his first experience with them. She placed them both on his chest so he knew exactly what was coming next, and then began rolling his nipples between her fingers. He didn't react much when she gave a gentle tug, so she decided to increase the pressure. Beth wanted to see how much pain it took for him to respond.

She got her answer on her third try. Based on his responses she knew she'd have to tighten the tweezer clamps almost completely. If he liked them, she might try something stronger next time.

Pinching his nipple, she placed one of the clamps on either side, and then slid the band of metal up the two arms until she saw him wince. Then she did the same on the other side. With both clamps in place, she noticed he had a look of total concentration on his face.

Beth placed a hand on his cheek, drawing his attention. "You doing all right?"

"Yes, Mistress."

"Remember you have your safewords if it becomes too much."

He nodded.

She reached for the small flogger. Unlike the larger one she'd used on him earlier against the wall, this had more of a stinging sensation. With the ring driving all the blood to his cock, it would be fun to see how he reacted to the flogger on that part of his anatomy.

Glancing up at his face to make sure he was still okay, Beth began working the flogger in random movements over his chest and legs before she took aim at his erection. With the snap of her wrist, she struck his cock right above the silicone ring.

He flinched, but then settled himself.

Beth took that as the green light to continue and began a series of blows on his cock, balls, and inner thighs. By the time she was done, the entire area had a nice pink hue to it. She tossed the flogger onto the floor and took hold of his balls in her left hand while lowering her mouth to lick and sooth the flesh she'd just abused. He moaned as her tongue made contact and widened his legs even more to give her better access. Beth saw his chest begin to rise and fall faster as she continued. His cock was hard and pulsing.

Before she moved on, Beth placed a wet kiss on the tip of his cock. It bobbed a little, which made her smile. He seemed to be enjoying what she was doing to him.

She stood, stuck her hand in the cooler, and removed an ice cube. Drew had his eyes closed. He seemed lost in everything he was feeling, so he startled a little when she brought the cold object to his lips.

He opened his eyes and looked up at her.

Beth rubbed the ice along his lips, and he slid his tongue out to lick the cool liquid. She held it there, letting him drink. When the ice melted enough, Beth allowed him to suck it into his mouth while she went to retrieve another cube. This one she ran along his forehead and then down his neck and collarbone. As she moved lower, she followed the path of the ice with her mouth—licking and biting—warming the skin she'd cooled moments before.

As she worked her way to his chest, she circled his nipples with the ice, and then one by one removed the clamps. Drew arched his back. He breathed through his nose as she eased the hurt with her tongue.

She palmed what remained of the ice cube and wrapped her hand around his cock while she continued to kiss her way across his abdomen. He gasped and tensed. Beth knew keeping still had to be killing him, but he was doing it.

Slowly she ran her hand up and down his length letting the warmth melt the ice. She looked up to watch his reaction and was pleased to see that he had his eyes closed and his head tilted back.

When she arrived at her destination, Beth straddled his hips. She waited until the ice was completely melted, and then guided his cock to the entrance of her pussy.

His eyes flew open as he felt her heat envelope his cock.

***

Drew had entered into the night with no illusions. He was giving up control to Beth and he knew what that meant. Because of that, Drew didn't know if he'd get to be inside her.

She lowered herself down onto his erection with excruciating slowness. Watching his cock disappear inch by inch into her pussy and not being able to touch her was torture—but he couldn't look away.

If that weren't enough of a visual, Beth released the hooks that held her corset together. He held his breath as she shed the garment and threw it down beside the bed.

"Give me your hands."

He moved quicker than he thought possible. She laced their fingers together, using their connection as leverage. When she moaned, he transferred his attention from where she was grinding away on his cock to her face. Beth's eyes were closed and her head was thrown back. She was totally assured in what she was doing. It was amazing to watch.

Her breathing became more labored. She picked up her paced, slamming down onto him as she chased toward her goal.

The fevered pace had all the blood rushing to his groin. He felt his balls tightening, readying for climax. But he didn't know if that was going to happen. Again, that decision belonged entirely to Beth.

He didn't want to look away from her. Them. But he had to. If he didn't concentrate, he was going to come whether he wanted to or not. It was right there—he could feel it beckoning.

Suddenly, Beth tore her right hand from his, and reached between them. A second later, he felt the vibrations. "Shit!"

Her only response was to place both his hands on her tits. Drew was so thrilled to be touching her that he began playing with them in earnest. From their previous encounters, he knew what she liked. It amazed him how focused he was on her considering his body was so close to betraying him.

"More," she said. "Pinch my nipples."

Drew did as she asked, doing his best to give her what she needed.

The intensity continued to build as she rode him. He was sweating but it was the least of his worries. Like it or not, he was going to come if she kept up the way she was. Between the feeling of her wet pussy pulling and squeezing him and the vibrations at the base of his cock, he was seconds away from losing it.

Beth must have realized how close he was because she leaned down, bringing their foreheads to rest against each other. Her mouth hovered only centimeters from his—so close their breath mingled together. Their eyes met and held as Beth matched her breathing with his. Everything outside the two of them fell away.

Her breath hitched in her throat and he felt it deep in his core.

Beth caressed the side of his face as she continued to move against him. He could feel every intake of breath, every exhale.

"Come," she whispered.

Instinct took over. Drew released his hold on her breasts and dug his fingers into her ass, thrusting his hips. They both gasped, and he felt Beth's muscles clamp down. Her face contorted with pleasure as her orgasm claimed her.

Seeing her come undone—feeling it—was the last straw. With one last jerk of his hips, a burst of energy shot up his cock as he experienced one of the most explosive climaxes of his life.

He was vaguely aware of Beth reaching between them to turn off the vibration and remove the cock ring before she collapsed on top of him. Neither of them moved for a while after that. Her chest rose and fell with his. Feeling her against him in the aftermath of what they'd shared was almost spiritual. Was it the kink, or was it because it was with Beth? Could he even separate the two? Lucky for him, he didn't have to.

"What are you thinking so hard about?" she asked.

"Is it always like that?" She turned her head to look at him. "So intense, I mean?"

Beth smiled and ran her hand down the length of his chest. "When it's with the right person."

Drew brushed the pad of his thumb along her cheekbone. Her face was flushed and her hair was wild. She'd never looked more beautiful. He pulled her in for a lingering kiss.

She hummed and rested her head against his shoulder. "How are you feeling?"

It wasn't funny, but he laughed anyway. "I'm not sure I could be any better than I am right now."

He felt her smile.

"What about you?" he asked.

Beth gazed up at him with both eyebrows raised. "Did you think I was faking that orgasm I just had?"

Drew grinned. He'd never been this happy in a relationship before. "No. If you were faking it, then you deserve an Academy Award. I meant did I do all right? I've seen scenes at the club, but . . . well, it's different when you're the one that's in it."

"Yes, it is." She propped herself up on her elbow, but kept the length of her body pressed against his. "Did you enjoy what I did to you?"

With their scene over, he took full advantage of his freedom to put his hands wherever he wanted. "I did. It was . . . liberating."

"For me as well."

He cocked his head to the side. "How?"

She ran her fingers through his hair. It made him want to curl up against her and never move. "It's a release for me. I can let go of all my stress and be in the moment."

Drew guessed that made sense. Being a top wasn't something he'd ever desired to be, and after the experience he had, he didn't think it would be in the future—especially if that future involved Beth. "I guess that's good since I very much like being dominated by you."

"Yes, that's a very good thing." Beth kissed him. "We should go get cleaned up."

"I don't want to move. I like lying here with you like this."

"So do I, but you'll thank me in the morning."

Before he could protest, she was getting out of the bed. He felt a sharp pang of loss as she distanced herself from him. It didn't last long, however, since almost as soon as her feet hit the floor, she was reaching for him.

It was in the process of climbing out of the bed that Drew felt the first real signs of soreness. His ass felt as if he'd sat on a heating pad for too long.

"Sit on the edge of the bed and I'll remove your collar."

He looked to find Beth standing only a foot in front of him. "Sure."

Drew lowered himself down on the edge of the mattress. Her hand brushed against his chest as she reached to unclip the leash that he'd completely forgotten was there.

He waited while she walked to the other side of the bed. She returned with the key, and leaned over to unlock him. The position placed her bare breast within an inch of his face. Drew couldn't resist, so he latched on and sucked it into his mouth. Beth moaned, but then leaned out of his reach as she turned the key and the restriction of the collar pulled away.

Beth tilted his chin up so that he could look at her. She was still naked and it was impossible for him not to take notice even though he'd been inside her less than twenty minutes ago. It had never been like this for him before. Granted, he wasn't sure if he could go again so soon—he wasn't Superman after all—but that want was still there.

She gazed into his eyes for several minutes before running her fingers over his mouth. He parted his lips, hoping to convey that he was ready and willing for anything she wanted. Beth closed her eyes and sighed.

Taking her hand, he kissed the tips of her fingers, and then her palm. A feeling of warmth flooded his chest at the tender moment. Beth was different in more ways than he could count, and so were his feelings for her.

When she opened her eyes, he saw the same tenderness reflected there that he was experiencing. He'd known he was falling for her—that he was already halfway gone. Now he was positive that the falling was over. Although he doubted she was there yet, he knew there was no longer a question as far as he was concerned. He loved her, and he would do everything in his power to show her just how much.

Chapter 21

The next morning Drew woke up to the sound of Beth's alarm. She groaned, rolled over, and hit the snooze button. When she plopped back down on the mattress, he slid up behind her and gathered her into his arms.

"Mmm. Good morning."

Drew kissed her shoulder and nuzzled his nose against her neck. "Definitely a good morning."

"Not too sore?" she asked, turning to face him.

It was true that his backside was still somewhat tender, but overall he felt great. "No worse than I would be after a good workout at the gym."

Beth grinned. "I wish I didn't have to go to work. It would be nice to stay in bed with you like this."

He couldn't agree with her more. Spending the day in bed with her sounded pretty close to perfect to him. "Too bad Tommy can't cover for you today."

"Oh, I meant to tell you. I decided to hire someone else. It's just becoming too much for me and Tommy by ourselves."

"I think that's a good idea. You both need to take some time off once in a while. Plus, I'd like to take you camping with me one of these days and we'd definitely need more than two days." He pressed his lips against hers in a teasing kiss before moving his attention down to her neck.

She hummed. "Camping, huh?"

"Yes," he said between kisses. "Don't worry. I'll be sure to keep you nice and warm at night."

"Is that so?" Beth tangled her fingers in his hair as he worked his way lower.

"Promise," he murmured before tracing around her nipple with his tongue.

Unfortunately, their fun was interrupted by her alarm going off again.

Beth took a deep breath and stared down at him. "I have to start getting ready or I'll be late."

Drew knew he should let her go. He knew how much the café meant to her. Instead, he pushed himself up until he was at eye level with her.

"Be late." The words were whispered, but that didn't decrease the emotion behind them.

Everything around them seemed to stop as he waited to see how she'd react.

She placed her palm flat on his chest. Drew was sure she was going to push him away from her, but then she hit the off button on her alarm with her free hand and reached for his cock. "Make it fast. And you don't come until after I do."

His morning wood grew with her words. "Yes, Mistress."

The tip of his erection pressed against her pussy as she guided him right where she wanted him. Beth raised her hips and he took it as an invitation to thrust forward.

She was tighter than she had been the night before. Considering how little experience he had with morning sex, Drew didn't know if that was normal or if it meant that he needed to do more to get her aroused—maybe both. To be sure, he molded his hand to one of her breasts and sucked her nipple into his mouth. Little by little, he kept going until the base of his cock was pressed against her.

"More," she urged as she bent her knees to give him better access.

He gave her more. Releasing her breast, he propped himself up on his knees and grabbed hold of her hips for leverage. The new position drove him deeper, and the look on her face every time he plunged forward had him determined to please her no matter what.

When he noticed her breathing begin to change, he debated whether or not he should provide additional stimulation to her clit. Beth took the decision away from him when she grabbed hold of his hand and positioned his thumb where she wanted it. "Touch me."

Drew had learned a few things in his wilder days. He had no issue putting that to use in making sure Beth felt good. Widening his legs a bit, he timed his thrusts with a firm pressure to her clit. It only took three times before Beth arched her back and came undone before his eyes.

He picked up his pace as she rode out her orgasm. Knowing he didn't have to hold back, Drew concentrated on the feeling of her, hot and wet around his cock. Beth was an amazing woman and she was all his.

A handful of thrusts later, Drew felt his climax within reach. He was right there.

Beth took both of his nipples between her fingers and twisted hard. That was all it took. Drew felt his orgasm all the way down to his toes.

Blood pounded in his ears as he fell forward, bracing himself on his forearms. "Now, that's a great way to wake up."

Lacing her fingers behind his neck, Beth grinned up at him. "Enjoy yourself, did you?"

"With you, always."

"You're good for my ego." Beth shifted beneath him. "But I really do have to get ready."

Reluctantly, Drew flopped over onto the mattress beside her.

He thought she'd scramble out of the bed as soon as he'd removed his weight from her. That's why he was surprised when she turned toward him and ran her index finger from his collarbone to his navel. "Want to join me in the shower?"

"I thought you didn't want to be late."

She shrugged.

It looked as if the morning fun wasn't entirely over.

*****

Beth was almost an hour late, but for the first time, she didn't care. When she walked through the door, Tommy nearly attacked her. He'd been worried she might have gotten into an accident or something. After she explained that she'd just overslept, he calmed down and they got to work.

The day turned out to be one of the busiest they'd ever had. Beth had no idea how she and Tommy managed, but they did. Somehow. By the end of the day, though, she was dead on her feet. It only reinforced the need to hire some help. If days like this became the norm, she and Tommy would burn out quickly.

As it was, Beth didn't make it back home until after five.

"I was starting to worry."

She snapped her head up to find Drew sitting on her front porch. "Sorry. I probably should have called. Things were just crazy today."

They'd made plans for him to come over again for dinner and maybe even another play session. Beth knew with the way she was feeling there was no way she would be up for playing.

"I can go if you'd rather be alone," he said.

Although Beth was tired, she couldn't bring herself to send him away. "Stay."

He nodded and followed her inside.

Beth kicked off her shoes and started toward the kitchen.

Drew reached for her arm to stop her. "Let me cook for you. You can sit down on the couch, have a glass of wine . . ." He stepped closer and pressed his forehead against hers. "Let me take care of you."

"You don't have to do—"

"I want to." He cupped the side of her face and gave her a soft kiss.

"Okay."

He smiled. "What kind of wine would you like—red or white?"

"White, please."

"Coming right up." Before disappearing into the kitchen, he gave her another kiss.

It had been a long time since someone had offered to pamper her. Sure, there were times when she'd ordered Ben to do something for her, but it wasn't the same.

Thinking of Ben reminded her that she hadn't seen him since the day he'd shown up at her café. While she'd like to think that he got the message and would leave her alone, she highly doubted it. Ben could be very persistent when he wanted something. If he truly wanted to talk to her, he'd keep trying. Next time she would be more prepared. At least, she hoped she would be.

"Here you go." Drew handed her a wineglass that was filled almost to the brim.

She raised one eyebrow at him.

He kissed her nose and chuckled before walking off. "Dinner will be ready in about half an hour."

Taking a sip of her wine, Beth sat down, and stretched her legs out onto the couch. She tilted her head back and tried to relax.

Before she knew it, he was back. Drew placed two plates on the coffee table and then gently picked up her legs so that he could sit down. The care that he took to arrange her legs so that they were draped across his lap warmed her heart. How was she not supposed to fall for him when he did stuff like this?

She accepted the plate that he offered and took a bite. It was baked ziti and it was delicious. "Is there anything you can't cook?"

"I'm glad you like it." His smile melted her as it always did.

They ate in silence for several minutes before she decided that she needed to let him know that their plans for the night would have to change. "I know you were hoping we could play tonight, but I don't think I have the energy."

"I figured as much. You looked as if you were about to collapse earlier." He took a drink of the wine he'd poured for himself—a glass that wasn't even half as full as the one he'd poured her.

"Does that bother you?" She knew it would have bothered Ben. If they'd made plans for a session, then he expected them to play.

"Not really. There will be plenty of other opportunities. I am kind of hoping you'll still let me stay the night, though." That cocky grin was back.

"I don't know. I might have to think about that one," she said as she peered at him over her wineglass. "It's been a long day. I need my rest."

Drew leaned forward and placed his empty plate onto the coffee table along with his drink. Then he turned his attention to her feet. "Guess I'll have to convince you."

Beth moaned when his fingers pressed along the arch of her right foot. "What are you doing?"

"Giving you a foot massage."

He kept rubbing, and it felt heavenly. She soon forgot her food.

"Are you done?" he asked when he realized she'd stopped eating.

"I don't think I can eat while you're doing that to me."

Drew halted. "Do you want me to stop?"

"No. It feels too good."

He laughed and went back to what he was doing.

Beth set her plate and wine on the floor next to the couch, then leaned back to enjoy her massage. He worked every muscle in her feet and ankles with a circular motion that seemed to draw out every bit of stress. When he'd begun, her feet had been throbbing and tight. After his attentions, she was starting to feel normal again. "You're good at this."

"Thank you." He continued by dragging his hands along her calves and then down again.

It had been a long day and with the coaxing of his hands, she was becoming drowsy—so drowsy, she'd missed what he'd said entirely. "What was that?"

Drew dug his fingers into her skin as he traced a path from the back of her knee down to her heel. "I asked if you'd like for me to draw you a bath."

"You're spoiling me. Keep this up and I'm never going to let you leave."

She said the words in a teasing way, but his response and the look on his face were utterly serious. "That's the plan."

Beth swallowed. Was she misreading him? They'd only recently begun dating.

While she was still mulling over his words, Drew lifted her legs and stood. "Let me warm up the rest of your food so you can finish eating, and then I'll go start that bath for you."

He kissed the top of her head before bending down to retrieve her plate. As she watched him stroll out of the room, she tried not to read too much into what he'd said. Beth knew he was looking for something more than just someone to play with. He'd wanted a relationship. Considering she'd only ever played with one other person besides her ex, she was on board with that. While Beth understood that there were a lot of people out there who didn't mind playing casually with other members of the club, it wasn't something that had appealed to her. Then again, neither did casual sex.

She lifted her wineglass to her lips as Drew returned with her warmed dinner. "I'll come get you when your bath's ready."

Beth grinned up at him. "Thanks."

There was a slight hesitation before he jogged up the stairs to see to her bath. She really didn't know what she was going to do. The man had not only wormed his way past her defenses and into her heart, he was taking up residence there. Even though she'd meant it as a joke, she was wondering if it were more prophetic. When she'd found out about Ben's other life, she'd been crushed, but more than anything Beth had been embarrassed—betrayed. How could she not have known?

What she hadn't felt was all that heartbroken over the actual loss. Ben could be attentive, but looking back at the relationship she realized more often than not it was always a means to an end with him. It was a way to manipulate her.

If Ben had been the one waiting for her tonight, she doubted it would have crossed his mind to give her a foot massage. On the off chance that it would have, there would have been strings attached. Since they'd made arrangements to play, he would have most likely ended the massage by asking if she felt up to having some fun then.

Glancing toward the stairs, Beth had to admit that Drew and Ben were very different men. She knew now that Ben had been selfish. He was selfish in everything he did, including how he'd treated both her and his wife. Drew was the complete opposite of selfish. Whenever they were together, he made her feel as if she were the only woman in the world. Even his job reflected his unselfishness—he ran into burning buildings trying to save lives and people's homes.

Whether she liked it or not—and even though it scared the crap out of her—she didn't know what she'd do if Drew left her life. If he ever betrayed her like Ben had, Beth didn't know if she'd be able to recover.

"Hey. Is everything okay?" Beth looked to find Drew kneeling beside her.

She grinned. "Yeah. I'm good."

He still looked somewhat concerned, but he didn't press her. "Your bath's ready."

Beth nodded.

Drew helped her up and took her mostly empty plate from her. "Did you want to finish eating first?"

"No. I'm good. We were so busy, I didn't get to eat lunch until almost two." While that was true, her lunch had consisted of half a croissant and some roast beef eaten in between orders.

They made their way upstairs to her bedroom. Drew went to check the temperature of the water again while she got undressed. Beth was tempted to forego the bath and crawl into bed, but she didn't want to seem ungrateful. She plucked her robe from the closet so she'd have it for later, and trudged into the bathroom.

When she walked in, she could hardly believe her eyes. Drew was on his knees next to the large tub. He had lowered the lights and had several candles lit. It was very romantic and peaceful.

He got to his feet and crossed the short distance to where she stood in the doorway. Without a word, he took her robe from her and hung it up on the door. Then he reached for her hand.

She placed her palm in his and let him lead her over to the bubble-filled water. Drew helped her as she got in and lowered herself down into the tub. It felt wonderful. The scent of lavender surrounded her and she wondered if it was from the bubble bath, the candles, or both.

"Would you like another glass of wine?" he asked.

Beth shook her head. "If I drink much more, I'll fall asleep. I'm not far from it now."

Drew smiled.

"You didn't have to do this, you know." She felt as if she needed to put it out there.

"I wanted to. Besides, you can pay me back one of these days." He brushed a strand of hair from her face and winked at her.

She chuckled.

"Relax and enjoy your bath. I'm going to run downstairs and clean up, then I'll be back to check on you."

Beth sighed and slid further down into the water as she let the warmth pull the tired ache from her body. She loved baths and she wondered how Drew had known, or if it had been a guess.

The sound of something moving off to her right made her open her eyes. It was Drew. He was blowing out the candles. When had he returned?

"You're back."

She stretched. That's when it dawned on her that she must have dozed off. "Guess I was more tired than I thought."

He reached for a towel and then for her. She took the offering, and stepped out of the bathtub. Beth had to admit that she could get used to this type of attention.

After unfolding the towel, he slowly dried her off. It wasn't meant to be erotic, but it was. Although her mind wasn't remotely in the mood for sex, Drew was able to get her body to respond. Like it or not, her body wanted him.

She closed the distance between them and pressed her naked body against his fully clothed one. Drew stared down at her, unmoving, but he was unable to hide his body's reaction. She could feel his erection straining against his jeans. Beth wrapped her arms around his neck and pulled his lips down to hers.

"Beth . . ."

His whispered plea only made her body yearn for him more. "Shh. Take me to bed, Drew. Make love to me."

There was a moment's pause, and then he scooped her up and carried her into the bedroom.

Chapter 22

Beth held tight to Drew's hand as they approached the entrance to Serpent's Kiss.

"Nervous?" he asked.

There was no reason to deny it. "A little."

He gave her hand a gentle squeeze.

"What about you?"

"Not at all. In fact, I'm thrilled that I get to walk in there with you." Drew turned her to face him and placed his free hand on her hip. "I've only been dreaming about this since I first saw you across the room."

She rolled her eyes.

"What?" he asked, pulling her closer. "You'd rather have another hot stud by your side?"

"A *hot stud*, huh?"

He shrugged. "Gotta call 'em like I see 'em."

Beth ran the tips of her fingers along his jaw. "I might have to borrow one of Katrina's paddles and spank some of that cockiness out of you."

"My ass is all yours any time you want it." He punctuated his words by palming her behind.

Before she ended up doing something completely inappropriate in public, Beth took a step back and resumed her progression toward the door. "I'll keep that in mind."

They strolled into the foyer and she realized that her nerves had almost completely disappeared. Beth knew she had Drew to thank for that. He'd been able to tease her out of her funk. At every turn, he'd been there for her. Even earlier that day, he'd proved his devotion by showing up at the café in time for the lunch rush. She was able to stay in the back and make the sandwiches while Drew ran them out to the customers and helped Tommy with the soups and pastries.

Later, when they were cleaning up, she asked him why. His answer was simple. *I figured you could use the help.*

He realized she'd stopped again. "Beth, if you're not okay with this—"

She shook her head. "No. I'm fine. Let's get this over with." Not waiting for him to comment, Beth swiped her membership card, opened the door to the lobby, and marched through it.

Bridget was behind the coat check. She smiled, started to say something, and then closed her mouth just as quickly when she noticed Beth was not alone.

Taking a deep breath, Beth decided to acknowledge the elephant in the room. "Drew, you know Bridget, right?"

"Yes. We've met."

"Y-yes," Bridget stuttered.

If Beth was being honest with herself, the young woman's response was almost comical. She kept blinking like there was something in her eyes. Maybe the night wouldn't be that bad if everyone's response was similar.

After checking the light jacket Beth had brought along for later—it was still a little too chilly for her liking late at night—she and Drew made their way into the club. They'd intentionally timed their arrival so that most of the regular patrons would already be there. It would be easier to blend in that way. At least, that's what she'd been hoping.

It took less than a minute for her bubble to burst. One by one everyone in the room turned their attention in Beth and Drew's direction. "I guess this means the cat is officially out of the bag."

He chuckled. "I'd say so."

She straightened her shoulders. "Here goes nothing."

***

Drew stayed by Beth's side as she worked her way toward the bar. He glanced around to find that most of the people following their progress had smiles on their faces. When he caught sight of John, his friend gave him a thumbs-up. Seeing confirmation of John's approval, and what appeared to be that of most of the club's members, had Drew grinning from ear to ear. He picked up his pace and placed a reassuring hand on Beth's lower back. She glanced over at him and then continued on.

Chad was behind the bar. Drew had only met him once before. Chad was okay, though. He didn't joke around with the members as much as Brandon did, but he wasn't part of the lifestyle either.

"Lady Beth, what can I get you this evening?" Chad greeted as she stepped up to the bar.

Drew stayed behind her, letting her lead.

"I'll have a Coke and Sprite, please." She turned to Drew. "What would you like?"

"Just a water. Thanks." While he typically had a beer on the nights he came to the club, this evening was all about Beth. He wanted her to be comfortable with their new status—their new, very *public* status.

Chad nodded. "Coming right up."

Beth turned around so that her back was against the bar. "You're sure you don't want anything besides water?"

He traced a line up her arm with his fingers. "Nope. I'm good. Besides, I need to stay hydrated, right?"

"I don't know if I'm up for playing in public yet," she confessed.

"It's up to you. I'm fine with whatever you decide."

"You're being awfully submissive tonight."

"Isn't that what I'm supposed to be—your submissive?" He edged closer, crowding her a little, acting anything but submissive. It was a bold move considering where they were.

She grinned and an evil glint appeared in her eyes a moment before he felt her hand grab hold of his junk. It wasn't painful, but the threat was there. "Make sure you remember that."

Drew smiled. "Yes, Mistress."

Chad returned with their drinks, and she released him. This was a gray area when it came to their arrangement. Outside the club, he was only her sub when it came to sexual things. Inside the club, however, the lines were blurred. He liked serving her last night—rubbing her feet, drawing her bath. Drew had also expressed an interested in kneeling at her feet and having his head in her lap. Before spending time at Serpent's Kiss, he wouldn't have thought something like that would appeal to him, but when he'd seen the level of devotion between John and Allison, it made him curious.

Because of that curiosity, they'd decided to play it by ear for the time being. He was always supposed to show her respect while inside the club walls. Outside that, they were still negotiating. He promised that he would communicate if he wanted more, and she had done the same.

When he began researching BDSM, he'd thought that everything took off at full speed from the start. Drew supposed that had a lot to do with porn. Of course, now he knew just how inaccurate those videos were. Even still, he'd somehow imagined things with Beth being hammered out swiftly with no question marks. While their relationship had hit the ground running and he had no complaints, it was evolving and changing the more things they tried.

The night before came to mind. Beth had surprised him when she asked him to make love to her. Their sex up until then had always had some element of dominance and submission. He'd worried that their lovemaking wouldn't be as fulfilling for him if he was the one in control—it never had been in the past. What he found, though, was that knowing that he was doing what she wanted, how she wanted it, gave him pleasure. It was submission in a way he'd never imagined it.

He followed her over to where Nicole, Jeff, Daniel, Brandon, and two subs he recognized but whose names eluded him at the moment, were congregated. They all had knowing smiles on their faces as Beth and Drew sat down on one of the love seats.

"I was wondering if you were going to make it," Nicole said.

Beth met her friend's gaze and responded with a level of confidence he knew she didn't feel. "Busy day."

"Well, we're glad you're both here," Daniel said, tipping his glass in their direction.

Trying to divert some of the attention, Drew addressed Brandon.

"Enjoying your night off?"

"I am. As much as I like being behind the bar, sometimes it's nice to sit back and let someone else take care of everything for a night."

Nicole leaned toward Brandon and whispered, "That's what you have a sub for."

All the Dominants in the group chuckled. Beth's tension seemed to be ebbing. She was no longer holding herself rigid. Drew rested his left arm along the back of the love seat, and placed his right hand on hers where it lay on her leg. Beth flipped her palm over and grasped his fingers. She leaned back against his chest, and he inhaled the scent of her shampoo.

He was so caught up in Beth that he almost missed the switch in conversation. "There haven't been any more sightings of *you know who*, have there?"

Beth shook her head. "No."

"Do you think he'll show up again?" Daniel asked.

Nicole jumped in before Beth could answer. "You can pretty much count on it. Ben isn't one to give up."

Drew's head was spinning with this new information. Beth's ex had contacted her—or tried to, at least? Why hadn't she said anything?

Eventually, the conversation shifted again but he lost track of what they were saying. He was too busy mulling over the realization that his girlfriend's lying ex had made contact with her. Drew wasn't sure if he was hurt or angry that she hadn't told him—maybe a little of both. Sure, they had only started dating in the last week, but they were supposed to be friends. Her other friends knew about it. Why hadn't he?

It was hard to tell how much time had passed when he felt Beth elbow him. Drew found her staring at him with a strange expression. "What? Something wrong?"

"I was going to ask you the same question."

He frowned. "You didn't tell me about your ex coming to see you."

Beth shifted to face him. She cradled his hand in her lap, caressing the ridge where his palm and wrist met. It was distracting, but he couldn't bring himself to ask her to stop.

"I didn't mean to keep it from you. It just never came up."

"When did he come to see you?" he asked.

"It was almost a month ago. And then I was told that he showed up here at the club two months before that. Katrina kicked him out."

He blew out a breath. "Good."

"I don't know what he wants. But if he's already tried twice, he's likely to do it again."

"I don't like it." That was the understatement of the year. Drew hated it. Although he hadn't known Beth back then, he knew that if he had, he would have wanted to rearrange Ben's face for him. Even thinking the man's name made him see red. He wasn't sure he could be held responsible for his actions if he ever saw him face-to-face.

"I don't like it either. Trust me, I'd much rather go the rest of my life without ever having to see or talk to him again. Unfortunately, I doubt that's going to happen. The first time he caught me off guard. That won't happen next time."

Drew saw movement out of the corner of his eye and realized that their little group had broken away to give them privacy. He glanced down at their hands. "How did this night turn out to be about your ex?"

"Because my best friend doesn't have a filter."

Despite the seriousness of their conversation, he chuckled. Everything he knew about Nicole supported Beth's assertion. "She's worried about you. So am I."

She kissed him. It was one of those barely there kisses, but it still had his heart kicking up a notch.

"You don't have to worry about me," she whispered against his lips. "I can handle Ben."

Their eyes locked, and he was reminded of the night before when she'd been looking up at him as he'd filled her. "I don't think it's possible not to worry about you, Beth."

Neither of them moved until the music changed from the slow sultry number to something with a driving beat that reminded Drew of sex. The air around them began to change, and thoughts of Ben took a backseat to his desire to get his hands on the woman right in front of him.

Beth stood, and Drew followed.

Without a word, she led him by the hand up to the second floor. Had she changed her mind about playing?

They stopped briefly for Beth to talk to Cooper, one of the

Dungeon Monitors. It didn't consist of much more than her checking to see if a room was available. He nodded, instructed them to give him ten minutes, and then disappeared through a side door that Drew hadn't noticed before. Less than two minutes later, he reappeared with a large bag and entered one of the playrooms. When he returned to the hall several minutes later, he gave Beth another nod, and she led Drew into the room Cooper had vacated.

He felt he needed to ask. "Did you change your mind?"

She released his hand and strolled over to peruse the implements hanging on the wall. "I thought we needed a distraction. Tonight was supposed to be about you and me."

Drew couldn't disagree. Excited to find out what Beth had in mind, he waited to see what she'd do next.

"I want you to pick out five of these that you'd like to try," she said, pointing to the array of impact devices along the wall. Beth turned to look him in the eye. "No scene. And you can keep your clothes on. But I want you to have an idea what they feel like."

"All right." Walking over to the wall, he scanned his choices. Some of the toys were scarier than others. There was a lot of leather, of course.

He knew he liked the flogger that Beth had used on him on Wednesday night. After their shower, he'd had the chance to get a better look at it. There were a few on the wall that appeared to be of similar construction, but there were plenty that had obvious differences. One had knots tied into the ends of the falls.

"That one has more bite to it than the one I used on you the other night," she said.

Drew nodded and moved on. The thing he'd loved most about being flogged was that it was a solid thud against his back. While he hadn't minded the leather strap she'd used on his ass, it had felt a lot different from the flogger. There was a sting to it that Drew wasn't sure he was crazy about. "I think I'll skip it, then."

Beth hummed.

"What?"

She smiled. "Nothing."

Something told Drew that whatever she was thinking, he wasn't going to like it.

Shaking it off for now, he removed a wooden paddle and a flogger that looked heavier than the one Beth had used. He placed them on the table and then returned to his task. Drew knew from watching what went on at the club that no two implements were exactly the same, even if they looked similar. Every subtle variation made a difference.

For that reason, he tried not to stray too far from what he'd tried on Wednesday. His next two selections were made of leather. One was flat with three flaps that overlapped. The other was also flat, but it had a slit down the middle. Drew couldn't remember what it was called, but he'd seen it used before. Reactions from the subs had varied, which made him curious.

With only one item left to be chosen, he altered his original goal—to stick to the somewhat familiar—and ventured over to the selection of canes. John liked canes. A lot. Then again, John also enjoyed having his testicles tortured. That thought alone almost made Drew reconsider, but again, he was drawn by curiosity. This would be the perfect time to gauge if it was something he wanted to move up on his list or place in the 'hell no' column. Before he could talk himself out of it, Drew took one of the canes from the rack and placed it on the table beside the other toys.

Beth stood at the other end of the table and ran her hand over a couple of the toys. "Interesting choices."

"Good interesting or bad interesting?" he asked.

She ran her hand over three of the toys. "Just interesting. I figured you'd pick a flogger. You seemed to enjoy that quite a lot the other night. Almost as much as you liked me tying you up."

Again, Drew couldn't disagree. Although, there really wasn't anything they'd done so far that he'd disliked. He wasn't sure the leather strap would ever make it onto his favorite list, but one never knew. After conversing with people at the club, he'd learned that preferences evolved over time. What he didn't care for now could be his favorite thing in a few years.

While he'd pondered, Beth had strolled to the center of the room. She glanced up, and Drew followed her gaze to a set of cuffs hanging from chains.

"I'm not going to cuff you tonight, but I do want you to hold onto the ends. It will ensure that you keep your hands out of the way and help you hold position."

That made sense. He walked over to stand next to her and reached up to take hold of the dangling cuffs.

Beth ran a hand down the length of his back before cupping his backside. "I'll give you four swats with each, two on each cheek, so you can tell me what you think of them."

He nodded.

She removed her hand, and Drew wanted to call her back. There was something about her touch that affected him in an elemental way. It made his pulse quicken, yet was comforting at the same time. He'd heard about the intense connection that could develop between subs and their Dominants. Even though their relationship was new, he felt it. Drew could only imagine what it would be like once they'd been together for a while.

"Are you ready?" she asked.

Drew couldn't see her. She was standing behind him on his left side. That didn't mean he couldn't feel her. "I'm ready. Do your worst."

Beth laughed and a second later, a loud smack reverberated in the room as she landed the wooden paddle against his right ass cheek. She rubbed her hand over the area she'd hit and leaned in to whisper in his ear. "It's never wise to tempt your mistress."

Three more quick hits of the paddle and he was beginning to feel the burn. By the time she picked up the fourth implement, he was starting to think she was right. Issuing your mistress a challenge moments before she was going to take a paddle to your ass probably wasn't the smartest decision he'd ever made in his life.

Chapter 23

Beth had to hand it to Drew. He'd taken everything she'd given him. Which, granted, would have been worse had she ordered him to remove his clothing. As it was, he'd be feeling the aftereffects of their evening for the rest of the night, at least.

When she'd devised this little experiment, Beth had only planned to give him a few light swats with each of the items he'd selected. After his comment, however, she felt the need to remind him of just what position he held in this relationship. She'd landed four substantial hits to his ass with the paddle and then followed it up with four more of both the flapper and the tawse.

"How are you doing?" she asked when she picked up the cane.

"Fine."

She rubbed the cane across the back of his thigh before flicking her wrist. The rattan snapped against both of his butt cheeks, and she saw him tighten his grip on the cuffs. "Just fine?"

Before he could respond, she made contact again with his backside.

"Yes. Just. Fine."

Sliding her hand over his ass, she ran a finger along the waist of his jeans. "What do you think of the cane? Is it what you expected?"

He shook his head. "No. Not exactly."

"How is it different?" She moved around in front of him, but kept her hand inside his waistband, teasing.

"I wasn't expecting it to be so . . . intense."

"Hmm. Yes. There are subs that take great pride in being able to take their master or mistress' cane."

Drew didn't comment. Not with a snarky comeback, or even a grunt.

"Look at me."

He lowered his eyes and met her gaze.

"Do you want me to stop?" she asked. "You only have two more to go."

It took him a moment to answer. "No."

Beth removed her hand from his jeans and placed it along the side of his face. As he stared back at her, she saw some of that attitude returning to his features. It made her smile. "When we get home, I'm going to tie you to my bed and ride you until you beg me to let you come."

"Whatever you want, Mistress."

She let her hand drop from his face, repositioned herself behind him again, and flicked her wrist twice more in quick succession. He jumped at the unexpected contact of the cane striking his ass. "Remember you said that later tonight."

Ready to end this experiment, she tossed the cane down on the table, and picked up the flogger. It was heavier than what she normally liked to throw, but there was nothing wrong with mixing it up now and then. Taking two steps back, she held the flogger in both hands, and took aim.

His reaction to the flogger was worlds apart from how he'd responded to the cane. As she made contact for the third time with his butt, he dropped his head. Clothes or not, this was feeling more and more like a scene with every passing minute. Beth needed to end this. She needed to end it and get them both back to her place. While Serpent's Kiss was a sex positive club, she wasn't ready to do that with him here quite yet. No, she wanted him completely to herself for a while longer.

Beth lowered her arm and returned the flogger, along with the other implements, to the wall. Drew must have realized what she was doing because she felt him come up behind her.

"Everything all right?" he asked.

She turned and circled her arms around his neck before pulling his mouth down to hers. "No. It's not."

After a passionate kiss, he stared into her eyes as if trying to assess what she'd meant. "You wanna go home?"

She kissed him again. This time their lips barely touched, but the meaning behind it was clear. "Yes. I'm ready to go home."

Drew took her hand and led her out of the room. Although some Femdoms would have had a problem with him doing the leading, Beth couldn't care less. She loved how enthusiastic he was. And she hated to admit it—she certainly wouldn't to him—but she loved his cockiness a little, too.

They passed Katrina at the bottom of the stairs. "Leaving so soon?"

"Yes," Drew said without giving Beth the chance to answer.

Katrina laughed and waved as Drew practically dragged Beth through the club toward the entrance. "Have fun."

When they reached the lobby, Beth dug in her heels and jerked on Drew's arm to get his attention.

"What?" he asked.

She took a single step forward, pressing the length of her body against him. "You're going to have to learn some patience."

When he realized she wasn't upset, he dipped his head and shot her a sheepish grin. "I'll work on it."

Beth responded with a smile that was anything but sweet and then went to retrieve her jacket from the coat check.

Bridget was still in the alcove. The young woman already had Beth's coat in her hand by the time she approached.

"Thank you," Beth said.

"You're welcome. I hope you both enjoy the rest of your evening."

It was no longer light out, and as they made their way to his car, Beth found herself searching the shadows. The conversation about Ben was making her paranoid. It was as if she was waiting for him to jump out from behind one of the bushes or something.

They arrived at Drew's car and he opened her door for her. She gave him a peck on the lips and then slid into the passenger seat.

He waited until he was behind the wheel to say anything. "Did I do something wrong?"

She looked over at him and gave him a curious look. "No. Not that I know of. Why?"

"Just checking." He turned on the engine and maneuvered the car out of the lot. "You seem like you have something on your mind. And to be honest, I'm not sure my ass can take another beating tonight."

Beth let out a loud, very unladylike laugh.

Drew took her hand and brought it up to his lips. "I know I was . . . a little overzealous in there, but I couldn't help it."

"I noticed." She placed her hand on his inner thigh and let it drift closer to his crotch. "But in this case, you're safe. I love Serpent's Kiss, but the things I want to do with you right now . . . well, I'd rather not have an audience."

He swallowed and nodded.

They were both quiet the rest of the drive home. She didn't remove her hand from where it lay less than an inch away from the bulge in his pants. It was only common sense that made her keep her hands to herself, and even that was pushing her limits. Beth pressed her legs together seeking the friction she needed but couldn't have quite yet.

He pulled up to her house a few minutes past ten. Before she could blink twice, he was out of the car and standing there with his hand outstretched, ready to help her out of the vehicle. Beth took his hand, and they made their way up the front steps and into her house.

Once the door closed behind her, she turned to face him. "Go upstairs. Remove all your clothes, and lie face up on my bed. I'll be there in a few minutes."

Drew leaned down and gave her a kiss. It was soft and in some ways it destroyed her defenses more than all the hot and heavy make-out sessions. "Yes, Mistress."

She remained rooted to her spot until she heard him moving around on the second floor. Taking what she hoped was a calming breath, Beth began making her nightly rounds to double-check that everything was secure before she turned in. She took her time even though the urge to race upstairs was eating at her. Drew was addicting, and if she wasn't careful, Beth was going to find herself in a worse position than she'd been in before—a position where she couldn't imagine her life without him.

For good measure, and to prove something to herself, she did a second walk-through of the lower level of her home. Then she strolled into the bathroom, took care of business, and washed up.

Beth was stalling. She knew that.

Lifting her head, she took a long look at herself in the mirror that hung above the sink in her small half-bath. The past four months had been quite a transformation. She'd gone from someone who was relatively happy and content with her life, to someone who'd barely been able to get up in the mornings. There were no longer bags under her eyes from the restless nights, and a healthy color had returned to her cheeks. She felt normal again. Better, if she was being honest with herself.

She knew what, or who, in this case, was responsible for the drastic change. Beth had no doubt she would have rebounded on her own, but it would have taken time. Drew had coaxed her back into the land of the living. He'd made her think that there was still a possibility to have that future she'd dreamed of having. Granted, it starred a different leading man, but she was starting to think she'd cast the part all wrong the first time around. Ben wasn't half the man Drew was, and he never would be.

Shooting one last look into the mirror, Beth turned off the light, and walked toward the stairs. She had a submissive waiting. *Her* submissive. And she was going to make sure he knew exactly who he belonged to before the night was over.

***

Drew lay on the bed looking up at the ceiling. He was trying to slow his heart, which seemed to be trying to beat its way out of his chest. Following Beth's instructions, he'd gone upstairs, removed his clothes, and situated himself on her bed. The sheets scraped against his still tender backside. It added to his awareness. Not only of his own body, but of Beth as well—of what was still to come.

The sound of her feet on the stairs sent all efforts to slow his heart out the window. He turned his head toward the door, and his breath caught in his throat when he saw her enter the room.

She strolled over to where he lay and ran her hand down his chest to his thigh. His cock twitched as her hand came close, but she ignored it completely. Then she turned her back on him and opened the chest where she kept her toys. She'd showed it to him the evening before. It was a small collection compared to what could be found at the club, but more than enough for their personal use.

When Beth faced him again, she held a length of rope in her right hand. She had a knowing smirk on her face as she approached him. "Give me your hands."

Drew didn't hesitate. He presented both hands to her eagerly.

She maneuvered them so that his palms were facing each other and then began wrapping the rope around both wrists, binding them together. As the ropes secured his wrists, Drew felt himself becoming grounded. With the rope in place, Beth lifted his arms over his head and used a second section of rope to connect his bound wrists to the bed.

Beth leaned over him, her hands on his face. She traced the outline of his lips with her thumbs. He wanted to kiss her, but he didn't think that was going to happen. Not the way she was looking at him. Her eyes were almost predatory.

"The ropes aren't too tight, are they?" she asked in that seductive voice of hers. He could listen to it all day. Then, of course, he'd most likely be sporting a permanent erection.

"No, Mistress."

She came closer to whisper in his ear. It sent chills rippling through his body. "Is this how I had you tied up in your dream?"

"Yes."

"Yes, what?" She punctuated her question by pinching one of his nipples.

He jerked.

Beth asked her question again. "Yes, what?"

Drew swallowed. "Yes, Mistress. This is how it was in my fantasy."

"Good," she said as she scraped her teeth along his neck before sinking them into his skin. He didn't know whether or not he wanted to push her away or invite her to devour him some more.

It was interesting how being tied up like this made him pay attention to things more. Beth was still fully clothed, and he could feel the scratch of the fabric against his chest. It shouldn't be erotic, but it was. Her tits grazed his abdomen with a featherlight touch.

He was so focused on the feel of her body that he'd almost missed her words. "Tonight we're going to work on patience. Patience and obedience."

When she pulled away from him and climbed off the bed, he had to bite the inside of his cheek to keep from begging her to come back. Drew wanted her to touch him. He didn't care how. As long as her hands were on him in some fashion, he would be happy. It was almost comical to realize that even if it meant her grabbing him by his balls and inflicting some sort of torture on him that he'd take it as long as it meant she had her hands on him.

That line of thought was quickly shelved when Beth shimmied her jeans over her ass and down her legs. His heart had skipped a beat when he'd first seen her in them earlier. They molded to every one of her curves and the first thing he'd done upon seeing her in them was palm her backside and squeeze. Seeing that perfect ass of hers bending over in all its glory made him want to do it all over again.

"See something you like?" she asked.

"Yes." He cleared his throat. "Mistress."

Beth chuckled and continued to remove the bottom half of her clothing. She turned to face him as she removed the sheer top she'd worn over her corset. Before Beth, he'd never understood the fascination with corsets. They covered too much skin and took more time to remove than a bra. Seeing her standing there, though, with her breasts molded beneath the blue satin and lace . . . it made his mouth water.

With all her clothing removed except her corset, Beth sashayed back to the bed and lay down beside him. Drew could feel the heat from her soft skin and all he wanted to do was get closer.

"Shh," she said, caressing his face. "Patience, remember. If you're a good boy, I might even let you come tonight."

They'd talked about orgasm control. And while they both wanted it as part of their relationship, it hadn't been something she'd truly put to the test. Whenever they'd had sex, he'd been allowed to come. He knew that might not always be the case, but he wasn't sure if he was ready for that to be taken away yet. They'd only been together a week. He could still count how many times he'd had his cock inside her and felt that rush of fulfillment.

"Tell me what you're thinking." She searched his eyes as if she could somehow figure out what was going through his mind.

"Just hoping I please you enough to be allowed to come, Mistress." He didn't want to make her think he'd changed his mind because he hadn't.

She scraped the nail of her index finger over his left nipple, causing it to pebble. Again, the sensation was a mixture of both pleasure and pain. "I'm going to push you tonight. Some things you may like more than others."

"I understand, Mistress." A thrill ran through him every time he called her his mistress. She not only owned his body but his heart as well—even if she didn't realize it yet.

As if to test him, Beth scraped a line from his nipple down to his erection. She circled the base of his cock with her fingernail and then cupped his balls in her hand.

Drew held his breath. He had no idea what she'd do next.

The feeling of all five of her nails scratching along his testicles made him stiffen. Instinct made him want to close his legs for protection, but he made himself keep them open for her.

She hummed against his neck. "These belong to me as much as your cock does."

Her nails dug in a little more and he gasped. "Yes, Mistress. Yes."

Right when he thought he might have to safeword for the first time, she moved her attention to the underside of his cock. While it was still a sensitive area, he'd rather have her torturing his cock than his balls. At least, he thought he would. It was just a guess since—

Holy hell!

He arched his back as a single nail started at the base of his cock and trailed upward. Drew thought for sure that he would lose his erection, but that wasn't happening. He was just as hard—or maybe harder—than what he'd been before she'd begun toying with him. His body's reactions made no sense, but the evidence was there standing tall for all the world to see.

Beth shifted, and the next thing he knew she was straddling his face. Her ass was staring back at him. Her pussy inches from his mouth. He took the invitation and tugged at his restraints in order for his tongue to make contact with the moist flesh between her legs. She faltered briefly in her movements when he licked the first bits of moisture from her labia. He did it again, wanting to see what she'd do and needing to please her.

"More," she said as she lowered herself onto his face.

If she wanted more, that was what he would give her. Drew dove in with vigor, fucking her with his tongue and circling her clit.

As he ate her pussy, Beth continued to torture him with her

nails. It was as if two things were vying for his undivided attention. He was surrounded by Beth's scent, tied to her bed. His cock was quite literally in her hands to do with what she wished. For the first time in his life, he thought he might be able to come without a hand, mouth, or pussy adding friction. Was that even possible?

Drew knew she was getting close when she started grinding against his face. He doubled his efforts and concentrated on her clit. If he had his hands free, he would have added his fingers to the mix as well.

Out of the blue, Beth leaned forward. He felt her place one hand on his balls, pressing them to the side of his leg. Then, almost all in the next instant, one of her fingers was rubbing the skin on the underside of his testicles and another was skimming his asshole.

Her breath hitched and she jerked her hips violently against his tongue.

"Come," she yelled.

The last thing he felt was her lips wrapping around the head of his cock. After that, he saw a flash of light and then the world fell away.

Chapter 24

Beth pulled the sheet over both their bodies and curled up alongside Drew. She had untied his wrists and then dropped the rope on the floor next to the bed before curling up next to him. As she placed her cheek against his chest, she felt a tremor pass through him. "Are you all right?"

He didn't answer right away. She tilted her head up to see his face. Drew had his eyes closed and he was still breathing deeper than was normal. Unsure what else to do until he started talking to her, she held him tighter.

Drew lifted his arm and rested his hand on her hip. With his other hand, he caressed the side of her face. "I don't think I've ever come so hard in my life. Scratch that. I *know* I haven't."

She smiled and kissed the smooth column of his neck. "Are you thirsty?"

He swallowed and then nodded. "Yeah. I could use some water."

Beth reached behind her to grab the bottle of water she'd left on her nightstand. When she turned back around, she saw he'd propped himself up on his elbow. She handed him the bottle and then reached for candy that had been sitting next to the water. "You should suck on this as well. It will help."

There was a slight hesitation before he took the offered candy.

"Thanks."

She stayed close, but gave him some space as he downed almost half the bottle of water before unwrapping the hard candy and popping it into his mouth. "Are you feeling lightheaded at all? Cold? Jittery?"

Drew took another sip of water before reaching for her. "I feel a little off balance. And I feel a strong desire to wrap my arms around you."

She smiled. "That can be arranged."

They propped some pillows up behind them so Drew could still suck on his candy, drink his water, and get the connection with her that he wanted. Beth enjoyed being a Domme. There were so many things about it that turned her on. But this was one of the best parts for her. She loved the quiet moments after a scene when everything was still raw. It held an intimacy that she couldn't explain to someone who had never experienced it.

He traced a line with the tips of his fingers down her spine, and then curled his palm around her hip. "I guess I like CBT more than I thought I would."

Beth giggled. "While that may be true, that wasn't really what I'd consider CBT."

"It wasn't?" He seemed shocked by her statement.

"No. That was more me giving you a preview of what knife play is like without the actual knife." Drew was quiet for several minutes, and she remained silent allowing him time to process what she'd said.

"Interesting."

"That's it, just *interesting*?"

Drew grinned down at her. "Well, my head is still spinning from that out-of-this-world orgasm I just experienced. Maybe I'll be able to come up with something better in the morning."

Although she really was curious to hear his thoughts, now that he had more insight on what she had in mind when she'd talked about knife play, she understood that he really did need time to recover.

"Beth?"

She looked up at him. "Yes?"

"I never thought to ask before, but . . . what's your full name? I figure since we're now officially dating and you're going to meet my family soon, I should probably know something like that."

Burying her face in his shoulder, she couldn't help but chuckle. Given what they'd just done it felt silly, but kind of appropriate, too. "Bethany Paige Davenport."

"*Bethany Paige*," he repeated. "I like it."

She pinched his side and he laughed. "Glad you approve."

Finished with his candy, he slid down lower on the bed, and took her with him. "I'd wondered if Beth was maybe short for Elizabeth, but for some reason, you didn't strike me as an Elizabeth."

Having his arms around her—feeling the warmth of his body— could easily become an addiction all its own. She couldn't seem to get close enough. Luckily, Drew appeared to have the same problem.

"Mom had a friend in school named Bethany. She loved the name, so when she found out she was having a girl, Bethany it was." Beth lifted her leg and wedged it between his, aligning their bodies even more. "Paige was my dad's contribution."

She left it at that, and he seemed to sense there was something more.

"There's a story there."

Beth shrugged. "Dad had a sister that died. From what I understand, she never made it home from the hospital, but they named her Paige. My dad was old enough to remember her."

Drew kissed the top of her head. "It's a good story."

"Whenever someone asks, Dad just says it's a family name. He never goes into detail." She took a deep breath. "What about you? Since we're talking names, is Drew short for Andrew?"

He nodded.

"What about a middle name?"

She felt the rise and fall of his chest beneath her before he answered. "Raymond."

The way he said the name gave her the impression that he wasn't a huge fan of his middle name. "*Andrew Raymond Parker.* I like it."

"You wouldn't if the only time it was ever used was when you were in trouble."

Beth couldn't hide her amusement. "Got in trouble a lot, did you?"

"I was a boy. Of course I got in trouble. It's part of the job description.”

“Is that so?” She traced a line from his abdomen and along his hipbone. Placing her hand flat on his left butt cheek, she gave a gentle squeeze. “Sore?”

“Nothing I can’t handle. Although, I can feel it every time I move.”

“Good. Maybe it will remind you to keep that smart mouth of yours in check.”

Drew surprised her by rolling her over. “You love my smart mouth.”

“Nope,” Beth said trying to suppress a smile. She wasn’t doing a very good job.

The next thing she knew, his hands were at her sides, and he was tickling her.

“Drew! What. Do You. Think. You’re. Doing?”

By the time he let up, she was gasping for air. And he was beaming down at her. He looked younger and more carefree than she’d ever seen him before, and her heart skipped a beat. This felt so natural. It didn’t feel as if they’d only been in her bed together a handful of times.

Before she could analyze what she was feeling too closely, Beth took hold of the back of his neck and pulled his mouth down to hers. She attacked his lips in a not-so-subtle reminder of who was in charge.

Beth didn’t release him for several minutes—not until she felt him press his weight against her. Even then, the look in his eyes held things she wasn’t ready for, so she averted her gaze and pretended to look at the clock. “We should get some sleep. I still have to work tomorrow.”

He moved, bringing his cheek to rest above her right breast. “I signed up to do some volunteer work in the morning, but I should be free after lunch. Would you like some help at the café again?”

“If you keep coming by to help, I’m going to have to put you on the payroll.” She ran her fingers through his hair as they talked. “Sure you don’t want another job?”

Drew snorted. “Thanks, but I think I’m good. You see, I have this girlfriend that keeps me pretty busy on my days off.”

“She does, does she?”

“Oh yeah. She’s a real slave driver.”

Beth pinched him, and he laughed.

"Remember you said that the next time I have you tied up," she said.

His only response was to dip his head an inch or so and draw her nipple into his mouth.

She could have made him stop, but it felt too good. Besides, it was the perfect distraction to her thoughts and where they were leading. Taking hold of his wrist, she guided his hand between her legs. Beth opened herself to him and stopped thinking for a while.

***

Drew waved to Tommy as he ducked in behind some customers a little before one. Tommy nodded and then turned his attention back to the man standing in front of the counter. As usual, the café was busy. Drew only counted two empty tables and there were four people in line. It said a lot about Beth's food. Since he'd eaten it several times himself, he knew what all the fuss was about.

Beth was standing at the sink washing her hands when he strolled into the kitchen. She looked in his direction.

"You made it." The smile she gave him sent warmth spreading all the way down to his toes.

Unable to resist, he closed the distance between them, and gave her a kiss that was probably a little much for the workplace. Good thing he wasn't her employee.

She released a contented sigh as his lips left hers.

He waited until she opened her eyes and then glanced around the kitchen. "Now, put me to work. What do you need me to do first?"

Put him to work she did. Within minutes, he was loading food on trays and taking them out to customers. Things didn't slow down until it was nearly time to close. He liked working with Beth, mostly because every so often when she'd hand him a tray of food she would rise up on her tiptoes and give him a peck on the lips. It made the running back and forth worth it.

They were closing up when a woman stopped near the front of the café acting as if she wanted to come in but kept changing her mind.

"Beth." Drew yelled loud enough to get her attention in the

223

back.

"Yeah?" She appeared through the kitchen door, wiping her hands on a towel.

He tilted his head toward the front. The woman still looked unsure of herself. "Want me to see what she wants?"

Beth shook her head. "No. I got it."

When the woman noticed Beth was heading her way, she froze. He'd seen that look before from people who were standing across the street watching their home burn. It was a deer in the headlights kind of look—a mixture of panic and something akin to disbelief.

"Can I help you?" Beth asked, cracking the door open.

The woman spoke, but it was too low for him to hear. Beth nodded a few times. Whoever the woman was, she was obviously shy, or nervous, or maybe both. After several minutes, the woman left, and Beth locked the front door again.

"Everything okay?" he asked.

"She was inquiring about the job opening."

Even though the woman was nowhere to be seen, Drew looked behind Beth to where she had been. "Does she realize she'll have to deal with people?"

Beth smiled. "Yes. She worked in a diner when she was in high school."

He went back to the table he was cleaning. "So are you going to hire her?"

"I told her to show up Tuesday morning at seven and I'd give her a trial run."

"That was nice of you," he said.

She took a step forward and brushed the back of her hand along his arm. "I can be very nice. When I want to be."

Drew took a deep breath and met her gaze. "Are we going to the club tonight?"

"I haven't decided yet."

"I doubt it could be worse than last night. I'd say the hard part is over. Everyone knows we're together now. End of story."

Beth shrugged. "Maybe. But that wasn't why I was considering staying home."

He gave her a questioning look.

"It's your last night off. I don't want to wear you out when you have to be at work first thing in the morning." He opened his mouth to speak, but she cut him off. "Plus, I think I might want you all to myself tonight."

It was hard to argue with that.

As it turned out, they did make an appearance at Serpent's Kiss that night. They received a few lingering looks, but it was nothing like it had been the night before. For the most part, they hung out with friends and relaxed.

They headed back to Beth's house around ten thirty. Drew was feeling a little guilty that he hadn't really talked to Shawn since Wednesday morning. Other than a few quick texts, he hadn't communicated with him at all in the last four days.

"What's bothering you?" Beth asked as they lay in her bed that night.

"Just worried about Shawn."

"I've sort of monopolized your time off, haven't I?" She turned slightly so that she could look at him.

"Could be the other way around. I could be monopolizing your time."

Beth rolled so that she was facing him. "This is moving kind of fast, isn't it? I mean, we've spent nearly every minute I wasn't at work together."

He hated to ask, but he felt he needed to. "Are things moving too fast for you, Beth?"

Her forehead wrinkled as she considered his question. "I don't know."

Drew waited.

"I know it should. It's only been a week since our first date, but . . ." She looked him in the eyes. "I missed you Tuesday night when you weren't in my bed."

It didn't take a genius to know how much that admission cost her. The urge to tell her that he loved her was strong, but he resisted. She may have admitted that she missed him, but that didn't mean she was ready to hear that he had fallen in love with her.

"I missed you, too," he whispered. "I was lying in my cot remembering what it had been like to fall asleep with you beside me. It made it hard to go to sleep." Drew flexed his hips against her to make sure she got his meaning.

She gave him a gentle shove. "I'm sure you managed. Don't you have a shower at the station?"

He laughed. "If you think I'm going to go into a public shower room to jack off, you're crazy."

"So you just had to suffer, huh?" she teased.

"Yes." He buried his face in her hair. "I could hear all the guys around me and all I wanted was to be here with you. Tomorrow night is going to be torture."

Drew expected her to laugh, but she didn't. "I know."

Neither said anything for a long time, but Beth finally broke the silence. "What's your family going to think of me? Am I anything like the other girls you've brought home?"

He was grateful for the change in subject. "Yes and no. I've always been attracted to strong women, even in high school, so that won't shock them. I think the biggest difference will be our relationship itself."

Beth stiffened in his arms, and he knew he needed to clarify. "Not what we do in the bedroom. I'm talking about the normal stuff." He laced their fingers together and held them up close to their faces. "Like the fact that I like to be touching you. It doesn't matter if I'm holding your hand or if I have my arm around you."

She squeezed his hand. "So that's different. What else?"

"I've been thinking about sleeping arrangements. There is no way my parents are going to let us share a bedroom—they're old-fashioned that way."

"Mine probably wouldn't either."

Drew lowered their hands, but didn't release her. "What do you think about camping?"

She raised her eyebrows. "I thought we already covered this."

"True, but if you recall I presented you with an alternative that would make camping more appealing."

"You did. Although I'm not one-hundred percent convinced," she said.

Taking the plunge, he told her his plan. "Give me the chance to convince you. Sunday night you and I will camp under the stars. We'd be away from the house and completely alone. And best of all, we can share a sleeping bag."

Beth kissed the hollow at the base of his collarbone. "You think you have it all figured out, don't you?"

"I think I'd go insane if I knew you were sleeping in the same house and I couldn't be there next to you," he confessed. Let her take that however she wanted.

"Your parents won't get suspicious or want to come with us?"

"I don't think so. Mom doesn't camp. And Dad's back gives him issues now and then, so I doubt he'll want to chance it the night before the big party." Drew paused. "The only one we really have to worry about is Seth."

"You think your brother will want to tag along?"

Drew shrugged. "It's unlikely, but maybe. You never know with Seth."

"Do you and your brother get along? I know you've told me some about when you were kids, but what about now that you're older? Does he still treat you like you're his pesky younger brother?"

"I suppose we get along as well as most brothers do. He has his life. I have mine. We don't exactly travel in the same circles." Drew preferred physical work and getting his hands dirty. Seth was just the opposite. Drew was pretty sure the only time his brother broke a sweat was in the gym.

"So no meeting for lunch or dinner even though you both live in St. Louis?" she asked.

"Not really. As I said, we both have very different lives and we're both happy the way things are. I think we've met for lunch a handful of times since I moved to the city."

Beth sighed. "That's kind of sad. I'm not very close with my siblings either, but that's mainly because they're so far away. Still, we e-mail about once a week just to see how each other is doing."

He knew he shouldn't ask, but that little voice inside wouldn't let him leave it alone. "Have you told them about me?"

"Yes."

Knowing she'd told her family about him made Drew smile.

"Don't get all cocky on me." She poked him in the ribs. "It's not a big deal."

Whether Beth admitted it or not, it was a big deal. At least, to him.

He slipped his arm around her waist and cupped her ass in the palm of his hand as he tucked her head into his shoulder. It was a near perfect position and he didn't have any desire to move from it until morning. Drew kissed the top of her head and rested his cheek on her hair. "I'm glad you told your family about me."

She didn't say anything for a long time. He thought maybe

she'd fallen asleep. Then, in a soft voice she said, "Me, too."

Chapter 25

When Drew arrived for work on Sunday morning, the station was full of activity. The outgoing shift had recently returned from a fire and everyone was busy cleaning equipment and getting debriefed. As he walked by some of the guys, he thought he heard one of them mention arson, but didn't get a chance to question it before he heard his name being called.

"Parker!" He looked up to find Chief Franks peering over the second-story railing.

"Morning, Chief."

"I need to see you in my office at eight sharp." Chief Franks' gaze landed somewhere behind him. "You, too, Cameron."

Willis Cameron, captain of one of the ladder trucks, shot Drew a questioning look as they both headed toward the locker room to stow their things. "Any idea what that's about?"

Drew shoved his duffel bag into his locker. "I thought I overheard one of the guys downstairs mention arson. I'm guessing another building was targeted last night."

"Bomb and arson really needs to catch this guy already. What's it been . . . six buildings now? I wonder if there were any people in this one."

"I guess we're going to find out." Shutting his locker, Drew began walking toward the kitchen with Willis. "And even if this one wasn't, sooner or later there will be. His luck is going to run out."

"True that."

Lucky for Drew, Beth had brought home some of her amazing blueberry muffins on Saturday and he'd enjoyed them and a cup of coffee before leaving her house that morning. She'd gotten up to see him off even though he told her she didn't have to. Sitting there with her at her table eating breakfast had felt very domesticated to him. It had only been a week and yet it felt as if they'd done the same routine hundreds of times.

Drew smiled as he poured himself a fresh cup of coffee. He was taking his first sip when his crew found him.

"There you are. I thought maybe your big date had worn you out and you'd called in sick."

Of course, everyone in the kitchen heard Romeo. They all stopped what they were involved in and turned their attention on Drew.

He took his time, taking another drink of his coffee before he responded. "You think I'd let you off that easy, Romeo? Someone's got to be here to keep you in line."

Some of the guys chuckled. Romeo was a great guy, but he had the habit of talking first and thinking later.

"Come on, Parker. You've got to give us some details here. Let us live vicariously."

Drew took his coffee over to the table and sat down. Although he still felt protective of his relationship with Beth, he knew it was a lost cause to keep it from the guys he worked with, especially his crew—they were like family. Since he was planning to be with Beth for a long time to come, they were going to have to know about her sooner or later.

Before he could figure out what to say, Baily pulled up a chair beside him. "It's the café lady, right?"

"Yes."

Romeo whistled. "Oh man. You've got good taste. That is one hot piece of ass."

Drew gave him a hard stare.

"Oh wow," Irwin said, finally piping up for the first time. "It's like that, is it? Better watch what you say, Romeo. Looks like our captain here has it bad for this one."

Some of the other guys were still paying attention to their

conversation. Others were starting to drift out of the room. It was nearing eight and the previous shift was eager to head home— probably to get some sleep since they'd most likely been up all night fighting that suspected arson.

"You should bring her to Romeo's barbecue," Baily said.

They all nodded.

Drew shook his head and stood. He still had a few minutes before he had to be in Chief Franks' office, but he needed a breather from the interrogation. "No can do. I'll be at my parents' Monday for their big shindig."

"I'm surprised you'd want to leave your new girl that long. She may find someone else while you're gone."

Romeo thought he was smart, but Drew was about to make clear the position Beth held in his life. He strolled with coffee in hand toward the door that would lead him out to the bay and the stairs to Chief Franks' office on the second floor. "Not likely since I'm taking her with me."

He knew there would be a price to pay for that kind of admission, but seeing Romeo momentarily speechless had been worth it. For now he needed to concentrate on his job. Cameron was right. If last night's fire was by the same arsonist that would mean six buildings had been hit. So far no one had been hurt—not civilian or firefighter—but set fires were always more dangerous. They tended to burn hotter and spread faster than your typical fire. They really needed to catch this guy.

Four hours later, Drew was working on some paperwork while his guys did some general housework around the station. He shifted slightly and was reminded of Friday night when he'd been able to feel the residual effects of Beth's spanking. His morning had been full between his meeting with Chief Franks and a call about a hydrant not working properly. This was the first opportunity he'd had to decompress.

Every time Beth crossed his mind he would start grinning. It was impossible not to. Drew finally had the kind of relationship he wanted, and with a woman who kept him engaged and interested outside sex. He'd never had that before and he knew, even now, that he was never going to want to give that up. Beth was it for him. He just had to get her to see it, too.

A knock sounded on the doorjamb causing Drew to look up.

Jamison, a private on Willis' ladder crew, framed the doorway. "There's someone out front asking for you."

Confused, Drew nodded and set his pen down to go see who it was. Seth had only dropped by once in seven years, so Drew doubted it was him.

When he rounded the corner, he couldn't believe his eyes. It was Beth. "Hey."

"Hey." She looked uncharacteristically shy. "I hope you don't mind that I came."

"No. Not at all." He pulled her out of the main hall and into one of the side rooms so they could have a little privacy. "I'm just a little surprised. Everything all right?"

Beth reached into her pocket and pulled out a watch. *His* watch. "You left it on my dresser."

"Thanks for bringing it to me." He took the watch and secured it on his right wrist.

"You're welcome. I didn't know if you would need it today or not."

"I'm surprised I didn't realize it was missing." Drew was shocked really. It was a gift from his parents upon graduating from the fire academy. He rarely left home without wearing it, and it was as much a part of his work uniform as his dark blue pants and polo shirt were.

"Well, you have it now, so . . ."

Drew was torn. He didn't want her to go, but he knew she couldn't stay either. "Do you have any plans for today?"

It was a weak attempt to prolong her visit. "I'm meeting Nicole for lunch, actually."

He glanced down at his watch. "It's already after twelve."

"I know," she said. "I'm going to be late."

"I'll walk you out."

Beth nodded, and he followed close behind her as she walked down the hallway and out the front door. She turned, hesitating. Beth didn't act as if she wanted to leave any more than he wanted her to go.

Drew felt her press something into his hand. He opened his palm to find a key.

"Come over tomorrow morning when you get off work." Although she didn't pose it as a question, he knew she was really asking.

"Are you sure?" Giving him a key to her house was a big step—especially for her.

"I'm sure."

Drew searched her eyes to see if he could detect any hesitation or uncertainty on her part. He found none.

Closing his fingers around the key, he slipped it into his pocket. "I'll try to be quiet."

Beth took a step toward him. She grabbed a fistful of his shirt in her right hand and twisted, pulling him closer. Her lips were on his before he could think about the consequences. Then there wasn't much thinking at all as the memory of her mouth and her body against him the night before spread through every muscle of his being.

When she finally detached her mouth from his, she looked up at him with heavy-lidded eyes. "Don't be too quiet."

He blinked, and she chuckled before giving him another quick kiss and walking away.

Drew was still trying to get his bearings as he turned to go back inside. That's when he noticed that they'd had an audience. A handful of guys, including Baily and Romeo, were standing outside the bay watching his interaction with Beth. Ignoring them, he opened the door he'd exited a few minutes before and headed back to his desk. He knew what was coming, but he was going to try to hide from it for a few minutes more. At least until he could get his body's reaction to that kiss to go away.

***

"I gave him a key."

Nicole paused with her fork halfway between her plate and her mouth. Her face was completely blank as she stared across the table. Beth didn't know what to make of her best friend's reaction to her declaration.

"Would you say something? Am I being stupid?" Beth asked.

It took Nicole another few moments. She returned her utensil to her plate and placed her hands in her lap. "That depends."

"On?"

"On why you did it."

At least Nicole didn't immediately tell Beth that she'd lost her mind. "We've spent pretty much all our free time together since our date last Saturday."

"I know."

She glared at her friend. "Are you going to let me finish?"

Nicole waved her hand indicating Beth should continue.

"Anyway . . . I was surprised at how much I missed him Tuesday night when he had to work and that was after he'd only spent one night in my bed." Beth plucked nonexistent fuzz from her napkin. "He has to work tonight and I know I'm going to miss having him beside me."

Luckily, Nicole caught on to her train of thought. "And you don't have to work tomorrow so you were thinking he could come straight from his shift and maybe be there when you wake up?"

It was embarrassing to admit, but there it was. "Something like that."

"Do you regret giving him the key?" she asked. It was just like Nicole to cut to the chase.

Beth sighed. "No."

"Then what's the problem?"

"Everything is moving so fast with him. I mean, we just started dating and I want to be with him all the time. That's not normal," Beth said.

Her friend gave her a knowing smile.

"What?"

"You're falling in love with him."

She sat up straight in her chair, defiant. "No, I'm not."

Nicole picked up her drink and brought it to her lips. "If you say so."

"I can't be. It-it's too soon." When Nicole didn't respond, Beth asked, "Isn't it?"

"Only you can answer that, Beth. But let me remind you that while you've only been *officially* dating for eight days, the courtship has been happening for well over a month."

Beth didn't comment right away. "How did you know with Jeff?"

Her friend's eyes lit up at the mention of her man. "We were sitting in his apartment one evening watching a movie. He looked over at me and asked if I wanted any popcorn."

That didn't sound like an *aha* moment to Beth, but what did she know? With Ben, it had been a gradual thing. There wasn't a single moment she could pinpoint when she'd fallen in love with him. It just sort of showed up one day. "Him asking if you wanted popcorn doesn't sound all that romantic."

"It wasn't. And it wasn't just the popcorn. But it was at that moment when I realized that he wasn't like all those selfish guys I'd dated in the past. He was always asking if he could get me anything, or going out of his way to help me relax after a stressful day at work. It was then that I realized we clicked, and that I wanted to be with him long term. Being with him did, and still does, make me happy," Nicole said.

Beth thought back on her time with Drew. He did make her happy. But was that love or just hormones? She honestly didn't know.

"Look, you don't have to take my word for it. One of these days it will just hit you like it did me. You'll see."

"And if it doesn't? What if Ben broke that part of me and I can't get it back?" It might sound like a stupid question, but in her mind it made perfect sense.

"You gave Drew a key to your house, right?"

She rolled her eyes. "You know I did because me telling you that is what started this whole conversation."

Nicole picked up her fork and began eating once more. "A month ago you didn't think you'd be able to trust another man again. You wouldn't have given Drew a key to your home if you didn't trust him."

This was true. Beth did trust him. Whether that trust was misplaced or not remained to be seen.

***

Drew used his new key to let himself in Beth's front door. He'd hightailed it out of the station as soon as he could, but even still, it was getting close to eight thirty. The house was quiet, so he figured she was still asleep.

Hitching his duffel bag a little higher on his shoulder, he made sure the door was locked behind him, and climbed the stairs. It had been a rough shift. Not because of the calls—they'd only had two

235

after Beth's visit—no, it was due to the ribbing he'd endured from the guys. He tried to take it in stride. It was par for the course when you worked with fifteen other guys. The only thing he wanted to do was crawl into bed with Beth and feel her warm body pressed against his.

When he stepped into her bedroom, he was surprised to find her wide-awake and waiting for him. "I thought you'd be asleep."

"I didn't sleep all that well last night. It was lonely in this bed all by myself."

She threw back the covers. It was only then that he realized she was completely naked. He swallowed and dropped his bag.

"Come here, Captain." Beth spread her legs for him. "There's something that desperately needs your attention."

All the innuendo and suggestive comments he'd had to deal with over the past twenty-four hours disappeared as he crawled onto the bed and took up position between her legs. Her pussy gleamed back at him, already moist and ready for his attentions.

"I missed you, Mistress." He dipped his tongue into her heat and partook.

Beth placed her hand on the back of his head and lifted her hips. "I missed you, too."

He had no idea what she'd been thinking about before he arrived, but whatever it was had her very wet. Her clit was already peeking out from beneath its hood, and he teased it as he sucked and licked every inch of her within easy reach of his mouth. It was the perfect way to end his shift—start his day—however you wanted to look at it.

Her fingers dug into his scalp as she got closer. He flicked his tongue against her clit in rapid succession because he knew how much she liked that. Drew felt her legs begin to tremble, and then her breath hitched. A moment later, she arched her back and released a high-pitched squeal.

When she glanced down at him still perched between her thighs, he knew he had a shit-eating grin on his face.

"Thank you. I needed that," she said, caressing the side of his face.

"Anytime."

Beth sat up and stretched.

He was unsure what to do next. Their arrangement said they

would only play on his four-day-off stretches, but they'd already discovered that most of their sexual encounters involved some level of kink, even the more vanilla ones. There was nothing he wanted more after eating her pussy than to sink his cock inside her.

She patted his cheek and then turned to put her feet on the floor as if she was going to get up. "I'll use the bathroom down the hall. Get yourself ready for bed. I'll be back in a minute."

Although he was somewhat disappointed, he didn't argue with her. Drew went to retrieve his duffel bag and dug out his toothbrush and toothpaste. If all they were going to do was sleep, he might as well go through his normal pre-bed routine.

Ten minutes later, Beth strolled into the room still as naked as she'd been when she left. He was in her bed waiting for her. She climbed in beside him and reached for him.

Drew met her halfway, and his heart began to race as she drew his mouth down to hers. "I thought—"

Beth kissed him hard. "You thought what?"

"That you didn't . . . that you didn't want to." Talking was becoming less of a priority.

Any ideas he had of her not wanting to have sex with him this morning fell by the wayside as she wrapped her fingers around his erection and guided it home. Feeling her pussy milking his cock as he pushed inside her had him longing more than ever to blurt out that he loved her, but he knew he couldn't do that. Instead, he buried his face in her neck and repeated 'I love you' over and over again in his mind with each thrust of his hips.

Chapter 26

They slept until a little after eleven. Because Drew hadn't been all that busy during his shift, he'd been able to get a decent amount of sleep. That didn't mean that he was going to pass up the chance to spend a few more hours in Beth's bed with her softness pressed against him.

That afternoon, in need of some clean clothes, Drew took Beth with him to his apartment. He was surprised to find Shawn there. The last time he'd spoken to him, it sounded as if he'd found an apartment.

"You're home." Shawn glanced up from the television. When he realized Drew wasn't alone, he clicked it off and stood. "Hello. You must be Beth."

She smiled. "And you must be Shawn. I've heard a lot about you."

"Only good things, I hope."

Beth pressed her lips together, brought her thumb and index finger in front of her mouth, and then acted as if she was locking her lips closed and throwing away the key.

"Ah. So it's like that, is it?" Shawn glanced over at Drew. "I like her."

Drew rolled his eyes. "Glad you approve."

There was a lull in the conversation and a lightbulb seemed to go off in his friend's head. "Did you guys need me to make myself scarce for a while? I can go catch a movie or something. Give you some privacy."

"That's all right. We aren't staying. I just came by to get some clean clothes." Drew leaned in and gave Beth a kiss. "I'll hurry. Make yourself at home."

Leaving Beth in the living room with Shawn, Drew scurried into his bedroom and gathered up enough clothing to get him through the next three days. He was eventually going to run out of clean clothes, but he wasn't willing to sacrifice time with Beth in order to do laundry.

He was zipping his bag when there was a knock behind him. Drew looked over his shoulder to find Beth framing the doorway.

"Do you have a bag or something you could put your dirty laundry in? I have a washer and dryer at my place. You're more than welcome to use them."

"Are you sure?" he asked.

Beth strolled across the room and he was mesmerized by the sway of her hips as she walked toward him. When she came to a stop in front him, Drew had to remind himself that they weren't really alone and that he needed to keep his hands to himself. She traced a line down the outside of his jaw with the tip of her nail, reminding him of Saturday night. Almost instantly, there was a lot less space in his pants.

"I'm sure." The words barely left her mouth before her lips brushed against his.

"Okay." He tried to breathe through the temptation. "Beth?"

"Yes?"

"Shawn's still in the next room." As the moments ticked by, that fact was becoming less important. His friend was an adult and it was Drew's apartment. If he wanted to make love to his girlfriend in his bed, then he would.

To his disappointment, Beth put some distance between them. "I'll wait for you in the other room. Don't be long."

It might not have been a command—they weren't playing—but Drew still flew around his bedroom gathering dirty clothing wherever he could find it. In less than two minutes, he had his duffel bag in one hand and his laundry bag full of dirty clothes in the other. The only thing left to do was get Beth home as fast as humanly possible. If he was lucky, they could spend the rest of the day in her bed.

Over the next few days, the two of them spent what some might call an unhealthy amount of time together. If they weren't working then they could usually be found together. Beth had help at the café so she didn't need his assistance anymore. When Shawn had called to see if Drew could give him a hand moving into his new apartment on Wednesday morning, he'd jumped at the chance. It would be something to keep him occupied while Beth was at work.

Drew had never been in love before. The reality of it—the feeling as if he couldn't get enough of her—wasn't something he was prepared for. He'd experienced lust in the past. The physical attraction to Beth wasn't what bowled him over. It was the wanting to see her roll over and smile at him first thing in the morning or having her give him that look when he was acting a little too playful.

He pulled up to his apartment at noon. Shawn was inside, packing up the few things he'd brought with him. The rest was in a storage unit a few miles away.

The two didn't say much as they loaded everything into Shawn's pickup truck. Drew hopped in the passenger side while his friend got behind the wheel. "Thanks for letting me stay at your place. I appreciate it."

"Anytime. You know that," Drew said. "Not like I've been at my apartment much lately anyway."

Shawn pulled out onto the road and headed in the direction of the storage facility. "Can't get enough of each other, huh? I remember those days."

Drew didn't comment.

The rest of his afternoon was spent hauling the few pieces of furniture Jill hadn't wanted, and helping Shawn get his apartment ready for living. Drew didn't mind doing domestic chores. Housekeeping was part of being a firefighter. That being said, his friend's new place left a lot to be desired. It was a one bedroom like his, but everything in it appeared to have been transported from the seventies.

"I hope you got a good deal on this place," Drew said.

"What? You not digging the shag carpet?" Shawn chuckled and shrugged. "It's the middle of the month. Beggars can't be choosers. Besides, it's just me. I'm not out to impress anyone."

"Yet."

Shawn shook his head. "Not for a while. I think I need to take a break from women for a bit. Jill and I were together for ten years. It's going to take a while to get my mind wrapped around someone else in my life like that. "

At four o'clock, Shawn dropped Drew back at his apartment. Maybe he should have gone inside and stayed put for a while—give Beth some space. He didn't want her to feel smothered.

His good intentions lasted about as long as it took his friend's truck to disappear. Digging his keys out of his pocket, Drew opened his car door and got behind the wheel. With any luck, Beth would already be home.

She was.

Drew hurried up the walkway and knocked. A few moments later Beth opened the door. "Hey."

Without waiting for more of an invitation, he stepped over the threshold, and scooped her up in his arms. "Hey."

Beth laughed until he pressed his lips to hers. It was a slow, deep kiss that said more than words ever could.

She licked her lips and met his gaze. "Why didn't you let yourself in?"

He kissed her again. "I didn't want to assume. You might have been busy or something."

"I was starting dinner." She hadn't made any move to pull away. Hopefully, she didn't have anything on the stove or in the oven that would burn.

"Want some help?" he asked.

Only then did she back out of his arms. "Always."

Drew followed her into the kitchen and they spent the next hour working side by side cooking dinner. He wondered what his mom would think if she knew.

That night as they feel asleep, Drew let the excitement of the upcoming weekend take hold. He was bringing his girlfriend home to meet his family. Drew was almost positive his dad would like Beth, but Dad was easy to please. His mom and Seth would be the real test—Seth especially. His brother was naturally suspicious. Drew always figured it was a lawyer thing.

As Beth's breathing evened out, Drew let himself wonder for the first time what it would be like to be married to her. She was everything he wanted in a woman. He could see himself coming home to her every day for the rest of his life.

The only thing he had to do now was convince her. She'd come a long way, but there were still times when he thought she was second-guessing herself. The only time that didn't seem to happen was when they were in bed. Beth knew her role there the same as he did. It was everything else, the traditional boyfriend-girlfriend stuff that brought that look into her eyes every so often.

He'd noticed it a lot that first week, but as the days passed, it was less and less. Either Beth was beginning to relax and trust their relationship, or she was getting better at hiding it from him. He really hoped it was the former.

***

On Sunday morning, Beth woke up with a huge smile on her face. Drew was in the middle of another four days off and they'd spent last night having some fun with bondage. She'd had a long day at work and needed a release.

The smile lasted as long as it took her to remember that they would be going to see Drew's parents in a few short hours. It felt like a big moment for her—for them. She wasn't sure why every step forward in their relationship filled her with anxiety, but it did. Maybe it was because, deep down, she knew the significance.

Drew was important to her. Technically, they'd been together only two weeks, but in some ways she felt closer to him than she ever had to Ben. How was that possible? She'd been with Ben for three years. He knew her. Drew . . .

As much as she didn't want to admit it, Drew did know her. Maybe it wasn't in the same way, but considering how things turned out with Ben that was probably a good thing. Drew was honest. It was the only way to describe him. He held nothing back. It didn't matter if they were in bed or out of it, he gave her all of himself and it was hard to combat that.

His eyes flittered open, and when he saw her looking at him, he grinned. "Good morning."

Unable to resist, she drew closer to him.

The feel of his arms around her brought Beth comfort. He'd spent every night he hadn't been working in her bed. She knew some in the lifestyle would feel that there needed to be some separation. Maybe they were right, but she couldn't bring herself to make him sleep in the other room or even go home. Not having him beside her when he was at the fire station was bad enough.

"Are you ready for today?" he asked.

"Not really."

His chest vibrated with amusement. "It'll be fine. You have nothing to worry about."

Beth snorted. "I'll remember you said that when it's time to meet my parents."

"Bring it on."

They lay there for several minutes just enjoying each other. Eventually, though, they had to get up and begin getting ready. There was no use putting it off anymore as tempting as that might be.

Drew's parents lived roughly an hour east of St. Louis. As they drove farther into Illinois, civilization fell away and they were surrounded by nothing but fields. He'd said he grew up on a farm, but Beth was envisioning more along the lines of what she was used to in Ohio. There was nothing except fields for as far as the eye could see. She didn't even think they'd passed a house in the last ten minutes.

"You okay over there?" he asked.

"Yeah. I just thought there'd be more . . . houses."

He smiled. "That's southern Illinois for ya. Fields as far as the eye can see."

"Is it like this where your parents live?"

"Pretty much. There's a small town about ten miles down the road, so there are a few more houses if you head in that direction."

He said it as though it were the most natural thing in the world. Of course, to him it probably was. Beth couldn't imagine living so far out of touch from everything. She'd grown up in the suburbs and that's what she was used to. This felt as if one could get lost.

Fifteen minutes later, they turned onto a road that looked only marginally better than a gravel driveway. They seemed to keep going farther and farther out in the middle of nowhere.

Then she noticed a mailbox up ahead. Drew put on his turn signal even though there was no one behind them. She guessed it was showtime.

Beth reached for his hand as they drove up the long driveway toward the house. That, at least, was how she'd pictured it—an old two-story farmhouse with a wraparound porch. She wondered if Drew's parents ever sat outside on a hot day sipping iced tea.

He pulled up to the house and parked the car alongside a fence. "You ready?"

"No," she said.

Drew squeezed her hand and shot her that teasing grin of his. "Don't worry. I'll protect you."

She rolled her eyes. "So I need a big strong man to protect me from your family?"

"You never know. Mom might have some secret truth serum or something lurking in her cupboards. She'll make you tell her all your secrets."

Beth shook her head and laughed.

"Don't worry. We'll be alone tonight. Camping, remember?" Drew's eyes were sparkling. He loved teasing her as much as she loved teasing him.

Taking a quick look around, Beth confirmed that they were still alone before leaning across the console and whispering in his ear. "I'm going to make you beg for it tonight."

She saw the muscles in his throat move as he swallowed, making her grin. Drew could tease her all he wanted as long as he remembered that she would always get the last word. The only thing that kept her from pushing things right then and there was the fact that any member of his family could come out to greet them at any given minute. Beth didn't think finding her sitting in Drew's car with her hand wrapped around his cock would be a great first impression.

Reluctantly, she pulled back enough to meet his gaze. His pupils had dilated, and Beth wondered if she looked down at his lap whether she'd find him aroused. Her train of thought did nothing to help her current state one bit. "We should go inside. Your mom's probably wondering what we're doing out here."

He looked toward the house. "She's probably at the window watching."

"Oh, goody."

Drew chuckled. "Come on. We should go inside before I start tenting my shorts."

"We wouldn't want that now, would we?" Yet again, Drew had

managed to dispel her fears.

Beth met him at the front of the vehicle. He laced their fingers together before making his way toward the house. As they drew closer, she saw the outline of a woman in one of the upstairs windows. Drew had been right. She had been spying on them.

He opened the door and let Beth go inside first. Moments later, they heard someone coming down the stairs. They didn't have to wait long before a woman descended into view. She had brown hair the same shade as Drew's, but it was mixed with a fair amount of gray. Beth knew that this had to be Drew's mother.

The woman greeted them with a warm smile, then walked over to Drew and wrapped her arms around him.

Drew hugged her back.

Beth stood anxiously waiting for the introduction she knew was to come. From the conversations they'd had about his family, she knew this meeting was important. Whether Drew admitted it or not, Beth doubted a relationship between them would last if his family didn't approve. As they pulled apart, his mother's gaze settled on her.

"You must be Beth." Instead of the nod or handshake Beth was expecting, Drew's mother embraced her as well.

Startled, it took a moment for her to return the gesture. Beth looked to Drew for guidance but he wasn't any help as his attention had turned toward the door.

Things happened fast after that. Beth was quickly introduced to Drew's father, Bill, before being hustled over to the kitchen table. Nancy, Drew's mother, placed a towel-covered bowl on the table. "Help yourself. I'm sure you're hungry after the drive. Lunch will be ready soon."

Drew sat down beside Beth while Bill disappeared up the stairs. At home in his surroundings, Drew opened the towel and motioned for her to help herself to a roll. Since neither one of them had been eager to get out of bed, they'd been running late this morning. Because of that, breakfast had been nothing more than a bowl of cereal.

"Thanks," she said, picking up one of the warm rolls.

He smiled. "Mom makes the best rolls. I've tried to duplicate them, but they never come out the same."

Beth pinched off a section of her roll and popped it in her

mouth. The moment the taste and texture hit her tongue, she thought she might have died and gone to heaven. The rolls were a perfect balance of sweet and savory. No wonder Drew loved them.

"Good, huh?"

All she could do was nod. Beth's mind was already working to dissect what was in the rolls.

Drew placed his hand on top of her leg as he leaned in to whisper in her ear. "I'll give you the recipe when we get home. Maybe you'll have better luck making them."

She wasn't sure if she was experiencing some sort of high from the carbohydrates or if it was merely the fact that she could feel his breath caressing the side of her face, but Beth felt her temperature begin to rise. Placing a hand over his, she removed it from her leg.

He chuckled.

Unfortunately, anything Beth might have said was silenced when Bill joined them at the table. He reached for one of the rolls, took a huge bite, and asked, "My boy here tells us you're a pretty fine baker. You make anything as good as my Nancy's rolls here?"

Before she could answer, Drew chimed in. "Her muffins are the things dreams are made of."

Nancy appeared beside Beth with what looked to be a large pot of stew. "Yes, dear, we're all aware of how much you like muffins, but I do believe your father was referring to food."

Beth thought her eyes would pop out of her head as she stared up in shock at Drew's mother. Nancy only winked at her and turned to get the salad.

Fingers tangled with hers under the table. She knew it was Drew, but she was too stunned to speak.

He squeezed her hand, and she finally turned her head in his direction.

"They like you," he mouthed.

She swallowed and nodded. They liked her. Okay. That was good. Beth only hoped she could get used to their teasing and not die of embarrassment before they headed home on Monday night.

Chapter 27

Lunch was interesting, to say the least. Beth didn't know what she'd expected, but Drew's parents weren't anything like what she'd been picturing. They were older. His dad had to be close to seventy and his mom wasn't much younger, but they didn't act that way. As soon as they were finished with their meal, Bill got up from the table and offered to help Drew bring in the bags.

"Actually, I brought my camping gear. I figured Beth and I could sleep down by the creek tonight," Drew said.

A knowing smile spread across Bill's face. He knew exactly why his son wanted to camp out instead of spending the night under his parents' roof. "Well, then, I'll help you unload everything and haul it back to the campsite."

"Thanks." Drew stood and pushed in his chair. "Did you want—"

"You men go on ahead. Beth and I will clean up."

There was a finality in Nancy's voice that left an uneasy feeling in Beth's stomach. She didn't know the woman well enough to hazard a guess as to what was coming, but she knew something was.

Nothing was said at first beyond a few polite 'can you hand me that plate' or 'there's a container over there you can use' for the first couple of minutes. It was tempting to let her guard down.

"My son tells me you own a café."

It wasn't the line of questioning Beth had been expecting. "I do."

There was another pause.

"A lot of hard work running a business. Long hours."

"It is," Beth agreed, "but I enjoy it for the most part. Baking has always been a passion of mine."

Nancy nodded, reached for a dishtowel, and began wiping down the counter. Beth could tell there was something on her mind.

Not sure she wanted to know what Nancy was thinking, Beth decided to keep the conversation on food. "Drew tells me he gets his love of cooking from you."

His mother smiled. "My boy is very talented in the kitchen. Could probably have been a chef if he'd put his mind to it." Nancy pulled out a chair and sat down, inviting Beth to do the same. "But he's wanted to be a firefighter since the second grade. I thought maybe he'd grow out of it, find something a little safer he wanted to do with his life, but that didn't happen. Too much of his father in him."

There was no malice behind her words. She was only stating a fact.

"Are you disappointed he didn't choose to do something different with his life?" Beth asked.

"Oh, heavens no. I want my boys to be happy. Both my boys. If that means one of them has to rush into burning buildings on a regular basis, then so be it." It was clear Nancy had come to terms with Drew's choice of profession a long time ago.

"I haven't met Seth yet, but Drew's told me a little about him." In truth, Beth was extremely curious about her boyfriend's brother. Some of the things Drew said made her think Seth had a superiority complex. After meeting Nancy and Bill, however, Beth had a hard time believing that. They were very down-to-earth people. She had to imagine Seth couldn't have fallen that far from the tree. Drew certainly hadn't.

"Seth and Drew are very different. There's ten years between them, and where Drew always wanted to play outside, Seth preferred to have his nose in a book." Nancy smiled but there was a sad element to it. "It's good to see Drew has found someone that makes him happy. I can only hope that one day Seth does as well."

A weight lifted off Beth's shoulders at the compliment.

Whatever Drew's mom had been after in arranging this one-on-one time, she seemed to have found it.

Beth was about to ask more about Seth when they heard the front door open. She and Nancy both turned their heads toward the noise. Two seconds later, a man Beth didn't know strolled into the room. He was tall—maybe an inch or two taller than Drew.

Nancy scrambled out of her chair and went to hug the new arrival. "You missed lunch."

The man looked slightly abashed from the mild scolding. "Sorry, Mom. I had to go into the office this morning to pick up some paperwork."

"This is a holiday weekend. You shouldn't be working." Nancy shook her head, a look of disapproval on her face.

It was then that the man whom Beth deduced had to be, Seth, noticed her sitting at the table. "Hello."

Beth stood. "Hello. You must be Seth."

He nodded and gave her a thorough once-over. "I am. And you must be my little brother's new girlfriend."

Before she could answer, Nancy stepped in. "Beth, this is my oldest, Seth. Seth, this is Beth."

His gaze was scrutinizing and he showed no signs of extending the same welcome as Nancy and Bill had done. Trying not to let it bother her, Beth cleared her throat. "Well, it's nice to meet you, Seth. Nancy, thank you for lunch. I think I'll go outside and see if they need any help getting the tent set up."

"Of course," Nancy said.

As Beth reached the door, she thought she heard Nancy saying something about being rude but it was said so low Beth couldn't be sure.

She hurried outside and scanned the large yard. On the other side of the driveway was a huge barn. Beth doubted they were in there, so she headed around to the back of the house.

The first thing she noticed when she rounded the corner were the flowers. Drew hadn't been exaggerating. There were flowers everywhere—rows and rows of them in a variety of colors. Beth took a minute to enjoy the view before continuing her search for Drew.

When she passed the small wooden shed, she spotted them. They were farther away than she thought they'd be. It would be quite a trek in the dark if they needed to visit the house for any reason.

Unsure of her footing, Beth took her time crossing the grassy area that stood between her and the men. They had their backs to her as she approached.

"Seems serious," Bill said. Beth had no idea what they were talking about. Were they talking about the farm? Something to do with Drew's job?

Nope. He wasn't.

"It is. I love her."

At Drew's confession, Beth's heart skipped a beat. She knew then that they were talking about her.

Bill nodded. "I figured as much. Even with your mother's nagging, I doubt you'd bring a woman home to meet us unless she was pretty important to you."

If Beth thought Drew's last statement shocked her, his next one nearly had her running all the way back to St. Louis. "I want to spend the rest of my life with her."

She must have made a sound because they both turned their heads in her direction. A long silence followed and by the look on Drew's face, he knew she'd overheard.

With a subtle cough, Drew's father excused himself and left the two of them alone. Neither spoke right away. What was there to say? How did she respond to that? They hadn't even been together for a month yet. He couldn't love her. And he absolutely couldn't be thinking about marriage so soon. They didn't even know each other that well.

"Beth? Will you say something, please?" Drew asked.

"I'm trying to convince myself that I didn't just hear what you said."

He looked down at the ground and then back at her. "I do love you."

"How—"

"I've loved you for a while. Probably since before our first date. I didn't think you were ready to hear it so . . . so I didn't say anything."

She was trying to take it all in. A voice in the back of her mind screamed that he was lying—that he was saying it to manipulate her—but Beth knew that was only her fear talking. Drew had no reason to lie. She'd committed to their relationship. "And the other?"

Drew took a step closer to her. "The part about me wanting to spend the rest of my life with you?"

Beth swallowed. "Yes. You c-can't . . . you can't mean that."

The next thing she knew, he was standing close enough to touch her. Drew reached for her hands. "I do."

She opened her mouth to protest, and he cut her off. "I know you're not ready. Like you said, this thing between us is still new. But my dad always told me that one day I'd just know. He was right."

So many emotions were racing around inside her. She wanted to believe him. The part of her that had been falling for him since the first time he sat down beside her at Serpent's Kiss wanted everything he said to be true. Experience had taught her different, though. Beth had thought she was closing in on the dream before and had it blow up in her face. Dating Drew had been a huge risk for her. She couldn't give anything more. Not right now. It was just too soon. "I'm sorry. I can't . . ."

He moved closer. "I'm not asking you to. No pressure, Beth. I'll wait as long as you need to feel comfortable."

"And if I never do?"

Drew cupped the side of her face and looked her straight in the eye. "I'll still be here."

***

He'd thought she was inside with his mom. If he'd had any idea that she was standing close enough to hear what he'd said to his father, Drew never would have said it.

"You don't mean that."

"Yes. I do mean it." Drew wished he could make her understand. He'd played the field, as it were. At no point in time had he ever felt anything near what he felt for Beth with any other woman.

"Hey."

Drew glanced over Beth's shoulder. Seth was striding toward them.

"I need . . . I need to think," she whispered.

He felt her start to back away. Instinct made him grasp her hands tighter, but then he let go. Whatever was going through her

251

mind, they wouldn't be able to discuss it with Seth there. So like it or not, Drew watched as Beth turned and walked away, leaving him standing alone as his brother drew closer.

Seth tilted his head in the direction of Beth's retreating back. "Lovers' spat?"

"Not exactly." Drew returned to what he'd been working on before Beth's arrival—securing their tent.

His brother surprised him by pitching in to help.

They worked side by side making sure everything was set up properly. Seth was keeping his own counsel for the time being, but Drew knew that wouldn't last. His brother had an opinion about everything. He was sure Beth was no exception.

Finished, Drew tossed their overnight bags inside the tent and began scrounging the area for kindling. It was a warm day and should be a nice night. That didn't mean they wouldn't want a fire if they decided to sit outside the tent after the sun went down. It was always good to be prepared.

Seth followed him over to the line of trees, but made no move to help with the gathering of wood. "A little soon to be bringing someone home to meet Mom and Dad, don't you think?"

"Nope."

"Mom says she owns a business."

Drew shot a glare in his brother's direction. "Yes. A café."

"Is it solid? Have you seen her financials?"

That brought his progress to a halt. Drew turned around to face his brother. "Why in the world would I ask to see the financial records of my girlfriend's business?"

"To make sure she and her business can stand on their own two feet." The way Seth said it made it sound as if that should have been obvious.

"It's her business, not mine."

"I can do some digging when I get home. I'm sure I can find—"

"No." Drew was getting angry.

"No?"

"That's right. No. You stay out of her finances and anything else of hers. It's none of your business." Drew didn't even want to hazard a guess as to how it would look to Beth if she found out his brother had been digging around in her private life. Not to mention the very real possibility that his brother could make a connection with

Serpent's Kiss. Katrina was good at keeping the nature of the club under wraps but he wouldn't put it past his brother to stake out the place.

Seth frowned. "You can never be too careful. It's always good to err on the side of caution in these—"

"I said no."

He pressed his lips together in displeasure.

Drew didn't care. All he wanted to do was go find Beth and get her to talk to him. Instead he was here listening to his brother spout off some insanity about Beth and her money.

"Mom wanted me to ask if you and your girlfriend would be joining us for dinner or if you were planning to fend for yourselves tonight?" Seth's voice was tight, but Drew was happy that his brother was dropping the subject.

"We'll be there." At least, Drew was hoping they would be. That, of course, had a lot to do with Beth.

The sound of retreating footsteps was the only indication that his brother had left. While Drew continued to gather sticks, Seth's line of questioning lingered. Why would he care if Beth had money or not? It wasn't as if Drew was wealthy. He made a good living and had some savings, but that was about it.

Eventually he became frustrated with that line of thinking—it wasn't getting him anywhere anyway—and his thoughts drifted back to Beth. She said she needed to think. In his experience, when a female said that it was rarely a good thing. Granted, Beth wasn't like any of the other women he'd had in his life, but he wasn't willing to sit by and watch her fear convince her that they shouldn't be together.

He dropped an armful of wood near the campsite, cleaned the dirt from his hands, and went in search of her. There were a lot of places to hide on the farm. During his childhood, Drew had explored them all. He knew he'd be able to track her down one way or another.

It turned out that she wasn't that difficult to find. She was standing by a fence, petting one of the horses. Drew leaned against the weathered post about a foot away from her and waited. She dropped her hand, and the horse bent his head down to chew on some grass. It was peaceful except for the underlying tension in the air.

"Did you really mean it?" she asked. "That you love me and—"

"Yes."

She nodded.

"Beth, I'm not asking for anything more from you. I like what we have. None of that has to change."

"For now. But eventually you're going to want more." He opened his mouth to speak, but she cut him off. "Don't deny it."

"I wasn't going to." Drew wanted to touch her, but he forced himself to remain where he was. "Can you honestly tell me that you're never going to want more?"

She took a deep breath. "Yes. I do want more. Someday."

With that, he couldn't hold back any longer. Closing the distance between them, he turned her to face him. "Then what's the problem? Me? Can you not see yourself growing old with me?"

A smile tugged at her lips. "You know that's not it."

"I'll make you a promise, okay? When you're ready, you let me know. No pressure."

"No pressure, huh?" she asked, finally beginning to relax.

He circled his arms around her waist and pulled her against his chest. "None at all. But I should warn you. When you do give me the green light, all bets are off. I plan on going all out when I propose."

"It's talk like that that makes my blood pressure spike."

Drew kissed her neck and ran his nose along her jaw up to her ear. "Once we're alone in our tent tonight, I'm sure I can do a much better job at elevating your heart rate."

Beth tilted her head back, giving him better access to her neck. He took the invitation gladly. Within a few minutes, she was grasping the back of his head and rubbing against him. It was making it hard to remember that they were standing in the middle of a field on his parents' farm.

"Where are your parents? Your brother?" she asked.

"Mom and Seth are probably in the house. Dad's most likely in the barn." He said all this in between kisses. Beth hadn't stopped her very suggestive movements against him. He really hoped no one came looking for them anytime soon because he wasn't going to be able to walk if she kept it up.

"So we're alone?" She leaned back to look at him.

Drew glanced over his shoulder toward the house. There was no sign of his family. He had no idea what she had in mind, but at this point he was up for just about anything. "Yes."

Beth sank back against the fence and guided him to stand between her spread legs. With a mischievous smile on her face, she popped the button on her jeans. He swallowed as she wrapped her hand around his wrist and brought his hand to rest on her abdomen. Drew met her gaze, thinking she couldn't possibly want him to do what was going through his mind.

She reached behind his head again and jerked him closer. Beth grazed his ear with her teeth before she whispered her command. "Stick your hand down my pants and finger fuck me until I come."

Holy hell. This was really happening.

The thought that they could be caught crossed his mind for a split second, and then it was gone. After what had happened between them, the only thing he wanted to do was connect with her in the most elemental way. If they couldn't make love, then the least he could do was get her off.

He flattened his palm and slid his hand beneath the waistband of her jeans and underneath her panties. Drew had watched her get dressed that morning so he knew exactly what her underwear looked like—red silk with lace in the front that gave him a glimpse of what was underneath. He'd been trying not to think about it during their drive. Given that he could currently feel the scratch of the lace against the back of his hand, it was at the forefront of his mind yet again.

Moist heat coated his fingers as he reached the junction between her legs. Wanting to make sure she was ready, he circled her clit several times, drawing a soft moan from her before dipping his fingers inside her.

The space in which he had to move was limited, but it didn't seem to matter. Beth dug her fingers into his neck and began moving her hips in time with his fingers. Her breathing became labored as she got closer.

"Harder," she demanded.

Drew shifted a little, hoping to change the angle and get a little more leverage. She responded with a high-pitched whine that resonated from her throat. Then her knees begin to buckle as pleasure took over. With his free hand, he increased his hold on her, keeping her upright.

Less than a minute later, she buried her head in his neck and released a near silent scream. He could feel her heart pounding in her chest. To be honest, his was pounding as well. Drew didn't know a man alive who could do what he had just done and remain unaffected.

She hummed and turned her head to find his lips. The kiss was full of passion and promise. Drew may not have gotten off himself but that was all right. He was able to serve her needs.

He had no idea how long they'd been kissing when a throat cleared behind him. It was only then that he realized his hand was still shoved down Beth's pants. Trying not to make it obvious what he was doing and where his hand had been, Drew turned to the side, blocking his father's view. He was hoping his dad would think his arm was behind her back or even cupping her ass. Both of those options were less awkward than the reality.

"Sorry to interrupt, but I was hoping I could get you to help me with something in the barn before dinner." His father stood at least ten paces away from them, probably not wanting to get any closer once he'd realized they were making out and not merely talking.

Drew nodded, trying to clear his head. "Sure. I'll be up in a minute."

Not questioning why Drew didn't come right away, his father turned back toward the barn.

"Guess it's a good thing I didn't go down on you, huh?" Beth said, smiling.

Laughing, he removed his hand and helped her right herself. "Yeah. Good thing."

When he left Beth to go in search of his father, she was in much better spirits. He was hoping it would stay that way, but he wasn't naïve enough to think that her doubts wouldn't resurface in the future. Drew was beginning to realize that when she felt unsure of herself, Beth tended to go toward the sexual side—the place she knew she had control. He understood it, but he didn't like it. The only thing he could do was hope that one day she felt comfortable enough with him and herself to overcome whatever was holding her back.

Chapter 28

Seth was quiet during dinner, even for him. Drew had no idea what his deal was. He would like to think it was brotherly concern.

Beth, at least, seemed to be better. She was smiling and laughing at his father's jokes. It was progress.

They stayed to help his mother clean up and prep some things for the next day. Usually it was only him in the kitchen with his mom slicing things up the night before. Having Beth there working beside him felt good.

Once everything was as ready as it was going to get for the evening, Drew and Beth made their way back to the makeshift campsite. With a little bit of daylight left, he built a small fire for the two of them. The flames licked at the kindling, catching easily, so he added some larger logs.

She sat down on a large rock to his left. "I'm imagining you doing this as a little boy."

Drew smiled. "It never gets old." He leaned back on his heels and stared into the flame. There was something about fire that had always appealed to him—the way it moved and flowed.

For a long while nothing could be heard but the sounds of the night surrounding them and the crackling of the fire. He knew her mind had to be going a mile a minute and he wanted to give her time to work through whatever it was she was contemplating.

While she was thinking, Drew let his mind drift to the afternoon he'd spent with his father. It had been a while since he'd mucked out stalls and put new hay down, but it had felt good to exert some energy after getting Beth off like that. After he'd said goodbye to her, he'd turned on the hose his mom used to water her flowers and washed his hands. It had helped, but until he'd washed up for dinner there was still a faint scent of her on his fingers.

He heard her move and figured she must be chilly, and decided to scoot closer to the heat of the fire. Then he felt her run her hand along the inside of his leg. She wasn't cold.

Drew turned to face her and that's when she kissed him. This wasn't a kiss where one could mistake its meaning. Her mouth was pressing against his with such force that his teeth were hurting. Even still, his cock responded. How could it not? The memory of her coming by his hand earlier had been on his mind moments before. Of course, it didn't help that her palm was also pressed against his groin.

"Beth?"

She barely removed her lips to respond. "No talking."

Thinking was becoming difficult, but this didn't feel right. He'd let her sidetrack their discussion with sex earlier. Drew couldn't let her do it again. When Beth lifted her leg to straddle him, he knew he had to act quickly or all his good intentions would go out the window.

"Red," he gasped.

Drew knew exactly when what he'd said registered. Her entire body froze. She pulled back and stared at him with eyes wide.

He knew he had to explain. "We can't, Beth. Not like this. You're using this"—Drew gestured down to where her hand still hovered all too close to his erection—"not to talk about what happened earlier."

Without a word, Beth removed herself from his lap and stood. He'd wanted her to stop pushing him away emotionally with sex, not for her to physically go away.

She looked down at the fire. Drew waited, hoping she'd share with him what she was feeling. They would never make it past this if she kept it inside.

As the minutes passed, he began to think that maybe safewording hadn't been the best idea. Instead of opening up, she appeared to be shutting down.

"I'm going to bed. Good night." The words were uttered without looking at him. Drew knew she was hurting, but he had no idea how to make it better so he let her go into the tent without him.

He rubbed his hand over his face in frustration. This wasn't how he'd imagined spending the night with her.

When he couldn't stand it any longer, he doused the fire, and climbed into the tent. Beth was on her side, facing away from him. He kicked off his shoes and lay down beside her. She didn't move— not even a little—so he didn't think she was asleep.

Knowing he was going to have to be the one to break the ice, he rolled over and placed a hand on her hip.

Beth flinched. Any doubt he'd had that she was awake vanished.

Although he wanted to make her talk about it, he knew she had to do it on her own time and in her own way. Drew meant what he'd said earlier. He would wait as long as it took. All he wanted her to do was talk to him.

"I don't . . ." Beth sighed. "I don't want you to think that I don't care about you."

"I don't think that." Drew didn't want her to worry about what he might think. This wasn't about him. It was about her.

She turned to face him. It was dark inside the tent and he couldn't see her expression, but he heard the emotion behind her words and he was pretty sure she was either crying or close to it. "I wish I could say it back. I just . . . I can't."

Unable to resist, he reached out for her, and folded her into his embrace.

Beth tucked her head into his shoulder and shuddered. She put on a good front most of the time. Whether she realized it or not, letting him see her this vulnerable said more about her feelings for him than any words.

Drew held her until he heard her breathing change. Kissing her temple, he shifted them both so that he could lie on his back yet still hold her against him. Beth loved him. He knew it in the very core of his being. She might not be able to admit it to herself yet, but he knew she'd get there eventually.

Closing his eyes, he let the warmth of her body seep into his muscles and take everything negative that had happened that day away. He'd told the absolute truth when he'd said he wanted to spend the rest of his life with her. Beth was the first person Drew thought about when he woke up every morning and she starred in his dreams every night. He couldn't think of anything better than spending the rest of his days worshiping her in every way possible.

***

The rise and fall of Drew's chest was the first thing to enter into Beth's awareness as she awoke early the next morning. She had no recollection of moving into this position with her head resting over his heart. The last thing she did remember was feeling confused about everything except for how good it felt to be wrapped up in his arms. Crazy, considering that the whole reason for her distress in the first place was that she couldn't tell him that she loved him back. Knowing that she needed some space before she had to face him again, she carefully extracted herself from his warmth and crawled out of the tent.

It was a brisk morning. The wind blew just enough to make her shiver. Beth knew she could rebuild the fire he'd started the night before—there was still a small pile of wood to her right. If she did that, however, Drew would wake up and she'd be right back where she started. The day ahead would be stressful enough as it was. She didn't want to add to it.

With that in mind, she hugged herself and headed toward the house. Hopefully, Nancy would be up getting things ready for the party and Beth could help. Baking always relaxed her and she was counting on it to provide some much-needed balance before people started to arrive.

Drew found her almost an hour later rolling out piecrust. He walked up to her and gave her a kiss on the cheek. It was completely innocent, but it still made her pulse quicken.

"I woke up and you were gone." A simple statement full of meaning. He'd thought she'd left.

She looked up at him and lowered her voice so that only he would hear. "I needed some space. And I figured your mom might need some help getting things ready."

He scanned her face as if he could see into the inner workings of her soul. Instead of making her uncomfortable, it had her fighting to hold onto coherent thought. What was it about him that twisted her insides into knots?

Seth stumbled into the kitchen looking for coffee, pulling them both out of the bubble that they had created. Beth wasn't sure if she was happy with the interruption or not. She knew things weren't settled with Drew—not by a long shot—but she couldn't deal with her feelings right now. Not with his family around and everything else that went with it.

The morning flew by as they all worked together, even Seth, to set things up for the big party. There were two long tables placed in the side yard along with ten smaller tables surrounded by as many chairs as would fit around them. She'd thought for sure that the setup was more than enough for any barbecue, but she was wrong. A little before noon people began arriving. By twelve thirty, cars lined both sides of the long driveway and there were people everywhere.

"You doing all right?" Drew asked, coming to stand beside her.

"Yeah. I didn't think there'd be this many people, though." If she had to guess, there were at least fifty people present.

He shrugged. "In a rural area like this, a barbecue is a big deal and my parents invite all the neighbors and local farmers. There'll probably be a few more late arrivals before it's all said and done."

"More?" He couldn't be serious.

Drew chuckled. "Most likely. The Clarks are notorious for being late to stuff like this."

She felt like a fish out of water. Other than Drew and to some extent his family, Beth didn't know anyone here.

What she was feeling must have shown on her face because Drew laced his fingers through hers and squeezed. Beth was grateful for the support—especially after this morning. He could have easily left her to her own devices.

It turned out Drew was right. Three more families showed up with covered dishes and lawn chairs in tow. His dad fired up two separate grills and filled them with hamburgers, hot dogs, and brats. The smell of cooking meat filled the yard and seemed to animate the already lively conversations that were taking place among the neighbors.

By the time the last car backed out of the drive, Beth was exhausted. Over the previous eight hours, she'd met more people than she could ever hope to keep track of. Drew introduced her to everyone in attendance. He knew them all by name with the exception of two little girls that were new additions to their families. Beth didn't even think she knew that many people, and certainly not with the ease of familiarity everyone at the barbecue displayed.

"I wish you both didn't have to head back tonight," Nancy said as she and Drew walked toward where Beth was standing.

He gave his mother a kiss on the cheek. "Unfortunately, we both have to work tomorrow."

Nancy sighed as her husband came up to stand beside her. "Are you sure you have everything?"

"Yep. I loaded all our stuff from the campsite into the car this morning."

Seeming not to want to say goodbye, Nancy pulled her son in for a hug. "You take care of yourself, you hear?"

When she released him, Bill moved in to embrace his son. "Stay safe."

Drew's parents might both support their son's decision to become a firefighter, but that didn't mean they didn't worry about him. Then again, Beth knew her parents worried about her, too. It wasn't the same, but she figured all parents who loved their children worried about them to some degree.

Seth jogged down the front steps to join them. He'd been pleasant to her during the barbecue, but he still wasn't overly friendly. She had no idea why and wondered if maybe Drew did. They'd gotten sidetracked and she'd forgotten to ask him about it.

"Are you heading back to the city tonight?" Drew asked his brother.

"Nah. I'll get up early and drive back in the morning. These things always wear me out. I need a good night's sleep first." It was the most Beth had heard Seth say since she'd met him.

"I wish we could as well, but work beckons."

"You'll call me when you get home? Let me know you made it back in one piece?" Nancy asked.

Drew grinned. "Don't I always?"

It was getting late and they needed to get on the road. With that in mind, she addressed Nancy and Bill. "It was very nice to meet you. Thank you for having me."

The next thing Beth knew, Drew's mom once again had her locked in a tight, albeit brief, embrace. "You're welcome any time."

When Nancy stepped back, Bill surprised Beth with a hearty

hug as well. "Make sure my boy treats you right, now. If not, you let me know. I'll set him straight."

Drew's father winked at her, and she laughed. She liked Bill and Nancy. Not only because they were her boyfriend's parents, but also because they were good people.

Bill stepped closer to Drew and she discovered Seth standing in front of her. Beth really hoped he wasn't going to hug her, too. Although from Drew's parents it was a little awkward, from his brother it would have seemed less than genuine.

"Beth." He said it as if her name held some sort of hidden meaning.

Two could play at that game. "Seth."

Amusement lit his face and one side of his mouth pulled up in the closest thing she'd seen to a smile from him. "Have a safe trip."

Not what she'd been expecting, but she'd take it. "Thank you."

"You ready?" Drew asked.

She turned her attention away from Seth and nodded.

It took them another five minutes to make it down the driveway and head home as there was another full round of goodbyes from Drew's parents. He only made the drive home a few times a year and according to his mother, that wasn't enough. She got the impression that Nancy was hoping Beth could persuade her son to come see them more often.

The back roads were dark and there was even less to see than there had been the day before. Drew was quiet behind the wheel. It wasn't until they reached the highway that he spoke. "Did you enjoy the barbecue?"

"Yes. Everyone was very nice and welcoming."

He nodded. "That's a small town for you. I've known most of them all my life."

"Sounds nice." Growing up in the suburbs, most neighbors kept to themselves. Sure, you might see them outside mowing their lawn or tending to flowerbeds and you would wave, but it wasn't as if you invited them to dinner. Even if you did, it was nothing like what Drew's parents had put on.

Silence filled the car again for several more miles before Drew cleared his throat. "Did my brother . . . did Seth say anything to you?"

She shrugged. "Not really. In fact, I'm not sure he said more than ten words to me."

"Don't let him get to you. He knows how to push people's buttons. It's what he does for a living." Drew sighed. "And for some godforsaken reason, he thinks he has to look out for me or something."

"He's your brother."

Drew glanced over at her. "I'm twenty-eight years old. If I needed a big brother to look out for me, it was when I was growing up. Not now."

"I'm sure he has his reasons." Why she was siding with Seth—whom she hadn't really been all that impressed with—she had no idea.

"He does. Or at least, he thinks he does." Drew pressed his lips together. "Yesterday after you walked off, he was grilling me about you. Or about your financials anyway."

"Me? Why?" That made no sense. Beth had never met Drew's brother before he'd strolled into the kitchen.

"No idea. I got the impression that he thought you may be trying to take advantage of me or something."

Beth furrowed her brow.

"I wouldn't worry about it. It's probably just Seth being Seth. He's always been a numbers guy. Maybe he's only being like this because I brought you home. He knows if I did that you have to be pretty important to me." And they were back to the one subject she really didn't want to talk about.

But Drew didn't go there. Instead he reached for her hand and tangled their fingers together. It was a simple gesture, but it was exactly what she needed. How was she not to fall in love with him?"

It took them a little over an hour to get home. He drove up to her house and parked the vehicle along the curb. "Do you want me to come in?"

Did she? For all her insistence that she wanted space, the thought of him not being in her bed caused a lump in her throat. She should send him home. If for no other reason but to prove to herself that she didn't need him as much as it felt like she did.

She couldn't do it, though. "Yes."

He retrieved their bags from the trunk and followed her up the walkway to her front door. It wasn't too late. She could still tell him to go home.

Then she felt his breath on the back of her neck. Desire shot through her, settling at the junction between her legs. Last night was the first time they'd slept next to each other and not fooled around. She wanted him. And whether she liked it or not, she needed him.

Turning the lock, she opened the door and stepped over the threshold. As soon as they were both inside with the door closed firmly behind them, she faced him and brought his mouth down to hers.

Drew dropped their bags and circled his arms around her, resting one hand on her ass.

Beth drew back enough to look into his eyes. He'd rejected her last night. She was hoping he understood her need and wouldn't do it again tonight.

When she didn't see any hesitation from him, she reached behind her and took hold of the hand he had groping his favorite body part. As much as she wanted to fuck him and forget the swirl of emotions, she needed to make love to him. Everything else—all the analyzing of what it all meant—would have to wait until tomorrow.

Chapter 29

Things returned to normal over the next week . . . or as normal as they were going to get until Beth could figure out her feelings. Drew was trying to give her time. He hadn't brought up the subject of their future again, but she could tell he was frustrated. The stalemate they were locked in was entirely her fault.

Although he'd spent the night with her on Monday, he'd told her he had some things to do on his day off on Wednesday and might be out late so he didn't come over. With him working on Thursday, she didn't get to see him again until Friday. He picked her up for dinner and then they made their way to Serpent's Kiss.

It felt as if it had been more than a week since they'd been inside the club. She took a look around to see who was there. Jeff had some sort of work function, so she knew he and Nicole wouldn't be making an appearance. Drew's friends Allison and John were across the room and Daniel was at one of the bar tables chatting with a small group of Doms.

When Beth's gaze landed on Katrina, Beth blew out a breath and turned to Drew. "Why don't you go get us something to drink and see if you can find Allison and John? I'll join you in a few minutes. I need to talk to Katrina about something first."

He raised his eyebrows slightly, but after a moment, he nodded. "Do you want your usual?"

Beth nodded. "Yes, please."

She watched his retreating back and knew she had to figure this out soon. Drew was a great guy and she knew she could trust him. But knowing it and believing it were two different things.

Katrina was finishing up a conversation with a man Beth didn't recognize. She guessed he was a new member. He looked to be not much older than Beth, but he had a cane. Considering he appeared to be in fairly good shape, the cane seemed out of place.

"Beth," Katrina greeted. "I'd like you to meet Alexander. He just moved to St. Louis last week."

He shifted his weight to offer her his hand and Beth realized he must be recovering from some sort of injury. "It's very nice to meet you, Beth."

"You, too." Although she really did want to talk to Katrina, Beth was curious about this new arrival. It wasn't often that someone moved into town one week and joined a private kink club the next. "What brings you to St. Louis?"

Something passed across his face before he answered. "It's a long story, but I made a promise to a buddy of mine."

"And that promise was moving to St. Louis?" She knew she was being nosy, but considering his cryptic response how could she not be?

He chuckled. "Not exactly. It's more that he wanted me to give something to someone and I'm here trying to find them."

"Does that mean you're just passing through?" If that was the case, it still didn't make sense as to why he'd joined Serpent's Kiss.

"I haven't decided. So far, I'm enjoying the city. I might decide to stay and open a practice here."

"Lawyer?" she asked.

"No. I'm a doctor. Spent nearly ten years in the army before this"—he tapped his leg with his cane—"forced me out."

Beth supposed that explained the cane. And his age. "I'm sorry to hear that. Hopefully you'll like it here and decide to stick around."

"That is a very real possibility." He shifted his weight again as if his leg was bothering him. "Now, if you'll excuse me ladies. I need to sit down for a while and get off my leg. It's been a long day and I'm afraid I've pushed myself more than I should."

She watched him walk toward the bar and noticed a small limp. "Dom?"

Katrina nodded. "He'll be a good addition to the club, I think."

"If he sticks around."

"We'll see." Katrina shrugged as if it was no big deal either way. "And how are you and your new sub doing?"

"Good."

Beth drew out the word and Katrina picked up on it. "You don't seem too confident."

When she'd decided to talk to Katrina, Beth hadn't considered how she'd broach the subject with the club mistress. Nicole may have been her best friend, but she and Katrina had always had a good relationship. In the beginning, when Beth had no clue what she was doing, Katrina had helped her with Ben. Beth trusted Katrina's advice. "I wanted to ask you something . . . personal."

Katrina cocked her head to the side. "And what would that be?"

The more she thought about it, the more Beth thought this wasn't such a good idea. "Never mind."

"Beth. It isn't as if we just met. If you want to ask me something, ask me. I can always tell you it's none of your business." She smiled to soften the impact of her words.

"And you may very well do just that."

"Never know if you don't ask," Katrina said.

"Okay. Well . . . how did you know your husband was 'the one'?" Saying it out loud made her feel silly.

Katrina's eyes went wide and flashed in Drew's direction. "Really? That's wonderful, Beth."

"Is it? I don't know." Beth chewed on the inside of her cheek. "That's why I wanted to know how you *knew*."

It took Katrina a moment to answer. "I'm not sure I can really help you. My relationship with my late husband was complicated, especially during the last few years. But to answer your question, it was more a feeling that I didn't want to be without him. For all of our issues, he had a way of making me feel as if I were the only woman in the room."

Beth nodded.

Katrina placed a comforting hand on Beth's arm. "Are things not going well with Drew?"

"No. I like him. A lot."

"But?"

"But nothing, really. I want to be with him all the time even though I know that's probably not healthy."

She smirked. "So what you're saying is that you're in love."

Beth frowned.

"That isn't a good thing?" Katrina looked confused.

"It's just so fast. Everything with us seems to be going at lightning speed."

"Love takes as long as it takes." Katrina shrugged. "It isn't always practical. I learned that the hard way."

It was a lot to think about. As much as she hated to admit it, Beth was pretty sure she was in love with Drew. That didn't mean confronting it didn't scare her half to death.

"Look, don't stress too much about it. Things will work out the way they're meant to."

Katrina's gaze flickered to the right and Beth turned her head to see what had caught her attention. Nothing immediately stood out until she realized that Ryan was dancing with Madi, another one of the club's Femdoms. Normally this wouldn't be a big deal—Madi danced with a lot of the single guys, Dom or sub. The look on Katrina's face, though, made Beth think she was missing something.

Then she remembered the wax play demonstration Katrina did and her thinking it was odd that Ryan hadn't been involved. Something had obviously happened between Ryan and Katrina. Beth just had no idea what. She got the impression no one else at the club did either.

"Something wrong?" Beth asked. Since she'd been dumping her problems on Katrina, she figured it was only right to give her the opening to do the same.

She shook her head and smiled. "Not at all."

"Well, if you ever want to talk, I'm willing to listen. Heaven knows you've been privy to more than your share from me."

"Thank you. I appreciate the offer and will keep that in mind." Beth could tell the chances of Katrina reaching out to her were slim.

"I should probably get back to Drew. He's going to think I deserted him."

She started to walk away when Katrina's voice stopped her. "If it makes any difference, I like him. He's much better for you than Ben ever was."

Beth nodded and continued across the room to where Drew sat with his friends. His face was full of questions. She sat down beside him and leaned in to whisper in his ear. "I want you kneeling at my feet."

This was one of those gray areas in their arrangement. He could refuse, but he didn't.

Getting up, he moved to her other side, placed one of the pillows on the floor, and lowered himself onto it. He looked up at her, his eyes still questioning but trusting as well. As Beth combed her fingers through his hair, she felt him relax. Their connection was strong. She could feel the stress of the week melting away as he knelt at her feet.

***

After their conversation on Monday, Drew had had mixed feelings as to what to do. Beth said she needed some space and had shown that by hightailing it into the house to help his mom instead of waking him up. Then she had completely contradicted herself by asking him to stay over that same night.

Throughout his shift on Tuesday, he'd weighed his options. Things could go on as they were and he could pretend nothing had changed, or he could actually give Beth a little space and hope she figured out what she wanted. Neither option appealed to him. He didn't want them hanging in limbo for the rest of their lives, but that warred with his desire to be with her at every possible opportunity.

His crew helped to distract him most of the day, but it was at night when he was lying in his cot that this dilemma hit him full force. He needed to give Beth some time to figure out what exactly she wanted. If that meant putting a little distance between them, he would have to do it. Even if it wasn't what he really wanted.

With all his good intentions, Drew was only able to stay away from her for three days. Honestly, he wasn't sure he would have made it more than two had work not kept him from hopping into his vehicle and going over to see her. It wasn't the sex—although he missed that, too. No, it was Beth herself. He missed the feel of her hands in his hair and that mischievous smile of hers. It only reinforced that she was the one. Drew had never missed a woman like that before.

Beth played with the hair at the base of his neck while she talked with Allison. He was only half paying attention to what they were saying.

He felt something poke him in the leg and he shifted his attention in that direction. John had joined him on the floor and was grinning back at him. Drew could only guess that his friend was mentally saying 'I told you so.' The first night he attended the club the hardest thing for him was seeing the male subs kneeling at their mistress' feet. It felt wrong somehow.

During the course of the night, he watched John do the same thing. His friend had explained the best he could how freeing it was, but Drew wasn't convinced. Of course, then he met Beth and the draw to her had been difficult to explain, even to himself. He wanted to worship her in every way possible.

Drew rolled his eyes at John, letting him know where he could stick his smugness.

His friend chuckled.

"You should talk to Michael," Allison said. "He's a good teacher."

Drew knew who Michael was—everyone in the club did. He was one of the dungeon monitors. What Drew didn't understand was why Beth would want to talk to him. Then again, if he'd been paying attention to their conversation from the start, he would have had his answer.

"I probably should. Drew likes being bound and my experience with rope is limited."

He guessed that answered his question.

Allison lifted her drink to her lips with one hand and ran her nails down John's back with the other. He closed his eyes and let out a hum of contentment. "Haven't you ever seen one of Michael's demonstrations? The man is a true artist."

"No. My . . ." Beth paused. "My previous sub wasn't into rope bondage."

Unease seem to hang in the air for a moment before Allison spoke again. "That's too bad. John has come to enjoy it immensely, haven't you?"

"Yes, Mistress." There was almost a longing in his friend's voice, and Drew wondered if Allison and John would be heading upstairs before the night was over.

The topic of conversation soon shifted from bondage to some television show. Drew lost interest, closed his eyes again, and went back to enjoying the moment. Beth's fingers were hypnotic. It had been a long week, and he felt himself drifting.

"Drew?"

He glanced up. Beth looked worried about something. "What's wrong?"

"I was going to ask you the same thing."

Drew grinned. "I'm fine. More than fine."

She caressed the side of his face, and he leaned into her touch. "I take it you like sitting on the floor at my feet?"

"Yes. John was right. It's liberating." Speaking of John, he was no longer on the floor beside Drew. Allison was gone as well. When had that happened?

Beth bent down and brushed her mouth over his. "I quite like you there myself." She held his gaze and ran the tip of her tongue along the seam of his lips. He opened willingly.

By the time she broke the kiss, the position Drew was in was becoming uncomfortable. His erection was stretching his jeans to the limit.

She lowered her gaze, and he knew she could see how painfully hard he was. "Stay with me tonight."

Although it hadn't been phrased as a question, he knew he had the option. He could always say no. Even if he said yes, there was no guarantee they would have sex. Granted, since this wasn't one of his four days off, he could jack off, but that wasn't even close to what he wanted. It had been four days since he'd felt his cock inside her pussy. If there was the slightest chance that he would get to make love to her, he would take it. "I'll have to stop by my apartment to get some clothes for tomorrow."

Beth kicked off her shoe and brought her foot to rest on top of the bulge in his pants. He sucked in a breath as she started moving her foot in a back and forth motion.

"I'm sorry I ran away."

What? What was she . . .

"I should have stayed in the tent until you woke up."

Drew closed his eyes and tried to concentrate on what she was saying and not what she was doing to his appendage. "It's okay. I-I understand."

She increased the pressure slightly and he opened his eyes. "That's no excuse and I want you to know that I'm sorry."

"B—" He caught himself, but just barely. "Mistress? Please?"

Her breath tickled his ear, only adding to his arousal. "Please what?"

"You're . . . if you keep it up, I'm going to come." He hated to admit it, but it was the truth.

"And would you like that? To come here in front of all these people?"

He took a deep breath, trying to clear his head enough to give her an honest answer. "I don't know."

Beth licked his ear and removed her foot.

Drew stared up at her, not sure if he should be grateful or not that she'd stopped.

She grinned down at him and grazed the side of his face with her fingertips. "Think about it and let me know."

Swallowing, he nodded. It was like with the kneeling. Drew knew what she had done should embarrass the hell out of him. If they'd been anywhere else it would have, he was sure of it. But this wasn't just anywhere. This was a kink club and it wasn't as if he hadn't witnessed subs being made to come before. It didn't happen often on the main floor but Drew had seen it. On his third visit, he observed a female submissive who had been made to wear a chastity device with vibrating dildos filling both her pussy and her ass. Her Dom was able to control it remotely and had spent the entire night turning it off and on.

"And what are you thinking about?" Beth asked.

There was no reason to lie. At the time he'd felt kind of bad for the woman, but now, seeing it from the other side, he wasn't sure if he should have. "I was remembering seeing a sub being made to come here at the club."

Beth's smile grew wider, but she didn't comment.

They didn't stay long after that. It was already after ten and they both had to be up early the next morning. As they walked out of the club, Drew tried to ignore the fact that he was still hard as a rock. Following Beth out and watching her backside swaying side to side in that tight skirt of hers wasn't helping.

Somehow he made it to his apartment, ran inside to grab what he'd need for work the next day, and got back out to his car in under two minutes. Beth knew what was on his mind. She had to. The evidence was front and center for anyone to see.

When they turned onto her street, Beth instructed him to pull his car into her driveway. Normally he parked on the street at the curb, but he wasn't going to argue.

She reached into her purse, and the next thing he knew her garage door was opening. "You can park alongside me."

He shot her a quick glance, and then maneuvered his vehicle in beside hers.

Before he could put the car in park, Beth removed her seat belt and pushed the button to close the garage door. She waited until he shifted gears and turned off the engine before turning in her seat. "Take your seat belt off and push your seat back as far as it will go."

Chapter 30

Drew hesitated and Beth wasn't sure if he was going to do as instructed. Then he reached down and released the lever allowing him to push his seat all the way back. Smiling, she hiked her skirt up around her waist and climbed on top of his lap, straddling him. He placed his hand on her hips to stabilize her when she began sucking on his neck and moving her hips.

"Maybe . . . maybe we should go inside."

"No." She snaked her hand down the front of his shirt until she reached his waistband. "I want you, and I want you now."

He leaned his head back, giving her better access to his neck. "I want you, too, but . . ."

She scraped her teeth over his earlobe as she began working him free of his jeans. "But?"

He groaned and moved his hands down to her legs. Slowly, he started working his way higher until the tips of his fingers were brushing her inner thighs. It was getting hard to concentrate, but there was something she needed him to know first before they went any further. As much as it scared her, Beth knew she needed to own up to her feelings. He'd been nothing but honest and he deserved the same from her.

Taking a deep breath, she grazed the tips of her fingers over the head of his cock and went for it. "I love you."

It took a minute, but she knew exactly when what she'd said registered. Drew froze. The hands that had, moments before, been close to touching the part of her that was wet and throbbing for him were now motionless.

Beth's heart skipped a beat as she waited for his reaction.

Drew turned his head so he could see her. He searched her face and then looked into her eyes. "Say it again."

It wasn't a command. More of a pleading request.

She swallowed nervously, but held his gaze. "I love you."

Doubt flickered across his face. "Beth, please don't say it unless you really mean it. I don't want you to feel . . ."

Beth placed her index finger over his lips and he stopped talking. "I was talking to Katrina tonight and I realized something. When I overheard you telling your dad that you loved me and wanted to spend the rest of your life with me, I was overcome with fear. Fear that it was too soon. That if we admitted how important we were to each other after such a short time then the heartbreak would be even worse when it fell apart." She paused. "But she reminded me that love takes as long as it takes. It doesn't always follow the timetable we think it should."

Removing her finger from over his mouth, she caressed the side of his face. "I'm still scared out of my wits, but you deserve to know how I feel. That I'm emotionally invested in this relationship, too."

His lips curled up in a smile. "I never doubted your commitment, Beth. Never."

She smiled. "Thank you for that."

They sat grinning at each other, enjoying the moment, until he shifted beneath her, drawing her attention back to their current position. Beth's hand was still tucked down the front of his pants and she was still straddling him with her skirt up around her waist.

With a mischievous glint in her eye, she used her free hand to reach between them and push her panties out of the way. "Push your jeans down. I want your cock inside me and I don't want to wait until we get inside."

He swiftly moved to obey. Even in the confines of his vehicle, it didn't take him more than a few seconds to push his pants down around his thighs. His erection popped free and Beth's mouth watered. If they had more space, she would have gone down on him first. As it was, there just wasn't room. Plus, after opening herself up to him like she had, she really needed to feel him inside her.

Drew scooted down some to help with the angle as she positioned herself over his cock. She lowered herself down a little at a time, holding her breath as he filled her. When he was finally in all the way, they stared at each other. This was different. It felt different. Yet it was familiar at the same time. She recognized it for what it was, and also that never once had she felt this way with Ben.

Moisture pooled in her eyes and tumbled down her cheeks. Drew wiped the tears away as they fell. It was such a loving gesture and it only made her flood of emotion worse.

"What is it? Am I hurting you? Is the angle wrong?"

His voice was full of anxiety. She knew she had to do something, so she pressed her mouth against his. He kissed her back even though she knew he was bewildered.

Beth opened her eyes and met his gaze, her lips hovering a breath away from his. "Nothing's wrong. In fact, right now I'm pretty close to perfect."

A lightbulb seemed to go off in his head and he captured her mouth once more in a kiss—this one more passionate than the last— and pulled her against him. Beth could have chastised him or pushed him away, but instead she went with it, kissing him back with an equal amount of enthusiasm.

Gradually, their lower bodies seemed to get with the program and they began grinding against each other. Beth moved her hands under his shirt as she rocked her hips. She felt as if she couldn't get close enough.

Drew seemed to feel the same way. His hands were constantly in motion along her back, ass, and legs. It only drove the flames higher. She was quickly racing toward her climax. Part of her yearned to reach that peak, but there were other parts that didn't want it to end. Beth wanted to stay like this for as long as possible.

They kept kissing and touching. She had no idea how long it went on, but eventually the orgasm knocking at her door was impossible to ignore. Tilting her hips forward slightly, she increased the pressure against her clit with every downward movement. Drew caught on to what she was after and splayed one of his hands on her hip, helping to guide her movements.

As she got closer, she stared into his eyes, doing her best to match her breathing with his. "Breath with me. Come with me."

It was something Beth had read about, synchronizing your breathing with your partner's. She'd tried it once before—with Ben—but he'd never quite gotten it. Drew, however, followed her instructions perfectly. When she inhaled, he did. And when she exhaled, Beth felt his warm breath blow across her moist lips.

Everything else fell away as they moved. She'd always felt a connection with Drew, but this seemed to amplify it. Slowly they climbed, inching toward the finish. When she felt that tightening in her belly, she gasped and his breathing stuttered as well. It was coming, and Beth could tell it was going to be intense. She anchored herself, digging her fingers into his shoulders.

"Beth."

Her name came out as little more than a whisper, but there was so much emotion behind it. Her legs began to shake. Then her arms. It was as if the energy could no longer be contained and was leaking out through her limbs.

Beth's orgasm hit her with a force she'd never imagined to be possible. She screamed, needing to let it out and unable to keep it inside even if she'd tried.

Somewhere in the mental chaos, Beth felt a spasm work its way through Drew's body, but it was only when she floated back to earth that she realized they'd done it. They'd climaxed together, or pretty close to it anyway, and it had been better than she imagined.

Her heart was still pounding in her chest, so she buried her face in the curve of his neck until she was fairly sure she could speak normally again. "Wow."

"Yeah. *Wow*."

His hands roamed up and down her back, making her feel completely safe and content. It was too bad they would have to go inside soon.

***

If not for the cramped position, Drew could have stayed there in his car with Beth on his lap all night. That and the fact that he could feel the evidence of their activities leaking down the inside of his leg.

"We should go inside, but I don't want to move," she said.

Instinctively, he held her closer. "I don't either."

Beth was quiet for several moments. "I meant what I said earlier."

He knew what she was referring to and he grinned. "I know."

After a few more minutes, Beth sighed, and climbed back over to her side of the vehicle. He looked down at his lap and, even in the dim light, he knew that he was going to need a shower.

She rearranged her clothes enough to be decent, and leaned over to kiss him. "Now every time you get into your car for the next few days you're going to be reminded of what we just did."

Tangling his fingers in her hair at the base of her neck, he gazed into her eyes. "I'm not sure I'll ever be able to forget that."

She smiled. "Good."

He waited until she exited the vehicle before reaching into the back to get his bag. By the time he got out of the car, she was already inside. Drew waited at the bottom of the stairs while she walked through the downstairs, making sure the house was locked up for the night, and then followed her to the second floor.

As much as he wanted to ask her to join him in the shower, he didn't. It was edging closer and closer to midnight. Her alarm would go off at five. While he couldn't seem to get enough of Beth, Drew also knew that they both needed their sleep.

After toweling off, he didn't bother to put any clothes on as he made his way back into Beth's bedroom. She was turned on her side, facing away from him. The only part of her he could see clearly was the back of her head and the tops of her shoulders.

It wasn't until he was about to get into bed that he realized she was already asleep. He pulled back the covers and slipped under the blanket. Beth must have felt the movement because she rolled over.

Trying not to wake her, Drew positioned himself as carefully as possible. He thought he'd been successful until he felt her move again—this time she migrated closer to him. Her hand grazed his abdomen before sliding back down on the bed.

Drew lifted her hand—her left hand—and kissed her ring finger. After tonight, he was hoping that one day in the not too distant future she'd agree to marry him. Hearing her say that she loved him had warmed him down to his toes. He just needed to be patient.

He brushed the hair away from her face, and she released a contented sigh. Drew laid his head on his pillow and gently rubbed his thumb along her cheek. "I love you, Beth Davenport. I will burn for you for the rest of my days. All you have to do is say the word and I'm yours forever."

Lowering his hand, he closed his eyes and let sleep claim him.

When the alarm woke him the next morning, he felt the mattress shift under her weight as she reached up to the nightstand to turn it off. Blinking, he opened his eyes and was greeted with the most amazing view of her backside. "Now, that's something I could get used to seeing every morning."

Beth glanced over her shoulder and quirked an eyebrow at him.

He circled his arm around her waist and tugged her down on top of him. Palming her ass, Drew pressed his morning wood against her stomach. She looked so beautiful with her hair all mussed from sleep, which did nothing to help the state he found himself in.

"What do you think you're doing?" There was laughter in her eyes so he knew he wasn't in too much trouble.

"Getting my hands on your delectable ass." He gave her derriere a squeeze.

"Yes, well, this is the only way you're going to be getting your hands on this ass for the next twenty-four hours if we don't get a move on."

Drew groaned.

Beth laughed and extracted herself from his greedy hands. "Think you could use another shower this morning?"

It took only a second for him to realize what she was offering, and less time than that for him to jump out of bed.

She chuckled.

"Did you really think I'd pass up a chance to see you naked and wet?" he asked.

Lifting her tank top over her head, she tossed it into the hamper. His gaze immediately went to her tits. She knew what she was doing, of course, and smirked as she pushed the shorts she'd worn to bed down her legs.

He swallowed. His cock was standing at full attention.

She bent down to pick the clothing up from the floor, making sure she turned enough for him to get a good view of her backside. His erection pulsed and he clenched his fists together. If she kept this up, he wasn't sure he would be able to control himself.

Luckily, she must have realized he was hanging on by a thread because she strolled over to stand in front of him. "Do you like?"

"Very much."

She took hold of his cock and he closed his eyes. "If we had more time, I'd make you earn your release."

Why did the thought of that turn him on so much? "Yes, Mistress."

Beth ran the pad of her thumb over the head of his penis until it began leaking pre-cum. His breathing was already starting to become labored. He was so turned on. It wouldn't take much to send him over the edge. He closed his eyes, enjoying the feel of her hand on him . . . and then she was gone.

Drew opened his eyes and saw she was halfway across the room.

"Are you coming?" she asked.

He moved as fast as his feet would carry him into the bathroom behind her. Whether he came or not would be up to Beth. As they stepped into the enclosure, Drew realized that he hadn't masturbated since that first night with her. He hadn't had any desire to do so.

That wasn't entirely true. Pretty much every time he thought about Beth he ended up aroused. It was a given. The difference was that on some level, he didn't feel it was his right anymore. His body belonged to her as much as his heart did.

Water cascaded down on them and he reached for her loofah and body wash. It had become an unspoken rule between them that when they showered together, he would wash her. Only once had that not happened due to a lack of time and afterward, he'd longed for another opportunity so he could worship her body the way she deserved.

"A penny for your thoughts?" she asked as he ran the sponge up the inside of her thigh.

Drew grinned. "I was thinking about how much I enjoy this. Washing you."

She stepped closer, trapping his hand between them. "So do you like getting dirty or clean better?" Her mouth hovered over the pulse in his neck and he willed her to use her teeth.

"Both."

Beth hummed and sucked the beating flesh into her mouth. He groaned and dropped the sponge in favor of grasping her hips. She wrapped her leg around his waist and he moved his left hand to support her leg.

"Do you want me?" she asked, her teeth worrying his skin.

She raked her nails down his back and he gasped. "Yes."

The next thing he knew, she was anchoring her arms around his neck and pulling herself up. Instinct kicked in and Drew cupped her ass, bringing her in line with his erection.

"Put your cock inside me and show me what it is you want."

He didn't need to be told twice. Turning them, he used the shower wall as support and lined himself up with her entrance. Feeling her muscles contract around him as he pushed inside made him feel as if he'd died and gone to heaven. It was truly a spiritual experience.

Doing as she'd asked, he dug his fingers into her ass and thrust his hips upward. Beth clung to him as he pounded into her against the wall. Soon he was sweating and it had nothing to do with the steam coming off the shower.

Beth must have been as primed as he was because it didn't take long before she reached between them and began rubbing her clit.

"I love it when you do that."

She gripped the back of his neck hard. "You like knowing I'm pleasuring myself?"

"Yes." It was all he could do to hold on to his sanity knowing he was fucking her up against a wall while she was trying to make herself come.

Drew thought he felt her grin, but he wasn't sure. Her fingers were forked so that with each thrust, she rubbed him and her clit at the same time. He could feel his balls tightening.

Then, without warning, she threw her head back and released a loud moan as she reached her climax. He felt her muscles hug his cock and watched her face turn a bright shade of red.

He clenched his jaw, waiting, hoping she would give him permission to come. As he waited, he kept up a steady movement, not sure if he should stop or keep going. Finally, she met his gaze. There was something in her expression that he didn't like.

"Let me down."

Drew guessed that was his answer. He shouldn't be surprised. She'd let him orgasm every time they'd had sex so far. He knew sooner or later, she'd decide otherwise.

Once her feet were back on the ground, Drew tried his best to calm himself down. That was until she shocked the hell out of him with her next command. "Use your hand. I want to see you make yourself come for me."

She was serious, so after a moment, he reached down and took his cock in his right hand. Beth picked up the loofah, giving him another stellar view of her butt. He groaned and increased his pace. At this rate, it wouldn't take him long. He'd been on the edge when he'd been inside her.

With the sponge in hand, Beth began washing the evidence of their morning activities from her body. She made a show of it, teasing him. Man, he loved her.

When she reached between her legs, that was it for him. He came with a grunt, spilling his cum on the tile below his feet.

Getting out of the shower several minutes later, Beth handed him a towel. "Next time maybe you'll rethink molesting me first thing in the morning."

He was confused. Then again, he wasn't sure all the blood had made it back to his head yet. "Why?"

Beth wound a towel around her head and used another on her body. "Cocky boys don't get to come inside their mistresses. Remember that," she said as she strolled out of the bathroom.

Drew was left speechless for a moment, and then he laughed. He doubted life with Beth would ever be predictable, and he was perfectly okay with that.

Chapter 31

Beth managed to make it to work on time. How, she didn't know. Sex in the shower had taken longer than anticipated, but she and Drew had worked together to make breakfast and she was able to get out the door in record time. That was good because she had plans for her evening and she didn't want to be stuck at work any later than she needed to be.

Granted, that was happening less and less since Beth had hired Grace. She was a good worker. A little shy, but polite and more than competent. In her short time at the café, Beth had learned that Grace had lost her husband about six months ago. He was a soldier killed overseas. Beth hadn't gotten any details. She wasn't sure Grace could have held it together long enough to give them to her.

The woman in question walked into the kitchen with an empty tray. "We ran out of blueberry muffins."

Nodding, Beth motioned toward the sink. "It's too late in the day to make any more. That's the second time this week, though. I might have to reconsider how many we're making each day."

Grace did as instructed and then joined Beth at the counter. "Tommy says things are slowing down out there so he doesn't need me."

"Okay. Well, why don't you go check on the customers and then you can start getting things cleaned up back here. Maybe we can all get out of here a little early today."

Things worked in their favor, and they were able to get everything cleaned and closed down before three o'clock. Having a third person made a huge difference.

As Beth was leaving the cafe, her cell phone rang. She looked at the caller ID, but didn't recognize the number. It was local, though, and just in case it was Drew, she answered. "Hello?"

"Hello, Beth. It's Seth Parker. Drew's brother. I was hoping I could speak with you."

Beth wasn't sure she wanted to talk to Drew's brother after the way he'd been the weekend before, but she had to admit she was curious. "Okay. Go ahead."

"I'd rather talk in person."

Her defenses went up. "Your brother's working today, but I'm sure we could arrange—"

"I'd prefer it be just the two of us, if you didn't mind. I'm out in front of your business now if you have time."

He was here? Now? She glanced over her shoulder expecting him to magically appear, but no one was there. "All right. Give me ten minutes and I'll meet you out front."

She hung up the phone and turned around to find Tommy standing there. "Everything, okay?"

"Yeah. Everything's fine. You ready to go?" she asked.

They walked out the back door and she locked it behind her. Tommy climbed in his car, and she waved goodbye to him as he drove off. Grace had an appointment at three she couldn't reschedule, so Beth had sent her home as soon as they'd closed since they were caught up.

Beth waited until Tommy's car was out of sight before getting into her vehicle and driving around to the front of the building. Seth was there, leaning up against the ledge of one of the café's large windows. She parked along the curb and climbed out to see what he wanted.

"I was hoping I'd catch you before you closed but I had a meeting that ran late," he said, pushing away from the building.

He looked like an older version of Drew, but the way he carried himself was quite different. Drew could act full of himself sometimes, but he was also very approachable. Beth imagined Seth went after what he wanted and didn't take no for an answer. A profitable skill for a lawyer, no doubt, but completely undesirable in a mate as far as Beth was concerned.

"What can I do for you?" Beth figured it was better to cut to the chase.

"I'm told I owe you an apology."

That surprised her.

Clearly, her shock showed on her face because he continued. "After you left, both my parents laid into me about how rude I'd been to you. And then my brother called to harass me as well."

Drew had called him? When?

"I guess he didn't tell you that."

"No. He didn't." Beth wasn't sure if that was a good thing or not, but she wasn't going to let that sidetrack her. "So you came to apologize because your parents and your brother told you to?"

Seth grinned. "No. But I think you already know that."

She did. Seth didn't strike her as someone who bowed to pressure from anyone, even his family.

"I'm here because I wanted to see for myself if you were who you said you were."

"What's that supposed to mean? Who exactly did you think I was?"

He put his hands in his pockets. "I didn't know. That was the point. I didn't even know you'd be there until I walked into the kitchen and found you sitting at my mom's table."

"So what you're trying to tell me is that because my presence surprised you, you decided to be a jerk."

"You don't pull any punches, do you?" Seth chuckled. "I can see why Drew likes you."

Beth wasn't sure if she should be flattered or not.

"I do apologize if I acted like a jerk. Drew hasn't had the best history with women and it worried me when he'd suddenly brought one home to meet us. I wanted to make sure you weren't taking advantage of him."

As good as that sounded, Beth wasn't sure she believed him. "You were trying to protect your brother? Don't you think he's old enough to do that on his own?"

"You'd think so, wouldn't you, but my baby brother tends to see the best in people."

Beth knew there had to be a story there, but quite frankly, she didn't care. Her relationship with Drew was none of Seth's business. "If you have an issue with your brother being with me then you need to talk to him."

"Oh, I have. As a matter of fact, I just came from there. He wouldn't hear any of it. Told me to mind my own damn business." Beth sensed a level of pride there. She wasn't sure she would ever understand Seth Parker.

"Maybe you should listen to him."

Seth opened his mouth to comment, but someone came around the corner and cut him off. "Having an afternoon rendezvous? Is this your new boy-toy, then?"

She spun around to find Ben striding toward them. He looked determined, and Beth knew there was little chance she'd be able to get rid of him this time without allowing him to say his piece. "What are you doing here, Ben?"

"I came to talk to you." He looked Seth up and down. "Is this him? I heard you were with someone new."

Drew's brother didn't flinch. He stared Ben down with a level of contempt that had been missing from her first encounter with Seth. "And you are?"

"I'm her ex."

Seth crossed his arms over his chest and she had to admit it made him much more intimidating. "If you're her ex, then why are you here demanding to know who she's having a conversation with outside of her own restaurant?"

"That's none of your business," Ben snapped.

"Since you've barged into our discussion, you've made it my business." Seth never raised his voice. He was chillingly calm.

Ben continued to stare at Seth until he realized it wasn't going to get him anywhere and refocused his attention on Beth. "This is a waste of time. I need to talk to you."

"So you said." She sighed. "Go ahead. I'm listening."

He glanced over at Seth. "Alone."

She opened her mouth, but Seth interrupted her. "No. If you have something to say to her, then you can say it here in front of me. Otherwise, be on your way."

Ben got a smug look on his face. "Fine. Amy decided that I needed to see a sex therapist. It was the only way I could keep her from walking out on me after she found out about you and me."

Beth felt Seth stiffen beside her, but otherwise he didn't react.

"I'm supposed to confront my addiction and that included tracking you down and telling you that . . ." He glanced over at Seth and then back to her. "That letting you do those things to me was a way for me to get back at my wife. That was all it ever was."

She blinked. "Anything else?"

Ben looked to be considering his next words.

Seth must have picked up on the same thing she did. Ben was out to hurt her, embarrass her, or maybe a little of both. "I think you've said enough. You can leave now."

"Pfft." Ben rolled his eyes and took a step back toward the alley. "Good riddance. I did what I said I'd do. I hope you have fun with your new plaything while I'm having a *real relationship* with my wife."

With those parting words, he was gone. He disappeared around the corner, presumably to the back of the building where she'd been not long ago. Beth wondered if he'd planned to ambush her when she left the café or if he was planning to follow her home. Neither sat well with her.

"So that was your ex?" Seth asked.

"Yes. Unfortunately." At that moment, Beth realized that any feelings she'd had for Ben were long gone. She'd been able to view his words for what they were—an attack. He was angry he was being made to jump through hoops to save his marriage and he was lashing out. It didn't look like therapy was working. Then again, it only worked if the person committed to the process. Ben had proven that commitment wasn't one of his strong suits.

"Want to explain?" Seth asked.

"No." Explaining the meaning behind what Ben had said to Seth, someone who already didn't seem to care for her, was the last thing she wanted. Beth was starting to think that she and Drew had a real future together and she didn't want to create any more bumps in the road with his family than she had to. "If there isn't anything else, I have things to do tonight."

She began heading toward her car.

"Hot date?"

"No. I'm meeting a friend at a club. The only hot dates I have these days are with your brother and you already know he's working." She waited until she was at her car before addressing him again. "In case you didn't pick up on it, my ex is a vindictive, manipulative bastard. I think that is all you need to know."

Not giving Seth a chance to respond, she climbed into her car and drove away.

Beth was pulling onto her street when her phone rang. Not wanting to deal with Ben or Seth again, she made sure to check the caller ID. When she saw Drew's name on the screen, the stress of the last half hour disappeared. "Hello, handsome."

He laughed. "Hello. You sound like you're in a good mood."

Pulling into the driveway, she maneuvered her car into the garage. "I am now."

She heard some noise in the background and then movement. "Sorry. I'm upstairs trying to get some privacy, but that doesn't seem to have worked out very well."

"Don't worry about it."

"Anyway, I called to let you know that you might be getting a visit from my brother. He stopped by earlier today."

"I know," she said. "He's already been to see me."

A muffled sound came through the phone that almost sounded like a grunt. "I'm sorry. I was going to call you as soon as he left but a call came in and I couldn't."

Beth shook her head even though he couldn't see. "Don't worry about it. I can handle your brother."

"I have no doubt. Even so, I know he can be a pain in the ass when he has a bug up his butt about something."

She loved that Drew was feeling protective of her, but in this case, he didn't need to be. "Your brother may never approve of us, and I'm okay with that as long as you are."

"Seth's opinion doesn't matter to me."

"He's your brother." Beth felt the need to point that out. Especially considering that Seth was there to hear Ben's rant.

"And you're the woman I love." There it was. Right there. Her chest clenched and she felt moisture fill her eyes. When Drew said he loved her, she knew he meant it. The words weren't just window dressing or said because he thought it was what she wanted to hear.

"I love you, too."

This time she did hear an unmistakable groan come through the phone. "I wish I could hold you right now."

"Will you come over tomorrow morning? We can sleep in.

Maybe even spend the entire day in bed."

"You're on."

Beth grinned, but then she remembered that there was something else she needed to tell him. "Drew, something else happened today you should know about. While I was talking to your brother, Ben showed up."

Drew didn't comment for a few moments and she wondered if he was working to control his temper. Ben wasn't one of his favorite subjects—nor hers—for obvious reasons. "What did he have to say?"

She was surprised that Drew sounded rational. If she didn't know any better, she would have thought they were having a conversation about where to meet for coffee. "His wife is making him go to therapy and part of that was him confronting the people in his past. I'm guessing he was supposed to apologize and explain why he did what he did, but of course it didn't come out that way."

"He upset you." Beth could hear the anger in his voice. He was controlling it, but just barely.

"Not as much as you'd think. Honestly, I'm more concerned with Seth's reaction. Ben thought your brother was my new 'boy-toy.' Seth now knows that I dated a married man and that he let me 'do things to him'. Ben wasn't specific, luckily, but I'm sure your brother can use his imagination."

Drew didn't respond.

"You still there?" she asked.

"Yes." She imagined he was counting to ten. "Don't worry about Seth. If he says anything else, just tell him to come talk to me."

"I already did."

"Good." Drew sighed. "This is so hard. I want to be there right now to comfort you."

"I'm fine. Really. Regarding Ben? Well, seeing him again made me realize that he no longer has any hold over me. I've moved on and I've found a much better man to spend my time with."

"Yeah?" She was almost positive he was smiling.

"Yeah."

"Parker!"

"Coming!" Drew yelled back to whoever had called his name. "Sorry. I've got to go."

"I'll see you in the morning. I love you."

"I love you, too."

Then he was gone and something she'd been tossing around in her mind came to the forefront once again. Deciding to go with it, she dialed Nicole's number.

"Need something to keep you busy while your man's working?"

"Hello to you, too."

Nicole laughed.

"Do you have some time this afternoon? I could use your help with something," Beth said.

"Sure. What do you need?"

"I'd like your help picking out a collar for Drew. I want it to be something he can wear at all times." Nicole would know what he was allowed to wear and what he wasn't. Beth didn't want to buy something that he would have to take off whenever he went to work.

"I need to finish what I'm working on, and then I can come over. Say about an hour from now?"

"See you then."

Beth hung up the phone and headed into the house. She spent the next hour straightening the upstairs and making sure her bedroom was in order. Sunday began another four days off for Drew and she planned to make them memorable.

A little before five there was a knock on her front door. She went to greet Nicole. If they were going to get both a collar for Drew and make it to the club that night, they needed to get going.

Two hours later, Beth was in possession of Drew's new collar. To the casual observer it looked like a regular watch. Nicole had informed Beth that the only two pieces of jewelry he would be allowed to wear were a wedding ring and a watch. That narrowed down her choices considerably. In the end, however, she'd found the perfect watch and had the back plate engraved. A symbol of their relationship would be pressed against his wrist whenever he wore it.

With that objective accomplished, Beth and Nicole went their separate ways agreeing to meet back up at the club. Beth ran upstairs and tucked the watch in her top drawer before getting ready for a night at the club. Since Drew wasn't going to be there with her, she opted for a pair of black jeans and a nice top. She wasn't out to impress anyone and she needed to be comfortable.

Nicole and Jeff were already there when Beth arrived. She

stopped to say hi to the two of them and then excused herself to go find Michael. He was a master at rope work and she wanted to see if he'd teach her something. Drew loved to be bound and she wanted the night she collared him to be special.

She found Michael, who also happened to be one of the club's dungeon monitors, upstairs outside room number four. He was watching Daniel flog someone. She thought she recognized the sub, but she couldn't be sure since her head was down.

Michael acknowledged her arrival. He also noticed she was alone. "Flying solo tonight?"

"Drew's working."

"Ah." He turned his attention back to the scene in front of him. Considering Daniel was one of the more experienced Doms in the club, Beth knew Michael wasn't watching for safety reasons. "So what brings you upstairs without a sub in tow? You never were much of a voyeur."

It was true. The only time she came upstairs to watch was when she wanted to learn something new. "No. I was looking for you, actually."

He turned to face her. "I'm flattered. What can I do for you?"

"I was hoping you could help me with some rope bondage. Drew likes to be bound and while I can do some simple wrist ties, I was hoping maybe you could show me something a little more involved."

A huge grin spread across Michael's face. "Sure. Let's see if we can find an open room."

Chapter 32

Drew worked alongside his crew to clean the truck and make sure everything was stocked and ready to go for the next run. It had been a busy shift. Both lunch and dinner had been interrupted by calls. It was a good thing it was Sunday, otherwise they'd be scrambling to get the daily maintenance finished.

His brother's appearance that afternoon had been unexpected. Why he was so concerned about Drew's relationship with Beth was a mystery. It wasn't as if Seth had ever taken a great interest in the women Drew dated before.

Although his conversation with Seth, and his brother's subsequent visit with Beth, irritated Drew, it had nothing on what he was feeling toward Beth's ex. Fury ran through his limbs as he washed the windshield of the fire truck.

"I don't know what the windshield did to you, but I'm sure it didn't mean it."

He looked down to find Shawn standing there with his hands on his hips. Drew sighed and wiped off the last of the solution he'd applied before hopping down. "Stressful day."

"I can see that. Want to talk about it?" Shawn asked.

"Not really." Talking about it wasn't going to help. What he really wanted to do was punch something—preferably Ben's face. Since that wasn't an option . . .

Shawn was quiet for a moment. "You almost done here? I was thinking of trying to get a workout in if you wanted to join me."

Rolling his shoulders, Drew thought that might be the best idea he'd heard all day. He needed to release some of his pent-up energy. "Give me ten minutes."

Nodding, Shawn left Drew to finish his work. Luckily, most everything was done. His crew had finished washing down the truck and all their gear was cleaned and in place. The only thing he had left to do was check in with them and make sure there were no issues from the previous run to go over. Irwin had some problems getting the hose hooked up and Drew wanted to see if there was a way to keep it from happening in the future. In a fire, seconds counted.

He found all the members of his crew huddled together at the back of the truck. "Hey, Cap."

Something was going on. "What are you knuckleheads up to?"

"Not a thing," Romeo said.

Yeah. Drew didn't buy that for a minute, but he decided to ignore their strange behavior. "I wanted to talk about what happened with the hose connection today."

Irwin spoke up. "Not much to tell. Looked like some kids had been messing with it or something. I had a hard time getting the cap off."

"What do you mean? What was wrong with it?" Drew asked.

"Someone must have been trying to pry it open with something and whatever it was got wedged in there. The only way to get the cap off was to dig it out." Irwin shrugged.

Drew nodded. "I'll brief Chief Franks on the issue. I think I remember one of the other crews saying they had a problem with a hydrant recently as well. In the future, if you can't get whatever it is out after a few seconds use the sledgehammer. Anything else?"

Baily cleared his throat. "Just one more thing."

"Yes?" Drew asked when Baily didn't automatically spit it out.

"We." Baily pointed to Romeo and Irwin. "We're wondering if your girlfriend was going to be stopping by tonight. You know. To say hi."

Drew guessed that answered his question on what they'd had their heads together about. Figures it was about his personal life and not work. "No. Beth isn't stopping by."

"Well, you know, if you needed to work off a little tension, we'd cover for you," Romeo said.

"Good to know you all would go through such a sacrifice for me." Drew strolled over to the cabinet and replaced the cleaning supplies he'd been using. "See if you three can keep out of trouble for the next hour. I'll be in the gym if you need me."

He could hear them laughing as he left. They were good guys and a great crew. In all honesty, they probably didn't understand why he wasn't sharing details. He had in the past. Then again, his relationship with Beth was different. It had been from the start.

As promised, Shawn was waiting for him in the gym. They were alone. Apparently, no one else had felt the need to burn off any excess energy.

For the next forty-five minutes, Drew lifted weights, did leg presses, and spent some time on the treadmill. He was still angry, but at least he had it under control.

"Feel any better?" Shawn asked.

"Yeah. I do." His friend handed him a bottle of water and Drew downed most of it in one go. "How's the new apartment?"

"Quiet."

Drew nodded and followed Shawn into the showers. It was almost nine and things would be winding down. Considering the day they'd all had, Drew was guessing most of the guys would be crashing early tonight.

Freshly showered, he went to his desk and finished the paperwork on the small house fire they'd responded to earlier that day. Once that was completed, he placed the file on Chief Franks' desk and went to find a spot to read before going to bed.

By eleven o'clock, the station was quiet. Most of the guys were upstairs asleep or heading in that direction. Drew closed his book, tucked it under his arm, and began climbing the stairs.

He was halfway to the top floor when the intercom came to life. Drew froze and waited. You never knew if it was going to be an EMT-only call or if the trucks would be needed.

It wasn't meant to be. The dispatcher announced that a fire had been reported. Drew turned on his heels and made a beeline for the fire engine. He was still putting on his gear when the rest of the guys began filing into the bay. Less than a minute later, they were climbing into their trucks and driving away from the station.

Drew's crew pulled up to the building first, so he jumped out and began assessing the situation. Taking his radio with him, he jogged around the side of the building to get a look at the back. It was much the same as the front, unfortunately. The third floor appeared to be completely engulfed in flames.

Bringing his radio up, he relayed the information. "There's evidence of fire on sides A, B, C, and D. Request second alarm."

"Copy that. Dispatching additional trucks to your location."

By the time Drew made it back to the front of the building, everyone was in position and ready to go.

"Do we know if anyone is in the building?" Romeo asked as he came up beside Drew.

"No idea." He said it loud enough for everyone around him to hear. They all knew what that meant. They were going to have to go in and find out.

Shawn and his crew took the lead. When they first entered the building there was very little smoke. It wasn't until they came to the top of the second level that they began to encounter serious evidence of the fire. Drew and Romeo stayed on the second floor to look for anyone who might be inside while Shawn and Kelly continued on to the third floor.

As Drew began checking each of the rooms, an eerie feeling settled into his bones. The building was under construction. It was being renovated and it looked like apartments were going in. That meant the chances of there being people inside were slim, which was good. It also meant that it had the potential of being a target for the arsonist.

A shout came from up top and Drew and Romeo took off toward the noise. They ran up the stairs. As soon as Shawn saw them, he tilted his head toward the standpipe. "It's not working. We're going to have to get one of the ladders to feed us hose from the outside."

"On it," a voice came across the radio.

"Bring it to the second floor. I don't think we can get close enough to any of these windows on the third," Drew said.

The four of them hightailed it back downstairs and made it to the windows as the ladder was maneuvering up to the window. They pulled in two hoses. Shawn and Kelly took one, Drew and Romeo the other.

Out in the hallway, they met with the crew who'd searched the first floor. "All clear on one."

All six of them began their journey back up to the third floor. They could hear the water hitting the building from the outside. The aerial trucks must have arrived. That was good because this fire was a hot one. It only reinforced Drew's thoughts that this might be another fire courtesy of the arsonist.

It took a while to get the fire under control. Every time they thought they'd managed to get everything, they'd find another hot spot. It was a big building and unlike the others the arsonist had hit, this one was probably only a month or so from taking on tenants. Once the main fire was out, they had to go room to room to make sure there were no live embers.

Finally, they got the last of it and made their way back downstairs. When they reached the first floor, something caught their attention and they all turned. They couldn't see anything, but something or someone had made that noise. The first floor had been checked, so no one should have been down there.

"Hello?" Drew shouted into the darkness.

There was no answer, but they did hear what sounded like metal.

"We'll check it out," Shawn said. "You guys stay here."

Shawn and Kelly were halfway down the hall when the figure of a man appeared and bolted into one of the far rooms. Kelly took off after him.

"Kelly wait," Shawn yelled.

The rookie didn't listen. He took off after the guy and Shawn had no choice but to follow.

Drew clicked the switch on his radio. "We've got a civilian inside the building. Shawn and Kelly—"

The sound of an explosion ended the transmission. Drew and the other guys automatically ducked in reaction.

"Is everyone all right? What the hell happened in there?" came across the radio.

"No idea. We're gonna check it out. Shawn and Kelly are unaccounted for," Drew said.

"Were they anywhere near that explosion?"

Drew swallowed, trying not to think the worst. "Yes."

"I'm sending in the rapid intervention team."

By the time the RIT got there, Drew was already on his knees next to Shawn. His friend was unconscious. Drew checked for any major injuries, but couldn't find anything beyond some superficial wounds on his face from where his helmet had been knocked off. Chances were he had a concussion.

Romeo was beside him. The other team was checking on Kelly. It looked like the door had been rigged. When Kelly tried to follow the guy out, it had gone off. From what he could tell, Kelly's injuries were much worse than Shawn's were. Part of his jacket was torn and Drew could see and smell burnt flesh. Shawn had been collateral damage. Kelly had taken the bulk of the blast. The force of the explosion seemed to be concentrated near the door.

When he walked out of the building a few minutes later, the sun was coming over the horizon. They'd been at it all night.

Drew waited for the EMTs to load Shawn and Kelly into the ambulance and drive away with the sirens blaring before heading back to his truck and his crew. They had a couple of hours left in their shift and then he'd head over to the hospital to see how Shawn and Kelly were doing. It was a far cry from how he'd planned to spend his morning.

***

Something felt off. It took Beth a moment to realize it was because she was alone in her bed. Drew had to work last night. The only saving grace was that he was coming over this morning.

Sighing, she turned her head to look at the clock beside her bed. Beth was shocked to see that it was almost nine o'clock. She sat up and glanced around the room. There was no sign of Drew or the duffel bag he always brought with him.

Beth flung the covers off her and went downstairs to check her cell. Maybe he'd gotten held up at work or something—at least, that's what she was hoping. She didn't want to consider it might be something else.

The first floor was as empty as the upstairs. She went to the kitchen and removed her phone from the charger. There was one text message.

Went to the hospital. Call you later.

Her heart began pounding in her chest and all the air from her lungs seemed to disappear. Was he hurt? Of course he was. Why else would he have gone to the hospital? She hit the call button and tried not to hyperventilate while she waited for him to pick up.

But he didn't pick up. The phone went straight to voice mail.

She hung up, not bothering to leave a message, and then berated herself for even trying to call. If he was being treated for an injury in the hospital, then he probably wouldn't be able to answer his phone.

Beth knew she needed to calm down and think rationally. If he'd sent the text message, then he couldn't have been that badly hurt, right? Then the thought crossed her mind that maybe he hadn't sent the message. Maybe he'd asked one of the guys he worked with to send it for him. Before she could talk herself into a panic attack, Beth called the only person she knew could help her.

"Isn't this supposed to be your day off?" Nicole yawned in her ear.

"I need your help."

Her friend must have picked up on how desperate Beth sounded. "What's wrong? What do you need?"

She took a deep breath and explained. "Drew was supposed to come over this morning, but instead I got a text saying he went to the hospital. I tried to call him back but he isn't answering. I need to know what's going on and I know if I call the station they won't tell me anything."

"Okay. Hold tight. I'll see what I can find out and call you back, okay?"

"Okay."

Beth paced while she waited. Nothing could happen to him. It couldn't. She'd just told him she loved him. They had so much more to experience together.

When the phone rang, she jumped. "Hello?"

"Drew's fine. He's not hurt." Nicole must have known those were the words Beth needed to hear most.

"Then why did he go to the hospital?"

"They were responding to a fire last night and two other guys were hurt. One was Drew's former captain."

Beth swallowed. "Shawn."

"Yeah." Nicole gave her a moment. "I didn't get all the details, but apparently something happened as they were exiting the building and two of the responding firefighters were injured. I got the impression that Drew, along with most of the other guys from that station, headed over to the hospital as soon as their shift was over."

"What hospital?" Although Nicole had assured her that he was all right, Beth needed to see it for herself.

It took her almost a half hour to get dressed and drive to the hospital where Shawn was being treated. She was still trying to convince herself that Drew wasn't the one hurt as she parked her car and headed into the emergency room waiting area.

If there had been any doubt that she had the right place, it disappeared as soon as she walked through the sliding doors. There had to be a dozen firefighters taking up various positions around the large room. All of them were still wearing their dark blue pants and polo shirts with the St. Louis Fire Department logo.

"Beth?"

Beth turned to her left and saw Drew striding toward her. She released a cleansing breath when she saw he was perfectly fine. "Drew."

He pulled her into his arms and held on tight. "Not that I'm not happy to see you, but what are you doing here? Didn't you get my text?"

She still hadn't let go of him. "Yes. I got your text. Your text that said you'd gone to the hospital."

Drew leaned back and searched her face. Then his gaze softened as he realized how she'd taken the message. "You thought it was me? That I'd been taken to the hospital?"

"Yes, you insufferable man." Beth wiped the moisture from her cheeks. "I've never been so scared in my life."

"Aw, Beth, I'm so sorry. I never meant to make you worry. It didn't occur to me that you'd take it to mean I'd gotten hurt."

She tried to pull herself together—everyone was watching them. "How's Shawn?"

"How did you . . ." He paused. "Nicole."

"Yeah. I didn't know what else to do when you didn't answer your phone, so I called her."

He rubbed his hands up and down her arms, still trying to comfort her. "The last we heard he was still unconscious, but stable. I think they're trying to get him a room now. Kelly, though . . . they took him upstairs for emergency surgery. He got beat up pretty bad by the explosion."

Drew guided her over to a set of chairs in the corner. The other firefighters left them alone, but she knew they were paying attention. She took hold of both his hands and gathered them into her lap. "I was scared. I thought . . ."

"I know. And I'm sorry. I promise next time to give a little more information when I text you."

Next time. Beth knew there would be a next time. With his line of work, it was inevitable.

"What are you thinking?" he asked.

"I'm thinking how hard this is going to be going through this for the rest of my life." He grew really still, and Beth looked up to see what was wrong. "What is it?"

"You said the rest of your life."

She hesitated. "I did, didn't I?"

"Yes. You did."

Beth flipped over one of his hands and traced the lines in his palm. "I'm not ready to get married yet, but I want you in my life, Drew Parker. And one day, hopefully not too long from now, I will be ready to walk down the aisle with you, and have a family with you . . . the whole nine yards."

A huge smile spread across his face, and before she knew what was happening he was kissing her—right there in the waiting room. It was only when a couple of the guys whistled that Drew pulled back. They were both breathing heavily. She never thought she would get a kiss like that in a hospital waiting room.

"I love you. I meant it. I'll wait as long as it takes for you to be ready," he vowed.

She caressed the side of his face. "I don't think it will take that long. You seem to have a way of breaking through all my defenses."

He kissed her again. "Good. I'll keep chiseling away."

Beth grinned. "But you have to promise me something."

"Anything."

"You have to do everything in your power to keep yourself safe. I don't think I could handle it if something ever happened to you."

Drew brushed his lips against hers. "You got it."

Chapter 33

Beth pulled into her driveway and smiled when she saw Drew's car was already there. It had been ten days since she'd sat across from him in the emergency room and admitted that she wanted a future with him. She'd imagined going home after that and celebrating their new commitment with a long bout of kinky lovemaking. What actually happened was about as far removed as it could get.

Shawn didn't regain consciousness right away and Drew refused to leave his side until he did. She stayed with him as long as she could, but eventually he asked her to go home and get some rest. There really wasn't anything she could do there. All he was doing was sitting alongside his friend's bed waiting for him to wake up.

It took more than twenty-four hours, but eventually Shawn did open his eyes and start talking again. He had a concussion, of course. On top of that, they also found out that he'd dislocated his shoulder. Drew stayed with him at the hospital until he was released and then took him home. Since Shawn didn't have anyone else, Drew effectively moved in with his friend until he had to return to work. Even then, Drew checked on Shawn as much as he could, making sure he had everything he needed.

Needless to say, while he was watching over his friend, Drew and Beth hadn't spent much time together. They talked on the phone and sent text messages, but it wasn't enough. Not for him and certainly not for her. It scared her how much she needed him.

Parking her car and turning off the engine, she made her way toward the door that led into the house. Drew was staying with her for the next four days and she planned to make the most of every minute.

As she reached for the doorknob, she paused. Beth had a lot to be thankful for. Drew was safe and they were ready to start their future together—whatever that might be. Shawn was going to recover. He'd be on desk duty for a while, but from everything Drew had told her, that wouldn't keep him down for long.

Things hadn't gone so well for the other firefighter, James Kelly. He ended up having complications from his injuries and died in the hospital four days later. They'd attended the funeral. Drew had to work, but that hadn't mattered. All the guys from the station were there. The ones who were on duty showed up in their uniforms alongside their trucks. Beth met Drew at the gravesite, wanting to be there with him.

Taking a deep breath and pushing back the wave of emotion that was threatening, she opened the door and stepped inside. If all went right, she was planning to give Drew the watch she'd bought him tonight. She needed to feel that connection with him now more than ever. "Honey, I'm home."

Drew strolled out of the kitchen in nothing but one of her aprons. "You're early."

Beth chuckled and wrapped her arms around his waist, making sure to grab two handfuls of his bare behind. "And what do we have here?"

He smiled. "I wanted to surprise you. I'm making dinner."

"Hmm." She rose up on her tiptoes and gave him a lingering kiss.

"Do you like it?" he asked, glancing down at his attire. "I'm not sure it's much of a fashion statement."

She dropped her arms and motioned for him to turn around. When he did, he gave his tush a shake. Beth responded with a solid smack on the rounded flesh.

Drew reached for her hand and twisted them both around so that she was pressed flush against his front. She felt his arousal growing with every touch.

Raising an eyebrow, she ran a single finger down the side of his face. "Later."

His pupils dilated and darkened.

Beth grinned. "Dinner first."

He sighed dramatically and led her toward the kitchen. "I suppose it's only fitting. Me slaving away in the kitchen, serving you before I serve you in other ways."

Deciding to go with it, she strolled over to the kitchen table and made a show of sitting down in one of the chairs. "And what are you making your mistress this evening?"

Drew glanced over his shoulder before going back to chopping the vegetables. "Chicken enchiladas."

She sat and watched him for a few minutes. "Is it going to be a while before it's ready?"

He nodded. "At least another thirty minutes."

"I'm gonna go grab a shower, then." She waited until he'd laid the knife down before coming up behind him and reaching between his legs. He jerked and a few of the onions missed the skillet. "After dinner you're mine."

Beth could see the muscles in his throat move as he swallowed. "Yes, Mistress."

Leaving him alone, she climbed the stairs and ambled into her bedroom. Drew's duffel bag was near the door and she knew that was something else they needed to discuss. Beth wasn't ready for marriage yet, but she knew she wanted him with her. They would have to figure it out. Having him move in brought with it a whole other level of uncertainty, but whenever he wasn't around, her house felt empty. It hadn't been like that before.

She walked over to her dresser and opened the top drawer. Her gaze fell on the black case that held Drew's watch. Beth picked it up and placed it on the nightstand beside her bed. Then she stripped out of her work clothes and headed in to take a shower.

***

Forty-five minutes later, Drew sat across from Beth at the kitchen table. When he'd placed the dish in front of her, Beth had told him to remove the apron and have a seat. Although Drew could have said no, he didn't want to. He'd ached for her this past week.

He craved her companionship and her domination. If she told him to sit at her feet rather than at the table, he probably wouldn't bat an eye before complying.

"How was your day?" she asked as if he weren't sitting a few feet away from her in nothing but his birthday suit.

He shrugged. "I spent most of the day cleaning my apartment and doing laundry. Nothing terribly exciting. It made for a long day."

Beth shifted in her seat. She seemed suddenly nervous. "I wanted to ask you something."

Laying his fork down, he gave her his full attention.

When she didn't come out with it, he reached across the table and covered her hand with his. "It can't be all that bad."

He'd been trying to lighten the mood, and it seemed to have worked. She glanced up at him and gave him the smallest hint of a smile.

"No. It's not. But . . ." Beth sat up and took a deep breath. "I'd like you to move in with me."

Drew opened his mouth in shock. Whatever he'd been expecting her to say, it wasn't that. He'd thought it would be months before she was ready to consider them living together. Even still, he had to know what had prompted such a leap. "Are you sure? I told you that I'm willing to wait until you feel comfortable—"

"Yes. I'm sure." She met his gaze and although he could still tell she was nervous, there was something else there as well. "This house felt empty last week when you were gone. It feels like something is missing every time I come home and you're not here. I don't like not having you there beside me in bed at night. I want . . ." Beth took another cleansing breath and laced her fingers with his. "I want you here. With me."

Wow. He was flabbergasted and happier than he could put into words.

Obviously his stunned silence left her with the wrong impression. "You can say no. I know it's soon, but—"

"Yes."

She blinked. "What?"

He grinned and squeezed her hand. "I said yes. I'll move in with you."

"Are you sure?"

Drew chuckled. "Wasn't that my line?"

Her eyes twinkled with amusement. "Are you contradicting your mistress?"

Picking up her hand, he kissed the inside of her wrist. "Only when needed."

They both laughed before turning serious again. "So you're really going to move in?"

He nodded. "Only if you want me to."

"I do."

"Then I guess I'm moving in." He released her hand and they both went back to eating their dinner.

The rest of their meal was much of the same. She told him about her day at the café. Her new employee, Grace, was turning out to be a godsend. Beth was actually considering taking a day off during the week.

Once they were both finished, Beth told him to go upstairs and shower while she cleaned up. He was to meet her in her room in fifteen minutes wearing only a pair of jeans. The jeans threw him, but he did as she requested.

When he stepped into the room, the first thing he noticed was that the blanket chest that was normally at the end of her bed had been pushed against the wall. The next thing that caught his attention was that Beth was standing beside her nightstand. That might not seem all that unusual, but typically when they were about to play, she was at her dresser where she would have laid out the implements and toys she planned to use. He debated asking if something was wrong, but he held his tongue and waited. They were in her bedroom and it was during their agreed upon playtime. She called the shots. He'd have to be patient.

She turned around and pointed to a kneeling pad on the floor. He'd seen them at the club plenty of times, but he'd never used one. Whenever he'd knelt before Beth, he'd always done so with his knees directly on the floor. It made him wonder if he'd be kneeling for an extended period of time tonight.

He lowered himself onto the floor and placed his knees on the pad. His jeans strained a little as anticipation of what was to come began to build. That was one of the nice things about being naked—you never had to worry if there would be enough room to comfortably contain your erection.

Once he was kneeling, Beth walked behind him. He could hear her moving around, but couldn't tell what she was doing. Several minutes later, she touched his back with one hand and dragged it across his shoulders and chest as she made her way back around to his front. When she removed her hand, he had to bite back a whimper. He wanted more, but knew it was not his place to ask.

Beth lifted his chin with her index finger until he was looking up at her. It was only then that he realized what she'd been doing when he'd heard her moving around. She had stripped down to a red corset and a short black leather skirt.

"Are you happy with our arrangement?" she asked.

"Yes, Mistress."

"You wish it to continue?"

"Yes, Mistress. Very much." He had no idea where she was going with this, but he was excited to find out.

Turning on her heel, she walked back over to the nightstand and retrieved something from a black box. When she returned to stand in front of him, he could see it was a silver watch. "I found out from Nicole that you're only allowed to wear a wedding ring and a watch while you're working. That limited me as to what type of collar I could get you since I wanted you to be able to wear—to have a piece of me with you—at all times. Even while you're working."

His heart started pounding in his chest as what was happening hit him. Beth might not be quite ready for marriage, but she was making a commitment to him nonetheless. While there was an urge to blurt out yes as swiftly as possible, he didn't want to ruin the moment. Drew knew how important this was for both of them.

She turned the watch over and showed him the engraving. It was a fireman's axe with a rose wrapped around the handle. The rose had thorns, of course, and they were embedding themselves into the axe handle. It was such a perfect symbol for them.

"I had no idea what to make of you that first night when you came over to sit beside me at Serpent's Kiss. The last thing I wanted was another man in my life. Another submissive." Beth brushed the back of her fingers along the side of his face. It was a loving gesture and he leaned into it, enjoying both her touch and the love she was expressing. "You changed my mind. You changed everything."

There was so much emotion behind her words. His chest ached knowing how much of her soul she was revealing to him.

"I love you, Drew Parker. I want you to be my submissive as well as my partner in life. Will you give me your submission? Will you accept my collar and wear it as a symbol of our relationship and all that comes with it?"

Drew held up his right arm and presented her with his wrist. "Yes. I will proudly wear your collar, Mistress."

The cool metal touched his skin as she put the watch on his wrist. He normally wore a watch—most of the guys he worked with did. The only reason he didn't have his on now was because he knew they were going to play and Beth often had him in cuffs or sometimes even rope. Watches tended to get in the way.

With the watch secured, Beth took a step back. "Stand up."

He rocked back on his heels and did as he was told.

Beth strolled over to her dresser and picked up a length of rope. She was going to bind him. He was salivating already.

Folding the rope in half, she ran the cotton over his skin. He knew what was coming, and the feeling of the softness against his chest and back was almost hypnotic.

"We're going to try something new," she whispered in his ear as she moved behind him. Drew waited, holding his breath to see what it was that she had in mind.

Luckily, he didn't have to wait long. She took him by the hand and guided him to the foot of the bed. Once he'd sat down, she knelt and had him cross his ankles. As she began wrapping the rope around his feet and ankles, he felt his balance shift. It didn't take him long to realize that he wouldn't be able to walk. He knew for some that would cause a rise in anxiety, but instead he felt a calm overtake him as more of the rope encased his legs.

"How does that feel?" she asked, glancing up at him.

"Good. I can't move my legs, though."

"That would be the point." She smirked. "Scoot that cute ass of yours up further onto the bed. I don't want your legs hanging off."

It took some effort, but he was able to get his entire body onto the bed. Beth stood patiently by, watching as he moved. She seemed to be in no hurry at all. He didn't know if that should worry him or not.

When his head rested on the pillows below her headboard, Beth hiked up her skirt and climbed onto the bed. She straddled his legs and bent her head over his denim-clad crotch to scrap her teeth along his erection. He clenched his fist to keep from reaching for her.

"Do you like that?" The glint in her eyes told him she already knew the answer.

"You have no idea."

"Oh, I think I do." She did it again. Then she wrapped her lips around his length and began licking and sucking and using her teeth. By the time she sat up, his crotch was wet and his cock was painfully pulsing against his jeans.

Drew had no idea what she would do next. All he knew was that he wanted her and he was hoping she'd let him come. The how wasn't as important.

She crawled her way up his body, making sure to brush her tits seductively against his chest until his nipples hardened in response. Not touching her was becoming more of a challenge with every minute. It had been too long since he'd had his hands on her.

"Your turn," Beth whispered in his ear moments before she positioned her knees on either side of his head. He had a clear view up her skirt. She wasn't wearing panties.

Pushing her skirt up so that it was completely out of the way, she gripped the headboard and lowered her pussy down onto his face.

Drew didn't need any further instruction. He dove into the moisture that was already coating the outside of her labia. As he probed and licked, Beth began moving her hips. The more he flicked his tongue in and out of her, the faster she rode his face. He had to concentrate on his breathing, but it didn't matter. Drew was still in heaven. With every intake of breath, her musky scent filled his nostrils and he knew her juices covered his mouth and chin.

There was a hiccup in her movements as her legs began to tremble.

"More," she demanded.

He brought his arms up, hooked them around her legs, and started eating her out as if she were his last meal. Her clit brushed against the tip of his nose with every thrust of her hips. She was getting close. Drew knew she wouldn't last much longer.

Seconds after the thought crossed his mind, she threw her head back and gasped as a fresh flood of liquid seeped onto his tongue. He lapped it up greedily.

She let him continue to lavish attention on her swollen flesh while she floated back down to earth. When she did look at him from her perch above, he could still see desire in her eyes. Beth wasn't done.

All at once, she pushed herself away from the headboard and began working her way back down his torso. When she reached the top of his jeans, Beth popped the button and then lowered the zipper. "Lift your hips."

It wasn't a request. He lifted his hips as best he could with his limited range of movement. She worked them down his legs until she reached his knees. Then she abandoned them completely and straddled his hips.

Between what she'd done with her mouth and then having had her come on his face, Drew was more than primed. Beth, however, didn't appear to be in any rush. She placed one hand at the base of his cock, lining it up with her entrance. But instead of lowering herself down onto his erection, she stroked him against her clit.

Watching her was one of the most amazing sights. She was completely focused on making herself feel good. Knowing she was using him like that did nothing to calm his desire. By the time she lowered herself down on his cock, he was on the edge.

"Give me your hands."

He raised his hands and she laced their fingers together in a firm grip. Beth used his arms as leverage just as she'd used the headboard earlier. It didn't take long for her muscles to start quivering.

"Come for me." The words were soft and strained, but he heard them. His entire body heard them and began racing toward the finish line.

Drew tried to hold off until she came again, but it wasn't possible. Her permission had triggered a reaction that he couldn't keep a lid on. He closed his eyes and groaned as cum shot out of his cock and up inside her.

By the time he came to his senses again, Beth was still sitting astride him, but she had a shit-eating grin on her face.

"Did you?" he asked. The thought that she hadn't finished bothered him.

She leaned down and propped her head up on his chest. "Oh yeah."

He smiled and brushed a damp strand of hair away from her face. "I love you."

Her expression changed. The lighthearted air of moments before was gone. In its place was a look that warmed him down to the tips of his toes. "I know."

Epilogue

One Month Later

Drew made sure the back door was locked before heading into the foyer. They would be leaving for Serpent's Kiss as soon as Beth came downstairs. She'd wanted to take a shower before changing into her club wear. He had no idea what outfit she was going to put on. She said she wanted to surprise him, so he'd ducked downstairs to watch some television while she finished getting ready.

Living together had presented a few challenges that neither one of them had foreseen. He hadn't lived with anyone since his parents. And while Beth had technically shared a living space with Ben, he was often gone on 'business trips.' Drew's twenty-four-hour shifts were a lot different than Ben's two- to three-week jaunts.

They were working it out, but it was taking some major communication. In a way, their obstacles were a good thing. When something came up, they both had to figure out what it was about the particular issue that was causing the problem and then find a solution. It was ultimately bringing them closer and building more trust.

Hearing her heels on the stairs, Drew turned toward the sound. When he got his first glimpse of her, his mouth dropped open. Beth was wearing that blood-red top that he'd loved so much—the one that dipped down low in the front—and a pair of fitted black pants with heels. She looked downright sinful.

He reached out a hand and helped her down the last few steps. "You look amazing."

"Thank you," she said, slipping into his arms.

Drew took the opportunity to cup her ass.

She chuckled. "So predictable."

"What can I say? I adore your ass."

Beth kissed him. "I don't think anyone would argue with you."

He squeezed her backside, pulling her flush against his body as he relished the feel of her lips on his.

"Hmm. Are you ready to go?" she asked.

"More than ready. It's been a long week." Drew released her, and they made their way to the garage. What he needed was to get out of his head for a while. Nothing did that better than kneeling at Beth's feet. He was looking forward to a night of light conversation with friends and serving his mistress.

They walked into the club holding hands. It was the middle of July and even at nearly eight at night, the heat from earlier in the day was still making itself known. He'd spent some time earlier, while Beth was at work, helping to deliver fans to the elderly. They were expecting to see temperatures near one hundred in the next two weeks. He wasn't looking forward to fighting fires in that kind of heat. He'd rather deal with the snow.

Beth stopped right inside the door. They were alone in the small foyer. She didn't say anything, just simply ran her thumb back and forth over the inside of his wrist below the watch she'd given him. He needed to focus.

Nodding, he lowered his eyes getting himself into the right mindset. As they'd gotten closer as a couple, Drew found that he embraced his submission to her more and more. He didn't think he'd ever be able to submit twenty-four-seven like some, but there were times, even outside the bedroom, when he wanted and needed to let go of himself and just be.

Seeming satisfied, Beth swiped her card and led them into the main lobby. Ali was there reading a book. Given the rising temperatures outside, there wasn't much call for a coat check.

Ali waved at them. "Good evening, Lady Beth. Drew."

"How are you, Ali?" Beth asked. While Drew didn't have any

speech restrictions while they were at the club other than being polite and respectful, he tried to remember his place and defer to her whenever possible.

"Glad to be in the air conditioning. Mine's out."

Beth strolled over to the small alcove that surrounded Ali. "I hope you're getting it fixed. It's supposed to be pretty unbearable next week."

"I told my landlord. He's supposed to come over tomorrow and try to fix it. We'll see. He doesn't always do what he says he will." She shrugged as if it was no big deal, but Drew knew it was. When temperatures got this high, their EMT calls went through the roof with everything from heat exhaustion to dehydration.

"That's horrible." Beth sounded disgusted, and honestly, he was, too. "Hopefully your landlord will do the right thing."

"I hope so, too."

There wasn't much more to be said, so Beth wished the woman a good night, and they walked into the club.

As soon as they were away from Ali, Drew squeezed Beth's hand to get her attention. She met his gaze. "I might be able to get Baily to help Ali. He's a whiz at stuff like that."

Beth nodded. "That's a good idea. We'll ask her tomorrow night if her landlord was able to get it fixed. If not, then we can make the suggestion. Do you think he'd be willing?"

"I do. He loves working on appliances. His dad used to own an appliance repair shop years ago and Baily used to help his dad growing up. I honestly think if his dad still had that shop, joining the fire department wouldn't have even crossed Baily's mind."

She smiled and gave him a peck on the lips. "Come on. Let's get a drink. Then, I'm thinking a foot rub would be nice."

"Of course, Mistress."

Chad was behind the bar. "What can I get you tonight?" he asked Beth. Chad had been working at Serpent's Kiss long enough to know the protocol.

"One of my usuals and a beer." Drew was a little surprised to hear she was ordering him alcohol. Then again, it was early. It wasn't as if one beer was going to leave him intoxicated and unable to function.

"Coming right up." Chad quickly filled Beth's glass with half Coke and half Sprite before grabbing a beer out of the refrigerator and popping the top off it. The whole process took less than a minute. "Here you go."

Beth handed him her membership card to swipe, and then they were off to find their friends. Over the last month, there had been some rearranging. Allison and John had joined Nicole, Jeff, Daniel, and a few others, including the club's newest member, Alexander. Drew followed Beth over to their group. He waited for her to sit before tossing a pillow down on the floor and kneeling beside her.

"How's everyone been? I feel like this week went on forever," Beth said, getting comfortable and kicking off her shoes. Drew took a swig of his beer and then placed it on the coffee table in front of him so he could get to work on that foot massage.

Nicole apparently liked Beth's idea and kicked off her shoes as well. "It's the heat. Makes the minutes feel like hours." She paused and then sat up suddenly looking directly at him. "Oh. I almost forgot. I got a call this afternoon. They caught the arsonist."

Despite his desire to please his mistress, Drew halted his movement and gave Nicole his full attention.

"That's great news."

Beth bumped his hand with her foot, letting him know she wanted him to continue. He mumbled his apology and went back to work.

Nicole, however, didn't miss a beat. "Yes, it is. He's caused enough damage over the last few months. But they caught him red-handed. Someone saw him entering an abandoned building and the police found him in the process of starting another fire. He even had burn marks on his hands and arms. Although signature-wise they can tie him to the other fires, they are going to see if Madison can identify him as the man he and Kelly saw running from that building. If so, the DA will likely add murder to the charges as well."

Beth scratched her fingers along Drew's scalp in an affectionate gesture. He knew she was offering him comfort. He might not have been all that close to Kelly, but it didn't matter. Kelly was a firefighter who had been killed on the job.

***

There were some things Beth knew she would never fully

315

understand. The connection between Drew and his fellow firefighters was one of them. She didn't know what it was like to walk into a burning building and put your life and your trust into the hands of the men and women who were in there with you.

They'd talked a lot over the last month about what had happened to Kelly and even Shawn. The fear that something like that could one day happen to Drew was still there—it probably always would be—but she was learning to accept it and to trust in his training.

As they sat there with their friends, she tried to offer him what comfort she could. Gradually, she felt his tension ease. He rested his head against her leg as he continued to massage the muscles in her tired feet.

Alexander cleared his throat. He was the newest member of the club and had struck up an almost instant friendship with Daniel. They were both ex-military. Although Daniel had only served for four years back in his twenties, it was a connection they both seemed to be embracing. "Since we're sharing good news . . . I think I've finally located my buddy's wife."

A couple of weeks ago, Alexander had shared more information with them as to what had brought him to St. Louis. The same incident that had caused his own injuries had killed his best friend. When he got back Stateside, he started his search for his friend's wife. The only problem was that she'd moved—to St. Louis, apparently. He wouldn't go into detail, but from what Beth gathered, Alexander had a message of some sort to pass on to her.

"That's great news," Daniel said.

"It is." Alexander cupped his glass with both hands. Beth couldn't see what was in it, but she would bet it was something strong.

"Are you nervous? I mean you've been here looking for almost two months." Maybe it wasn't Beth's place, but there was an underlying anxiety in the way he held himself.

He snorted. "Terrified."

Daniel raised his glass of amber liquid. "To the end of Alexander's search. May all go well."

They all raised their glasses and toasted.

Katrina strolled over to the group and propped herself up on the edge of one of the couches. "Are we having a party over here?"

"Something like that," Alexander said, tilting his glass toward her. "The PI you recommended, Peter Monroe, found her. He found Grace."

Beth nearly choked on her drink. Grace? Surely he couldn't mean . . .

But the more she sat and thought about it, the more things added up. She debated whether or not to say anything, but decided to keep her mouth shut. It wasn't as if Alexander hadn't already found her. Any information she would provide wouldn't assist him in accomplishing whatever it was he meant to do. Besides, maybe it wasn't the same Grace he was looking for. There had to be more than one Grace in St. Louis, right? And who could have also lost their husband in combat. Even as she thought it, she knew the chances that there were two Graces in St. Louis with the same circumstances were unlikely.

She felt as if someone was staring at her. When she looked down Drew was gazing up at her with a concerned look in his eyes. "Are you okay, Mistress?"

The last thing she wanted was for Drew to think something was wrong. If anything, everything was right. She and Drew were living together. They had even begun to talk about marriage. Work was good. Her friends were happy. What more could she ask for?

Beth caressed the side of his face before tangling her fingers in his hair. "I'm not sure I could be any more perfect. I was just thinking about how far we've come in the last few months."

That brought a smile to his face. "Does that mean you're ready to say yes and marry me?"

She played with the hairs at the base of his neck. The words were there on the tip of her tongue. "What would you do if I said yes?"

His eyes went wide. "Are you serious? Are you really saying yes?"

All conversation around them stopped. She knew their friends had picked up on the fact that something big was happening. They might not know what it was yet, but she knew that would change in the next moment.

Beth worried the side of her cheek and nodded.

All sense of decorum left Drew as he all but tackled her, kissing every inch of her skin that he could reach. Perhaps she should have been upset—they were in the club, after all—but she was too happy. Surrounded by their friends, she kissed him back with just as much excitement.

"I'll make you happy for the rest of our lives. I promise," Drew declared.

She looked him in the eyes and ran the pad of her thumb over his bottom lip. "I'll hold you to that."

"Promise?"

"Oh yeah," she said as she brought him in for another kiss. Life might not always be a bed of roses, but as long as Drew was with her, she was more than willing to embrace the thorns that came along with it.

About the Author

Sherri spent most of her childhood detesting English class. It was one of her least favorite subjects because she never seemed to fit into the standard mold. She wasn't good at spelling, or following grammar rules, and outlines made her head spin. For that reason, Sherri never imagined becoming an author.

At the age of thirty, all of that changed. After getting frustrated with the direction a television show was taking two of its characters, Sherri decided to try her hand at writing an alternate ending, and give the characters their happily ever after. By the time the story finished, it was one of the top ten read stories on the site, and her readers were encouraging her to write more.

Nearly eight years later, Sherri is the author of eight full-length novels, and two short stories. Writing has become a creative outlet that allows her to explore a wide range of emotions, while having fun taking her characters through all the twists and turns she can create. You can find a current list of all of Sherri's books and sign up for her monthly newsletter at http://www.sherrihayesauthor.com/.